A Dance with the Fae

BOOKS BY KENNEDY KERR

Mistress of Magic

A Kiss from the Fae

Loch Cameron

The Cottage by the Loch

A Secret at the Cottage by the Loch

The Diary from the Cottage by the Loch

A Gift from the Cottage by the Loch

An Invitation to the Cottage by the Loch

Keepsakes from the Cottage by the Loch

Lost Memories of the Cottage by the Loch

Inheriting the Cottage by the Loch

Magpie Cove

The House at Magpie Cove

Secrets of Magpie Cove

Daughters of Magpie Cove

Dreams of Magpie Cove

A Spell of Murder

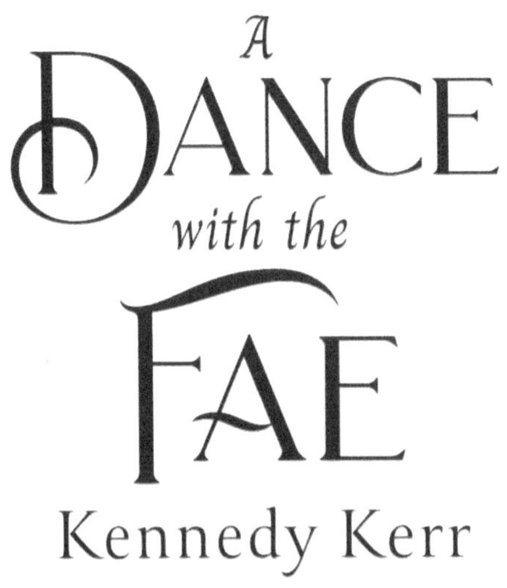

A Dance with the Fae

Kennedy Kerr

SECOND SKY

Published by Second Sky in 2025

An imprint of Storyfire Ltd.
Carmelite House
50 Victoria Embankment
London EC4Y 0DZ

www.secondskybooks.com

The authorised representative in the EEA is Hachette Ireland
8 Castlecourt Centre
Dublin 15 D15 XTP3
Ireland
(email: info@hbgi.ie)

ISBN: 978-1-80550-036-0
eBook ISBN: 978-1-80550-035-3

CONTENT AND TRIGGER WARNINGS

This work contains explicit sexual content and scenes with elements of dubious consent, as well as in-depth depictions of BDSM.

When thowes dissolve the snawy hoord,
An' float the jinglin' icy boord,
Then, water-kelpies haunt the foord,
By your direction,
An' nighted trav'llers are allur'd
To their destruction.

— ROBERT BURNS, 'ADDRESS TO
THE DEIL'

PROLOGUE

1590, NORTH BERWICK, SCOTLAND

Grainne Morgan stood on the rough wooden stage at the edge
of the stinking harbour. She was exhausted; she had been made
to stand inside a dank, dripping cell with no room to sit down
for three days until she was hallucinating from lack of sleep.
Dirt streaked her torn grey dress. Still, she would not confess
that she had done anything wrong.

It was Midsummer, usually a bright and joyous day for
feasting and celebration. Today, the heat was oppressive; she
had a harsh red burn across her nose and across her bare white
shoulders. Her dress had been slashed to the waist and her
breasts were also bare under the unforgiving, bleak Scottish sun:
exposed as punishment, as if to demonstrate her sluttish nature.
Yet, she did not wish that the villagers around her – those she
had lived alongside all her life – would look away. She knew she
did not owe them modesty. She would not beg. She would not
apologise for her body or her soul.

Tears streaked her muddy face; her long black hair had
come undone from its neat plait and was plastered to her neck
with panicky sweat. Next to her, five other women from other
villages stood lashed to the same rough-hewn poles. Three of

them were unconscious, hanging forward from the pole by their wrists. One of the unconscious was only a child: nine years old and there to implicate her mother.

In the crowd that jostled to get a better view, some of the friends and family who had known Grainne since she was a bairn held each other's hands tight and looked away, grimacing. Not to attend might mean that they condoned Grainne's actions, and the minister had made it very clear that there was no shortage of stakes for those who communed with the faeries. Many of the villagers, though, had always avoided her; many of them had always believed the gossip about her and her family. Many of them might have lashed her to the pole with their own hands, if they'd had the choice. Grainne had seen the slick of envy in their eyes, the silken desire that burned in their loins for her. Not because she was the most beautiful – though the Morgan women who had always kept their own surname and their own counsel had always been comely – but because she was free in her spirit and her mind. Free, independent and powerful. And those who are not free wish to fuck or kill those who are.

'Confess! Confess that ye are a witch and receive God's absolution!' The local sheriff was a barrel-chested, bearded, thick-set man wearing the colours of King James, who believed that Grainne and the others were responsible for raising winds to shipwreck him at sea. *Heavens forfend that a man should take responsibility for his failure*, she thought. The fact that the sheriff believed that ships at sea held any importance in the minds of the women before him was almost laughable. So full of their self-importance, they were. Fat with it.

Why would I bother to raise a wind to wreck any ships? she had asked, days ago, in her interrogation. *I do not care about your ships. I keep my mind on higher things.* Which she did: the language of the leaves and flowers, the messages of spirit, the appeasement of the Good Folk who lived alongside them all, though only some could see them, and only a rare few, like Grainne, would converse with them.

If you only knew how I have saved your life a thousand times, she thought as she hung there. *If only you knew how many offerings I have made to the Good Folk on your behalf. How many intercessions, barters and bargains have kept them from your door?*

Grainne knew she was close to death; she could see her faerie guides waiting for her, forming a line from the wooden stage over and out to the sea to the distant faerie city of Murias. They held out their hands to her as the sheriff's hot grasp encircled her neck. *'Confess, and ye shall go to your death godly. Not as the Devil's whore,'* he muttered in her ear; she felt him harden as he pressed up against her from behind. Bile rose up into her throat, but she choked it down. She would not be disgraced any further.

'I am no whore. I am Grainne Morgan, Beloved of the Good Folk!' she spoke into the jeering crowd before the sheriff's thick fingers could cut off her speech. She called upon all her remaining strength and reached her hand out for the faerie closest to her – a beautiful, mostly naked fae king; the fae king she had known so well, all of her life. She felt his spectral touch on her fingertips. The faerie king was surrounded with a green shimmer, like an aura of glitter that caught the sunlight and swirled around his perfect, larger-than-human form. His musculature was largely human-like, but Grainne knew that there were subtle differences between human and fae bodies. The fae were made of a higher, purer elemental energy, made for their individual planes of existence, and able to do things that humans could not.

Their touch was intoxicating, making a human feel the way that drinking a few cups of mead and then dancing a reel might. Their voices resonated at a frequency that, if the listener was not attuned to it, could induce hysteria or an uncanny sense of dread. They were always breathtakingly beautiful, their faces aquiline, their limbs long and well-muscled. They were free of the diseases and imperfections that beset humans. They were intensely sexual beings. To the fae, that was a normal part of life: to be enmeshed with sex, the creative force of the universe.

The intoxicating faerie energy entered her as the faerie king touched her, just as it had done so many times before, and Grainne felt warmed and enlivened by it. Though she knew she was dying, the fae's energy had the effect of plugging her into a source of pure life. It would be temporary, but it would be enough.

Come now, sweet Grainne, the faerie king spoke directly in her mind. They had known each other long enough now that they had communicated telepathically for some time. *Finally, it is time for you to enter the kingdom of Murias. You have served me well, these many years. Come, and find peace.*

'You do evil today by taking the name of the Fair Ones in vain! They are no devils; they are our own angels, part of our lands. That have always been in the streams and rocks and trees and moss, since before there was Man, and certainly before there was this village.

'They wait for me, though you cannot see them. Aye, I do not go to my death. I go to live in the hills forever; in the far castles of the fae that are full of sweet mead and fresh bread and dancing for all eternity,' she cried out, her final words in this realm. Grainne clasped the faerie king's hand. *Aye. I will go now,* she said, and the fae nodded.

Startled, the sheriff's hands loosened. Grainne had seen this moment in her dreams, and she knew that she would suffer no more in this world of pain. But she had one more task before the faeries would take her away forever. She raised her chin and drew in a deep breath, summoning all her power.

'But they will curse you, you men who bring pain to this land of magic! I curse you! In the name of the kings and queens of Falias, Gorias, Finias, Murias and the Crystal Castle of the Moon! In the names of earth and stone, air and winds, fire and hearth, water and sea, I curse you! Let no more the Good Folk help you. Let no more the wise ones negotiate with them on your behalf. Let a blight be on this land!'

Grainne watched as the waves outside the harbour walls rose and roiled higher and higher. The faerie king's energy gave her everything she needed.

Her breath had almost left her, and her eyes blinked shut. Her body slumped against the ropes that held her upright to the stake.

And as she left her body, she held out her arms for her beloved faerie king, who had been her lover and adviser for so many years, who folded her into his strong arms. But it was her spirit that met her king and not her body, which remained behind. Grainne felt her spirit merge with the faerie in a deeply erotic union. The atoms of her spirit – whatever spirit was formed of – thrummed in delight, like a struck bell. It was like the feeling that washed through her when she touched herself and found – oh so temporarily – the brief, heady bliss of orgasm, a feeling of floating, of vibration, of peace. She had known that bliss so many times already: she had become one with her beloved countless times. But, finally, she was his in spirit.

She was light itself now, a being made of love, unencumbered with the weighty body she saw on the gibbet before her. She was no longer limited by her mortality: released from her body, she was free. Finally, after so many years of communing with the Good Folk, she was able to know what they felt. How they experienced feeling, life, connection. It was remarkable. She felt more alive than she ever had, even though she had passed into death. Communing at this energetic level was like blossoming at the peak of an orgasm, but without any sense of tapering off or fading. The velvety delight of it thrilled Grainne.

If I had known this was what awaited me, I would have been so much wickeder, she thought, *and thus hastened my end. Or, perhaps, not worry about the little life I led here...*

As she transformed, Grainne felt herself become fluid. Her spirit thrilled with the sensation. Finally, as the faerie king held her firmly, she dissolved completely into him.

Come, my beauty, he said in his voice that resonated deep in her soul. *Know eternal pleasure in the halls of your king...*

She knew that the other women – and Joan, the child who had been denied the years to grow into one – would also be taken by the Good Folk, as a reward for their faithful honouring of the fae. The Good Folk would not let their favoured humans be strangled and burned.

She went willingly to Murias, the faerie realm of water. The King of Murias led her in an embrace over the waves to a distant, gleaming castle, and if she still had a heart, it would have exploded with joy.

1
____

'Annie, you can't drink all the wine. It's an offering for the sunrise.' Faye Morgan hugged the foil blanket around herself and pulled her scarf back over her nose. It was December and Faye and Annie – best friends since they were children – were camping out on Black Sands Beach, waiting for the cold sun to break over the black night horizon for the winter solstice.

Annie drained the insulated travel mug of the home-made raspberry wine they'd brought. Faye made it from the raspberry bushes in the garden behind her family's shop, Mistress of Magic; like any good witch, she maintained the ancient garden that had always been there.

Scabious, comfrey, lavender, dandelion, mugwort and nettles grew along the stone-walled edges of the long garden behind the house. Two apple trees stood like guardians at the end, and the raspberry and bramble bushes dominated the east side of the garden, drinking the sun into their ripe fruit every summer. On the west side of the garden, wild white and yellow roses clutched their wall like possessive lovers, not allowing anything else to grow there.

'Cannae let these good offerings go unappreciated.' Annie

burped. Faye and Annie usually came to the beach late on the night of the twenty-first of December, the shortest day, and camped there, ready to watch the sunrise and welcome in the new solar year. Faye liked presents and turkey dinners as much as the next person, but she had always celebrated the old ways in private – when her mother, Moddie, and her grandmother, Evelyn, had been alive, they had, too. Now, Annie had become her solstice companion.

Grandmother had died of a heart attack when Faye was twelve; Moddie had passed, suddenly, from a stroke when Faye was eighteen.

Moddie was too young to die. Everyone agreed on that.

Faye had found her mother in the garden, where she'd been picking fruit when she had been abruptly taken. Faye had run out into the street, crying, and hammered on the doctor's door – *Please help me, please help me*. When it was clear there was nothing to be done for Moddie, the doctor had gently steered Faye away from where Moddie lay among the flowers and made her a cup of tea. *Strokes can happen at any time,* she'd said, handing Faye a mug with a generous amount of sugar stirred into it. *I mean, it's something that happens in your brain, as you know. But it's like a lightning strike. Something as fast and savage as heartbreak. Or, falling in love in the first place.*

Faye, who suspected Moddie had been heartbroken over something in her past for some time, hadn't answered. But she thought of Moddie's death at every winter solstice, when the days were darkest, waiting for the sun to return. She thought that death was a door that seemed to swing open easily for some as soon as they approached it, but for others was slowly, creakingly pushed open after a long struggle. And for others, it seemed that they danced with one hand forever on the door, daring it to open, until one day, it acquiesced.

Moddie, for some reason, had prompted the door into the

next life to swing open suddenly and gather her into its velvety blackness at the first hint of her passing by.

Because Faye had been eighteen when Moddie died, and an adult in the eyes of the law, no arrangements had to be made to look after her; she had picked up sole responsibility for running Mistress of Magic. But she was still young, and Annie had taken to dropping in more to help and staying over at the house a few nights a week. Neither of them had ever talked about it, but Faye knew that Annie was substituting herself for Moddie in all the little spaces she had inhabited in Faye's life. And that included the solstices.

Every year, Faye and Annie brought Grandmother's grimoire with them and recorded their thoughts and impressions of the solstice in it. The grimoire was a book of old Scottish folk magic, added to by generations of Morgan women, who had always been witches.

In the blank pages at the back of the grimoire, after the pages of remedies, rituals and strange sigils, there was a handwritten section which was a combination of diary, recipe book and magical journal, where Grandmother and the Morgans before her had observed the moon and the seasons, and recorded the magic they did and how well it worked.

That aspect of the book was what people called a Book of Shadows nowadays: a kind of reflective journal of magic: a perpetual work in progress. Faye had found the grimoire a few years ago when she had finally cleared out Grandmother's room at the back of the cottage.

It had been convenient for Grandmother to be on the ground floor when she'd started to find the stairs difficult. Not that she gave up her mobility easily, Faye had remembered with a smile as she'd packed up the blankets, throws and nightdresses in Grandmother's wardrobe after she died. And, after walking became tough, Grandmother had taken up residence in the easy chair by the fire in the shop. From that chair, Grandmother had told stories, read palms and dispensed advice. Sometimes, Moddie had rolled her eyes, not wanting her mother in the shop all the time, but Grandmother wasn't going anywhere. Not then.

Faye had learned to be independent – fiercely so – since losing her mother and grandmother. She lived alone, she ran the shop, and she had grown accustomed to her own company. But she was also desperately lonely, a secret that she never shared with anyone. Despite her friendship with Annie, Faye longed for a deeper connection. She longed to be seen, to be held, to be special to someone. Life seemed to swell and embrace the people around her. They had families. They had loved ones. Networks of support.

Faye had nobody, not apart from Annie. And it hurt.

At the bottom of a drawer containing woollen socks, scarves and various hairbrushes – Grandmother had kept her white hair long, and still brushed it a hundred times every night, just like she had done with Faye and Moddie's deep auburn curls when they were children – Faye had found a large, brown leather-bound notebook. It was plain on the cover and wrapped with a leather thong. Inside, she found Grandmother's neat, copper-plate handwriting. *The Magical Record of Evelyn Morgan*, it read.

It started with some passages that concerned local faerie lore.

At Midwinter one of the faerie kingdoms of Murias, Falias, Gorias or Finias takes a child and, at Midsummer, a willing woman. The child must be under a year old so that it can be raised in the Crystal Castle with no memory of its mortal parents, and the woman must be fair and willing to join the faerie dance for evermore. In thanks, the faerie king and faerie queen will bless the land and grant boons

to the villagers of Abercolme for their generous
offerings.

There was a song that Faye remembered from childhood:

Midsummer, Midsummer, Midsummer delight;
go to the faeries on Midsummer night
Take thee a maiden, take thee a wife –
Take thee a bairn for the rest of its life –
Midsummer, Midsummer, Midsummer delight;
go to the faeries on Midsummer night.

Grandmother had taught it to her, and they'd sing it
together at Midsummer on the twenty-first of June every year.
They'd sing and dance and have all of Faye's favourite things to
eat, and lemonade to drink, but Grandmother would always
insist they were home by teatime.

Now, years later, on a different, darker solstice, Faye stared
out at the black sea and sky. Grandmother had said that faeries
were the reason that Abercolme seemed to have always been
blighted – at least, for as long as anyone could remember.

According to Grandmother, anything bad that happened in
the village was because the villagers no longer observed the old
ways: the old rituals and observances that were put in place to
respect the Good Folk.

That job, Grandmother lectured the young Faye, had been
left to the Morgan women, and it was a hard, ongoing task. The
Good Folk must be propitiated with bowls of milk, libations of
wine, flowers at their special places in nature; they must be kept
happy, or they would wreak havoc on the land. Cause droughts,
famines, diseases, floods, fires. In the oldest tales, the fae would
steal baby girls to raise in the faerie realm, *and, when they were*
grown, Grandmother had whispered, her eyes wide, *breed with*
them. Fill them with their half-fae babies.

That phrase had always given Faye a sense of tingling disquiet. *Breed with them.* As if a human woman was an animal, used only for her reproductive qualities. The thought had filled her with horror, but she remembered Grandmother's tone of voice when she had told her, which was low and filled with a strange longing.

But that is awful, Grandmother, the young Faye had exclaimed.

Yes, my dear, her grandmother had replied. *But there are some things in this life that you can only understand when you are older. Some consider that being the lover of a fae is a great blessing.*

When she was older, Faye had asked Moddie if she believed that the Good Folk bred with humans. She had expected her mother to say no, that it was one of Grandmother's more fanciful ideas, but Moddie had looked away, a blush on her cheeks. The thought of it returned to Faye sometimes.

Grandmother had tried to teach her, as a child, the old ways to appease the Good Folk, but Faye had never witnessed any evidence of them, and she had lapsed in her observances over time.

But, sometimes, now that she was a grown woman, Faye would dream of a fae lover, like a man, but larger, taller: his chest was broad, hard and muscled, his forearms corded and strong.

He had an aquiline face and yellow-blonde hair, long, to his shoulders. His face was beautiful in an otherworldly way, with piercing blue eyes, heavy-lidded with long lashes.

In the dream, her lover stroked her skin gently with his long fingers and murmured words in her ear that she had no memory of on waking. In the dream, he kissed her, held her in his huge, strong arms, and then, slowly, entered her, whispering that he was going to give her a baby, that he would fill her with his seed, that she was his pretty little brood mare, that they were destined to be together. The dreams always made her so wet and full of longing that she would wake up, gasping and frustrated.

Grandmother had also said that the Good Folk would swap a human baby for a faerie changeling, disguised so that the baby's parents would be forever unaware. The human parents would take care of the changeling as their own, until one day, it would be taken back into the fae realm. Sometimes, this was done if a fae baby became ill with an affliction that could not be healed in the fae realms, or if the fae kings or queens decided that the baby needed to learn certain skills in the human world.

Though Faye had believed this as a child, she'd questioned it as she'd grown older, and this part of Grandmother's teaching seemed a little far-fetched to her now. Still, she had showed the grimoire to Annie, and together they'd leafed through the thick pages. Grandmother had written down her dreams in it, as well as spells, healing she'd performed for various villagers, and accounts of her rituals at the new, full and dark moons.

Annie had always been fascinated by Faye's witch heritage: the fact that she could trace her family back to Grainne Morgan, who had been murdered as part of the now infamous witch trials in Berwick in the sixteenth century. Even before then, the Morgan women had been witches, Grandmother had told her. *Their blood is in yours, Faye. Never forget.*

But Faye didn't like to think about Grainne Morgan, being burned at the stake; every time she did, she could almost feel the fire licking up her own skin. The ancestral trauma from such a thing, she had read, lived on in the generations following. She could well believe it. She'd had nightmares as a child: of being shut in a dark, smelly room with no light or air. She would wake up from those dreams crying and with a sensation around her wrists as if they had been chafed by rope.

How to explain the crackling panic that engulfed her when she thought about those women?

Annie was leafing through the grimoire, lit by the lamps they had brought with them onto the beach.

'Every year, I find something new,' she murmured. 'There's all kind of things in here. Look – spells for health, luck... Look at this. Faerie kings and queens.' She showed the book to Faye, who frowned at the pages.

'I don't remember seeing that part before,' she said, leaning over and staring at the thick vellum parchment. The double page was arranged in a kind of diagram, like a family tree, with amateurish illustrations – done by Grandmother, or a Morgan woman before her, Faye guessed. The illustrations showed royal crests and crowns on each corner of the pages.

'In Murias, the realm of water, the king and queen are Fintanaeon, Master of the Tides, and Levantiana, Mistress of the Cup. In Falias, the realm of earth, the king and queen are Lyr, Master of Mountains, and Moronoe, Mistress of the Stone. In Gorias, the realm of air, the king and queen are Raphaeleon, Master of the Winds, and Tyronoe, Mistress of the Knife. And in Finias, realm of fire, the king and queen are Attis, Master of Flame, and Thetis, Mistress of the Staff.'

Faye read aloud, tracing her finger over the words written in a thick ink.

Each royal house's crown symbol was different: the crown for Murias, the realm of water, was a rose gold crown with six tall spikes and an inner cap of pearls and opals. The crown for Falias, the realm of earth, was square with four domed sides made of deep yellow gold, each holding a precious jewel in a different colour. The crown for Gorias, the realm of air, looked as if it was made of glass, with no jewels at all but with hundreds of tall, thin, transparent spikes around a glass circlet. And the crown for Finias, the realm of fire, was a thick black circlet without any spikes but studded with rubies in an abstract pattern. Whoever had drawn the crowns had taken a lot of care: the whole double page was a work of art.

'That's awesome,' Annie cooed. 'Look at all the work that must have gone into this. The page was stuck together, so I don't think it's been opened in a while.'

'That would explain why I haven't seen it before. I must have flicked right past it,' Faye said as she studied the names of the fae kings and queens. 'Isn't it wild that someone believed in all of this enough to write it in the family grimoire?'

'Your grannie was all about the faerie world. Maybe there's something in it.' Annie shrugged.

'Maybe,' Faye said. 'Look. Rules for interacting with the faerie realms.' She ran her finger down a list of commandments, written in a neat, copperplate hand.

One. Never eat or drink in the faerie realms. Taking in their food and drink, while delicious, will alter a human body forever and make it more of the fae, less of the human. This can result in a greater susceptibility to illness and bad luck while in the human world, though it can confer great power in the worlds of faerie.

Two. Following on from One. The Rule of Balance applies between the faerie and the human worlds. Each world depends on the other to exist, and there is a natural ebb and flow between the realms. If one realm seeks to overpower the other, chaos reigns. If they work harmoniously together, peace reigns.

Three. Faerie powers must be propitiated by the humans assigned the task, who we call witches. To maintain peace with the faerie realms, witches must care for their places of power in nature, leave regular offerings and remain in communication with the fae.

Four. Do not ask special boons of the fae. The Rule of Balance demands payment, and if a human asks the fae for help, know that it will be given, but the price demanded in return will be high.

Five. Observe the rites of the seasons: Beltane, Samhain, the solstices and the equinoxes.

Six. Study the faerie realms and know them before entering them. Keep your wits about you at all times when in the realm of faerie. The fae realms are not like the human world; the fae do not operate as we do. Morality does not exist in the faerie realms. Tread carefully there.

Seven. Wear charms to resist faerie enchantment, or risk being lost. The fae, though they confer power to witches, are perilous and will seek to seduce, possess and impregnate witches for their own ends.

Eight. Know that the longer a human spends in the realms of faerie, the more difficult it will be to return to the mortal world.

Nine. A faerie cannot force a witch to stay in its realm, and a witch has free will. If you enter faerie, it is because you choose to, and you can leave when you wish, as long as you have not partaken too much of the faerie food and wine, or stayed away for too long. The fae will lie to you and tell you that you are their prisoner. You are not. But the fae are persuasive and can make it seem that you cannot leave. Beware.

'That's a lot of rules, eh.' Annie took the book from Faye.

'Hmm. Whoever wrote that really believed in the fae,' Faye said thoughtfully. 'Maybe, in years gone by, they were more present. Different times.'

'Aye, maybe,' Annie said, and flicked further through the thick, handwritten pages, absorbed. 'Things've moved on. Wouldn't blame the faeries fer retreatin' back tae their lands, what wi' all the chaos humans have brought tae the world.'

'*Impregnating witches.* That's kind of intense.' Faye's eyes widened. 'Do you think that ever happened?'

'Naw. Old legends. I'd say all that's a code fer *respect nature, 'cause she has no respect fer you.*' Annie made a face. 'Good advice.'

'I guess. Still, it seems kind of... like this person thought that was real.' Faye stared out to the black night sea.

'You don't know who wrote that. How they saw the world

would be different to how we do,' Annie said distractedly. She was still flicking through the pages, until she exclaimed and jabbed her finger down on the paper. 'Ha! Knew it. Spell for love. To summon passionate love, aye, that's what we want! Good on ye, Grandmother Morgan.' Annie pulled out her glasses and slid them onto her nose. 'We're gonna do this.'

'Why?' Faye replied. 'Love is...' She trailed off, frowning.

'What?' Annie poked her.

'Disappointing. Leads to heartbreak and pain. Pointless.' Faye shrugged, trying to seem unbothered. That was what Moddie had taught her. *Never trust a man. They will break your heart. Your father broke mine.* 'I don't want to do a spell for love.'

'Oh, come on. Don't be such a stick in the mud.' Annie held her torch up to the book again. 'Says here that the first step is to make dolls. *The object of your desire is to be rendered as dutifully as possible, with the hair and fingernails if it is to represent one person in particular.*' Annie read it aloud in her actress voice, as if she were a television announcer from the 1950s. 'Wow. D'ye think Grandmother Morgan was out and about, picking toenails out of people's bins, aye? Not for me. But it says here ye can just make one up that represents your ideal partner. I'd be well up for that. Why not? We could ask Aisha to do it with us, she's single.'

Aisha worked part-time at the shop with Faye.

'I don't know. I'm not sure I want that. It's... I dunno. More trouble than it's worth,' Faye protested. But the truth was that even though she had been raised to fear love – even though Moddie had schooled her in all the ways that a man would betray her and break her heart – Faye was lonely. And her heart yearned for love.

'Course ye do. You're always moonin' around like a lost faerie, Faye. Look at ye. Made for romantic hair-whippin' in the wind, moonlit seaside rendezvous.' Annie shone her torch into

Faye's face. 'Look at that face, aye. If no one takes ye soon, I'm going to try and convert ye to a lesbian.'

Faye shrugged. 'No offence, but I don't think I'd be a very good one.'

'Aye well, don't rule it out. But the spell? Come on, Faye. What d'you have to lose? I know you're shy. I know ye don't want to get hurt. You're afraid. But it doesn't have to be earth-shattering, okay? Ye could just have a little fun. Ye need some fun, sweetheart.' Annie put her gloved hand on Faye's shoulder and looked into her eyes in the dim light of the torch. Their campfire was burning low, and the coals were only a dim glow in the dark.

'I am having fun. I'm here with you on a sub-zero beach, waiting for the sunrise. Honestly. Who else is doing this?' Faye argued, but she knew Annie was right. And that Annie normally got what she wanted, one way or another.

'Promise me, sweetheart. You need this. I bloody need it, too.'

'You get a new girlfriend every other week.' Faye rolled her eyes.

'I know, I know. But I want someone I really like. That I can trust.' Annie looked at Faye out of the corner of her eye. 'Not just to sleep with. I want someone to love.'

'Are you being serious?'

'Aye. Why not?' Annie looked away wistfully at the black sea. 'I've only been in love once, and that was a long time ago.'

Faye narrowed her eyes at her friend; she was an actress, so she could roll out the drama if she wanted to. But Faye knew her well enough to know when she was being real or not, and she thought that in this case she was.

'Fine, fine. We'll do it. Anything to stop this emotional blackmail.' Faye took the grimoire from her friend. Grandmother's handwriting was so familiar; neat copperplate, spidery with time. She felt the tears spring to her eyes as the memory of the woman she had loved so much came back, breathing and vivid. 'Let's see what we'll need.'

As she peered at the book, Faye noticed the light had changed, and she could see the page better. She looked up and saw the first faint rays of the sunrise reaching out over the horizon, and nudged Annie.

'Come on. We'll look at this later,' she said, holding out her hand for her friend.

They walked down the beach together, foil blankets tied around their shoulders like magicians' capes.

'Happy solstice.' Annie hugged her and they stared up at the sun, blanketed by dawn-pink clouds, glinting on the grey-green sea. 'May all our wishes come true this year. Make a wish on the new sun.' She raised her flask to the sun and closed her eyes. Perhaps Annie really was wishing for someone she could love.

Faye held up her own flask and made her own wish on the new sun before taking a drink and pouring a small libation of the wine into the sand by her feet. She had, in previous years, wished for her health and for the shop to be successful. She was about to do the same again, but as she closed her eyes and felt the faraway warmth of the new sun caress her skin, a sense of bravery overtook her. *I too wish for love. True love to come to me*, she thought, and was surprised at how much she truly meant it.

2

'So. Are we all ready?'

It was past closing time in the shop, and Faye looked at the other women in turn as they sat in a circle on the sheepskin rugs in front of the hearth, candles flickering around them, sweet incense in the air. Annie, her many-ringed hands folded in her lap, sat cross-legged, the firelight reflecting on a pair of oversized reading glasses. Next to her was Aisha, wearing a vest top that said *WITCH, PLEASE* in bright pink on stretchy black fabric, grinning excitedly.

'I can't wait! This is awesome. We shoulda done this years ago,' Annie cooed.

As it was, it had taken Annie a month to persuade Faye to enact the love spell they had found in the back of Grandmother's grimoire, and another two weeks to wait for a propitious new moon to occur. A new moon was the time to wish for something new; a dark moon was the time to end something.

Faye's mum, Moddie, had made the downstairs of their family home into a shop in the seventies. Flower power had made its way to Abercolme, a tiny village in Fife, and, stubbornly, despite Grandmother telling her that no one would come, Moddie had filled the windows and wooden shelves with crystals, her home-made incenses, books about witchcraft and tarot packs. Faye remembered standing behind the glass counter as a child, watching Moddie talking to her customers about astrology, spell casting, runes and the phases of the moon.

Tonight, Faye had laid out a circle of candles and three cushions in front of the shop's tall stone hearth, blackened on the inside and topped with the original stone mantle.

'Let's do it,' Aisha muttered. 'I have needs, ladies.' Aisha had been working part-time in the shop for the past year, while working on her PhD at Edinburgh Uni, job-sharing with Annie. It worked well, as neither Annie nor Aisha could commit to full-time hours and, anyway, Faye couldn't afford to pay them both to always be there. Aisha was a huge music fan and had slowly been trying to educate Faye, playing new bands in the background as they worked. Usually, she came to work in jeans and scruffy band T-shirts, although she couldn't ever quite disguise her small waist, delicious curves and glossy black hair, which she usually tied up in a knot. Tonight, though, it was loose.

Annie gave her a long look. 'Scrubs up well, this one, aye.' She raised her eyebrow at Faye. 'Seems like my troubles might be over.' She winked theatrically at Aisha.

'I wouldn't stop your search just yet.' Aisha grinned. 'Faye said to come in the mood for love, so I thought putting a bit of lippy on wouldn't hurt.'

'Your hair *is* lovely, though, Aish. You should wear it down more often,' Faye said.

Aisha blushed, but looked pleased. 'Thanks,' she said shyly.

Faye had always had certain *abilities*. Like Moddie and Grandmother, she had precognitive dreams: she would dream something, and then it would happen, a week or so later. She had inherited her grandmother's healing hands, being able to lay her hands on people and channel what felt like high vibrational pure love into them. Annie swore by it when she had a headache.

She was able to see energies in nature as well as in people, too. Sometimes, particularly at the local beach – Black Sands Beach, so named for the darker colour of the sand to the beach around the corner from it which was called White Sands Beach – Faye saw figures moving at the edge of her sight, sometimes shadowy, sometimes in light of different colours. Sometimes, she heard things: singing, words spoken in a language she could not recognise. Sometimes, it was a glimmer or an energy haze in the air; sometimes, it was just a feeling, a change in energy somewhere that could be like a click, a sudden transition of vibration.

And Faye had always been able to detect the colourful auras that hovered around people. Tonight, Aisha's aura was bright orange, and Annie's was blue. As well as colour, there was a kind of frequency that Faye could detect in the energy of others. There was also a feel – sometimes energy could feel buzzy and fast, sometimes slow and hot, cold and rigid – all people had a feel, a weather, a combination of colour, texture and sound that made them who they were, from moment to moment. Some people were always the same; others were changeable.

'Come on! Let's do this. The night's auspicious.' Annie wriggled her shoulders in excitement. 'It's a Friday, the best day for love spells. And it's a new moon. Ach, I'm horny. Bring me someone, moon! I'm not even fussy by now.'

'Hey. I thought you wanted your next great love?' Faye raised her eyebrow at Annie.

'I do. Just saying, nothin's off the table. Or floor, in this case. Shall we get started, then? You going to clear the space, call the powers in?'

Annie knew almost as much as Faye about witchcraft; Moddie and Grandmother had taught Faye, and later, when

Grandmother had passed on but Moddie was still alive, she had treated both of them as her daughters. *Ah, my witchlings, come in and learn*, she'd say sometimes when they tiptoed into the kitchen, trying to get a glimpse of Moddie's spell-making.

Moddie had relied more on the modern witchcraft books that she stocked in the shop than Grandmother's family wisdom, though Faye never knew why. When they were teens, Moddie had taught them how to cast a circle according to modern witchcraft; Grandmother sniffed at what she considered her daughter's modern notions. *No point calling in the powers like you're in the theatre, standing there, waving your arms like an idiot. The powers would be there all the time if ye were living rightly with them*, she'd say, glaring at the purple-and-blue-covered paperbacks that featured elegant women's profiles against crescent moons. *Hell mend ye if ye conjure some kind of foreign spirit in the house...*

Faye practised a combination of magic that Moddie and Grandmother had taught her, though she tended more towards the modern. Some of Grandmother's old ways, like her fervent belief in the Good Folk – and the perils that would come by not observing their traditions – seemed archaic, but Faye still used a lot of the recipes from Grandmother's grimoire in the shop to make incense, magical teas and body washes and spell candles.

Tonight, Faye was following the ritual in Grandmother's grimoire at Annie's insistence. She picked up a rose quartz wand – the stone for love – and walked around her friends, imagining herself drawing down moonlight and starlight from the clear black Scottish sky.

She felt the power fill her from above, then brought the power up through her from the earth: the rich black earth under the worn flagstone floor, the wet green of the woodland, and the dark, rained-on sand of the beach that she had felt between her toes so many times that she almost missed it when it was gone. The power of earth and stars filled her and met in her middle, spiralling into each other and building heat through her body.

Faye felt the power flow through her, through the wand, and, with her eyes half-closed, she saw it light up the stone-flagged floor, making a circle of light that glowed in the same pink as the crystal wand.

Next, Faye called in the elements: north for earth, east for air, south for fire, west for water. Going to each point in the circle where she had already placed the candles inside their glass lamps, she spread her arms wide and called out to the spirits of each element to protect them in their work.

When she turned to west to invoke the power of water, she envisaged a wall of water, like a waterfall, flowing to her; to the south, a wall of fire that crackled and spat. When she faced the east and opened her arms to connect with the power of air, she imagined standing on top of a mountain with the wind pushing at her from against the drop below. And when she turned to the north, she felt the steadfast power of earth spiralling around them.

The women gripped each other's hands. In the middle of their circle Faye had set up an altar for their love spell. In the centre she had placed two carved wooden figures, inherited from Grandmother. They usually stood on the stone mantle-piece above the hearth, but she had taken them down tonight. One of the figures was a horned goat-man, with a shaggy chest and cloven hooves on an otherwise human man's body, covered in leaves. The other was a naked feminine figure with long hair that swirled around her body, holding a goblet in one hand and a flower in the other.

Grandmother had always called the male figure Old Hornie, and the female one was called merely Queenie, for she was the Queen of Elphame, the faerie queen, Grandmother said. Around the deity figures Faye had scattered shells and pebbles collected from the local beach; a vase of red and pink roses stood behind them. It seemed appropriate to use Old Hornie and Queenie in their ritual, representing masculine and feminine energies. Faye knew that putting them there wasn't about representing men and women in heterosexual relationships, per se – Old Hornie epitomised one force of nature, the masculine, and Queenie represented the feminine. Grandmother had taught that everyone held both energies within themselves, and both were the stuff of life itself.

She had lit pink and red candles, two of each, and benzoin, rose petal and jasmine incense burned fragrant smoke around them from where it smouldered on top of a charcoal disc in an earthenware holder. In preparation for their ritual, Faye had also filled a blue-painted pottery chalice inscribed with a pentagram with half of a mini bottle of champagne. *A lover's drink to entice a lover*, she thought as she watched the bubbles burst on the surface of the golden fizz. *Why not.*

'Let us first set our clear intention in our work. That we will attract romantic love to ourselves in the best way possible for us, individually; that we trust the gods to bring us exactly what we need,' she said, opening Grandmother's book. The ritual additions were hers, to set the mood and create the space; the spell itself noted only the bare bones of what was needed: desire, and a poppet doll. In preparation for the spell, Faye had told them to each make a poppet of their ideal partner.

'They should be sexy. The men. And women,' Aisha added.

'Okay, okay. We'll attract romantic love and great sex to ourselves, and we trust the gods to bring us what we need.' Faye smiled and raised her eyebrow at her friend. 'Good enough?'

'Aye.' Annie wriggled on the rug.

'Let's get started, then. Get out your poppets.'

Each woman laid a doll onto the rug in front of them. Aisha put hers in front of her shyly. She had drawn a big red heart in marker pen on the white T-shirt material she'd made her poppet of. 'He's got a good heart,' she explained. 'And I stuffed him with cut-up copies of *Rolling Stone*. So he'll be intelligent and into music.'

'Okay, well, that makes sense. Annie?' Faye turned to Annie. 'What have you got?'

Annie placed a Barbie in front of her. 'This is her.'

'Barbie?'

'She's got big tits, she's blonde, she's into fashion and she's, like, had about a million professional careers. What's not to love?'

Aisha laughed. 'That's so cool. I love it.'

Annie picked up the Barbie and smoothed out its little T-shirt, on which she'd written *GIRLS RULE*. 'So, I gave her a kind of activist T-shirt because I want someone who cares about politics. And I gave her this miniskirt and cowboy boots because she still needs to be hot. And she's carrying some little books I made because she's intelligent and she likes reading. And, look, I coloured in all her chakras.' Annie pulled up the doll's T-shirt to show exploding stars in the colours of the rainbow going from red at the Barbie's groin to dark blue on her third eye. 'So, she'll be spiritual. Into yoga or something at least.'

'Cool!' Faye nodded. 'Okay. So, we present these poppets to the Good Folk and ask them to bring these qualities to us, or something better.' She placed hers next to the other dolls.

'Faye, that's beautiful!' Aisha gasped. 'How long did it take you?' She picked it up and turned it over gently in her hands.

'Oh, not long,' Faye murmured, and looked away, embarrassed. Her poppet had actually taken a week to make; she'd neglected restocking the shop because she'd been sitting at the shop counter, stitching it for days.

She had made a man's shape; tall, long-legged, strong in the shoulders, but not too meaty a figure. It had dark-blonde hair made of a golden wool with a dark copper fleck in it that she'd found in Moddie's old mending basket, which she'd woven into braids. She had embroidered blue eyes and, as it had turned out, quite a pouty mouth. She had taken inspiration from the man in her dreams; the one she had had such erotic dreams about.

On the body of the poppet she had sewn her wishes in blue and gold. The stitching was fine and delicate; as a child, Moddie had taught her how to embroider: chain-stitch, cross-stitch, open-leaf, fishbone.

In a fine running stitch she'd written a long line of rhyming words, wrapping around the doll's body. *Let him be kind, beautiful, magical, free; let him be loving, gentle and in love with me.*

Aisha read out the words; the fire crackled as her voice wove the magic that had already begun with the stitching.

'That's lovely, Faye.' Annie smiled gently and took her friend's hand. 'I hope he comes for ye, I really do,' she said.

'Thanks.' Faye blushed, and placed all three poppets on the altar. 'Right. So, now we've created our poppets, we charge them with the elemental energy to give them life. Starting with air in the east, go clockwise and imagine all four elements flowing into your poppet.' Faye closed her eyes and saw each element immediately, flowing and combining into a golden-white light that surrounded and filled her little doll. 'Now! Say with me:

Bring love to me; so mote it be.

Fill my heart; so let it start.

Satisfy my desire; by earth, air, water and fire.

Blessed faerie realm, bring love to me.

Blessed Good Folk, bring me the satisfaction of my desire.'

Faye took each poppet and wafted it through the incense

smoke, then replaced them on the altar, then she took up the blue chalice of champagne and drank. She focused as hard as she could on the desired outcome, but her mind shifted every time. It was like trying to look through bevelled glass. She knew she wanted someone. A lover, someone who would pull her heart open and deserve the love that lay there, dormant, waiting. A lover who would dispel her loneliness and fill her life with companionship, sweetness, affection... yet, her mind kept straying. She couldn't seem to focus.

Still, she had made the doll at least. That would do its work if Grandmother's book was to be believed.

'So mote it be,' she intoned, and passed the cup to Aisha.

'So mote it be,' Aisha repeated, and passed the cup to Annie, who sipped twice before passing it back to Faye. 'What now?' She looked at the door as if she expected someone to walk through it immediately.

'Now, we close the circle and wait,' Faye said quietly, feeling the magic spiralling around her, big and powerful. Something would come of this. She knew it, deeply, inside herself.

'Do you think they'll come?' Aisha whispered.

'Hopefully.' Annie stretched out her legs and knelt, preparing to get up. 'Magic works.'

'It will be what it's supposed to be,' Faye said as she banished the elements from the circle, imagining each one disappearing: the fire dying and going back to the ground, the water drying away, the mountains receding, the strong breeze dropping to a light breath. Closing the circle by walking around the outside of the space and smudging at the circle of light with her foot, she took care not to disturb the rose petals. 'The altar can stay up overnight. I'll take it down before we open in the morning,' she said. 'Let it have as much time as it can.'

Aisha murmured to Faye, 'Will it really work, do you think?' Her wide, long-lashed brown eyes searched Faye for reassurance and, for the first time, Faye saw something she hadn't seen before in Aisha's eyes: a raw need, a yearning. Perhaps Aisha needed this more than Faye had expected.

'I'm sure it will.' Faye reached out shyly and touched Aisha's soft cheek. 'Have faith,' she murmured, and Aisha nodded.

Annie knelt in front of the altar and bent her head for a moment, no doubt adding an extra prayer to the Good Folk. Faye watched her friend trace her fingertips over the words of the spell in the book. If Grandmother had cast this spell, had it brought her Moddie's father? Had Moddie cast it to summon Faye's own father? And, if so, how good was a spell that summoned lovers who would desert you?

Suddenly, the door swung open and an icy winter blast of wind blew in. The bells next to the door jangled in alarm, and the old pebble hagstone charm that hung there, made by Grandmother as protection, shook violently.

'What the...?' Aisha was the closest to the door and instinctively stepped out into the street. As soon as she did, the gusting wind died away and the streetlights painted shining streaks on Aisha's long black hair.

Faye ran to close the door, goosebumps prickling her skin. She had been so sure she'd locked it. As she did so, she felt a kind of presence pass her and go out through the door. The incense smoke which had built up in the room billowed out into the night air, but it was more than that – as if the spell had been truly released into the world.

Faye's heart beat in a panic as she pulled Aisha inside and closed the door again hurriedly behind them both. She felt for a moment that the stone-flagged floor had dissolved under her, and now she was falling.

Aisha's face wore an odd expression; her wide eyes dreamy and staring. Her cheeks were flushed and hot, even though it was cold outside.

'Aisha! Aisha! What's up?' Faye shook her friend gently, realising that she was also hanging on to Aisha to stop the disorienting feeling of the floor slipping away under her. The roses faded from Aisha's light brown skin. Her eyes cleared, and she met Faye's gaze. Faye felt the room right itself and her feet firmly back on the stone.

'Nothing... I...' Aisha gazed through the glass door outside onto the street, which was almost as bright as daylight, and smiled quietly, as if she had a pleasurable secret. 'I'm fine. I don't know why you locked the door in the first place.'

But Faye felt something other than pleasure at the languid yellow moonlight outside. There was a strange atmosphere out there, like the heavy warmth before a storm.

Faye pulled the blind down on the door, blew out the remaining candles in the shop and turned on the harsh electric light.

'Back to real life,' she said as cheerily as she could, but her voice wavered. She could feel something, now that they had released the spell into the world. Something was coming. Something big.

3

There had been a strange magic in the air ever since the three witches had cast their love spell – a lush, brooding, fragrant miasma of roses that Faye could smell at the edge of her awareness and a sense of pressure in the air, like a storm was coming.

It was a week after they had cast the spell – early February, just past Imbolc, an ancient Celtic festival signifying the first stirrings of new life in the land – and Faye he had awoken from a dream where she had been standing naked on Black Sands Beach, with rose petals cascading over her naked skin. The petals were everywhere, being blown on a breeze like standing under a cherry blossom tree in spring.

She had to open the shop soon, but she liked to walk down to the sea in the morning with a coffee and just sit, taking in the sea air, rich in ozone. Or, she would look for feathers and stones, or walk and think. She liked to be alone on the beach, and she often was: Black Sands Beach was often deserted, apart from the odd dog walker or jogger, but Abercolme wasn't in general a village of joggers or exercise fans. Mostly, it was older people who had lived there their entire lives and were more likely to be found in the pub or the community centre.

Often, Faye came to the beach with a spell ready to cast into the waves; sometimes, she came just to be with the sea, loving its strong, elemental force. The air at the beach was always so *good*, so healing – regardless of the weather. She loved the salt spray on her face; she loved the wildness of the water and the way it changed colour, from grey to dull green to blue-black and even turquoise, in the summer.

Today, she had followed her instinct. She needed to be at Black Sands Beach. Her heart yearned to be there: the dream was a sign.

The feeling – and the smell of roses – had become stronger the closer she had got to the beach. Here, the sky was roiling – dark clouds hovered over the sea, which was as slate-grey as the sky. Perhaps a storm *was* coming, Faye thought, but it hadn't been forecast. This felt different, somehow. There was no wind, just the clouds rolling in, and a sense of waiting, of hiatus. She closed her eyes, and the vision of decadent, blowsy pink roses crowded the space behind her eyes. Rich hued, velvety, soft and sensuous, like soft, full lips, languorous kisses, thick with sweetness, waiting to be ravished.

She shook herself, opening her eyes, the fragrance of roses still lingering. Was it strange that the feeling in the air – around her, in the shop, in the village, since the spell has been cast – felt so... delicious and dangerous at the same time? Was it strange that a kind of lassitude had overtaken her, on the beach, as if she herself was a rose, soft and full of pleasure?

As she brought herself back to the present, she saw a figure walking up the beach towards her: a man – tall, heavy-set but powerful, brown-skinned and unshaven with probably a week or more of beard, and longish black hair. He was wearing a black knitted hat and a plain white T-shirt over black jeans. He was broad-shouldered and muscular, with thick biceps and strong forearms. His thighs stretched the jeans a little as he walked. He reminded her of a bull: there was something in his sheer physicality that was pure primal masculinity.

As he drew closer, Faye took in the details of his face: he had thick, heavy brows, high cheekbones, and a strong jaw under the dark beard. Dark eyes regarded her curiously; he had an intense stare, not aggressive but... direct. Faye got feelings about everyone, and even as he walked towards her, she could *feel* him: focus, groundedness and a kind of delicious warmth that thrilled something within her.

She was sure she hadn't seen him around the village before, and she felt strangely exposed, standing there.

A flash of light to her right made her look away for a moment. One of the windows on a nearby house that faced the beach was open at just the right angle, reflecting sunlight into her eyes exactly at that moment. The house was all steel and glass, that ultra-modern look that had been popular when it was built. Most of the villagers hated it; it didn't fit in with the rest of the village, which was full of the old-style Scottish stone houses. But Faye had always thought it belonged there, some-how. The glass reflected the sea and the sky in all its changing moods and colours, and on full moon nights when Faye had been at the beach, the house, dark and uninhabited, had caught the lunar light like a glass temple.

It had been built in the sixties by some rich architect who was drawn to Abercolme for the coastline. Moddie had told Faye that the architect had unknowingly built the house on a ley line, or some other sacred ground. Either way, once it was built, Grandmother had said that the local faeries were displeased and had cast a curse on anyone who lived there. Whatever the reason, it had been bought a few times but always sold soon after, so had been empty for as long as Faye could remember.

She stared at the house for a moment, shielding her eyes

from the bright glare. She saw that a few of the windows were open, in fact, and when she looked harder, she could see the blinds that were usually closed had been opened, meaning she could see into the house.

Inside, people were moving furniture; she watched as two men carried some kind of desk up a set of stairs. Someone was moving in.

I wonder if there really is a curse on it. She smiled to herself, pulling the tartan wool shawl around her shoulders to keep out the cold.

She remembered asking her mother about it one day when Moddie was plaiting her hair for school. *But IS there a faerie curse, Mummy?* She had watched as Moddie's deft hands braided the three hanks of the deep auburn hair that fell in natural – but often wild and knotted – ringlets around Faye's shoulders. But when she gazed up to her mother's face from the edge of her bed, mirrored in the glass of the dressing table opposite, Moddie had a strange expression. *Just Grandmother's tales. Go on and get dressed for school now, little one,* was all she had said, but she had hugged Faye fiercely before she let her go.

'Great view out here!' the man called out as he approached her.

'It certainly is!' she called back.

He was holding a sheaf of papers, but just then the wind came up unexpectedly and blew them out of his hand.

'Oh, shit!' His dark eyes widened, and he started running after the papers, which had turned the quiet beach into a sudden storm. Instinctively, Faye collected the ones nearest to her and realised they were flyers of some description. She watched him as he ran around, trying to catch the others. There was a sudden greenish glimmer of light around the man, as if it was chasing him, tormenting him. It was as though there were sprites in the wind, pulling the papers away from him right at the last minute, curling and parading them around him. Faye blinked, watching the energy. It appeared to want to distract the man from Faye, because every time he got closer to her, the green light – which curled and danced lazily in the air – pushed the papers further away. Curiously, she watched for a few moments before moving towards him and collecting some more of the papers. As soon as she approached, the shimmer disappeared.

'Here.' She handed him the ones she had collected.

'Thanks. I don't know what just happened. There's no wind.' A smile played on his lips as he looked up at her.

'You're welcome.' She found herself smiling back, taking him in as he stood up. Close up, he seemed even larger. Faye was very aware of the aura of masculinity that surrounded him; she could almost breathe it in, and it made her giddy. She had the sudden impression of this man holding a baby pink rose softly against her cheek, and then taking her in an embrace, his rock-hard biceps pressing her close to his chest.

He handed her a wet flyer. 'Here. You might as well have the last salvageable one.'

ABERCOLME ROCKS, Faye read. Underneath, there was a list of what she assumed were band names, then *MIDSUMMER EVE* written at the bottom. *Midsummer, Midsummer, Midsummer delight; go to the faeries on Midsummer night* – the old rhyme played in her mind.

'What's this?' She looked back up at him. Close up, his eyes were such a dark brown they were almost black; his eyelashes were long and soft.

'Abercolme's first music festival. That I know of, anyway. Hi. I'm Rav Malik.' He held out his hand; Faye shook it politely, feeling a glow of warmth from his skin and a sudden shiver of desire at his touch. 'I'm promoting a festival up here. I was supposed to be plastering these all over town.'

'You managed the beach.' She smiled shyly. Faye was unused to interacting with men like Rav Malik. He exuded some kind of primal pheromone that she could feel herself responding to, and she had no idea how to deal with it. She had never, ever met a man and been this attracted to him on sight before.

The smell of roses was now quite pungent in the air. Faye wondered if she was going mad or if Rav could smell it.

'Yeah. Not quite the plan, but maybe a few snails will buy tickets.'

'Snails don't live on beaches. The salt would kill them.' Faye chuckled. 'You're not from around here?'

'You got me.' He looked boldly at her: a look that she felt between her thighs, as if he had touched her there. Her eyes widened; her lips parted. She made a noise in the back of her throat, like a moan, and disguised it as a cough.

Faye pushed her hair out of her eyes and tried to compose herself. 'Who's moving into the big house? Do you know?'

'Me.' He smiled at her. He had a nice smile. 'Just moved my company up from London to Edinburgh. Amazed it's been empty so long.'

'You? *You're* moving into the house?' Faye did a double take. She didn't know how much the house was worth, but it would have to be a lot, given its size and location, right on the beach. Rav didn't look particularly wealthy, dressed casually with his week-old beard, but then, she supposed, what did a wealthy person look like?

'Aye.' He smiled at her again, the grin tugging at the edge of his mouth. 'I'm moving into the house. Anything wrong with that?'

'No... I guess I'm just surprised that... you're not... old,' she blurted out, and blushed instantly. 'I mean... most people who live here are.'

'Hmm. I've got a few years in me yet.' He chuckled. 'And you are?'

'Faye Morgan.'

'Nice to meet you.' He gestured at the remaining flyers that still littered the beach.

'I'm going to have to pick this lot up, aren't I, Faye Morgan? Or the village elders will curse me.'

She laughed. 'The village elders would tell you it's not them you have to worry about.'

'Oh. Who do I have to appease with burnt offerings?'

She started picking up the stray flyers, mostly wet with seawater. 'Me, probably,' she said over her shoulder. She caught a glimpse of his thick, muscled back under his T-shirt, which had ridden up as he crouched down, and looked away, feeling a heat spread through her, from her thighs, deep into the core of her and up into her stomach.

He stood up and stared at her. Faye felt his intense gaze, again, as if it was penetrating her. She shifted, swallowing.

'You? Why?'

'I'm the local witch, you could say. My family's been here for generations.'

'Witch? What, eye of newt and toe of frog?' He frowned at her now, his brow becoming heavier, and Faye was reminded of a bull, sizing up an intruder in its field. Overhead, the seagulls circled and squawked.

'No. Herbs, plants, the moon, magic... that kind of thing.'

'Right.' He smiled, then, crinkling his eyes against the hard late winter sun, and the sense of peril passed. 'I don't think I've ever met a real witch before.'

'You probably have. You just didn't know it.' Faye ran for three flyers that were caught at the tideline. Rav followed, picking up more.

'So, you're local? D'you know anything more about the history of the house? The agent was pretty clueless.' Rav appeared next to her and stuffed another handful of mulched flyers in his pockets.

'I run a shop in the village – Mistress of Magic, and I live above it. I've lived here all my life. Yeah, that house has a history. My grandmother used to tell me stories about it.' She didn't break her gaze away from the water, but only because she didn't know where to look: Faye was deeply, almost painfully aware of Rav. Of his aura, which was a deep red. The colour of sex. Of the smell of him, which was clean, woody, but also somehow overpoweringly masculine.

'I'd love to hear them sometime.' Rav's eyes met hers, and held her gaze. *He's probably nice to everyone*, Faye thought reflexively. *He's not flirting with me.*

'Well, pop into the shop. I'm open every day except Sunday,' she said, looking away hastily. 'Anyway, I've got to go and open up. Good luck with your festival.' She bent and picked up a dry flyer from a few feet away. 'I'll put one up in the window if you like?'

'I do like. Thanks.' He caught her eye again and his eyes twinkled. 'I'll look forward to seeing you again soon, Faye Morgan. Or should I call you *Morgan Le Fay?*'

'Just Faye will do,' she said, picking up her forgotten coffee. She made her way back to the footpath, feeling his eyes on her. Once she was far enough away, she waved, and he waved back.

I can't believe I waved, she thought.

She wondered whether meeting Rav at the beach – in all its strangeness, with the glimmering light chasing him away from her, and the scent of roses – was a result of the love spell. Surely, that was just her imagination.

Let him be kind, beautiful, magical, free; let him be loving, gentle and in love with me.

That was what she had asked for.

Faye didn't know much about Rav other than that he was gorgeous, was moving into the house on the beach, and that he worked in music. Whether he was kind, magical and available, she had no idea.

Would the spell work that quickly? Faye had cast spells before, but the outcomes were never that exact. Was meeting Rav a coincidence?

Or had she just got what she asked for?

4

———

'Good morning. May I come in?'

The bells tinkled as the glass door pushed open. It was the day of the full moon, another week after Faye had met Rav at the beach, and Faye was pouring loose incense through a funnel into the small glass jars that she sold in the shop and didn't look up, but called out a cheery good morning as she always did to any customers who entered.

Even so, at the edge of her awareness, there was a feeling of strangeness. An unknown presence. The faint smell of the sea in the rain, even over the incense that burned in the corner of the shop.

Faye was playing gentle folk music from her phone and through a small digital speaker. Suddenly, the music stopped, and the shop was dead quiet. She looked up, frowning at the sudden pause.

The man stood in the doorway, smiling at her in such a way that suggested he knew her.

'Good morning. May I come in?' he repeated in a low, musical voice.

'Oh! Morning.' Faye pulled her glasses onto her nose from where they held her auburn hair back from her face. 'Please do.'

The man gave her an odd look, and gazed around him before stepping through the doorway into the shop. Faye shivered as he did so, unsure whether it was the blast of chilly, wet air that came in with him or something else.

It was then that Faye noticed that Grandmother's old hagstone charm – nine pebbles with natural holes in them, held together with string – was missing from where it usually hung by the door. Puzzled, she wondered where it was.

'Welcome,' she added with a smile, to reassure him – it wasn't unusual for visitors to the area to be a little unsure about the shop.

'Thank you,' he said.

Tall. That was her first thought. He must have been six foot five or more, because he had to stoop his head to come through the doorway. She watched him as he walked in with long, easy strides and the air of a king inspecting his realm.

Faye's second thought was that he was beautiful. She was absolutely sure that she hadn't seen this man before. Handsome was a poor relation to the kind of heavenly perfection of his face, which was slightly long and high-cheekboned but perfectly proportioned. His blue-green eyes transfixed her; and when he spoke, his mouth had a slight sulky fullness. Lips that wanted to be kissed; a bottom lip that deserved biting. His eyelashes were long, and his manner was languid but purposeful. Faye had the impression of strength kept in reserve, just under the surface, coiled and ready under his slightly cat-like demeanour.

He had said something, and she had no idea what it was.

'I'm sorry?' she asked, befuddled.

'I said, nice shop you've got here.' His voice was slightly accented; she half frowned, trying to place it.

'Oh. Thanks.' She smiled, her heart racing. Faye was suddenly very aware of her own breathing.

'How long has it been here?' He smiled at her again, and his eyes lit up with an odd glow when he did. They were strange, luminous: exactly like the sea on a cloudy day, when the sun came through the clouds and the colour of the sea changed from grey-green to jewelled blue.

'Oh. It opened in the seventies. It's always been our house, though. Belonging to my family, that is.' Faye took a deep breath while pretending to take a sip of coffee. 'You're not local. What brings you here?' she managed to ask over the rim of her mug.

'Adventure.' The stranger ran two long fingers along the glass counter, looking down at the pendants and rings show-cased underneath. Faye stared; he was rough-shaven, and his clipped beard was a dark blonde like his shoulder-length dark blonde hair. He leaned in closer to her. He didn't have the air of a young man – he was too centred, too present for that. Yet, he had few lines on his face; no grey hair that she could see.

'This one is beautiful.' His voice was low, and his face was inches from hers. Ordinarily, it would have been an invasion of personal space, but the idea didn't even cross her mind; she was spellbound.

He looked up, and time seemed to slow. Faye felt his gaze on hers, and it was as though a mist descended, obscuring the shop, leaving only her and the stranger in the middle, like the eye of a storm, the quiet inside a tornado. She felt a sense of shifting, as if she was not secure on the ground at all but instead had her feet in wet sand as the tide washed in and out, pulling her in, burying her feet deeper and deeper. Dimly she remembered a similar sensation after the love spell, when the door had flown open in the wind. But while that had been fear and disori-entation, this was a kind of pleasant fugue.

She didn't know what he was pointing to; she couldn't look away from his eyes. It was exactly how she'd felt before, in the seconds before kissing someone for the first time: a sweet anticipation, a sense of an incredible longing filling the tiny inch of air between their lips.

How would it feel to kiss that full-lipped mouth? The hint of a smile played at its corner; Faye's own soft lips parted involuntarily. She had never felt this kind of sweet, hot crackling energy as there was between them, making her light-headed. A heat that lit her up from the tips of her toes to her forehead.

She noticed a tattoo on his tanned neck, half hidden by the collar on his T-shirt. It was blue and looked like an animal head. Her gaze dropped to his well-muscled chest which was obvious even under his T-shirt. He was rangy but strong, like he spent a lot of time outdoors.

Without meaning to, Faye sighed. Somehow, the introduction of her breath into the small space between them blew away the mist that had hidden the rest of the world. Her return to the mundane was hard and unwelcome, like a sudden change in the temperature.

Faye fumbled with her cup and dropped it, spilling coffee over her laptop which was open on the counter. She had been meaning to start the quarterly accounts but hadn't been able to bring herself to focus on it yet.

'Oh, no. Oh god. Sorry. I...' Hurriedly, she picked up the mug and looked around for a rag to soak up the coffee from the computer. 'No, no, no!' she muttered. Not finding anything to hand, she tore off her green long-sleeved T-shirt, thankful she had a short, tight yoga top on underneath, and used it to dab the laptop.

Faye was glad Annie wasn't here. She'd take great pleasure in teasing her about this for years to come. *Faye, remember when that gorgeous blonde guy came in? Ye can't be trusted with a hot drink. Faye, we're gonna need to get ye oven gloves for when the fellas are around!*

'Don't apologise. Accidents happen.' He smiled, watching her: he didn't seem to share her panic over the spilled coffee.

'Oh... you must think I'm such an idiot...' she muttered as she tried to soak up all the coffee from the keyboard. The laptop made a fizzing noise, and the screen went black. 'Oh no!' she wailed. 'No, no, no!' Faye held down the ON button, but nothing happened. She swore under her breath. She couldn't afford a new laptop right now; takings were steady, but Mistress of Magic wasn't exactly a multimillion-pound business.

'Is it all right?' He leaned over, looking at the screen.

'I think it's gone...' She stopped mid-sentence as the tall stranger reached over and touched the keyboard gently. 'Oh, no, please...'

'It'll be all right. Give it a minute,' the man said, moving around the counter. Faye was vividly aware of his presence next to her. She found herself gauging where her head would rest perfectly on his chest if she lay next to him, or if she melted into his lean body in an embrace...

In the strange way that happens in times of misfortune, she felt in that moment that, somehow, they had already moved on from being strangers to something more. But later, when she looked back at their first meeting, she would know that it was in fact something else entirely that had made her feel that way.

The man touched the laptop again, and Faye thought for a second that she saw a spark of electricity between his finger and the computer. And then the laptop screen flashed blue, and the usual start-up screen appeared.

'Oh, thank god,' she breathed as the spreadsheet reappeared, apparently unharmed.

'There you are. The way they make these things now, it's hard to break them,' he said, that twinkle in his eyes again. She knew that was absolutely wrong, but she smiled along with him, nonetheless.

'Thank you! Thank you so much!' She gaped at the laptop and then at him. 'What did you do? That was like magic!'

'You'd know.' He gave her a mysterious smile. 'Ah, it was nothing. Probably just a loose circuit, or something needed a moment to dry out.'

'Well, I don't know about that...' she said doubtfully. 'You touched it, and it came back to life.'

'Just luck. I have a way with things sometimes.' He glanced out of the window. 'Oh, look. The sun's out.' The man beckoned her towards him, and she found herself following obediently. 'See? Everything is fine,' he said in a low tone, the rich, musical timbre of his voice making all of her body thrill. 'Come and see.'

As if she was hypnotised, Faye followed the man to where he stood in the shop doorway, in the sun: it blazed down unexpectedly from between the grey clouds.

'Good girl,' he said, in that same low, unhurried tone, holding his hand out for hers. Faye's eyes widened at the phrase. *Good girl.* No one had ever said that to her before, and it had a strange effect. She ought to be offended – she was a grown woman, not a little girl – but it felt strangely... comforting, but also... erotic. Deeply erotic.

Why? She had no idea why those words had seemingly enchanted her.

She desperately wanted to slide her hand into his; wanted to feel the strength of his touch, the comfort of his body next to hers, but she resisted. It was ridiculous to want these things with someone she didn't know.

As if he knew what she was feeling, he took her hand and brushed it with his fingers.

'Shh, now. Everything's all right,' he repeated, and the combination of his deep, resonant, reassuring voice and the feel of his soft touch on her skin made Faye draw in a sudden breath. Heat flowed through her body; she felt herself grow wet.

Just listening to his voice, just touching him, caused pleasure to erupt and spiral through her body.

She couldn't help it.

As Faye stood next to him, she could see that it was still raining on the beach just a few minutes' walk away, but here, at least, there was a brief interlude in the weather. Not really an interlude, but there seemed to be some kind of sphere of sunlight over her shop and the shops either side of it.

The man stood next to her and looked up in pleasure at the sunlight; Faye breathed in its warmth, a smile spreading on her cheeks. A similar warmth emanated from him. Irrationally, she still wanted to lean into him, wanted to feel his body against hers.

'See?' His warm voice caressed her like the sun itself. 'Things have a way of working out, even when you don't expect them to, Mistress of Magic.'

'Yes... I...' she stammered, completely thrown off balance.

He gave her an intense, long look, and turned to go. 'Goodbye, Faye Morgan. I'll see you again soon.' He smiled, and bowed theatrically before he left the shop, pulling the door closed behind him.

She was back inside the shop when she realised that she had never told him her name.

5

———

'Did you *hear*? The whole village's talking about it!' Aisha burst into the shop and startled Faye, who was stacking new books onto the shelves: two new spell books from an American publisher, a guide to psychic self-defence, and a book about Scottish faerie lore.

Mistress of Magic was a destination in itself for witchy folk across Scotland, and even wider; last week she'd had American tourists in who had chosen Abercolme for a stop on their holiday just because of the shop. *All thanks to you, Moddie.* And, Faye had to admit that her own magic had also been partly responsible for the shop's success. Since she had taken over running the shop, every month on the new moon Faye cast a spell. Sometimes, it was to attract money, if she had a big bill to pay; sometimes, it was for more customers; sometimes, it was for inspiration, or healing for a customer. But the intended result always tended to manifest, one way or another.

'Did I hear *what*? You're the second one to startle me today. I'm going to need some sort of herbal remedy on a drip at this rate.' Faye slowly slid the books onto the wooden unit and noticed it needed dusting. She was still half enchanted by her mysterious visitor – she felt at once strangely floaty, as if half of her was somewhere else, and still aroused.

What *had* actually happened? It all seemed like a dream: somehow, the tall man had managed to hypnotise her into some kind of lust-ridden fugue. At the time, it had made sense, and she had felt perfectly safe in a kind of bubble of closeness with him, a complete stranger. And then he had left, as mysteriously as he had appeared, and Faye felt confused.

'Dal Riada! They're coming!' Aisha danced around the faded blue high-backed chair by the hearth. 'I'm so excited! I've got both their albums. They're going to play at the festival!'

'You're saying that like I'm supposed to know who they are.' Faye raised an eyebrow at her friend, who was scrolling her phone screen.

'You *do* know. Dal Riada. You've got one of their albums somewhere. Here, listen.' Aisha's phone played a fast, folky Celtic tune.

'Oh, that.' Faye went to the counter and rummaged in the drawer where she kept CDs for the shop's sound system. Aisha had given her a couple more a few weeks ago and she'd slung them in without much thought. 'I haven't played it yet.'

'Oh, Faye! There's a world of new music out there, you know.'

Faye listened to the tune for a minute.

'Celtic folk isn't new. We play it in here all the time,' she replied, though she liked the fevered drumming and the fluted voice of the singer. It reminded her of Moddie: of being swung around in her mother's arms, Moddie's red hair flowing around both of them like flames; of Moddie singing along with the fast lyrics, of her feet drumming on the stone floor after they'd shut up shop and the moon glinted through the windows.

'You know what I mean. Thank the goddess for Abercolme finally making it into the twenty-first century!' Aisha was beaming ear to ear. 'And who knows, eh? Maybe that's how we meet our new lovers!'

'Maybe.' Faye smiled, thinking of the tall man and blushing at how easily she thought again of kissing him.

But men were dangerous. That was something she had learned from Moddie.

Faye had never known her father. He had disappeared just before she was born, and Moddie never spoke of him. But sometimes, if Faye asked, a haunted look would cross her face. All Moddie would say was that he'd had to leave Abercolme.

Just once, though, Faye had come downstairs, woken by a bad dream. Moddie had been sitting at the kitchen table with a friend of hers, a woman from the little coven she ran at the shop – Faye couldn't remember her name. There was a bottle of wine on the table between them, and Moddie's cheeks were flushed.

Faye's bad dream had been of her father; only, in the dream, all she could see of him was a looming shadow. She had described the dream, held in Moddie's warm embrace, sniffling into her mother's comforting soft flannel shirt.

Ah, well, that's all he'll ever be, sweetheart, Moddie had replied, stroking her hair. *A shadow. He didn't want us, child, so don't waste another tear on him.* And, to her friend, she had said, *That's one mistake I'm never making again. Almost killed me.*

Almost killed me. When Faye had gone back to bed, she had stared at the ceiling for what felt like hours with the phrase turning around and around in her head. What did Moddie mean? Had her father tried to *kill* her mother? Was she the daughter of a murderer? A picture began to form in her eight-year-old mind: a tall man, made of shadow; a scowling man, a man who wanted to hurt Moddie.

The next day Faye asked Moddie what she had meant, but her mother shook her head impatiently. *Nothing, little goose.*

Turn of phrase. There was no more explanation than that, except being told not to worry. He wasn't ever coming back.

'Any progress on the spell, anyway?' Aisha picked up the rose quartz crystal wand Faye had used in the ritual. 'Has something happened? You look... I don't know. You're blushing.'

'No... nothing.' Faye knew that she sounded completely unconvincing. Had it been Annie asking, she wouldn't have been able to lie, but she didn't know Aisha as well. Yet, Aisha gave her a perplexed smile.

'Are you sure, Faye?' Aisha had returned to her usual look: hair tied up, no make-up, ripped jeans and a Pink Floyd T-shirt. Yet, Faye noticed her beauty more today, her long lashes, dewy skin. Either Aisha had always had this just-been-kissed look, or something had changed with her, too.

'No. Well...' Faye considered telling her friend about the tall blonde man who had come in earlier, and Rav Malik at the beach. Two men? Were they the outcome of her love spell? But she didn't know what to say about the man who had reduced her to a mass of quivering flesh by calling her his good girl and brushing her hand.

'What?' Aisha looked up. 'Something's up. I can tell. Surely something's going to happen soon?'

'It's the full moon today...' Faye wrote on a tiny price label and stuck it on a carved wooden wand, then picked up another to price. She knew that spells could work more quickly, but there was a part of her that was afraid of her spell actually working. The fact that it might have worked *twice* as well as it was supposed to and brought her two men seemed... unbelievable. Yet, now that she thought about it, she realised that the tall blonde man who had hypnotised her earlier looked quite a lot like the poppet doll she had made. 'So, I guess it could manifest something around now. Anytime from now.'

'Nothing has happened to me. Not yet.' Aisha sighed.

'Hmm. Take some rose quartz home. It draws love to you.'

'I've already got some.' Aisha sighed again. 'So. What's up? I can tell it's something. What?'

'Oh, nothing.' Faye cleared her throat.

'Faye. Spill it.'

'It's nothing.'

'FAYE!'

'Oh, fine. I... I met a man on the beach,' Faye muttered. There had been some oddness about her interaction with Rav Malik – the green light that had followed him around, seeming to blow his leaflets out of his hand, the smell of roses on the beach that Faye couldn't explain – but, somehow, that experience seemed easier and more sensible to talk about than the man who had appeared mysteriously in the shop out of nowhere, who had a very strange aura about him – it was unlike anything Faye had seen before, in fact, gold and glittering – and called her *good girl*. In whose presence she seemed to melt and lose control of her normal self almost completely.

Aisha smiled and put the rose quartz wand down. 'Oh, REALLY! What man? Why is this the first we're hearing of it? The spell's working!' Aisha squealed. 'Have you told Annie?'

'No. It was only this morning. I haven't seen her yet.'

'She'll want to know. I'm texting her,' Aisha declared, getting out her phone.

'Aish. I'll tell her. Chill.' Faye laughed. 'It might not be the spell. He's just some guy. He's bought the big house there. You know, the one that looks onto the beach.'

'I know the one. So, what's he like?'

Faye considered what to say. 'Nice. Our age, I guess. He has his own business of some kind. Just moved up from London.'

'When you say nice, you mean...?' Aisha prompted her. 'Hot? What did he look like?'

'Oh, for... Okay, yes, he's good-looking. Tall. Dark. Handsome. Looks... strong, like he works out. Big,' Faye added, with a little sparkle in her eye. It wasn't a lie. Rav was a big, bullish man and she had liked him. There was nothing wrong in saying that.

'Ooh! And when're you going out with him?' Aisha raised her eyebrow archly.

'We're not *going out*. We just met on the beach, that's all.'

'D'you think it's the spell?' Aisha clutched Faye's hand. 'I mean... it can't be a coincidence, right? You ask for a man, and then this big guy appears... what, like, out of the blue?'

'Pretty much. We were both walking along the beach.'

'It just feels like magic, doesn't it?' Aisha asked, her eyes wide.

'I don't know. Maybe.' Faye chewed her lip. She didn't want to say *Rav Malik doesn't look like the doll I made. Another man does. But I don't know who he is or if I'll ever see him again.* 'Oh. He's organising that music festival your favourite band are playing at,' she added, pointing to the same flyer in the window as Aisha was still clutching in one hand.

'Dal Riada. Only the best band I've ever heard. And the absolute sexiest, too. Look.' Aisha pulled out her phone again and tapped the screen. 'Here. You can't tell me they aren't supernaturally good-looking.' She sighed again, and passed the phone to Faye.

There were four members of the band: three men, one woman. Aisha was right – they were all remarkably beautiful. The men were well-muscled, fit, tattooed; the woman stood like a faerie queen among them.

And the man standing on the left and looking unsmilingly into the camera was the same tall, blonde man who had made Faye melt only hours ago.

6

———

'You're gonna love them!' Aisha shouted over her shoulder as they made their way into the crowded bar. Taking Faye's hand, Aisha snaked her way expertly through the bubbles of space that opened and closed between people.

Faye had agreed to come with Aisha to see Dal Riada play in a club in Edinburgh. As soon as she had realised that the tall, dirty blonde man who had visited the shop was their singer, she had been intrigued to see him again.

Finn Beatha. That was his name. Aisha had told her, and ever since, his name had resonated in Faye's mind.

Aisha pushed her way to the bar and waved frantically at the barman until he craned forward; she shouted for two beers over the noise and handed one to Faye.

'It's so busy!' Faye shouted.

'I know! They've got such a following. No one even knew anything about them a year ago. They just came out of nowhere,' Aisha yelled back. 'Just look at the lassies in here. Obsessed. Just like us.' She grinned and took a long drink from her bottled lager.

'You're the one obsessed,' Faye shot back, smiling at Aisha's excited face, but she was lying. Ever since Finn Beatha had come into the shop, she hadn't been able to stop thinking about him. Not only that, but she had dreamed about him every night, waking full of longing for him.

Each dream was different, but in every one they were making love.

In one dream, Faye sat astride him, naked. In the dream, she could feel her wetness, her readiness for him. She wanted him so badly that she couldn't wait any longer.

Finn's hands held her hips, caressed her bottom and thighs, as she lowered herself onto him, crying out in pleasure as she felt his thick, lengthy cock enter her.

That's it. Good girl. Take all of it. I know you can. I am your destiny.

Shuddering with the delicious feeling of him filling her so completely, she leaned down to kiss him, moving against him in just the right way that meant the whole, long shaft of his cock stroked the most sensitive, aroused parts of her.

Faye had awoken with the first stirrings of her orgasm rippling in her belly, crying out for Finn, desperately missing the sense of his girth and fullness inside her. She'd had to bring herself to orgasm with her fingers, pushing two of them inside her and circling her clit with the fingers on her other hand. It had brought her some relief, but she yearned for the way she had felt in the dream. There had been something so right in the way that their bodies connected; something so complete that it filled her heart with a deep pleasure as well as her body.

In another night's dream, Finn had held her tight in his muscled arms, her head against his strong chest. He had whispered in her ear, *That's right, just let me play with you like my own little doll, my princess, my queen, good girl, let me take what I want,* while he stroked her clit gently. She had felt so safe, and yet so aroused. Over and over, his fingers circled her clit in maddeningly slow movements until she felt her orgasm widening across her hips. As she stiffened, he stroked her entrance, then gently plunged two long, thick fingers inside her, pushing up exactly where she needed it, before slowly drawing them out, then repeating the action until she was moaning loudly against his chest, desperate for release.

Stay with me, Faye, he had crooned in her ear. *Good girl. You're safe. I'm here. Who do you belong to?*

You, she had moaned: in that moment, she would have said anything. *You, I belong to you. Please.*

You belong to me. I own you. I own this hungry little pussy, he had replied. *I am your lord and master. Say it.*

Yes, you own it. Please, I want...

I am your lord and master, he prompted her.

You are... my lord and master, she repeated, wild with want and need. She would have said anything if it would mean he would allow her release.

You don't even know what you want. Not yet. He chuckled, and took his hand away.

Please, please, she was groaning as she woke up, her orgasm denied just at the last minute. In desperation, she had ground her hips against a pillow while touching herself, moaning into her bedcovers as her orgasm had come, finally. Yet, again, she had felt denied of the real ecstasy that was Finn: the smell of his skin, like sea salt and honey. The touch of him, and his voice in her ear.

There had been other dreams, one every night, in which their bodies had entwined, in which she had felt that same delight in submitting to him, in which he had held her, positioned her, licked her, kissed her, touched her and fucked her, and each time, her orgasm had been denied, inside the dream. Each time, she had had to wake up and pleasure herself, which was a poor substitute. It had left Faye yearning for Finn. Craving him. And she knew that it was totally unhinged and unreasonable to do so.

For Faye, the prospect of seeing Finn Beatha again was intoxicating.

Every one of her nerves tingled to be in the same room as him, even though he wouldn't know she was there. As far as Finn knew, he was just playing a gig with his band. He had no idea that Faye had developed some kind of strange, obsessively sexual crush on him. Yet, Faye wondered... the dreams had been so intense, so real... it was as if she had managed to connect with Finn in the astral realm – the world of dreams, magic and imagination.

She knew it was possible to connect with others in the dream world; she had been raised a witch, by witches, after all.

But it had never happened to her before.

Was that what had been happening? She didn't know.

'Nobody knows much about any of them,' Aisha shouted as she swayed to the background music that was coming from the speakers. 'Just that they do these amazing gigs. The one I went to before was like an out-of-body experience. I'm not even kidding, Faye. It was like a religious thing.'

Faye had not told Aisha about Finn coming into the shop. Something in her had been compelled to jealously guard that information. It was her secret, though she didn't know why she felt that way. It was almost as if something outside of her was compelling her not to say anything: to keep silent. Plus, the strange dreams that had starred him had shaken her. It was an oddly intense connection, and she almost felt embarrassed to be in the same room as him now. Even though he had no idea: her dreams were hers, and hers alone. *Weren't they?*

Faye had noticed that some of the guys in the bar were staring at her; one or two smiled. She looked away. She wasn't used to the attention – not because she wasn't a beautiful woman, but because she lived such a hermit-like life in Abercolme. Tending her garden. Working in the shop. Meditating alone on the beach.

Perhaps the dreams had somehow opened her up to a new energy that she was embodying, because the men at the bar didn't seem to be able to keep their eyes off her. But though she was uneasy with the attention, at the same time it awoke a similar sensation in her body as her dreams of Finn had: her lips felt fuller, her body tingled with pleasure as if she could feel the men touching her, adoring her. She had a sudden flash of an image in her mind's eye of the four men who had been looking at her, two on their knees, taking turns to lick and adore her, the others kissing, sucking and caressing her breasts.

She blinked and looked away. *Goddess*, she thought, shocked at her own lustful thoughts. She had never thought anything like that before. *What is happening to me?*

The lights in the bar dimmed and the band walked onto the small stage. There was a deafening roar from the crowd as the stage lights came up and bathed all four in a shifting green, gold and white light. Faye stared up at Finn Beatha, her heart quickening.

There he was, in all his glory, taller and more muscular than she remembered. She gulped, looking up at him, her whole body aflame with the denied desire that had built up in those dreams where she and Finn Beatha had explored every part of each other's bodies, where he had possessed her so totally that it left her breathless.

She couldn't believe he was real. Part of her had assigned him to a dream. Even the day that he had come into the shop seemed tinged with a dreamy unreality.

But he was definitely real.

On stage, Finn was stripped to the waist, and Faye could now see the whole of the tattoo she'd only glimpsed at his neck, that day in the shop. The tattoo was of a horse, appearing to ride up his body from the right side of his waist, up under his arm and with its head resting on his shoulder. She couldn't quite make it out from where she stood, but the part she had seen was the eye of the horse, which was designed as a well of spiralling water. Faye was reminded of the legend of the kelpie: Scottish water spirits, usually appearing as horses, that could shapeshift into humans. Grandmother had taught her all the faerie lore, while Moddie had taught Faye what she considered more practical witchcraft: spellcraft, herbs, astrology, divination.

Faye took in the defined lines of Finn's stomach and chest. A kilt sat on his hips, and he was barefoot under that. His eyes were closed as he played; the music swirled into the audience like a spell itself, weaving the people together.

Lust overtook her, and a sense of intense and illogical jealousy. Faye had spent all of twenty minutes in the company of this man, but there was something in her that said *mine*, and she couldn't help but feel deeply connected to Finn Beatha. She looked around her, at the rapt faces of the men and women in the crowd, watching him, and a part of her raged against them.

Mine. He is mine, my... my... She shook her head. It was as if she was enchanted, obsessed by a force beyond herself.

He is not my anything, she rationalised.

The drummer, in a kilt and wearing what looked like a wolf pelt around his shoulders, started pounding out a fast rhythm with his hands on two large drums.

Finn cried out, a kind of animal whoop, a silver flute in his hand, and put it to his mouth. He started playing a fast jig, following the quick drumbeat; Faye felt herself going into a kind of trance as the other instruments joined in and the singer began singing over the top; Faye thought the words were Scots Gaelic, but she couldn't be sure.

As the song picked up momentum, Faye watched as the individual auras of each musician shone bright around their heads. Finn's was the same glittering gold as before – in fact, all of the band members' auras were gold. It was odd. Faye had never seen that before.

The singer was tall, with long black hair in convoluted

braids arranged on her head and cascading down her back. The plaits were ornamented with silver clasps in the way the Celts had worn their hair, and tattoos wove their way down her arms; it looked like they had been done in blue woad. All of them had spirals and other symbols painted on their faces in the same style.

Then, the band's auras started to merge.

Faye had never seen the merging of auras before, and she watched with a sense of wonder as a field of gold light intensified around the band. And, now, as the drum beat in the core of her, Faye watched as the light started to form a spiral, reaching into the crowd.

Faye closed her eyes and let the music and the gold spiral energy come towards her, let the rhythm reverberate into the deepest caverns of her body. She had no fear of swaying and falling over, because she was so tightly packed in there was nowhere else to go. The music entranced her. It made patterns in her mind, whispered secrets into her in words she did not consciously understand, yet her body understood them all too well. Dal Riada were weaving a song of lust, and pulling every single person in the audience into it, like a sticky web of throbbing, wet and aching desire.

As soon as Faye closed her eyes, everything changed. She was immediately somewhere else, with the same feeling as when she was doing magic: it had the same vividness, the same sense of almost-reality. Her eyes fluttered open in surprise; no, she was still in the pub, with the band on stage. Yet, when she closed her eyes, she was on Black Sands Beach, and Finn Beatha was playing the flute.

There was no one else there. It was night, and a full moon sat pregnant and heavy in the clear black sky above, reflected in the black water.

Finn took the flute away from his lips and looked straight at her. She felt her whole body come alive, like a pleasurable fire engulfed it. He started singing, and she knew he was singing to her. To summon her to him.

She didn't speak much Gaelic, so she couldn't exactly tell what the song was about, but she didn't need to know: the call in her blood was unmistakable.

In the dream-vision, her feet sank into the black sand, pressing between her toes. Even though it was a vision, a waking dream, she had the same feeling of erotic lassitude that she had in the dreams with Finn.

Finn continued to sing, never looking away from her. In her waking dream, she came to him, as if she were attached to Finn Beatha by a golden rope and he was pulling it in, closer and closer.

Finally, she stood in front of him. In this dream-vision, she was wearing a flowing white dress and an elaborate rose gold pearl and opal necklace. It was long, with many strands of jewels that framed her breasts, the lowest opal resting just above her navel. She was aware that she was naked under the gauzy material, but not cold; the dress fluttered against her skin in the light, warm breeze.

He did not seem human. There was something so odd about him; otherworldly.

Finn stopped singing, pulled her to him and kissed her.

Faye experienced a strange sense of falling when their lips met, a sweetness and an underlying sense of longing, as if he was in some way a faraway home she had never imagined she would find. One of his hands was on her cheek, the other, softly, on her neck, and his touch made her dizzy. She was no longer aware of her feet on the black sand, only of him, his smell, like smoke and seawater, and the feel of her hands in his hair.

The same gnawing, hungry desire that Faye had felt for Finn Beatha in her nightly dreams returned, and as he pressed her to him, he paused kissing her to murmur in her ear: *That's it, my sweet one. I knew you would come. Let yourself open to me.*

Now, he wrapped his hands around her waist and held her tight against him. She could feel him harden immediately, the long, thick shaft of his cock pressing against her. She moaned, involuntary noises of need and want as he kissed her again, more deeply.

Good girl. Open for me, he murmured, as he reached between her legs, through the deep split in the gauzy, white dress. His hand found her dripping wet; she was so wet that she was ashamed by it. Like an animal in heat, Faye seemed unable to control her body, which responded to Finn Beatha in lustful desperation. He growled in lust.

Look at you. So wanton. So in need of me, he murmured, his eyes dark and lidded with desire.

She wanted him so badly. She wanted to be filled completely, taken and held and possessed by him.

Please, she murmured. She could still hear the music caressing her, see and feel its patterns weaving around her. She wondered how Finn was able to be playing on stage and be here with her, here, on Black Sands Beach, but part of her knew that it was magic, and part of her didn't care. All she wanted was him. Was he human, or something else? She had been raised to believe in magic; she had been taught about spirit and elemental beings. She knew that there was all kind of magic in the world – and other worlds – that most people would struggle to understand.

Please, what? he replied, his fingers stroking her gently. She was so wet that his fingers slid easily from her swollen clit to the slick opening of her: up and down, up and down, he stroked her, so gently that it was hardly a touch. She groaned, pushing against his hand, wanting more.

Please, she moaned. *Please. I want...* she trailed off, not wanting to say it. Not used to saying these words out loud. Unused to articulating her desire.

What do you want, sidhe-leth? he asked softly, his strong

hand still stroking her. Spirals of pleasure intensified in her abdomen and started to reach out into her back, down her thighs. His touch was like multiple soft mouths, licking, sweetly devouring her.

She did not know what those words meant: *sidhe-leth*. It was Scots Gaelic, that she could guess, since Dal Riada sang in the ancient language. She knew *sidhe* meant faerie hill or barrow, a place where the fae lived, or could just mean faerie. Grandmother had said it sometimes. But she had no idea what *sidhe-leth* meant.

Nor did she care now. All Faye wanted was Finn.

I want you... inside me, she breathed, closing her eyes, the music spiralling around her, thumping in her heart and her abdomen, her wetness, a song of desire and want and need. *Please.*

Soon, my sweet girl, he replied, as his strokes grew firmer. She cried out, wanting release, wanting him. She was so close; she wanted to come so desperately. *That's it. Scream for me*, he said, as the first wave of orgasm started to rise. *Say my name. Beg me to come. Beg me for your orgasm.*

Finn, she cried out. *Please, please.*

You do not have the privilege yet of calling me by my first name, he growled, his voice thick with lust. He took his hand away. *In time, my darling. In time, if you are a very good girl for me, then, perhaps, I will allow it. But I have much to tell you about who I am and who you are, and why we have come together. All of which will come in good time.*

Someone nudged Faye hard and she opened her eyes, returning to her body in a sudden shock of weight and heaviness. She gasped and reached out for Aisha, who was still next to her. For a minute, she didn't know where she was or how she had got to this noisy place from Black Sands, and she felt faint and wildly frustrated. Again, Finn Beatha had built her pleasure up to an unbearable degree and then refused to satisfy her.

'Hey. Faye! You all right?' Aisha held her by the shoulder and looked into Faye's eyes. 'Ach. It's too hot in here. Let's get some water and go somewhere to cool off,' she said, and guided Faye out of the bar.

Faye sat at an outside table and waited while Aisha went to the bar for two pints of tap water. She returned and handed one to Faye.

'You okay? You went peely-wally there for a second.'

Faye took a long drink of the cold water. 'Yeah. Thanks. I don't know what happened. I went into a kind of trance,' she admitted, not wanting to explain what had actually happened, which was that, somehow, Dal Riada's performance had acted as a – what? A gateway into a waking dream in which Finn Beatha had seduced her, yet again?

'It's that kind of fast drumming. Like a rave. It puts you in a trance headspace. I read something about it... like, at a certain number of beats per minute, it has that effect.' Aisha drained the rest of her water.

'Hmm. Maybe.' Faye looked back inside the bar which was full of jumping shadows; she saw other people with the same glassy stares as she knew she'd had. It was as though the band were enchanting everyone there. She wondered if everyone at the gig was having their own erotic visit from someone in the band, and, if so, how exactly that would even happen. Thinking that Finn Beatha might be making love to other people as well as her – even if only in her dreams, or a waking vision – filled her with that same, illogical, unhinged jealousy. *He's mine.*

Her what? What was Finn Beatha? He had said something about telling her who he was and who she was, which was an odd thing to say. Faye knew who she was. There wasn't any particular mystery about that.

And why we have come together, his voice repeated in her mind. That was the strange part. That was what she didn't understand.

'It was strange. I went... somewhere. That man, the one singing...?' She closed her eyes and saw Finn again in her mind's eye.

'Finn?'

'Yeah. I saw him on Black Sands Beach. He was... with me there. It felt so real.' Faye blushed, not wanting to say more.

'Lucky you.' Aisha smiled tightly, but then looked away. She probably didn't want to admit that she, too, had been enchanted by the band. Faye wondered if she, too, had had some kind of erotic daydream. 'I wish I could find myself on a beach with Finn Beatha. He's... he's like a dream, isn't he?' Aisha looked wistfully through the open door back at the band.

'You'll find someone real,' Faye reassured her. 'He's coming. I'm sure of it.' She had to try and right herself, try and come back to reality, even though she wanted nothing more than to find a way back into the dream-place, the dissolved state where she could meet Finn and feel his hands on her, feel the ecstasy that he built in her every time he came to her. Her panties were dripping wet, and she crossed her legs self-consciously. He brought her to the edge of extreme pleasure, over and over again, and then he had always disappeared, or the dream had ended, at the point just before her orgasm.

Faye had no idea what was happening with Finn Beatha. How she was connected to him, and why she was having these intensely erotic fantasies. Maybe it was something to do with the spell she, Annie and Aisha had cast. But whatever it was, she was becoming more and more obsessed with him. In the dreams, it was as if he was dangling her on the edge of his string, like a puppeteer, like a toy, playing with her, building her pleasure up and up and refusing to satisfy her and give her release. She had seen the look in his eyes before the dream-state had ended, just now, and it was a calculated and glittering desire.

Aisha sighed and fiddled with a button on her jeans. 'I guess. It's just that...' She trailed off, looking embarrassed.

'What? You can tell me.' Faye reached for Aisha's hand. Aisha had worked in the shop for a year now, but still Faye knew very little about her. She had sought out the shop and asked Faye if she was looking for help one day the previous summer; said she'd heard of it as one of the best places in Scotland to get supplies. Impressed with her knowledge, Faye had taken her on. But Aisha had never spoken about her personal life, and Faye hadn't pried further. Annie had, but with little success.

Aisha looked uncomfortable. 'I... I haven't ever been with anyone. In that way. You know?'

'With a man? Or woman? I mean, you made your doll a man, so I'm guessing...?' Faye asked gently. 'You're a virgin? Aisha, that's nothing to be worried about.' She smiled. 'I haven't had many boyfriends. Or one-night stands, come to that. It's okay. Just because Annie's confident in that way doesn't mean everyone is,' she added. Which made all of this – the dreams, the visions, the fantasies – all the stranger. Faye wasn't sexually experienced. She wasn't a virgin, but she had never really understood what people meant when they talked about wanting sex so badly. It had always been kind of *blah* for her. Forgettable, sometimes awkward. Never, ever like this.

Aisha blushed; clearly, it was hard for her to talk about this. 'I wanted to go to university. I'm going to be a geneticist. But my parents would rather that I married one and concentrated on popping out babies like my sisters are. And that's cool, y'know? That's fine if that's what you want to do. But I don't.' Her tone was quietly fierce. Faye imagined that it would be pretty difficult to get Aisha to do anything she didn't want to do.

'Of course! I so admire your brains, Aish. There's no way I could do what you do,' Faye replied, though she was struggling to concentrate on the conversation after what had just happened. *Get it together, Faye,* she reprimanded herself.

'Well, sure. Though there always have been women doing

important work, it's hard to get to the top, is all. You have to marry the job. Good news if you don't want to marry an actual person, I guess.'

'But you still want someone. You're human.' Faye finished the thought for her. She allowed herself to remember a moment from her strange dream experience: the moment when she had pleaded with Finn for her pleasure.

Her proximity to Finn had inspired desire in a way that she had never known she possessed. It had been a strange, magical experience. All of her dreams with Finn were inexplicable. And yet, she felt more human than she ever had as a result.

'You're human,' she repeated to Aisha, but she was also speaking to herself. 'You have needs. And desires. And that's okay.'

'I guess so.' Aisha sighed. 'Doctoral study is hard. And I haven't met anyone I like at uni. Or I'm too shy to meet men when I go out. Like tonight.'

'I know.' Faye laughed. 'Look at us. A pair of wallflowers. At least, we've got each other.'

Aisha smiled. 'But you're beautiful. You don't know how many guys look at you. You don't even see it.'

It was Faye's turn to blush. 'I don't know about that,' she said quietly, though she had always noticed it, and found it made her uncomfortable. 'And you are a beautiful, intelligent, interesting young woman, don't forget. Your time will come, Aish. Remember the spell.'

'D'you really think it'll work?' Aisha asked again, like she didn't really believe, but she wanted to.

'Is this your scientist brain making you doubt magic?' Faye asked, with more of a smile in her voice than she felt.

'No. The more you study genetics, the more you realise how magical humans really are. Anyway, the wisest of us know that we still have so much to learn.' Aisha stood up, chafing her hands together and looking back into the bar. 'God knows what's encoded into our DNA. No, it's just... I dunno. Human frailty. Not daring to believe, I guess.'

'You don't lose anything by having faith,' Faye mused. It was true, but she felt like a fraud for saying it. At the moment, she didn't feel like she had a decent grip on reality, never mind *having faith*. Having faith in what? she wondered. Could she have any kind of faith that what was currently happening to her was real? Could she have faith that she wasn't, in fact, going mad?

'I guess. D'you want to go back in?' Aisha shivered.

'Sure.' Faye stamped her feet on the ground; it was cold, sitting outside at night in Edinburgh; the spring equinox was approaching, but warm nights were a long time away still.

'And... thanks. Sometimes, I feel really alone, y'know? It helps. Having you and Annie around.' She leaned forward and gave Faye an awkward hug.

'That's okay, Aish. Any time.'

Faye took a deep breath and followed Aisha back into the bar.

This time, she would be more prepared.

Dal Riada were still playing. The song wove around her, and she could still see it as a magic in itself, enchanting the crowd. She watched the faces of the others around her; some were so entranced that their eyes were almost rolled all the way back; they swayed, totally unaware of where they were. She could sense that they *were* somewhere else, to all intents and purposes. The combined, spiralling, turquoise-blue energy of Dal Riada was transporting the whole crowd somewhere – maybe to their own individual beaches, to be seduced, or into another fantasy, Faye didn't know – and the whole crowd were completely at the mercy of this band.

Part of her yearned to run straight back into Finn's arms: she still wanted him so badly, and her body resonated with the unmet desire he had lit in her.

And, yet. Finn Beatha seemed to be playing a game with her. A game of cat and mouse, a game of desire that she had been thus far powerless to resist.

It had made her feel human, alive, wanted. But it also made her angry.

How dare this man – this person, who had appeared out of nowhere – think that he could enchant her in whatever way he wanted?

I don't think so, she thought angrily. *I can resist you. I am a witch, I was raised by witches, and no one plays with me. I am nobody's puppet.*

Standing at the bar, Faye imagined herself cocooned in a black cloak with a hood; she imagined drawing it over herself, and closing the seven energy centres in her body, the rainbow-hued chakras that everyone had, head to groin. Instantly, she felt better, more grounded. For good measure she imagined tree roots growing out of her feet and down through the sticky wooden floor of the bar and into the dark Edinburgh earth.

Now grounded, she let herself look at Finn again: he was just as beautiful, otherworldly, even. His hair was a lighter blonde in the stage lights, and the horse tattoo on his side seemed to writhe with the music.

'Aish. We should go and get the train,' she shouted to her friend, knowing somehow that it would be dangerous for her and Aisha to stay at the pub and get sucked in to whatever magic Dal Riada were weaving on stage. Aisha already looked half hypnotised again; Faye shook her arm. 'Aish. Come on. We need to go. Avoid the crowd when they finish.'

It was an excuse, but Aisha nodded, looking confused.

As Faye looked up to the stage one last time, she had the impression that Finn was searching for her. His blue-green eyes scanned the crowd, but she could tell that he hadn't seen her.

The defence was working, then.

Faye needed to take back some control. Her visions with

Finn had been intensely pleasurable. But she needed clarity. How and what was happening? She wouldn't know by allowing herself to get pulled under, into whatever bizarre, shared fantasy they were having.

Faye raised her hands to her long auburn fringe. Though she was only wearing an imaginary black robe, her hands grasped the edge of where the hood would be, and she brought her loose fists down in front of her face, as if to veil herself completely.

The music pooled around her in sharp, quick drifts, like snow; Finn had brought the flute to his lips again and the female singer with the dark hair in so many plaits keened a gentle melody over it. Faye's heart surged; the tune was haunting yet mournful, and she felt an overwhelming longing take her over, though she could not have explained exactly what she was yearning for. It was as if she was homesick or longing for a love she had never lost.

'Come on, Aish.' She steered her friend out of the bar, and as the door closed behind them, Faye felt the spell break again. She stamped her feet on the pavement. *Come on*, she thought. *Come back to earth, Faye.*

'You okay?' she asked her friend, who looked a little dazed.

'I'm okay. That was... strange,' Aisha said, hugging her coat around her.

'It was. An experience, to be sure. But not one I'm sure I'd like to repeat.' Faye frowned.

He has no power over me, she thought as they walked away. *Finn Beatha, you have no power over me. I resist your enchantments, whatever they are.*

Faye pulled the imaginary black robe tight around herself.

Her grandmother had taught her the first rule of spellcraft, when she was a child and just learning her first spells, learning about the elements: air, water, fire and earth, and the fifth element of spirit, which was a combination of all of those things.

Later, when Faye was older, Grandmother had taught her about the planetary forces, the stars, the powers beyond the earth and beyond earth, air, fire and water that made up all of life in this realm, too. Those were the important basics. But there were rules, and the first rule was *Be sure.*

To work a spell, the first thing to know was that you would likely get what you asked for. But, did you really want it? Grandmother had taught her to look inside herself, and think, *If I got what I thought I wanted, would I be happy?*

Faye had asked for a lover, and one had appeared. But it was so far beyond strange – this wasn't what she had asked for. She had wanted someone normal, nice, available. She hadn't asked for some kind of astral-plane headfuck.

This wasn't what I wanted, she thought as she and Aisha walked away from the pub. *How is this anywhere near what anyone would want?*

Be careful for what you ask for: you might get it, her grandmother's voice rang in her head. *And what will you do then, my darling? What will you do now?*

7

Faye stood in a town square looking out to sea. She knew it was Scotland – but it was different; everyone wore different clothes: old-fashioned, no jeans, jumpers or parkas. She didn't know any of the people there, but they were all standing in a crowd, watching a priest sprinkling holy water over a number of women who were lashed to wooden posts on a raised dais in the middle of the square.

I'm dreaming, she thought.

In the dream, Faye looked down at her own feet to find them encased in rough leather boots. She wore a dress of brown rough-spun material with a dirty, once-white apron over the top of it. She reached up and felt her hair, plaited and pinned up at the back of her head in a way she had never worn it. *What is this? What's happening?*

There was a man dressed in a fancier style than everyone else. He was on the dais, talking to the women. She heard him say to one of them, *Confess, and ye shall go to your death godly. Not as the Devil's whore.*

'I am no whore. I am Grainne Morgan, Beloved of the Good Folk!' the woman cried. The crowd gasped.

Faye shuddered in recognition. Grainne Morgan was her ancestor. Grainne Morgan had been burned as a witch.

It was about to happen. She was about to see it happen.

Faye's heart was in her mouth. *If this is a dream, let me wake up*, she thought, willing it all to stop, but the dream stayed, heavy and insistent.

'No!' she cried out, but her voice was subsumed in the noise around her.

'You do evil today by taking the name of the Fair Ones in vain! They are no devils; they are our own angels, part of our lands. That have always been in the streams and rocks and trees and moss, since before there was Man, and certainly before there was this village,' Grainne cried out.

Faye's eyes streamed with tears. Grainne Morgan had the same auburn hair as she did, the same high cheekbones that Faye and Moddie had shared.

'Please, please, save her, someone, help!' Faye cried out, turning from one person around her to the next, but no one seemed able to hear her.

'Aye, I do not go to my death. I go to live in the hills forever; in the far castles of the fae that are full of sweet mead and fresh bread and dancing for all eternity,' Grainne continued. The sheriff had lit the kindling at the bottom of the stake, and the branches and logs were beginning to flicker orange-red.

'No,' Faye cried out in desperation. 'Please, someone, help.'

In that moment, Faye saw someone else on the dais. A tall, blonde man dressed in elaborate blue and gold clothes stood next to Grainne; he appeared to be slightly translucent – real, and yet not real – yet, Faye saw her ancestor take his hand.

Grainne raised her chin and drew in a deep breath.

'But they will curse you, you men that bring pain to this land of magic! I curse you! In the name of the kings and queens of Falias, Gorias, Finias, Murias and the Crystal Castle of the Moon! In the names of earth and stone, air and winds, fire and hearth, water and sea, I curse you! Let no more the Good Folk help you. Let no more the wise ones negotiate with them on your behalf. Let a blight be on this land!'

Faye watched as Grainne slumped forward. The flames had not yet reached her, but Faye could see Grainne's spirit leave her body and merge with the spectral figure next to her. She blinked; even in a dream, it was strange.

See the fate of your ancestors, a voice intoned in her mind. *See the bond we have always had, sidhe-leth. For you are half fae; born in love, as was always the bond between the Morgan women and the kings of Murias.*

Faye jumped, startled, and turned to see Finn Beatha standing next to her. He looked deeply into her eyes.

Reclaim your power, Faye Morgan. Reclaim your position at my side, he said. *And reconnect your people to the protection of the fae. Or see your people perish.*

You will know my words are true when I see you again. It will not be long before we are together again.

Faye awoke. Her heart was hammering in her chest. What had she just witnessed? And what did Finn mean? *For you are half fae; born in love, as was always the bond between the Morgan women and the kings of Murias.*

She was a normal person. The Morgan women had always been witches, that was true. But half fae? That had to be a fantasy, conjured in her dream for reasons of her own.

Reconnect your people to the protection of the fae. Or see your people perish.

It was just a dream, she told herself. Just a fantasy.

But what if it wasn't?

8

The bell jingled as the shop door opened and Faye looked up hopefully. She knew it was silly, but Finn Beatha's last words to her in that vivid dream still rung in her memory: *You will know my words are true when I see you again. It will not be long before we are together again.*

But, it was just a couple of tourists. Faye smiled at them and went back to her book, disappointed.

She wanted to see him. She wanted to hear the bell jingle as the shop door opened and see him there, in the doorway. She craved him, and she hadn't been able to stop thinking about the dream. In it – if Finn had really been there – he had told her that she was half faerie. How was that even possible? She was human. Moddie and Grandmother were human. She didn't look in any way unusual, or have unusual faerie powers. *Sidhe-leth.* Half fae. Now, she knew what it meant. She had looked it up.

The fae were an archaic Scottish legend, a part of Grandmother's folk belief, nothing more. It didn't hurt anyone to believe in the Good Folk, but Moddie had raised Faye to consider the fae as outdated. They weren't *real*, not in the way that Finn Beatha was real: he had walked into the shop and talked to Faye. She had watched him perform on stage. He had a solid, human body – albeit he was very tall and supernaturally good-looking. He dressed in normal clothes.

Yet, Faye had also seen a spectral being take Grainne Morgan's hand just before she died, in her dream. And that spectral being had looked very like Finn.

What did that mean?

There was one answer, but she didn't want to believe it.

Dreams and nonsense, she told herself. Yet, she didn't believe in her own cynicism.

If she was *sidhe-leth,* half fae, what did that tell her about Finn Beatha? A man who was supernaturally good-looking and larger than life, who appeared in her life out of nowhere and had haunted her dreams. Dreams that were so powerful, Faye could hardly concentrate on her daily life.

She looked up at the door again, frowning. There was something else.

Grandmother's hagstone charm was hanging in the doorway again.

It hadn't been there when Finn Beatha had entered the shop. Afterwards, she'd looked for it for over a week to no avail: she'd asked Aisha and Annie, and neither had taken it down or noticed it had gone. Neither knew where it was. Faye had assumed that a customer must have stolen it, or that it had somehow got lost in the shop. And, now it was back. Nobody had said they had found it.

That was odd. *It must have been lost, and one of the girls found it and forgot to tell me,* she thought.

Faye returned to her reverie about Finn Beatha.

She opened her grandmother's grimoire and flicked through it. She didn't often read it, nowadays, but it was on the shop counter from when she had used it for the love spell and hadn't put it back in its usual place on a shelf behind the till.

She flicked past rituals for the equinoxes, observances for the different phases of the moon, spells for money, good luck, to silence an enemy. Then she came to the section she had been looking for.

The Faerie Kings and Queens.

She traced her finger over their names, their royal crests and the illustrations of their crowns. She didn't quite know what she was looking for, but something had been nagging at the back of her mind since seeing Finn on stage.

In Murias, the realm of water, the king and queen are Fintanaeon, Master of the Tides, and Levantiana, Mistress of the Cup. In Falias, the realm of earth, the king and queen are Lyr, Master of Mountains, and Moronoe, Mistress of the Stone. In Gorias, the realm of air, the king and queen are Raphaeleon, Master of the Winds, and Tyronoe, Mistress of the Knife. And in Finias, realm of fire, the king and queen are Attis, Master of Flame, and Thetis, Mistress of the Staff.

Fintanaeon, Master of the Tides, King of Murias.

It was a very close coincidence. *Fintanaeon. Finn.* Just a coincidence, surely.

Because Finn Beatha looked like he was in his thirties. Whichever Morgan woman had written and drawn the pages about the faerie kings and queens, it was either Grandmother or someone before her, meaning that Finn wouldn't have been born then. It didn't make sense.

Yet, something made Faye look more closely at the page.

Each faerie realm had a royal crest. Falias, the realm of earth, featured a tree and a mountain on its crest. Finias, the realm of fire, featured a blazing sword and what looked like a salamander or some other type of lizard. Gorias featured a bird's wing and a tornado.

Murias's crest was of a kelpie: a mythical water horse.

It was the same kelpie, the same water horse that Finn

Beatha had tattooed on his chest. The same water horse that reared up his chest, its head resting on Finn's muscular neck.

If Finn Beatha was Fintanaeon, King of Murias, he must be many hundreds of years old. That made no sense.

And Faye couldn't think of any way that she could possibly be half faerie. Wouldn't Moddie and Grandmother have told her? Wouldn't she have noticed some odd traits about herself – though she didn't know what they might be?

It was an outrageous suggestion. It wasn't real life.

So, why did Finn Beatha insist on calling her half faerie?

The doorbell tinkled again. Faye looked up to see Rav enter the shop. She closed the grimoire, her heart beating. For a brief moment, she had thought that Finn Beatha might be the faerie king of Murias. What a ridiculous thought.

'Good day, Mistress of Magic.' Rav Malik tipped an imaginary cap to her and looked around at the shelves of incenses, tarot sets, books and a row of brightly polished brass cauldrons. 'I hope I'm not disturbing you.'

Faye had temporarily forgotten about Rav. She had forgotten his large, wide, strong frame and his heavy brows; had forgotten the primal, bullish sense of him. Now that she saw him again, she was reminded of his inherent strength and masculine grace.

Rav was so different to Finn, so much more earthy, whereas Finn had a sense of transcendent beauty about him. Yet, Rav moved with care in the little shop, as if mindful not to disturb anything. Faye looked at his hands as he carefully picked up a tiny glass jar of incense. The jar appeared like something from a doll's house in his wide, strong palm. He read the label with interest and put it down again, looking up to catch her eye and smiling slowly. Faye felt her cheeks redden at being caught staring.

'Ah, no... you surprised me, that's all.' She smiled.

'You do know that this is a shop? Probably best if people do come in, I'm guessing?' He came up to the counter and picked up a novelty spell book next to the till. Like the jar of incense, it looked like a toy in his hands. 'How's business?'

'Not too bad.' Faye wondered what it would be like to be held in those vast arms; a bear's embrace. She let out a long breath at the thought of being so completely safe.

This is real life, she thought. Not myths and strangeness and old legends in dusty old books.

'Thought I'd drop in on the village's mysterious enchantress.' He raised an eyebrow, his black, long-lashed gaze holding hers. Faye was drawn to him. 'Who is even more beautiful than I remembered.' He seemed totally at ease, paying her a compliment, flirting with her unashamedly. He was very confident. Not in a flashy way, she could see that. But confident in himself, of his masculinity.

'Um. Thank you.' Faye blushed. 'Is there anything in particular you were looking for?'

'Apart from you?' He gave her that same, lazy smile that took her breath away.

Caught off guard, Faye was at a loss for words. 'Umm...' she stammered.

'I imagine people must come in here all the time just to see you,' he continued.

'Well... yes... but only for spells, readings, that kind of thing,' she blushed.

'Indeed. How have you been?' he asked, maintaining eye contact.

'Fine. And you?' she asked, wanting to look away, but somehow unable to.

'I was hoping for some advice, actually,' he went on. 'The thing is – don't think I'm deranged or anything – but I think... my house might be haunted.'

'Haunted?' she echoed his words.

'I know, I know. It's a mad thing to say. But ever since I moved in, there's been these weird noises in the night. Running footsteps in the hall. Sounds of laughing. And when I go downstairs, there's been a few times when the fridge door's been left open and stuff pulled out. Food all over the floor.' He looked chagrined. 'I just thought... if anyone would understand, it would be you. Hence, the visit.'

'It's not mad.' Faye frowned. 'You know there have always been stories about that house. No one ever stayed there long, not since it was built.'

'Really?'

'Yeah. My grandmother always said that the fae were close by, here in Abercolme. She would blame anything on the fae. Someone's dog was ill. Getting a cold. Stupid things, really,' Faye thought for a moment. 'But I do remember her talking about that house, too. She said that it had a lot of fae activity, because it sits on a ley line. That was why no one stayed in it too long.'

Rav gazed into the hearth, frowning. 'Hmm. Well, whatever it is, it's scary, Faye. I mean, I'm embarrassed to say it, but I don't want to sleep there right now.'

'You don't have to be embarrassed. These things happen all the time. Spirits that haven't moved on – occasionally people with powers they don't know they have, affecting their environments. The local minister would probably do you an exorcism.'

'*Should* I have an exorcism?' Rav ran a hand through his long, dark hair.

'You could. But I'd be happy to come and have a look for you first. See if we can't give the place a good cleanse. That might be all it needs.'

'A cleanse? You think so?'

'I can come and see, anyway. Take it from there.'

'That would be great.' Rav looked relieved. 'Honestly, I haven't had a good night's sleep since I moved in.'

She looked at the antique clock behind the counter; it was almost four.

'You can show me now, if you want,' she said.

'Now?'

'Sure, why not?' Her heart was beating a little faster than usual at the prospect of being close to Rav, and going with him to his house, but she was going with her instinct. And, she had a responsibility to help. She was the village witch, and, sometimes, people asked for help. It was what the Morgans did. 'Real witches are better than novelty spell books, and you have a real witch at your disposal.'

'I do?' It was his turn to look wrong-footed.

'You do.'

Smiling shyly, she held the door open for him, keys in hand. 'What're you waiting for?'

'Nothing! I had no idea that witches had this kind of immediate response time. I mean, I'm going to have to rethink my next 999 call.' A smile played around his full-lipped mouth.

'I don't come out for less than a level-three haunting. Just so you know,' Faye joked back. There was a pleasant vibe between them; Rav's aura, a dark red, was deeply masculine, grounded, calm, sexy like some kind of chivalrous knight intent on doing right by his lady, but still a huge man – a warrior – under his fearsome armour. Faye had the overpowering sense that Rav could pick her up and put her over his shoulder whenever he wanted to. And she would be able to do nothing about it.

It made her feel good. She liked Rav. He made her feel ladylike, feminine, and yet he seemed to respect her as a woman with her own power.

Rav's hand brushed hers as they walked up the high street, and Faye fought an impulse to take it. Yet, as they walked along, she also felt a sense of apprehension. She didn't know what was wrong with the house on the beach, but she could sense something dark there, waiting for her.

9

The house was cold. That was the first thing she noticed. The late afternoon light streamed through the floor-to-ceiling windows, showing up dust motes in the air. Faye hugged her coat around her – an old dusty-pink one of Moddie's with a rounded collar and big pink buttons down the front. Faye liked it because it hung loose like a cape, and it had deep pockets for collecting stones and shells and feathers from the beach.

'Sorry it's cold. As much as I turn the heating up, I just can't get it warm in here.' Rav ran his hand over one of the white-painted vintage radiators that sat against a white wall. He pulled his hand away. 'It's boiling hot to touch. Just won't spread to the room. The perils of a house made of glass by the Scottish coast, I guess.'

Faye frowned. 'I'm not sure. It's more likely that the cold is connected to whatever is happening here.' She walked into the steel and glass kitchen; it still looked unused. The cold was worse in here, and as soon as she walked in, she got a sense of being watched, and a prickling on her skin.

'Connected to the haunting?' he prompted her.

'Hmm. It very likely isn't haunted. Real hauntings are

pretty rare.' Faye peered at the temperature on the modern display, mounted discreetly on the wall.

'Are they? That's not what film and TV would have you believe.'

'Film and TV: that unassailable source of accuracy and fact.' Faye raised an eyebrow and smiled.

'Fair,' he chuckled. 'So, what do you think it might be?'

Rav opened the fridge and got some milk out. 'Coffee? Think I still have enough.'

'Coffee would be great, thanks.'

'It could be anything. Old spirits attached to the house that need to be moved on. A poltergeist. A curse. A malfunctioning witch bottle.'

'Witch bottle?' He frowned.

'An old folk custom. To protect your house, put rusty nails in a bottle, pee on them, close up the bottle and wedge it up the chimney.'

'Nice.' Rav raised an eyebrow as he spooned ground filter coffee from a packet into a silver cafetiere.

'But my grandmother always told me that this house was built on a ley line. Faerie land,' Faye continued. 'I mean, I don't really believe that, but... you should never discount the old ways. I... I have been reminded recently that magic isn't something you can predict.' She caught his eye briefly, then looked away. She still didn't know if the spell had brought Rav Malik to her, but she felt it was more than possible that it had. 'Or it could be you, sleepwalking. Night terrors,' she added.

'Well, I've never sleepwalked as far as I know.' He poured hot water into the jug and let it stand.

'Mind if I take a look around?' Faye felt drawn to the glass hallway that ran down one side of the house, connecting the kitchen with the lounge that looked out to sea and three large bedrooms.

'Go for it. I'll come and find you.'

Faye stepped into the glass corridor, and her world changed instantly.

Instead of standing in a modern glass-walled corridor, she was ankle-deep in a sea of grass. Small, twinkling lights and orbs, like a child's blown bubbles, bounced in the air and rose and fell in anarchic fashion on the grass, which was long and green-blue, like the shifting colour of the sea.

There was no glass on either side of her, but a metre or so away from where the outer edge of the house had been was a row of tall white stones, painted in blue spirals and other strange markings. Faye saw that they marked a path towards a radiant green-gold light just over the brow of the headland. To the left, the sea was still there, but the muddy, dark sand of Black Sands Beach glowed white.

She was also not alone on the pathway. As she stood there, adjusting to the strangeness of the vision, she became aware that the grass held legions of small faerie creatures. Some of the ones in the grass were a little like the faeries she'd seen in the books Moddie had read her as a child: tiny, winged creatures with petals for clothes and twigs in their hair. Some were half caterpillar, half fae; butterflies with faerie faces flew past her, and there were large, iridescent beetles.

But there were also taller creatures that pushed past her; some were singing, dancing, laughing; many didn't progress in a straight line but circled around her, pulling at her clothes. Some had a greenish skin. Three faerie-women passed her on horseback with a procession of courtiers before and after them. They were beautiful, in draping, diaphanous garments, but their expressions were forbidding. One horse was black, one white, and one was blood-red. Each of the horses had silver ribbons plaited into their long manes.

One creature, a bearded half man, half goat, tweaked her nose, and then, unexpectedly, her nipple, through her coat.

Blessings, sidhe-leth, he said, bowing. *We are honoured. You are as beautiful as the legends say.*

Before she could respond, the half-man, half-goat creature laughed and ran away towards the green-gold light.

Sidhe-leth. Half fae. The same name as Finn Beatha had used in her dreams.

Was she dreaming now? Had she somehow slipped into sleep while at Rav's house?

Rav's hand touched her on the shoulder, and she blinked. The grass disappeared under her feet, and she was back in the long passageway.

Faye could only stare through him as she tried to process what had just happened.

'What?' He gave her a strange look.

'I... I just...' She couldn't find the words – any words – at that moment. She felt outside herself in a different way than she ever had before, even when doing magic. Her hand went to her breast, which still tingled from where the goat-man had cruelly tweaked her nipple.

'It feels weird out here, doesn't it? I knew you'd pick that up.' He handed her a mug. Faye took a sip, instinctively, and then again as she felt the drink reconnect her to her body again.

'I just... I wasn't here, just then. This is a faerie pathway' – she pointed outside the house to the edge of the beach where scrubby grass gave way to the sand – 'to about there, where the sand starts. It leads over the hill, there. To the headland.'

'A what?' Rav gave her a look.

'A faerie road. I saw them. The fae, the spirits of nature. So many different kinds. This was all grass. It was... beautiful.' She felt a wave of exhaustion come over her, and she slumped against the wall.

'Wow. Okay, let's get you to a seat.' Rav took her coffee and guided her to the lounge where she fell back into a yellow leather sofa. He didn't seem to have done much moving in except for a tall, wide box-shelved unit that held what looked like thousands of vinyl LPs.

'So, I don't really understand what you're telling me. Faeries? I thought that was just made up for kids.'

'Of course not. Few things that are talked about that much aren't real. Even if they weren't real to start with, they become it because of being so intensely imagined. Magic 101,' Faye shrugged. 'I'm the expert, you wanted my opinion. That's my diagnosis.'

'Faeries?' He raised an eyebrow at her questioningly.

'Yes.' Faye stared at him, unblinking. *Sidhe-leth. Am I really half fae? If that was real... which I am telling Rav it was... which I feel it was... then how did that creature know, and how did it know to call me that name?*

'But, like... and I'm not disrespecting you, Faye. Really. But, as far as I know, faeries are these little, tiny, winged things. Like the ones in the flowers. My sister had those books. *C is for the Cinquefoil Fairy, D is for the Dandelion Fairy...* It doesn't feel like they'd be the ones trashing my kitchen and pounding the house so hard it sounds like an army passing through.' Rav sat forward, awkwardly, on the orange leather easy chair facing her and put his coffee down on a packing crate that was positioned as a table between them.

'No. That's not what they are.' She felt exhausted, as if all of her life force had been sapped from her.

'What are they, then?' Rav asked patiently. 'Sorry. I'm clueless with this kind of thing.'

'Okay. Faerie is the realm of the spirits of nature. There are all kinds of faerie, but as I understand it, they're organised into four elemental kingdoms: earth, air, fire and water.'

'Right. I guess that makes sense. Have you seen them before? Or was that the first time?' He sat back a little, and Faye could see that Rav was trying to take in what she was saying.

'Not really. As I say, my grandmother was the expert. She

taught me and my mum all about how to keep the Good Folk happy, otherwise they would cause havoc.'

'The Good Folk?'

'The fae. That's the old name for them.' Faye took a sip of coffee and felt some energy return to her body.

'Is that what they're doing in my house? Causing havoc?' His eyes widened. 'You saw them?'

'Yeah. I saw a grass road. All sizes and types of faerie, walking along it, running, dancing... I could see them all. They could see me, but most of them left me alone.'

'So...?'

'So... I think that maybe this house is sitting on a faerie road of some kind. As weird as that sounds.' Faye shook her head. 'Believe me, when I came up here, I didn't think that was what I'd find.' She shivered, and Rav came to sit beside her and put his arm around her shoulders.

'Faye. I'm so sorry. I had no idea,' he said quietly.

'I'm so cold,' she whispered. 'And... that was... really weird.'

'I can imagine. It sounds weird. You went completely blank. Like your spirit had disappeared, and only your body was left. I was talking to you, and you didn't respond.' Rav hugged her to him. 'That really scared me, too.' He took off his coat and draped it around her shoulders. 'Here.'

'Thank you.' She pulled the coat around her, and Rav replaced his arm around her shoulders. His touch made her feel safe, but the weight of his heavy, muscled arm on her inspired another feeling: a warmth and a a tingling across her thighs and a soft throbbing inside her. There was something so solid, so grounded and animalistic about him. She wanted to melt into his arms.

'I think all the disturbances you're getting are because of the faerie traffic going up the hill to whatever that glowing thing is up there. Which would explain why no one's ever settled here. The fae must have been livid when this house was built. Grandmother used to say that they were very protective of what they consider to be their land. Faerie mounds, roads, passageways.'

'Hmm. How do you know that?'

'There are documented cases of people having to placate faeries when they've built on their territory. In Iceland they build roads around their elf-hills. They wouldn't dream of knocking them over.'

'Really?'

'Yeah. There are people who are brought in specially to negotiate with the elves when a new road is to be built.' Faye was warming up now, but she didn't want to move.

'So, what're you saying? That I need to pacify the faeries?' he breathed, speaking quietly, as if he didn't want to spook her.

'I would say so.' She snuggled into him, and he tightened his grip on her, as if he knew that she needed the physical reassurance of his body. He smelled lightly of sweat and some musky, woody scent. Faye wanted to nestle her face into his neck. Neither of them were openly acknowledging what was happening between them, but Faye had the sense that they were following their bodies.

'Well, what are we talking about? Saying a prayer or something?' he asked huskily.

She looked up at him, and met his dark eyes, which were heavy-lidded with desire.

'Maybe.' She wet her lips with her tongue. He groaned and looked away.

'Faye. I know this isn't the time, but... you must know that I'm attracted to you,' he muttered. 'I... I know it's a strange time to say it, but... having you in my arms, I... I just can't control how I feel. You're so... I don't know. Mesmerising. Feminine. I just...' There was a desperate look in his eyes. 'I want you. So badly.'

'I don't know what to say,' she said quietly, not breaking eye contact. She wanted Rav, too, but it was a fraught moment. Faye didn't know whether what she was feeling was desire, or a light-headedness that came from being suddenly jolted onto the faerie road.

What she couldn't say, or even explain to herself, was that in that moment when she stood on the faerie path, she had felt at home. What could she say to Rav that would help him understand that? She hardly understood it herself.

'Perhaps I'd better go.' She stood up, caught between the desire to dissolve into Rav and a need to be alone to process what had just happened.

'Don't go.' Rav stood up and placed his hands on her shoulders. 'I... I really like you, Faye. All of this is kind of crazy, too. I just feel like ever since I met you, I've been enchanted and... it's really weird. But I can't stop thinking about you.'

'Oh.' She put her hand to his on her shoulder and they shared a long look. Faye felt the attraction pull between them, as if she was being immersed again in the heady mist of faerie; intoxicating and overwhelming. 'I... I don't know, Rav. What happened just then... I've never... it was a lot.'

'I know.' He gazed into her eyes. 'What just happened... I have no frame of reference for it. But ever since I met you, it's like I've been plunged into this world of magic and I'm just... enchanted. Lovestruck. I don't know what's happening.' He rubbed his eyes with the edge of his sleeve.

'I know. I feel strange, too,' she breathed. 'Maybe we should get out of the house.' She could still hear, still sense, a high-pitched whine. The power of the faerie road, so close to them, was undeniable.

'I think that's a good idea. Come on. Let's go for a walk.' Rav guided her out of the house, and pulled the door closed behind him. Instantly, the intensity of feeling decreased in Faye's whole body: she didn't realise how keyed up she had been until the energy changed, like a switch being flipped.

It was a relief, but it gave Faye a chance to think more clearly.

It couldn't just be a coincidence, witnessing the faerie road, and dreaming of Finn Beatha. If Finn was a faerie king – as unlikely as that might seem – then, was he causing all this strange stuff to happen? What was the connection between the Morgan women and the faerie world of Murias? And where did Rav fit in with all of this?

Faye's heart was heavy as she stepped onto Black Sands Beach. She felt as though she had a foot in two worlds: one normal and familiar; and one perilous, unpredictable and riven with desire. Had the spell caused this break in her reality? Had the spell brought her Finn and Rav, and somehow opened up the door to faerie? None of this had ever been her intention.

Be sure, Grandmother's voice reminded her. *Be careful what you wish for: you might get it.*

But I didn't ask for this, Faye thought, looking up at Rav. *I don't know what this is.*

This is magic, said a different voice in her ear. *If you knock at the door, don't be surprised when it opens.*

10

The evening spring sun hung over the sea like a spell.

Faye detected a faint smell of roses in the clean sea air. The rose smell had been here, before; Faye still didn't know where it came from. If it was coming from anywhere at all, and not some kind of hallucination.

'That's some beautiful sky.' Rav whistled as they stood there, taking in the view: the line between the heavens and the earth, grey-blue sky and sea that seemed to meet and merge seamlessly. There was an unusual hush on the beach. Faye felt the heartbeat of the land pounding through her toes. She took off her shoes and sank her bare feet into the sand. It was the spring equinox the next day: a time when the days and nights were of equal length, when a sacred balance ruled the land.

'Yes... it's... um. It's bonny,' she replied, without knowing how to say how she felt. She felt the surge of life in the earth under her: nature was waking up, and when she was with Rav, she also felt suddenly awake and alive and deep in her senses. Rav exuded masculinity, like a bestial, primal animal. He, too, was of the earth, full of strength and power and sex. The sunset cast his shadow onto the sand, looming over her.

Faye gulped, remembering the way he had held her, back at the house.

'Cream and milk,' she said out of the blue. 'That's what my grandmother said you should leave out for the fae. As an offering. And we should make an altar in your house, so they know you respect them. Shells, feathers, flowers, that kind of thing.' She looked away awkwardly, feeling silly. But it had just popped into her mind; an old bit of fae knowledge from Grandmother.

'Okay.' He looked at her askance. 'Whatever you say, my enchantress.'

They walked along the beach together, picking up shells.

'I sometimes wonder what I'd have been if I hadn't been a Morgan. An enchantress, as you say. I... I feel the legacy of my ancestors a lot, sometimes.' She thought about her dream of Grainne. Faye bent down to pick up three iridescent blue mussel shells; there were so many on the beach that the small, broken bits of shell gave the sand a jewelled sheen in the twilight.

Grandmother had told her that Grainne Morgan, a beautiful woman – Faye had seen her, and she knew it was true – had 'enchanted' several local men so badly that she 'possessed their minds, turning them aside from their wives'. That she was a witch was true, but her power – her magic – was intrinsically connected to her sexuality, and Faye had seen in her dream how much the people of Abercolme had resented it.

Grandmother said that when it came time for Grainne's execution, an army of faeries had swept in with the sea, flooding the harbour at North Berwick.

Faye thought back to her dream, witnessing Grainne lashed to the stake. At her cursing the people who watched her die, who persecuted her for her power. *I am no whore. I am Grainne Morgan, Beloved of the Good Folk.* Then, the fae who took her hand and spirited her away.

'Would you have been a witch, you mean?' he asked.

'I guess so, aye. I wonder that sometimes.' Faye picked up a flat, round stone and skipped it into the sea.

'I think you would. You just have... something about you. Something magical. Sexy. Alluring.'

He held his hand out for hers. Immediately, she felt a heat rise between them, even though the evening was cool and the wet sand was cold on her feet.

Rav's gaze caught hers and refused to let it go; he leaned in to kiss her.

As he kissed her, Faye saw in her mind's eye faeries riding on the waves towards them, laughing, catcalling, watching them kiss. She opened her eyes, startled, but there was nothing there except the setting sun gilding the soft waves with pink. She closed her eyes again and melted into the kiss.

She was suddenly filled with a kind of velvety, warm wickedness which dispelled any doubt and anxiety she had been feeling – about Rav, about Finn and what had happened on the faerie road – like a shot of morphine. A pleasurable lull relaxed her taut muscles; a sweetness filled her blood and she reached for Rav, wrapping both arms around his neck and pulling him to her. Nothing mattered now. Suddenly, it was as if a switch had been flicked again, but this time, it was her pleasure that had been switched on.

Faye wanted him badly. And, perhaps, it was the built-up frustration of all of the dreams with Finn that had taken her to the brink of orgasm and then denied her; she wanted *someone*, a man, and Rav was here.

Rav was here, and he wanted her, too. He looked down at her with unmasked lust in his eyes. She reached for him, desire hot in the core of her. Desperate to finally be satisfied, filled and physically dominated by a man – such a huge man – who could give her what she so desperately craved. Did she want Finn most of all? Perhaps. But Finn was a spectre, a fantasy, not real, or, at least, continually absent from her waking life. Rav was here, and he was real.

Without saying anything more, she kissed him fiercely.

As she closed her eyes, Faye was overcome with sensation. Rav kissed her back, harder, taking control. She felt his barely contained passion.

His fingers stroked her cheek, and then came to her bottom lip. It felt *right*, delicious: the kiss became hot, slippery, wet. Faye had the sudden sense they were not alone; for a moment, it was as though they stood on a beach thronged with people. She heard laughter, snatches of speech she didn't understand, giggling. But when she drew back briefly from Rav and opened her eyes, they were alone.

'What is it?' he asked huskily, his face close to hers still.

'Nothing, I just... thought I heard something.' The moon was rising already.

He kissed her again, and now Faye felt a sense of urgency thronging deep inside herself. All of those times Finn had worked her up to fever pitch and then refused to satisfy her; she had touched herself, but it wasn't the same. She wanted... needed... to be taken, to be fucked, to be... she didn't even know what she wanted. The things that Finn had said to her had been unlike anything anyone had said to her before. *Just let me play with you like my own little doll, my princess, my queen, good girl, let me take what I want.* The idea of a man taking his pleasure from her body – using her in exactly the way he wanted, bending her over and fucking her unceremoniously like an animal, or forcing himself between her lips – was so alien that she didn't know where the hot delight of the idea came from. And yet all of the desire and *need* she had felt in those dreams with Finn returned to her now in a rush of sensation.

'Come back to the house,' Rav murmured against her ear. Faye looked up at the rising moon and shook her head; she wanted to stay outside. She knew that she wouldn't feel safe in the house.

'Let's stay here,' she whispered.

Rav kissed her again, his lips tracing the line of her neck now; she felt his hot mouth on her collarbone. He pushed her clothes away from her skin and started to unbutton her blouse underneath the pink coat. Trails of pleasure followed his kisses over her skin, like fireworks. She moaned and wrapped her legs around him, needing more, relishing Rav's worship of her body. She was hungry; she had been starved of affection for so long.

She pulled him down to the ground and he made a sound that was part moan, part growl. He swore under his breath.

'Damn it, Faye. You don't know what you do to me. You make me feel like an animal.'

She reached into her pocket and took out a large, creased cotton scarf and spread it over the sand under them.

Then, she reached for him, lying back on the sand. His body covered hers, and the weight of him thrilled her. She wanted his skin on hers, so she pushed up his black sweater and the soft tartan shirt underneath it; she placed her ripe mouth on his stomach, feeling the electric buzz of connection between them.

He moaned as her kisses covered his chest. Both were heedless of the cooling temperature, but an aura of roses still hung in the air, at the very edge of Faye's perception.

He reached for her greedily, pulling her up towards his face for a deep kiss; he bit her top lip gently.

'Take this off,' he ordered, and she took off her coat. He slid his hand under her half-opened blouse and bra and stroked her breast, pushing its lace to one side.

'Rav... Oh, oh god,' she murmured as he ran his tongue over her soft skin. He brought her down to straddle his hips, and she leaned forward so that her full breasts, skimmed with the white lace bra, were in his face. He moaned as he licked her nipples through the soft lace. She reached behind her, unhooked the bra and pushed it up so that her rounded, soft breasts were his to adore. She could feel him harden and push instinctively against her as she ran her fingers in his black hair. She felt wildly alive; she was so wet already from his mouth on her that she felt she would climax with just a few strokes of him inside her, or with a touch to her clit.

As if he could sense her thoughts, Rav reached under her and stroked the crotch of her jeans: already, they were soaked. She unbuttoned and unzipped them, taking them off and throwing them to one side, and rolled beside him so that he could touch her more easily; his gentle sucking was intoxicating, and her body had now entirely taken over with its urgent need for pleasure. Rav pulled her knickers to one side and stroked his finger over her clit, maddening her with his deliberate slowness.

'Oh god, oh god...' Faye began moaning, having no control over her voice now. She closed her eyes and, just for a moment, had the sense again that they were not alone on the beach, that she could feel eyes on her dishevelled clothes, on her naked breasts. As Rav moved his mouth towards her stomach and continued stroking her softly, she closed her eyes and spread her arms out on the scarf, her palms on the sand. Shapes and shadows formed and dissolved on her eyelids as if figures stood by, watching her pleasure build, but she felt no shame or embarrassment. Indeed, as Rav quickened his stroking and pleasure filled her even more, she spread her legs wide. Just the act of doing that aroused her further: she wanted to be seen. She felt the gazes of the shadows feeding her. Their desires building hers.

Come and watch me, come and feel this, witness my pleasure. Worship me, adore me, she thought, the words coming from nowhere. She felt his finger enter her, moving slowly in and out of her, and then, as she was so wet, he pushed two fingers into her. She gasped at the sensation of them stretching her in just the right way: he twisted his two fingers into her slowly, and then pulled them out again in a gentle corkscrew motion. He moaned with lust.

'Fuck, Faye. I want you so bad,' he murmured. She reached for his crotch and felt how hard he was; how big he was.

'Please,' she gasped, touching him, knowing that he knew exactly what she wanted. But he shook his head. 'No. I want to taste you first,' he murmured.

His hot tongue met her clit, and she moaned louder as the warmth of his mouth covered her. She grabbed his head and pushed it into her, opening her eyes wide and staring blindly up at the evening sky. Her pleasure grew as he licked her gently, listening for her cries and whispered instructions for where it felt the best – *up, up, there, more, don't stop* – until he hit the perfect spot with a growing intensity of soft pressure, his tongue caressing her over and over again, and Faye felt as though she was going to pass out, so deep was she engulfed in ecstasy.

She felt the crest of her pleasure starting to rise, but she wanted him inside her. She needed it so desperately. To come, held down by his body, filled with his hard, throbbing cock, in a moment of pure, primal lust.

'Please, Rav. Please,' she begged. 'I want you... inside me.'

'As my enchantress commands.' Rav looked up at her and sat back on his heels, pulled down his jeans and, without hesitating, plunged his long, thick cock deep inside her in one motion. She cried out, loudly, in surprise and pleasure. She was so wet that he entered her completely, stretching her pleasurably with the girth of him: he was significantly bigger than any man she had been with before. She could feel the head of his cock deep inside her, far inside, in a place she couldn't remember feeling pleasure before. She moaned with the intensity of just feeling him inside her. He bent his head down and kissed her.

'Is that what you wanted?' he murmured. 'Is that what you

were dying for? A real man's cock inside you?' He started to move, then, gently pushing into her and then drawing it out. 'Fuck. You're so wet. And tight.' His fingers gripped the wet sand on either side of her head, and he growled again.

Having him inside her, hard, thick, filling her, was almost more than she could take. All the built-up frustration of the past weeks had reached fever pitch in her body, and she so desperately needed the release. As if knowing how close she was, Rav reached down between her legs and stroked her clit with his finger as he pushed deep inside her.

'There. Do you like feeling me filling you? Is that what you want?' he moaned. 'Oh, god. You feel so good, Faye.'

'Yes. I want it. All of it. More. Harder,' she moaned, clenching her muscles tight around him, feeling his rhythm build, touching the innermost parts of her and suffusing her with a deep, resonant ecstasy that she was powerless to resist. Her body met his rhythm instinctively and she started to feel the wave of ecstasy overcome her, like a hardness and a softness at once.

She cried out at the surging plateau of intense pleasure that made her gasp, cry out, kick and convulse as it took her over.

Her whole body was alight, from the soles of her feet to her heart and her head. White-hot pleasure filled her lungs, her throat, her blood. She'd had orgasms before, but this, with the strangely rose-scented air on the beach, the salt of the sand and the evening sun on her skin, was different. She cried out, a wordless, animal cry halfway between a moan and a scream.

As she rode the orgasm, she felt Rav stiffen, and heard him grunt and growl. His hips thrust into her, burying his cock deeply inside her and he made a noise that was somewhere between pleasure and pain.

'Fuck. Fuck. I'm coming. Oh, fuck... Faye, Faye...' he growled lustily, and his whole body shuddered.

Panting, he rested his head on her breasts for a moment, and they lay together, entwined.

'That was... Fuck. I don't know what that was.' He sounded bewildered for a moment, then chuckled. 'That was amazing. Wow. What have you done to me?'

Faye had been so focused on their lovemaking that she had temporarily forgotten the strange notion she'd had that she and Rav were being watched, but now she came back to earth a little and realised that they were lying on Black Sands Beach in full view of anyone who might be out for an evening stroll.

He propped himself up on an elbow and reached for her coat and jeans next to them, and draped her coat over her.

'Here, don't get cold.'

'Sorry, I... I don't know what happened, either. It was like... being possessed.' She sat up, feeling herself come back to earth, and reached for her jeans.

'You've got nothing to apologise for, except being unbearably sexy, Miss Morgan.' Rav kissed her forehead, nose and lips and hugged her in closer. 'I don't think I've ever ravaged anyone on a beach before. It's not even *dark*. That was just...' He blew out his cheeks and whistled. 'Yeah. That was insanely hot. You... I just felt like we were the only two people in the world. Like I was under a spell.'

Under a spell. Was it a coincidence that she and Rav had just made love under the rising moon, on the beach where Faye and Annie had found the love spell in Grandmother's grimoire in the first place? Was it at all surprising that the spell had brought Rav to Faye?

I don't think it was, she thought.

She pulled on her jeans and put her coat back on, shaking the worst of the sand out of the old scarf and stuffing it back in her pocket.

Faye watched the sea as Rav took her hand. She felt odd, suddenly, as if they had wandered into another time and place here, with the way that she had reacted to him, with the smell of roses in the air. The whole thing had been otherworldly; she had seen, or thought she had seen, faeries in the water.

While the sense of being watched had aroused her earlier, now, she felt vulnerable. What if, when Rav had been touching her, they really had been watching? She had seen the faerie folk in his house, and felt the cold they had cast about the place; she knew from the old stories that they were not always pleasant or kind.

She looked around, peering into the dark, but she couldn't sense any other presences now. Yet, she felt a sudden disinclination to go back into Rav's house and be among those energies again. In her ecstasy, she hadn't cared if they watched her pleasure. In a more sober state, she really didn't want that at all.

'Actually, thanks but I'm going to go home.' She turned abruptly, pulling her hand away from his. 'I've got some things I need to do at the shop. Just remembered.'

'What?' He turned in surprise. 'But... we just... I mean...' He looked dumbfounded.

'I have to go. I'll see you,' she said, feeling stupid but not knowing how to explain. The beach was different now, but she couldn't describe how; this had been her place of worship for so long, and she was sensitive to its energies. She had often drawn on the elemental power of the beach in working magic, but whatever she had felt just now was different. Sex had brought a different energy, maybe that was all it was. But that feeling of being watched – and of her own wicked, sexual response – had unsettled her.

'I need to go home,' she repeated.

'Okay.' Rav cleared his throat, as if there was a lot he wanted to say but was choosing not to. 'Will I see you again soon?'

'Oh. Yes...' She felt awful then, but it was too late. The energy had changed between them now. 'I'm sorry, I...'

'No, it's all right...' He smiled carefully at her, and gave her a little wave. 'See you around.'

No, no! Not see you around! she berated herself, and watched him take the path up the beach to his house.

Faye turned her back on the sea and started for home, pulling her coat tight against a wind that had whipped up suddenly. And as she stepped carefully around the rocks where the grass met the sand – where, she often thought, the real world met this in-between place of power – she heard strange voices calling her name. *Faye, Faye.* The wind seemed to carry an echo of someone calling her. *Faye Morgan.* But when she looked over at Rav's house, there was no one there.

11

———

Annie knew instantly when Faye opened the shop door the next day; it took her all of three seconds to look Faye over and make up her mind that something had happened.

'Morning.' Faye stood aside and let her friend in; today, Annie was wearing a belted red trench coat over a baggy Breton stripe shirt with flappy pockets, a denim miniskirt and thick orange tights with biker boots. Faye felt dowdy in comparison in her jeans and sweater, though the cornflower-blue colour of her top sat nicely against her auburn hair.

'Don' give me yer *morning*, Faye Morgan, like nothing's going on. Somethin's happened. I can tell.' Annie threw her coat on one of the easy chairs and stalked around her friend like a cat. She peered at Faye's neck and grabbed hold of the frayed collar of the old sweatshirt, pulling it away from Faye's skin and scanning her skin.

'What are you doing, you madwoman?' Faye pulled away, laughing at Annie's manic expression.

'Looking for love bites, my sweet dahhhling,' Annie trilled in her actress voice. 'Remainders of the love act. The shadow of a kiss.' She stood back and narrowed her eyes. 'You've had sex. Haven't you? I can tell.'

Faye laughed out loud. 'My god. What are you, like, some kind of sex detective? Yes, I did. Happy now?' She straightened her sweatshirt and tried to look normal, though she didn't feel it.

'Ye *didn't*. Tell me yer not makin' this up!' Annie screeched, lapsing back into her normal accent.

'I'm not making it up.' Faye fiddled with a basket of crystals, sliding her fingers between the cool smoothness of the clear quartz.

'Who? When? *Where?*' Annie demanded, letting out a whoop of delight. 'I cannae *believe* it! This is big.' She sat down behind the counter and leaned forward, drumming her fingers on the glass. 'C'mon. Tell me. I want it all. As the actress said to the bishop.'

'You *are* an actress.'

'I know. Meta.'

The door opened and Aisha strode in, smiling. The bells tinkled, and Grandmother's hagstone charm that hung by the door twisted gently in the breeze. Faye realised that she still hadn't discovered what had happened to the charm when Finn had come to the shop, that day, or who had put it back in its place: she reminded herself to ask Annie and Aisha about it. However, right now, that seemed unimportant.

'Aisha. Yer just in time, sweetheart. Seems that the spell's worked. Faye got laid last night.' Annie nodded to Faye, who was feeling increasingly uncomfortable.

'Annie, I don't think...' she began, but Annie glared at her.

'I hope yer not tryin' to weasel out of telling us, Faye Morgan. When we're the ones that did the spell with ye. Grandmother Morgan would frown on that, ye know. She didnae have anyone to share her magic with except your maw and you. We're a coven now, aye. Ye share yer magic. In fact...' Annie opened the store cupboard and drew out Grandmother's book. 'Here. We should be writin' this all down. Keepin' a record.'

She took a pen from the counter and sat down again, leaning forward.

'Annie! You are NOT going to write about my sex life in Grandmother's book!' Faye snatched the pen from her hand and closed the covers of the thick volume.

'We should put in the details of the ritual, though. An' the results,' Annie replied sulkily. 'It's only common witchcraft practice.'

'Fine. But only the ritual, and the fact that it seems to have worked,' Faye insisted.

'Tell us, then.' Aisha perched on the closest easy chair. 'This is so exciting!' She grinned, but there was a catch in her voice. Faye remembered their heart-to-heart outside the bar. Perhaps Aisha was sad that something had happened for Faye, and not her. Annie uncapped the pen and waited expectantly.

'Well, there's not that much to tell,' Faye lied. After all, there was a lot she could say: about the strange feeling of being watched on the beach; about the fact that she thought she had seen faeries in the waves, watching her and Rav make love; about the way Rav had looked at her, the fact that he had said *I feel like I'm under a spell*. About the primal animal lust that had overcome them both... But those things were private. And her wild pleasure was also hers, not for gossip. 'I told you I met someone at the beach, the other week. Remember?'

She had mentioned it to Annie the day after meeting Rav, but had played it down at the time.

'Ye told me ye had a chat tae some guy. Not that he was some kinda new sex puppet for ye.'

'Annie! He's not a sex puppet.'

Annie waved her hand dismissively.

'Aye, he's a mega-brainy yogic philanthropist, I'm sure. Get on with it.'

'He's new to the village. He moved into that big house on the beach? You know the one?' Annie and Aisha nodded; they both knew Black Sands Beach well. 'His name's Rav Malik. He's from London originally, he's just moved up because he's organising this new music festival in the village. He thought his house was haunted, and when I told him it was the fae that were displeased... That house sits on a faerie road, d'you know that?' Her friends shook their heads; Annie raised an eyebrow.

'Explains a lot, though,' she said. 'Continue.'

'Yeah. Well. When I said that, his first reaction was, like, *this is mad*. But then he took it seriously. He tried, anyway. I mean, I don't think we have that much in common. His whole life is music; I'm not really that into it. And I don't know what he thinks of me being from a family of witches. But I really like him.' Faye was aware that she had been gabbling a little; usually, she didn't say as much.

'He's probably fascinated with the witch thing,' Aisha replied. 'And you don't need to have that much in common. You just need to have... I dunno. *The feelings*.'

'D'you have *the feelins*?' Annie demanded. 'What happened, anyway? Ye went over there tae look at his haunted hoose? An' then what? Which, by the way, is a new one on me, aye. Goin' to have to keep that one in the bank for when I'm tryin' to seduce a witchy type in the future.'

'We kissed. And...' Faye felt shy saying much else. 'One thing led to another, I guess. On the beach.'

Annie screamed and punched the air. 'Yesss! On the *beach*? Seriously? What time was this?'

'I don't know. Evening time.'

'Christ. It's not even dark, then.' Annie exchanged glances with Aisha. 'That's intense.'

'Is he like what you asked for? What does he look like?' Aisha asked.

'He's... not exactly what I asked for. He's... bigger. Like

some kind of animal. I wouldn't usually go for someone like that. But... yeah. I like him.' She shrugged.

'I take it yer going to see him again?' Annie prompted.

'Maybe. I don't know.'

Annie looked concerned and wrote something in the book. 'Oh, sweetheart. It wasn't any good?'

Faye smiled, thinking of the way that Rav had brought her to the intense ecstasy of the night before.

'No, no... it was very good.' She felt her cheeks colour. 'He's... I don't know if he's like what I asked for. He's tall...' Faye remembered her doll. The wool hair with golden flecks that she'd braided; the way she'd tattooed its skin with her words. It wasn't Rav... but it *did* look awfully like Finn Beatha. So, why was it that she had made love with Rav last night? Where was Finn?

'I feel like there's a "but" moving in the general direction of this conversation,' Aisha said.

'There might be a but,' Faye conceded.

'Why? He's nice?'

'Yes.' Faye smiled.

'He made you come, aye?' Annie looked concerned. 'Tell me he made ye come, sweetheart.'

'Annie, that's none of your business!' Faye glared at her friend.

'Just say yes or no,' Annie prompted. 'I'm not going to write it down. Look.' She put the pen down. 'I just wanna know. Yer my pal. I want to know ye had a good time.'

'Fine. *Yes*,' Faye hissed, grateful they didn't have any customers in the shop while this excruciating conversation was taking place.

'Good! So, what's wrong with him? Ugly, is he?' Annie made a sympathetic face. 'Ye might get used to it. If he knows what he's doing, like.'

'He is very good-looking! Stop asking questions.'

'So, what is it, then?' Annie and Aisha were frowning at her, and Faye couldn't explain it to them. She was still unsettled that she had acted out of character in going so far with Rav at the beach. And she couldn't shake off the suspicion that they'd been watched by the fae – had they influenced their passionate abandon somehow?

As she talked to Annie and Aisha, her thoughts strayed briefly back to Finn Beatha. She had asked for someone kind who wanted her, and Rav had arrived....

But was he the one she wanted?

12

———

'Blue-rinse brigade out in force, I see,' Aisha murmured to Faye as they walked into Abercolme's community centre a week later. Folding chairs had been set out in lines facing the front of the room where the local minister stood, talking to the butcher. The front half of the hall was already full, mostly with the older members of the community.

Everyone had been summoned to a community meeting about Rav's music festival, Abercolme Rocks, and Faye had assented; she was nervous about seeing Rav again, but she knew she had to see him at some point. And Aisha was curious to see him. Annie had wanted to come, too, but she was away on an acting job.

Faye smiled at the people filling the rows; these were people she'd lived alongside all her life. Some had an uneasy relationship with her and her family. Some, like Annie, were enthusiastic about witchcraft. Faye recognised some of them from the circles Moddie would hold in the shop on a Friday night, where they would honour the old gods in the flickering candlelight.

'Don't know if I'm helping or hindering you, being here, you know,' Aisha said as they sat down.

'What do you mean?'

'You know what I mean. Villages like this one don't like outsiders. Especially not ones like me.' Aisha touched her brown cheek. Faye sighed.

'I wish it wasn't like that for you. It's not fair. But, yes. I know.'

'Tell me about it. I was born in Scotland. Not good enough for some of them, though.' Aisha smiled too brightly. 'Most people are lovely. Just, occasionally, I get that *where are you from* question. Baffles them when I say Glasgow.'

'They're very suspicious of new people to the village. Or people who have been here for generations.' Faye sighed. Many villagers still avoided the shop altogether. And there had always been whispering and sideways glances when Faye had been out and about with Moddie or Grandmother, though they had held their heads high and ignored the whispers.

Faye had learned this from a young age. On her first day at school, after she had bid a tearful goodbye to Moddie, who had mussed her hair affectionately and told her that she'd have a wonderful day, she'd gone inside and hung her coat on the peg with her name on it. Bel McDougall, her mud-brown hair in two scratchy plaits, had peered curiously at the bulge in the cream lining of Faye's coat.

'What's that?' She'd touched the rounded shape of the black tourmaline Moddie had sewn into Faye's coat for protection.

Faye, accustomed to Moddie's ways – crystals and lavender bags under her pillow for good dreams, herbal tinctures for coughs and colds, searching for faerie toadstool rings for making wishes – had shrugged. 'Black crystal to keep the bad spirits away,' she'd explained quite naturally, smiling at this new friend. But Bel's eyes had widened, and she'd run into the classroom calling out, *She's a witch, she's a witch*, laughing but casting baleful glances back at her at the same time until Faye felt she was being made fun of, though she didn't know why.

Tears had welled up in her eyes until she felt a small hand in hers, and turned to see five-year-old Annie's earnest face topped with a mop of unruly dark blonde hair staring into hers.

'Ye can sit with me.' Annie had led her to a green hexagonal table where two boys were sat, and they'd begun a discussion about what their favourite colours were. After that day, Faye learned that there were plenty more Bel McDougalls, but there was also Annie, who, rather than run away, always seemed to be propelled towards Faye with a combination of fierce curiosity and even fiercer love.

But Annie wasn't here to fight for Faye today; she was away at another audition. *I hope she gets something soon*, Faye thought as the minister banged the table for attention. Still, it was heartening to have Aisha with her: not for the first time, Faye thanked whatever fair wind had blown Aisha to Mistress of Magic's door.

The minister began the meeting.

Aisha looked over Faye's shoulder.

'What?' Faye mouthed, and Aisha signalled with a nod to the back of the hall where Rav Malik stood with his meaty arms crossed across his huge chest.

'Is that him?' Aisha whispered.

Faye blushed, looking away quickly. Those huge arms had recently pinned her to the ground on Black Sands Beach; those wide, muscular thighs had parted hers and thrust between them, making her lose herself in an ecstasy she had never known. Faye's heart started pounding. 'Yeah,' she whispered.

'He's fit.' Aisha turned back round to look at Rav. 'Jesus. He's huge.'

Faye elbowed her. 'Shh.' She was mortified and wished she could sink into the ground. What if someone from the village had seen her and Rav having sex at the beach? Oh god. How had she and Rav thought it was a good idea to throw all caution to the wind in the way that they did?

Someone at the back of the hall called out.

'Ma customers aren't happy with it. More and more unsuitable bands going on the list, aye. Village is going to be full of layabouts an' hippies, mark my words!' one of the shopkeepers exclaimed.

'I asked Mr Malik to be here with us, as I thought many of you would have questions about the festival,' the minister explained. 'Perhaps he can provide more information?'

Rav made his way to the front of the hall; Faye caught his eye as he walked past her, and he shot her a quick smile. Just for a moment, there were only the two of them in the community centre, and Faye was vividly reminded of the way it felt when Rav kissed her. She didn't allow herself to think about the rest of it, because she knew she would blush so deeply that everyone would notice.

'Hi. I'm Rav. I'm the promoter organising Abercolme Rocks.' He stood at the front of the hall, planting his feet confidently slightly apart and resuming the stance with his arms crossed over his chest. Faye couldn't look at him without getting a lump in her throat; his sheer animal magnetism made her eyes glaze over; instantly, she felt herself getting wet, just listening to his deep, sonorous voice. 'Thanks for having me here today. I know some of you have concerns about the festival and that you haven't had anything like it here before, so I thought I'd come and give you some information and answer any questions you might have.'

'Why do we have to have a music festival here at all? We were perfectly happy without one.' Mrs Kennedy, in her seventies, with a flowered scarf knotted around her head and dressed in a fleece of indeterminate colour, stood up and flicked her hand dismissively at Rav. 'Ah don't know who ye spoke to, to get permission in the first place, aye. Nobody wants ye here.'

'Well, you can take it up with the council. They put out a tender for a festival and my company won it; it's part of their regeneration project. I've produced a lot of festivals and music tours all over the world. I can promise you that this will be a good opportunity for Abercolme. Your businesses will benefit – accommodation, taxis, catering, retail; and I'm going to be creating some temporary jobs in terms of site services.' He opened his arms in a welcoming gesture. 'Honestly, I know it's new, but you're going to find that this helps Abercolme rather than hinders it. I promise,' he replied politely.

There was a general murmur, neither positive nor negative in tone.

'So, we've got some amazing bands on the schedule: Science Fiction Pulp Novel, Dal Riada, Green Apple: Red Apple, Kollectiv and Call of Sirens so far. Tickets are selling really well, but we have limited them to five thousand because of the space in the castle grounds,' he continued.

'It's going to ruin the castle! That's ancient, ye know. That's our heritage. We don't want hippies runnin' around it with no clothes on, spray-painting the stone, breaking things. It isn't respectful.' Mrs Kennedy wasn't going to let it go, clearly.

Rav smiled nicely and nodded, waiting for her to finish. 'Of course, I understand your concerns. I will say that a festival audience for an event like Abercolme Rocks will be responsible people who love good music. I imagine there will be quite a few parents bringing children. It's a pleasant outdoor festival event that starts in the afternoon and finishes around eleven, so won't keep anyone up too late into the night.' Rav ran his hand through his hair. Faye liked the way his fringe fell in his eyes.

'We will have proper security attached to the event. We'll be holding the festival in the castle grounds, away from the main building; people will not be allowed access to the castle for the duration of the festival,' he continued.

Rav's tone never wavered from a practised, steady pleasantness; he had a grounded, in-control energy that Faye found unutterably sexy, but she also sensed his frustration under the professional veneer. It couldn't have been the first time he'd had to deal with a difficult crowd, and Faye supposed that diplomacy was part of an event manager's skill set. Yet, she noticed that his left hand was clenched into a fist. As Rav caught her eye, he smiled subtly, knowing that she'd noticed his tell, and stretched out his fingers, returning his hand to his side. Looking at his clenched fist also made Faye even more turned on than she had been already; the suggestion of the brute force he commanded made her bite her lip with desire. She wanted him again, wanted to be completely overwhelmed by that muscled, heavy body. Held down, penetrated, possessed totally.

'All necessary risk assessments have been done. I think, if you came along, you'd enjoy it.' Rav twinkled a sweet smile at Mrs Kennedy, and Faye was amazed to see her look slightly mollified.

'Well, I still don't like it, but I see I've not got much of a choice, aye,' the woman muttered and sat down.

'Tell you what, you can have two free tickets so you can come and see for yourself. How would that be?'

Faye snorted with laughter and coughed to disguise it.

'Get on with ye! I wouldn't want to come.' Mrs Kennedy sounded scandalised, and Faye wished she could see her face from where she was sitting.

'All right. Well, if you change your mind, let me know,' Rav said. 'In fact, if anyone's not sure about the festival, come and talk to me about it. And I'm happy to provide free tickets to anyone here who would like to come.'

'Right. Thank you, Mr Malik.' The minister stepped forward. 'I'm sure we're all very excited about what will be a wonderful new event in the village. If anyone has any more questions for Mr Malik, please do ask him, or I believe he is going to leave some leaflets with contact details, if you'd like to phone or email him.'

Rav nodded. Faye watched him, wondering whether to approach him and say something. But what would she say?

Everyone started filing out of the village hall.

At that moment, the village door banged open, blown by a sudden wind. Faye, Rav and the minister looked around in surprise at the rain which had come out of nowhere.

'Scottish weather.' The minister shivered as the rain drummed on the windows. It had grown suddenly dark outside.

Faye looked up at the rain on the high windows. For just a second, she thought she saw faces in the water, looking in at them; otherworldly faces with large, watery eyes and open mouths. As if they were laughing. Or something more savage: as if they were hungry.

She walked cautiously out of the hall, through its thick, old double doors.

'Weird weather.' Rav was standing by the doors, adjusting the collar on his blazer.

'Oh. Yeah.' She looked away, embarrassed. Faye was painfully aware that they had been shockingly intimate so recently; the feeling of having been exposed returned to her, and she swallowed awkwardly. What must he think of her? *I don't normally do that kind of thing*, she wanted to say. *I wouldn't usually be so... abandoned. We hardly know each other.* She wasn't puritanical. It was more that it had just been strange. The whole time – on the beach, at his house – in retrospect, she had felt odd throughout.

'Good to see you, Faye.' He reached for her hand. 'Hope you're okay? You kind of rushed off the other night. And I realised I didn't have your number.'

Aisha was standing a few feet away, subtly staying in the background.

'I'm okay. Thanks,' she replied. It wasn't getting any less awkward: in fact, holding his hand just made it worse. Being anywhere near Rav Malik set Faye's whole body aflame with desire... 'Buying your way into their good books, are you?' Faye blundered on. 'The free tickets, I mean.' *Oh god, what am I saying?* she berated herself. *Sorry. Just say sorry for running out on him.*

'Oh... right.' Rav shrugged and let go of her hand. 'Worth a try. That woman with the headscarf, what's her name?'

'Mrs Kennedy. She does the flowers in the church.' Faye's heart sank. The moment had gone; if she was going to say anything, she should have said it by now. Rav was trying to talk to her, trying to connect to her, but she was doing it all wrong.

'Mrs Kennedy. Okay. Thing I've learned about places like this is, go for the ringleaders and the rest fall in line. I'll make friends with Mrs Kennedy, and we'll see how many complaints there are about the festival after that.' He smiled warmly at her, and she felt awkward again.

'Oh. Well, good luck.' She opened the doors; getting drenched was better than making a fool of herself with Rav. 'And... I'm sorry. For... you know,' she blurted, confused, and ran into the rain. *Get back in there and talk to the man, idiot!* Annie would have said. But Faye couldn't.

'Faye!' Rav called after her. He sounded confused and a little annoyed. She tried to wave over her shoulder, but it came out wrong and she looked like a flailing madwoman as she ran away.

It was nice that Rav still wanted to know her but, after that performance, Faye doubted she'd be seeing him again anytime soon. Letting herself into the shop, she berated herself again. *Stupid, stupid.* She'd had a chance at something. A real romance with a real man. But she'd blown it.

Summoning love with a magic spell might have worked. But magic wasn't responsible for what happened afterwards, Faye was learning.

13

A week later, Faye woke in the middle of the night.

She lay on the oak double bed that had once been Moddie's and stared at the ceiling for a moment. She had been dreaming of the faerie road; of the goat-man who had reached out and tweaked her nipple; of the fae that had skipped and danced past.

Blessings, sidhe-leth. We are honoured. You are as beautiful as the legends say.

When she closed her eyes, she was back there instantly, walking the grass road that existed somehow inside Rav's house. But this time, instead of Rav making love to her on the beach, Finn Beatha stood at the top of the hill, and he was beckoning her to come to him.

She opened her eyes again. She knew she was still in her bed, safe in the grey stone house of the Morgans.

She felt a sudden need to be at Black Sands Beach; her heart yearned towards it, her special place of magic.

Well, I'm not getting back to sleep anytime soon, she thought as she swung her legs out of bed. *So I might as well go.* Experience had taught her to obey her instincts when they were this insistent. It was times like these when she imagined the spirits of her ancestors pulling at her hand, compelling her to act. It would be rude to deny them.

She got dressed quickly: leggings, a heavy long woollen dress over the top, socks. Downstairs, she wrapped a thick blue and green tartan scarf around her neck and put the long pink coat on again, then pulled on her high, practical walking boots. They had a thick sole and she knew she could walk through water in them, and climb wet rock if required. She grabbed a pair of thick fleece gloves from under the counter and let herself out of the side door, grabbing a torch as she did so.

The street was deserted. She looked at her watch: 1.30 a.m. – no time for anyone to be awake in Abercolme. Even the pub shut just before eleven. Or, if people were up, they were sensibly indoors.

It wasn't that cold. It was a quarter moon, and when she got to the beach, the clouds parted so that the soft moonlight reflected on the flat water. She looked up at Rav's house, but it was in darkness. She felt embarrassed and hoped he wouldn't see her out here. She didn't know what she would say to him.

Instead of going to a rock to sit and look out to sea, she went to where she imagined the beginning of the faerie road might be – outside of the house, but aligned with it, a little way from the front door – and closed her eyes.

It was there, immediately, as if it had been waiting for her. The long grass where she knew there should only be sand, the twinkling lights that floated around her like stars in a tide of light mist. She had walked this place so many times and never known.

Or perhaps she *had* known. Black Sands was a magical place. It had always been that way; Moddie had brought her here as a child to make simple shell shapes on the dark sand.

She had squatted down on her bare heels next to her daughter. *Make a wish, Faye. When the tide takes your spell, it goes to the faeries.*

Moddie made shapes Faye recognised: circles, spirals, stars. She often wrote things within the shapes with her finger – symbols and letters. And, occasionally, she would dispatch Faye to collect as many shells as she could from around the beach to make one large heart shape which she would always trace the same name into: Lyr. *What is Lyr, Mummy?* Little Faye would watch Moddie draw the looping script into the sand. *Nobody, darling. Just a memory*, she would reply.

Faye and Annie had spent hours here as teens, asking all manner of boons from the sea and the wind and the air: to pass their exams, to get people to like them, to get the new boots they'd had their eye on in the one village shoe shop.

She closed her eyes and followed the sparkling path. She was no longer cold, and she took off her gloves and coat, letting them fall to the ground.

The fae were around her again, in varying sizes and colours and types. The butterfly fae fluttered past, moonlight glimmering on their wings. The quarter moon was still there and the sea rippled calmly to her left. There was a distant sound of hoofbeats on grass, and a pleasurable thrumming rhythm that vibrated up from the faerie earth into her body.

This time, she followed the path to the top of the hill where the golden light shone as it had before. And when she reached the top, she took a breath of wonder.

Before her, far out at sea, was a huge golden castle, ringed by a vast green maze. In reality, if you stood on Black Sands Beach and looked out, it was onto the Firth of Forth that ran into the North Sea; there was a small island off the coast that monks had once lived on, and before that, druids.

But now there was no island: instead, tall towers plunged

upward through the dark Fife sea, looking as if they were formed of golden seawater. The maze that led to it was impossible. There was no way that such a strangely manicured puzzle could just *be there*, dotted with flower gardens, fountains and strange golden statues. And yet it was there, made of a kind of hedge which ran at head height. Faye could see many small faeries scurrying about in it, the hedge towering above them. It seemed that the maze was the only way to the castle, and it seemed to reach on forever.

The air was scented. Faye could pick out rose, jasmine and lavender. She remembered the smell of roses when she had made love with Rav on the beach. It was the same smell, the same perfumed air.

Faye approached the entrance to the maze. In front of her, floating into the maze opening, was a beautiful fae woman about Faye's height. She was wearing a green skirt but was naked from the waist up, and her golden hair floated down her shoulders like a cloak. Yet, when her skirt swished to one side, Faye saw she had black goat legs underneath.

'Through the maze, this and there, the faerie castle is here. Beware!
Beware, humans, ere time is lost! Beware the years that the faerie realm cost!
Through the maze, this and there, the faerie castle is here. Beware!'

Two little men with beards – rather like the gnomes Faye had in the garden behind the shop – sang the song as she trod past. One looked up and nodded at her.

'Blessings, miss. Ready to try your luck in the faerie maze?' He chuckled rather unpleasantly. 'Most humans don't come back if they go in. But there's fine food and dancing to be had.

Don't be shy, little miss, in you go!' And he reached out a little hand and tickled the back of her calf so that she leaped forward.

'Hey!' she cried, not sure what to do. She didn't want to get lost, wherever she was. Moddie had read enough faerie stories to the young Faye for her to know that getting lost in the realm of the fae was no laughing matter. The realm of the fae was dangerous – faeries were capricious, changeable; they might grant your wishes or help you around the house, or they might try and drown you, steal from you or hurt you in a thousand little ways.

And of course there were the tales of unlucky villagers who, on moonlit evenings, had come across a faerie ring of toadstools or a faerie mound – the ones that the farmers preserved in the middle of their fields so as not to upset the Good Folk. They were transported into the land of the fae where they might have been treated well or badly, but when they returned, it was many years later and their family had all died of old age and no one knew them.

She stepped back, but the other little gnome-man followed her and looked up into her face.

'No, no! She's not one of them. She's *sidhe-leth*. Let her pass,' he said, and bowed deeply from the waist. 'Many apologies, madam. We have not seen your like for many years.'

Faye was confused.

'But I don't want to be lost here. It was a mistake. I'm going.' She turned away and followed her footsteps back to the beach, though she really didn't want to at all. Everything in her being sang out for the faerie castle; she wanted so much to go, to be in it. It was more than wanting, in fact – it was a need, a sense that it was part of her.

'You will not be lost, madam. You can pass.' The gnome bowed again. 'You will know the way.'

Faye turned again and looked at the castle before her; it seemed to loom even more golden and bright against the strange sky. Though it had the same quarter moon as above the beach, it was neither day nor night but a strange pink-orange in between, like sunset or sunrise.

She wanted to, but she was afraid.

Then, as she looked into the maze, at the end of the first turn, she saw Moddie.

14

Without thinking, Faye ran forward.

'Moddie!' she cried; she hadn't called her *Mum* since she was small. Moddie had preferred her own name; she'd been a young mother, only twenty-one when she'd had Faye. When Faye was in her teens, they had been more like sisters.

Moddie's hair was loose and curled and reached her waist in long ringlets. She wore a white dress with a full skirt and long, bell-shaped sleeves. Her feet were bare, and she wore a golden circlet on her head. She beckoned to Faye, smiling, then turned a corner.

Faye ran into the maze and turned left as Moddie had. The hedge of the maze wall was fragrant – Faye thought she smelled eucalyptus or bay – and brushed against her legs as she ran.

'Moddie! Wait!' she cried again, but her mother moved fast through the turns and twists, not looking back. Faye followed as best she could, being careful not to crush the small faeries as she passed them: ladybirds the size of cats; leather-apron-wearing, bearded goblins who carried metal tools; more diaphanous, beautiful fae who seemed to float by without touching the earth. They were all heading for the castle, and there was an excitement among them that Faye picked up on. As she grew nearer, her heart beat faster; she felt a pleasant sense of anticipation, though she didn't know why.

Will I be lost? she wondered, but she felt that Moddie wouldn't lead her astray. There was that strange sense of familiarity again, though she didn't understand how that could be. And the more she breathed in the strange faerie air, the more a kind of lassitude entered her veins. She felt the same light-headedness and pleasure at everything as she would after two glasses of wine.

Faye followed the turns of the maze as best she could, trying to stay focused, fighting the lulling influence of the air and a growing disinclination to hurry at all. Moddie led her through long, dark, tunnel-like passages where the hedge seemed to have almost completely grown over at the top, making a leaf-hatched ceiling; on other stretches the hedge was replaced by long walls of sandy brick or red stone, and one section was made completely of a thick blue-tinted glass through which Faye could see the black ocean under her feet.

Further on, when the hedge had returned, small, winged faeries fluttered around her head, singing, and she found herself laughing, holding her hands out for them to land on. She was fascinated with them all, shivering delightedly as four white faerie horses ran past her, their flanks covered in sweat, their hooves pounding on the flattened dirt. Faye stopped walking and let the scented air overpower her. There were other voices that joined in the singing; she wanted to sing, too. She felt her eyes closing, and pleasure washing over her. Moddie had died and left her long ago. It probably wasn't her mother who was leading her through the maze; most likely, it was another type of faerie who looked like her. Who wanted to trick her.

Come to us, Faye, come to us, sidhe-leth, the voices sang to her, and as her eyes closed, the edges of the maze seemed to melt away, leaving Faye in a slow, soft kind of dance with all the creatures undulating around in a circle, this way and that. *Come to us, be with us, Faye Morgan, kindred soul.* She felt caressing touches alight on her legs, tickling their way up pleasurably to the inside of her thighs. Something that felt like kisses, a mouth gently inching its way upwards.

Faye felt a pinch on her arm and opened her eyes; the dream, or whatever it had been, of the faerie dance disappeared and she was alone again. She rubbed the sore spot on her forearm, frowning; it was like a sudden hangover come way too early after the pleasant tipsiness of a moment ago.

Faye. Wake up. It was Moddie's voice. Even though she hadn't heard it for eight years, she knew her mother's voice as well as she knew her own skin.

As she looked up, Moddie's foot and the hem of her dress flickered around the far corner. Faye's head cleared; she knew it was Moddie, and that if she should put her trust in anyone or anything, here in the realm of faerie, it should be her mother. *The fae realm is treacherous*, Grandmother and Moddie had told her so many times. *They are beautiful, but you cannot trust them.*

Faye ran after her mother around the next turn, but Moddie had disappeared, and Faye didn't know which of the three possible openings she might have gone down.

Panic replaced the giddy pleasure of just moments ago. Faye peered into each opening, but each one was empty and shadowed. She stopped and rested her hand on the thick hedge. She was lost again, and this time, it didn't feel so good.

Moddie, please help me. I don't want to be lost here, she thought, but there was no answer, no flickering of a dress in the distance, and no further pinches on her arm. She had to choose one of the ways forward, and she had nothing but instinct to go on.

Taking a deep breath, Faye chose the middle path. And as

soon as she stepped into it, the open doors of the golden faerie castle towered, vast, above her. And slowly, they opened.

The walls of the faerie castle seemed to reach to the moon, which glowed above Faye in the coral-pink sky. Its golden towers, when she gazed up at them, seemed to lean towards each other to join under the moon, the golden petals to its glowing centre.

The moon was far larger here than Faye had ever seen it in the ordinary world. Dimly she remembered reading once that the moon would have looked much bigger than it did now to people in the Stone Age, because it was closer to the earth then. Was it the same moon here as the one she was so used to? Or was this another, different, faerie moon that pulsed with a different kind of fierce and sweet power?

Intricate Celtic decoration covered the castle doors and, she saw as she walked through them, the walls inside. Spirals and Celtic knotwork scrolled over the gold and stone, similar designs to the ones on the jewellery she sold at the shop. There were words, too, but Faye recognised they were in Scots Gaelic, and her grasp of it was shaky at best. Yet, as she passed through the doors, she lost the thread of comparison to the real world altogether; it was like passing deeper into a dream, and whatever grasp she still had of her shop, of Abercolme and Annie and all the things she knew, disappeared.

Faye found herself in an open-air courtyard. Faeries of all kinds milled around market stalls, which sold all manner of beautiful fruits. Faye remembered the old poem about the dangers of eating the faerie food – *Morning and evening, Maids heard the goblins cry: Come buy our orchard fruits, Come buy, come buy!* But she felt thirsty, and goblets of some rich red liquid were being poured by a bearded centaur from what looked like a crystal jug on the stall closest to her, with its bright red-and-white striped awning.

The centaur held out the drink to Faye with a wink.

'Drink for my lady, *sidhe-leth*? Thy beauty surpasses all, but this drink will make thee beautiful for ever,' it said in a seductive tone that thrilled Faye and made her shiver with pleasure.

Sidhe-leth. They all seemed to know her – or, at least, recognise that she was half faerie, which was strange. She still had absolutely no idea if it was true – and, if she was half faerie, how that had ever managed to come about – but, clearly, there was something about her that these faerie creatures recognised as familiar.

She reached out before she knew what she was doing, then pulled her hand back sharply and shook her head.

'No, thank you,' she said politely, and looked around for Moddie. The throng was getting bigger and busier, and she was being pulled into the crowd. She started to feel threatened instead of delighted.

The singing, catcalling and shouting was starting to ring in her ears; it was increasingly loud, so Faye pushed through the crowd as best she could, aiming for one of the three entrance-ways leading off the courtyard. She couldn't see what lay beyond, but a soft gold light shone in each one.

She managed to elbow and *excuse me* her way through the crowd until she had passed through the closest doorway and emerged on the other side, where the noise of the courtyard faded away quickly.

The room was lit by candles, and their warmth licked the carved stone walls from which hung ultramarine and emerald-coloured tapestries. She couldn't see anyone else in the room, so she approached the nearest one and stroked it with the tip of her finger. It was soft, made of something velvety, and beautiful. The pattern wasn't one she recognised, but there was a sense of movement in it; as she gazed at it, she thought for a moment she could see horses in the waves, then decided they were seals on rocks.

A hand on her elbow made her jump.

'I see you like the wall-hangings. They were made by our most talented weavers,' a deep, musical voice said, and Faye turned to face Finn Beatha. 'Welcome, Faye Morgan, *sidhe-leth.*'

15

'Oh!' She couldn't think of anything else to say and felt stupid straightaway.

Finn let go of her elbow and bowed to her, though his eyes never left hers, and his smile was mischievous. 'The faerie realm is pleased to have you here.'

'You? How did you get here?!' Faye spluttered, shocked. For a brief moment, a clear vision of Mistress of Magic replaced her opulent surroundings: it was a dark day, rain battering at the windows, and she had been arranging the stone mantelpiece which displayed her biggest crystals. A row of large amethyst crystal clusters sat next to a number of extra-large yellow-gold citrine and smoky quartz crystals that had been polished into pyramids and pillars. On days like that, the shop was a snug, safe haven, with the hearth fire flickering cosily. She clutched at the memory as if it could steady her.

'I am of this place,' he replied, as if that would explain everything. 'I hoped you would come.'

'You're... faerie folk?'

'You know that I am.' He fixed her with an intense gaze. 'And you should know by now that you are, too. If you were in any doubt, your admittance to my kingdom should have made all things clear.'

'I... I didn't think about that. It just happened.'

'It just happened because you are half faerie. Our stock runs in your veins. Hence, you were able to breach the membrane between your world and ours. Hence, the guardians let you come,' he continued, his face serious. 'It is a great privilege that you hold. You should be more grateful.' He raised an eyebrow haughtily. Faye gazed at his perfect, beautiful and yet slightly androgynous face. He was so gorgeous, so perfect, that he seemed slightly unreal. There was no imperfection in Finn Beatha, as far as Faye could see. His high cheekbones were perfectly angular, his eyes luminous, large, long-lashed. His chin was strong, perfect, and, as her eyes followed the sinuous line of his neck down to his collarbone, she could see the rise of his muscled chest under his clothes.

Now, he wore a dark blue jacket with gold piping on the shoulders which looked somehow military; fitted trousers of the same material highlighted his strong thighs and calves. His dark blonde hair had the same golden flecks in it as she had noticed before – exactly the same colour as the wool she had used on her poppet doll in the spell. But this time, he wore a golden crown, studded with pearls and opals.

'I am grateful. But I didn't exactly choose to be here. And... I am not a faerie. I am a human.'

Moddie. She remembered that she had been following her mother through the crowd. 'I have to go. I need to find my mother. She's here...'

'She resides with us now. You will see her again in due course.' Finn took her hand, and she felt the return of the light-headedness that had overcome her earlier, but this time, at a much greater intensity. Instinctively, Faye fought his power, though it was strong.

She tried to do what she had in the Edinburgh bar – to shut

down her energy centres and cloak herself in darkness to regain some kind of control, but it was impossible to retain enough focus to do it properly. She kept finding her mind wandering, and the focused power she was used to raising and directing in spells and ritual eluded her, like snow blown into drifts and eddies by a strong wind.

'What do you mean? How can she... How can I...?' But Faye's words trailed away as Finn drew her to him, his lips inches from hers.

She could feel his strength, and she knew that she was powerless to resist him. He held her effortlessly in a tight, hard grip. She struggled, but it only made a cruel smirk play around his mouth.

'Try to get away all you like, *sidhe-leth*. You are mine, and you are within my kingdom now. Here, I am all-powerful. You only breathe here because I will it. The blood only continues to course in your veins because I permit it to. Say it.' His grip tightened on her.

'S-say what?' she stammered. Being this close to him was like a drug; something raw and wild swept through her. She felt, suddenly, as though nowhere else in the world existed, and as if she herself was changed: her old self was sloughed away, and some new yet original, as yet unknown self remained.

'Say that I am your lord and master. That you only exist here with my permission.' His blue eyes glittered with desire, and something darker. *Ownership*. Faye felt a dark thrill run through her body at the thought. In her dreams, he had told her that he owned her. That he owned her pussy. And in those dreams, she had readily agreed, so deep in desire had she been.

'I only exist here with your permission,' she repeated dutifully, looking up into his eyes. He still held her tightly in his grasp, and she could feel the hard strength of his body against hers.

'And?' He raised an eyebrow.

'And... you are the lord and master of this realm,' she added, reluctant to say that he was her lord and master. Whatever he was, he was not that. Faye had only ever met Finn once, and seen his band play in a bar. Granted, there had been many times when they had seemed to meet in her dreams, but she was still not sure whether they counted as real or what the purpose of the dreams were.

'You *are* half faerie. Believe me when I tell you that our meeting is fated, and that yours is an important destiny in the faerie realms,' he said. 'Hmm. I see that I have some work to do to make you realise your true purpose, and your position under me,' he drawled. He stroked her face with one hand, tracing the line of her full lips with his fingertip. 'No matter. You are a wilful one, it would seem, but I am stronger.' He released her, and stood in front of her, appraising her. 'Still. I am not so much of a monster to know that this all must seem very strange to you. So, temporarily, I will grant you some... kindness, as you adjust.'

'Thank you.' She raised her chin defiantly. 'But you haven't answered me. What is my mother doing here? Is she safe? Is she here in spirit? Did she... become fae, in some way?'

Faye needed to know, even though her very being felt enrobed in lassitude, even though she knew that for every moment she spent in the faerie world, she was being sucked deeper and deeper into its magic, and it would be more difficult to get back to the human world. She remembered some of the other rules she had read in Grandmother's grimoire: *Do not eat or drink in the faerie worlds. Leave offerings. Keep your wits about you.*

'I will answer all of your questions, Faye Morgan,' he said, a wry smile returning to his lips. 'But first, follow me. I will show you this great land of mine.'

He released her from the embrace and took her hand again. She didn't want to follow along, and yet she did. She wanted Finn to answer her question, wanted to know where Moddie

was, how she was here, why she was here. If that had really
been her mother. And yet, Faye followed, mute.

There was a part of her that knew she was being entranced,
that this was a strange place where she very well might get lost.
Faye fought it as hard as she could, and, just for a moment, as
she focused hard on Mistress of Magic and on the rain on the
windows and the leaping firelight, she felt her own power
return a little. She pulled her hand away from his, concentrating on the vision of the shop to steady herself, but he took
her palm in his again, chuckling in amusement, and Faye lost
what brief advantage she had gained.

*Know that the longer a human spends in the realms of faerie,
the more difficult it will be to return to the mortal world.*

All Faye could focus on was the energy coming through his
palm and into hers. It was a tingling wave of headiness she'd
never felt before, and it circled her, so that she felt she was
walking in a cloud. Finn's touch was electric; as well as putting
her firmly in a dream state, she realised that she was also
violently, shockingly full of desire for him. Again. She realised
how wet she was. He chuckled.

'My sweet one can hardly contain her excitement at being
here,' he observed, casting her an amused glance. 'Do not think
that you can conceal anything from me, Faye Morgan.'

They walked through room upon room filled with tapestries
and treasures; each one flickered with that strange candlelight
and hummed with a distant music.

'Do you know where you are?' he asked her, as they stood in
front of a vast tapestry. It depicted two grand fae seated on
thrones. On one side sat Finn Beatha, dressed resplendently in
blue and gold robes. On the other throne sat a terrifyingly beautiful fae queen. Around them swirled a pattern of interlinked
creatures: sea serpents, kelpies, mermaids, eels, shoals of fishes,
gilled creatures that she didn't recognise.

The faerie queen's hair was the same dark blonde, flecked

with gold, as Finn's, and she had the same prepossessing blue eyes as he did. Faye found that she could hardly look at the queen's face without an odd feeling descending over her. It was a different feeling to being with Finn; when she looked into the faerie queen's face – even just in the tapestry – as perfectly beautiful as she was, Faye felt an inexplicable sense of horror.

Both Finn and the faerie queen next to him wore the same crown of rose gold, with six tall spikes and an inner cap of pearls and opals. Faye remembered it from Grandmother's grimoire, and the memory made her shiver with recognition. Somehow, she had thought that what her ancestor had written was fictional. Or, at least, from another time, when the worlds were different, and faerie was closer to the human world.

But the grimoire had depicted the crown perfectly. What did that mean?

'Do you know where you are?' Finn repeated, breaking into her reverie.

'Y... yes. I think so. The faerie realm of Murias,' she responded, the name feeling strange on her tongue.

'Indeed. Murias, the Castle of the Cup. The Palace of Water. This is my royal court, where my family has always resided.'

'*Your* court?' she asked, noticing that the noise – clapping, laughing, and the wild music – was growing louder.

'Yes.' He smiled at her; his eyes were like warm sapphires.

'So... you *are* a... king?' She already knew the answer to the question but asked it, anyway.

'A faerie king. My sister is the queen of this place.' He pointed to the tapestry, at the terrifyingly beautiful woman sitting on the throne. 'The Queen Levantiana.'

'How long have you been here?' she asked wonderingly. Grandmother had told her that the fae were as old as the world itself.

'Many moons. Many centuries, in your time.' He smiled,

raising her hand to his mouth and kissing her palm. 'I was a child once, but long ago, in your eyes. We do not age as you do in the human realm. I played here, with my pets and the other faeries of the court until I grew to be king. When we could not sleep, my sister and I, the faerie pipers played us lullabies. When our hearts were broken, in the days when we were foolish in our love with mortals, they played to cheer us and mend our sorrows.' He smiled at her expression. 'You do not think our hearts can be broken? The fae creatures have suffered much at the hands of humans.'

'I... I don't... I mean, I didn't...' Faye shook her head. 'I don't know. I've only ever heard about faeries enchanting humans, not the other way around.'

'Well, *sidhe-leth*, believe me, it can happen.' He gazed meaningfully at her, and Faye had the same sense of disquiet as before.

She pulled her hand away from his. Immediately, her head started to feel a little clearer; she looked around her at the room they were in. It was as grand as the others, but when she looked harder, she could see that the walls and the floor had shadows of tree roots within them.

Faye peered at the scene on the tapestry again and saw that in the background, there appeared to be a great ball or revelry of some kind happening. The figures of Finn and Levantiana had initially commanded her gaze, but when she really looked at the whole picture, she realised that several human figures hung upside down among the creatures of the water, by ropes attached to their ankles, their faces obscured. And, under the feet of the faerie revellers, there were skulls and bones.

16

A warning sounded in Faye's mind, a sense of foreboding.

'Am I dreaming?' she asked, turning to him. 'I know this is Murias. I know you are the faerie king. But we have... we have met before, in dreams.' She blushed as she said it, knowing everything they had done together. 'How do I know that this is not a dream?'

'You are not dreaming.' Finn's voice pulled her gaze from the tapestry and back to him. He reached for her hand again, but she refused him and held it to her side, suddenly unsure. 'Give me your hand,' he commanded.

'No. I need to try and keep my head, here. Keep my wits about me. I know the rules of being in the faerie realms. If I touch you...'

'You know nothing,' he scoffed. 'If you fully understood where you are, then you would be far more grateful than you are.' He took her hand forcibly in his.

She tried to fight the sleepy desire that came over her instantly, but it was impossible. When Finn Beatha touched her, she was under his spell. 'I... I shouldn't be here. I want to... I think I should go,' she protested, but Finn drew her to him again.

'Those were not dreams, sweet one,' he murmured, a smile playing around his lips once again. 'Those were real. And merely a hint of the pleasures that await you in my realm.'

Faye swooned, feeling herself fall helplessly into him. A wave of sweet, delicious pleasure overcame her. She felt as though she was being held underwater, if the water was desire. Some part of her knew that she needed to keep sharp, keep her head above water. And yet the feeling of submersion – of the sweet submission of allowing herself to go under and be a slave to her own desire – was too strong.

There was a knock on one of the doors and, frowning, Finn stalked across the room and flung it open. Immediately, as he let go of her, Faye felt like she awoke.

'What?' he shouted as he opened it; his demeanour had changed, suddenly, in a fraction of a moment; there were sharp edges now, where there had been none before, and Faye felt fear overtake the desire that had just filled her so completely.

There was a murmured conversation which she couldn't really hear. Faye stepped quietly towards where Finn stood, curious to see who he was talking to. In the shadow beyond the carved wooden door, she could see a tall figure standing in a corridor. Dim candlelight in the hallway gave just enough light to ascertain that whoever it was, they were dressed in some kind of reflective material, a little like armour.

'I don't care. Just do it!' Finn barked at the intruder, making her jump. He slammed the door and stood with his back to her for a moment, tense. Faye didn't know whether to ask what was wrong. She felt confused again; it was so changeable here. *I should go home, I don't belong here. What am I doing?*

Finn turned to her, scowling, and, without warning, reached up and tore the tapestry she had been staring at off the wall, letting out a shout of frustration as he did so. Faye, startled, shied away from him. He glared at her fiercely for a moment and, in that brief second, all his former warmth was gone. His deep blue eyes narrowed.

Faye ran to the other side of the room and tried the door.

'This was a mistake, I shouldn't have come here,' she muttered. 'I... this isn't right, I... I want to go home.'

But before she could open it, his hand was on her shoulder, and sweetness began to suffuse her whole being again.

'Forgive me, Faye.' Finn's voice was honey again. 'It was bad news. I apologise if I made you feel uncomfortable.'

She was still tense; despite his soothing presence, her body had kicked into fight or flight response. Finn stroked her arm.

'You... startled me,' she protested, pulling away from him.

'Please accept my deepest apologies, dear Faye. I would never intend to alarm you. My kingdom is in conflict with Falias, the realm of earth, and Gorias, the realm of air. That is something we must speak of. You will play a key part in it, whether you understand it or not just now. But I should not have shouted, my sweet one.' He clasped her to his chest in a hug that felt tinged with desperation. 'Dearest Faye, I should never have lost my temper. Please forgive me.'

Faye wondered at his changeable mood. 'You frightened me.' She felt that it would be politic to keep Finn happy, whether she meant it or not. He was keeping her here – when he wasn't touching her, she realised that. But when he laid his hand upon her in any way, she was helpless, at the mercy of her desire.

Finn released her from his arm and, reaching past her, gently opened the door she had been struggling with. Immediately, a blare of music pierced the room.

Faye found herself looking down from a balcony onto a large, ornate hall below where a party seemed to be in full swing. Faeries of all kinds sat at long tables which were piled with food and drink, and a band played on a raised circular stage in the middle of the room, which Faye recognised as the music she had heard distantly all the way through the castle.

It was a little similar to the music Dal Riada had played that night in the bar: a kind of fast, folky music with fiddlers and flutes, but this was performed on unusual wooden instruments and was faster and louder than Dal Riada's, and the dancers who circled around and around the stage were frantic and crazed. There were no dance moves that she could discern in particular, just fierce running, jumping, skipping and howling along with the music. As she watched, one slight-looking female faerie fell down as she skipped wildly to the music and was trampled by at least ten others before she got raggedly to her feet again. Faye's eyes widened in amazement.

'Come.' Finn took her hand and guided her to the top of some golden stairs which led from the balcony to the hall below. He was not barefoot, as he had been on stage at the gig, but wore some kind of gold slippers on which he walked soundlessly.

'Oh, no. No, I couldn't,' she murmured, and stepped back into the room, but Finn held on to her hand.

'Will you not take a dance with me in my own royal hall?' he asked, and as he touched her again, that golden lightness entranced her, and the music outside filled her with a wild delight. 'And I will answer all your questions. I promise.'

At that moment, the song came to an end and the musicians launched into something slightly slower. Faye certainly had questions, but her body had caught the rhythm of the new tune and she felt herself nodding.

Hand in hand, they descended the golden stairs and reached the ballroom. Finn bowed and clasped her around the waist and swung her into the outer throng of dancers that had formed around the wildest ones closest to the stage. Faye followed Finn's lead as they danced in a much more stately fashion, though it still made her dizzy.

The other dancers made way for them as they circled and dipped around the room, and Faye saw that many of the fae nodded and bowed as they spun past.

'What were you doing in that bar, in... in the real world? Your band. If you are... what you say you are?' Faye asked him, trying to keep up.

'You can hardly doubt that I am anything else,' Finn replied seriously as they danced. 'But you are correct. The fae sometimes go forth into your world. Not very often, now. Once, human and fae intermingled happily. It was a golden age; I remember it with such fondness.' He sighed. 'Now, everything is different. Everything is wrong, out of balance. We all mourn the passing of that time in the human world, where your kind knew us and honoured us in the correct ways. Even though we dance and laugh, sadness is in us all.'

The pipers and drummers paused again and commenced a much slower song.

'My grandmother said we had a house faerie called Gussie, who kept the hearth swept for us and the milk fresh, but he was very particular about how we honoured him,' Faye told him. 'As a child I left a bowl of the creamiest milk and a slice of bread out for Gussie every night, but one night I wanted to put out a scone. Grandmother said no, Gussie would take that as an insult in the same way as if no offering was left at all,' she said, feeling a blush on her cheeks as she looked up into Finn's strange eyes. He was disquietingly beautiful. His hair was a dark gold in the light of the ballroom.

'Your grandmother was a wise woman.' Finn smiled. 'The fae have their ways that humans used to respect. Now, they have all but forgotten us and built upon many of our dwelling places. Disrespected our sacred places.'

Dwelling places. Faye thought suddenly of Rav and his house on the beach. Was that what Finn meant? She wondered if *disrespecting our sacred places* meant that Finn knew what she and Rav had done on the beach. A wave of shame washed over her. No. Surely not.

Yet, she had felt eyes on her that evening. She had seen the fae in the waves, watching.

Faye blinked hard. It was very easy to forget the real world completely, but the mention of dwelling places had given her a key, a way to connect with reality, a reminder to keep her wits about her here. She was also still not totally convinced that she wasn't dreaming especially vividly, and might wake up in her own bed any minute.

'Grandmother taught my mother the old ways, and they both taught me,' she said, instead. They danced slowly now, and the rhythm of the tune patterned her heartbeat in a delicious, sensual repetition. Finn's face was close to hers, and their breath met between them. She was aware of breathing in when he breathed out, him following suit as she exhaled in an intimate synchronicity of air between them.

'Yes, I know,' he murmured, his lips so close to hers that she wondered if he was challenging her not to kiss him. She wanted to. The desire to lose herself in his kiss was so great that it took everything Faye had not to dissolve into him. He seemed to know it, and chuckled, grazing her lips with his softly. 'And I also know what you desire, my sweet one. Have patience. Good things come to good girls.' He cocked an eyebrow, then drew her around by her waist, smiling at the many dancers who called out a blessing or a greeting to him as they twirled around the dancefloor.

'You didn't answer my question,' she breathed, desperately trying to stay focused.

'I didn't?'

'About why you play music to humans. In the band,' she panted. The dance was having some kind of hallucinatory effect on her, and she thought she was catching glimpses of things in the corners, in the shadows – gaunt bodies, hanging flesh. Like in the tapestry, it wasn't what she noticed first, but when she blinked, echoes of a more threatening nature were all around her.

He gave a little laugh.

'You *are* persistent.'

I'm not nearly as persistent as I should be just now, Faye thought. Her head was spinning.

'Hmm. Well, perhaps I like the audience.'

'You have all the audience you need here, surely?' The hall was full of hundreds of faeries, feasting and dancing.

He raised his eyebrow and smiled. 'Quite so. Well, then. Perhaps it is that we need humans. We need your attention to survive. We need your love.' He looked at her deeply, and she felt her breath catch. 'We were banished from your world, or near enough, when you stopped paying us our due. As the spirits of the land. As the ones who give you good luck, help you, keep your babies healthy. We didn't ask much, but it was too much for humans in the end, and it broke our hearts. Now, we are mostly confined to our own places. But as I am king, I can choose whether to go forth into your world or not. And I choose to be loved again, and give love. It is no more than an act of a broken heart looking to be healed, my time with Dal Riada.'

Faye didn't know what to say in reply. She thought of the rules, in Grandmother's grimoire:

The Rule of Balance applies between the faerie and the human worlds. Each world depends on the other to exist, and there is a natural ebb and flow between the realms. If one realm seeks to overpower the other, chaos reigns. If they work harmoniously together, peace reigns.

Finn nodded to another couple that danced next to them. The woman – or, as Faye corrected herself, the faerie-woman – was dressed very grandly in a violet and silver dress with a bodice and full skirt reminiscent of fashion from many hundreds of years ago. She wore red roses in her dark golden-blonde hair, which was plaited intricately around them. Her partner was, as far as Faye could tell, human – a dark-skinned young man with a dazed expression who couldn't take his eyes from the faerie queen in his arms. She was high-cheekboned and full-lipped, and her eyes had the same oddness as Finn's – as if they were made of jewels that held great depth but still remained somehow impassive and cold.

'Greetings to you, *sidhe-leth*.' The woman nodded imperiously to Faye, and her human partner smiled briefly before he swung the golden-haired beauty away.

'Who was that?' Faye murmured to Finn, though she was having trouble focusing on anything apart from Finn and the music, which had entered her blood; it felt as though it was powering her actions from inside a formerly hidden part of herself. A part of herself that was as wild as the trees and the rivers, and wanted to sing and dance and – most of all, as Finn pressed her against his firm, well-muscled chest – submit to him. The thought of submitting to him made her thrill with a dark passion that she had never known. She thought about what it would be like to kneel before him; obey him.

Their faces were so close together now that their lips almost touched. Faye's awareness of the dancers around them dimmed so that it was only the two of them moving as one inside the music. If she inclined her head less than an inch, her lips would meet his; the idea thrilled her more than she had ever thought possible.

'My sister, the Faerie Queen Levantiana, Queen of Murias, Mistress of the Cup,' he breathed.

'And the... the person with her?'

'Her lover.'

'Is he human?' she murmured. 'Like me?'

'Yes.' Finn smiled, and lightly traced the line of Faye's cheek with his fingertip, causing a pleasurable fire that lit her whole body up in desire for him. She sucked in her breath. 'But not like you.'

'Are you... close to your sister?' Faye was curious about the faerie queen, and Finn's relationship with her. His eyes had glowed when they met hers, and Faye had felt something pass between them: an unspoken understanding, a deep connection.

'Of course. She is queen, I am king,' he replied dismissively, but on seeing Faye's expression, he explained a little more. 'She is made of the same stuff as me, the same as all faeries, just as other humans share much in common with you. But she and I are of an old, old family: our forebears are the spirits of the first oceans. What is between us cannot be between anyone else – it is impossible for you to understand. We are Murias, and Murias is us. This is one of the mysteries of my kingdom, *sidhe-leth*: it would take you many more lifetimes than the one you have to understand.'

She had so many more questions. But, rather than speak anymore, Finn brushed her lips with his fingertip and gently kissed her

17

———

It was like being underwater, but without fear of drowning.

Faye's eyes fluttered closed, and she was subsumed by the kiss, pulled under into tumultuous waves. She felt as though she was dissolving into Finn, and he into her, as they kissed deeper, and the sky rolled back into indigo nothingness above them.

Dimly she was aware of them walking away from the dance-floor, but they were both already somewhere else. They *were* something else other than what they had been separately: combined, even in a kiss, they had begun to merge and both felt the fierce pull of elemental power.

The music quietened, and Faye's eyes cleared a little as she climbed the golden stairs up again to the room with the balcony where they had started. She had no sense of time, or how much had passed while she had been in the faerie world. But she didn't care. The occasional flashes of her real, human life seemed like trivial memories. Compared to Finn, compared to the strange music that inhabited her blood, it was that life that seemed a dream now.

He led her down a corridor and into a bedroom. Faye followed, her hand in his. To refuse now felt like madness.

The dreams she'd had, the dreams where Finn Beatha had played games with her, pleasured her, raised her ecstasy to levels she had never known before, and then refused to satiate her – those dreams had been intensely erotic.

But being here in the faerie realm itself, where Finn commanded ultimate power, was another thing entirely. If she had felt enchanted before, that was nothing compared to the complete abandonment she felt now.

In the centre of the room, a golden four-poster bed was covered in green and blue silk and velvet coverings; the walls of the room were decorated with the spirals and carvings that were everywhere in the castle. One whole wall was glass, and looked out over a waterfall outside the castle. Faye was so deep inside faerie now that the pull of the human world was very weak. She was heedless of the danger she was in; the link to her old life was fragile now, and it would take very little to sever altogether.

Finn pulled her unceremoniously to the bed and she obeyed.

He kissed her again, deeply, and Faye felt the full power of the faerie realm close over her like a cloak of soft seawater. She pulled back from the kiss and gasped as she felt the strangeness come over her, but when Finn kissed her again, she dived grate-fully into it.

'Now, you will obey me, won't you, sweet one?' he demanded, pulling away from the kiss.

His lips found her neck, and she moaned in pleasure.

'Yes,' she breathed.

'Do you remember what to call me?' he asked, as his hand caressed her breast through her clothes. The sensation of his touch on her was like lightning on a black sea. She shivered in rapturous delight as his lips found hers again and they went under, merging with water.

'Y... yes. My lord and master,' she replied.

'Good girl. That's correct.' His breathing grew deeper.

She closed her eyes and watched a storm roll over the same unfamiliar sea. Her hands were in his hair, on his chest.

'Take off my clothes,' he ordered her. Wordlessly, she unbuttoned and peeled off his jacket and then his trousers. Underneath he was bare-chested, but his golden skin held the tattoo she had seen when he stood shirtless on the stage, a horse that reared up his body in a blue the same dark indigo as his jacket. Spirals followed his shoulders and continued down his arms.

'Strip. Take your clothes off. Those disgusting excuses for garments are not fitting for my consort,' he growled. 'You may respond *Yes, sir*, when I give you an order.'

'Yes, sir.' Faye pulled off the woollen dress she only dimly remembered putting over her vest and leggings when leaving the house. Finn kissed her collarbone and followed the line of lace along the neckline of her vest, then moved his mouth lower. She felt his warm breath as he kissed her breasts.

Faye moaned louder, then, and felt herself grow slick and wet with desire; now, she was completely naked on the bed. The material under her, like silk but something different, seemed to kiss her skin.

'Kneel in front of me, as your lord and master,' he commanded. She obeyed, gasping at his unnaturally long and thick cock, which was rock hard in front of her. 'Do you see that? Do you see that I want you?'

'Y... yes, my lord.' She wet her lips, wanting desperately to put it in her mouth.

'You want it, don't you, my little slut?' He gripped a handful of her hair and pulled her head away from his thighs. 'You want this. You're so wet and desperate for me that you'd do anything to have this inside you. For me to fill you in the way that no one else can. Fill you with my seed. Impregnate you, make you full and ripe and round, like you were made to be.'

'Yes, sir,' she breathed, meeting his eyes. His words were

tapping into something deeply primal in her brain, a pleasure centre that had nothing to do with all the things she'd been taught to value in a partner – kindness, friendship, equality – and everything to do with a forbidden, dark part of her psyche that wanted to be totally and utterly dominated. To relax into the sweetness of being nothing but desired and taken.

He smiled, his eyes half closing in pleasure.

'You will pleasure me with your mouth, first. Beg me for it,' he commanded.

There was a part of Faye that was appalled at being told to beg. Somewhere, in the back of her mind, she knew that she was a normal human woman and not some kind of mindless slut. Yet, Finn's power was so intense that it overpowered everything. And, deeper than that, there was her own desire. She wanted this. She had never known that she wanted it, but she did.

'Please, sir. Please, give me your...' She blushed, not used to saying the word.

'Say it.' His fingers in her hair pulled a little tighter. 'Say the word.'

'I want it. Your... hard... I can't say it.' She looked up at him, chagrined. He shook his head and reached down with his other hand, cupping her breast with his wide palm.

'I know you want it, sweet one,' he said. 'Worry not. We will make a slut of you yet.' Using the hand that held her hair, he pushed her head forward. 'Open wide,' he commanded, and thrust it between her waiting, wet lips.

It was so large that there was no way she could get all of him into her mouth, and she choked as he pushed it into the back of her throat.

'Good girl,' he said, his voice husky with pleasure. 'Oh, very good.'

He started moving his hips, drawing his cock almost all of the way out of her mouth and then pushing it back in roughly. She moaned in pleasure: even though it was challenging, and it was hard to breathe, the sense of oblivion and complete submission that taking Finn in her mouth gave Faye made her so aroused that she could feel her own wetness moistening the tops of her thighs.

He made a deep groan, thrusting into her mouth, and then pulled out completely. She sat back on her heels, catching her breath.

'You did very well, *sidhe-leth*. But that's not how I'm going to have you this evening,' he said. He pulled her onto her feet, picked her up in his arms and carried her to a throne-like chair that sat at the edge of the room.

Placing her into the chair, he knelt in front of Faye and parted her legs. She looked away, suddenly embarrassed at her nakedness. She felt exposed.

But Finn took her chin in his hand and stared solemnly into her eyes.

'Never be ashamed of your body. Of your pleasure. It's beautiful. You are beautiful,' he said, his voice firm. 'I am your lord and master, am I not?'

'Yes, sir,' she answered faintly.

'So, open your legs for me without shame,' he ordered. She did so, controlling her expression.

'Good. Now. Tell me what you want,' he said, still hard as he knelt in front of her, inspecting her.

'I want you,' she breathed, unable to look away from the sapphire depths of his eyes, knowing nothing other than this dreamlike ecstasy. 'I want... I...'

'I know what you want.' He smiled cruelly, his eyes full of lust. 'But you can't have it. Not yet. First, I am going to enjoy you, just as I would enjoy a ripe oyster. And I forbid you to orgasm. Are we clear?' He fixed her with a firm stare.

'Yes, sir,' she stammered, tingling with anticipation and aching to be pleasured.

His hands were warm on her thighs as he pushed them

further apart, and bent his head to her openness. He looked up at her and smiled, and then lowered his head to her and began to caress her with his tongue.

Faye moaned loudly, instantly feeling a wicked, wild pleasure start to erupt in the core of her being. Finn's mouth and tongue was unlike any she had experienced before; he seemed to know exactly how to touch her, what pressure to use, what movements to make. Faye felt herself approach orgasm almost immediately; she was so very ready, but, as if Finn knew that she was close, he tapped her on the thigh as if to remind her that she wasn't allowed to climax until he said so.

'Please, sir,' she made a loud, yearning cry. 'I want to come. Please, Finn.'

He moved his head gently from left to right: *No.* 'I told you. You are not permitted to call me by my first name.'

Even the motion of his refusal brought her to the edge of oblivion. Faye tried to pull away from his mouth, knowing that she was too close, that she wouldn't be able to help her coming orgasm, that she was so suffused with pleasure that it was impossible, but he gripped her naked bottom with both hands and drew her back into his mouth. Faye screamed with pleasure.

He began running the length of his tongue up and down her, from the opening of her to the top of her clitoris, lapping her gently like a thirsty dog. He knew that soft, regular movements and a gentle growing intensity of pressure was what she liked, what felt good to her, and somehow it continued to feel to Faye as if she was reaching a plateau, approaching an orgasm that never came. Instead, every moment, every breath, was a continuing orgasmic moment.

Suddenly, he stopped, and stood up. He held out a hand for her, and guided her gently to the bed. Laying her down on the silky material, he kissed her, and she tasted herself on his lips.

'You did very well,' he murmured. 'I know that was difficult for my little sweet one. She has been so patient with me playing with her. But I enjoy playing with my little doll so very much,' he breathed.

She wanted him inside her so badly by now that she could no longer control herself at all. She kissed him deeply, and reached for him. He was hard with desire for her, and he moaned deeply as she moved her hand gently up and down.

'Faye. Faye, *bruadarach, neach-gaoil,*' he murmured, opening his eyes to meet hers. His fingers stroked her, but she was so wet now, so swollen and ripe and full of pleasure, that they could find no purchase except to slide inescapably inside her.

'Not yet,' he said, and pulled her back to him. He took one nipple in his mouth and licked and caressed it with his tongue, while stroking her clit gently. Faye felt herself close to orgasm almost immediately, and he seemed to know, because he stroked her more slowly and returned to kissing her mouth and neck.

'Please. I want...' she gasped.

And as she was moaning loudly, lost on the waves of desire and pleasure, he pushed deep into her.

He filled her totally, and their bodies fit together as if they were one. He groaned, growled, deep in his chest and held her tight as he thrust inside her deeper and deeper.

'Now, you may come,' he whispered in her ear.

Faye had no consciousness apart from pleasure; the hot, sweet orgasm rose from her like an unstoppable wave, reaching higher and higher as Finn stroked in and out of her slowly, deeply. She was with him under the waves again, in the rolling of the salt water that was their sweat and saliva; they were the power of the ocean, and they were life and death and pleasure combined.

Finally, she shouted for him to come into her as hard as he could, and felt herself clutching and biting his shoulder as her climax came, bigger than she had ever had before.

Her whole body was aflame; pleasure screamed and sang in her stomach, in her elbows and toes. She was screaming his name and other words she had no awareness of. She came again and again against him, feeling him deep and hard within her, returning his urgent, hot kisses as he called out her name, mixed with the Gaelic words she did not understand.

And yet, at the same time, woven among her cries of ecstasy, Faye felt an undercurrent of danger. Perhaps it was because they were in the faerie realm, where time operated differently, but there was an uncountable moment when Faye saw a darkness open up around her. It was like being at the bottom of the ocean, and she felt the terror of drowning. And in the second before she opened her eyes to return to her body, Faye remembered the expression of Levantiana's human lover, lost in a desire he could never control.

The moment of darkness was fleeting, but Faye came back to her body with a sense of foreboding that nestled alongside the pleasure of being next to him, feeling his skin against hers, and dismissed the visions – of drowning, of the ocean, and of Levantiana's human lover – as a moment of mindlessness.

They lay entangled in each other; he kissed her forehead, the end of her nose, her fingertips. Her heart felt as it never had: open, raw, like a rose that had bloomed before time, and it hurt a little from the intensity of their connection. She felt tears start in her eyes, and wiped them away. But the ache wasn't pain or regret; rather, it was a sadness that she had waited all this time to know this kind of pleasure.

He kissed away her tears.

'What troubles you, *neach-gaoil?* You are safe with me. Do not be frightened. You are my lover now; remember, mine is a broken heart that needs to heal. Be happy that you are doing that.' He put his hand on his heart, then on hers. 'Here. To here.' He kissed her again tenderly. 'There is a bond now, not easily broken. I enjoy playing with you, just as you enjoy being played with, my sweet one. But our union is more than that. You know that it is.'

'I... I haven't known that before,' she stammered, trying to grasp on to some kind of clarity.

'The love of a faerie king is not something that many mortals will ever experience.' He gave a soft chuckle.

'Why me, then? I am half faerie, so you say. Why is that so significant, if it's true?'

'It is true. And it is very important. You are important: to the future of Murias, and the future of all the faerie realms. You have a special magic in you, Faye, that I doubt you know exists,' he murmured. 'And we can make each other whole, if we let ourselves trust each other: human and faerie, in balance, as we should always have been.'

'There was something in my Grandmother's grimoire about the rule of balance,' she said groggily.

'The Rule of Balance applies between the faerie and the human worlds. Each world depends on the other to exist, and there is a natural ebb and flow between the realms. If one realm seeks to overpower the other, chaos reigns. If they work harmoniously together, peace reigns.' He quoted it exactly as she remembered reading it. 'This rule is the most important of all. And it is, sadly, a balance that has been lost.' He sighed, and circled his fingertip lazily around her right nipple. 'This is causing great conflict between the faerie realms. A war is here, because of it. A war that humans know nothing of, but that cannot be kept from your mortal lands for much longer.'

'A war?' she asked sleepily. Though somewhere inside her she was deeply troubled by what he was saying, she was struggling to stay awake.

'Yes, my sweet *sidhe-leth*. A war that you must help us end.' She felt him kiss her gently. 'But that is for another day. Sleep now, my love.'

She started to dream as he was still talking. Images flitted in her mind's eye, nonsensical combinations of faerie creatures, cartwheeling, dancing, twirling. Faeries fighting, with long swords, terrible, savage weapons.

'I will adore you, Faye Morgan, if you do me the same kindness,' he whispered. 'Give me the whole of yourself and I will give you the world. I will give you everything that my kingdom can command.'

But in her dream, Faye was at sea on board a boat built for war, and Finn's voice was the sound of screams in the water.

18

She woke up on what she thought was the third day, feeling sick.

After the first time she and Finn had made love, she had fallen deeply asleep, only to wake still in his bed.

She had been unable to leave it since then. A deep desire for Finn, like an addiction, filled her totally. All she could think about was him – pleasuring him, and being pleasured. She had not thought of home at all in that time. It was like being in a dream. Perhaps it was a dream; she still didn't know.

On the second day, Finn had commanded that they be served with faerie wine and deliciously sweet, luscious faerie fruits. They were nothing like anything found in the human world, but Faye had found herself ravenous, and had taken her fill of them. Finn had watched approvingly. *Eat, eat, my sweet one,* he had purred delightedly as she had reached hungrily for one thing, and then the next, slurping from an ornate golden goblet of a rich, purple-hued wine. He had fed her, like a pet, and she had let him.

Whatever the faerie fruits were, they had kept her and Finn

awake – feasting and making love – for what felt like a long time. But they had not been alone.

Flashes of memory, of contorted faces, twining limbs, of bodies and lips, slid in and out of her mind. Faye felt a wave of revulsion as the realisation hit her of what they had done – what she had done, willingly. She couldn't remember how many of them had entered Finn's chamber, but she knew that he had tied her ankles and wrists to the bed with long, supple golden chains, and had been teasing her again, making her beg him for her pleasure, when they arrived.

Our visitors wish to watch the sidhe-leth and the faerie king, he had said with amusement, and lowered his head to her dripping wet pussy. In front of the faerie host, he had licked her again, unhurriedly, as she felt shame and mortification mix with a dark and wicked desire to be watched.

But now, a sudden, searing headache came over her, and her mouth was completely dry. She closed her eyes and felt her stomach heave.

Faye made it to the bathroom in time and retched until there was nothing left to come up. She slumped against the wall, the luxurious rugs under her legs, and tried to steady her breathing. Slowly, she got up, went to the sink and poured some water from a pink crystal jug into her hand and gulped repeatedly until she felt a little clearer.

She was a mess. Her face was pale, smudged with food and stained with wine. Her wrists and ankles were bruised.

How long had she really been here, in the time of the human world? She covered her face with her hands as she felt her humanity, her body, fight back against the drunkenness Murias had seduced her with. She was sick again.

It was a purge of everything she had swallowed without question. A sudden, vivid memory of making love to Finn in his bed while a host of faeries watched, laughed and pleasured themselves came back to her, and she stared at her reflection in the mirror in shock. What had she done? Finn hadn't made her do it, she was fairly sure of that. She had done as she desired; deep down, she knew that.

She started to cry. She felt the shame for what she had done. This wasn't who she was. Faye Morgan, daughter of Modron Morgan, granddaughter to generations of strong, practical, magical Morgan women. Had they come to Murias like this? Had they lost themselves in lust and excess?

And yet, even though she was miserable, she also started to feel more awake than she had since she had first entered Murias. Anger gave her clarity; perhaps anger was a tool that could be used against faerie enchantment.

Faye remembered Annie talking about how she made herself cry on stage: *All ye got to do is think aboot somethin' really sad before ye go on. Like, really get yourself goin'.* She could do the same thing. Faye reached into her memory to the few times she had been really furious and tried to place herself back in the moment.

'What are you doing, *sidhe-leth*?'

Finn Beatha stood in the doorway to the bathroom, rubbing his eyes. He was naked, his hair tousled, but otherwise as golden and beautiful as he had ever been; not dirty and bruised as she was. 'Come back to bed.'

'No. I'm leaving. Going home.' She stood defiantly, trying to look stronger than she felt. 'That was... what we did – I was not myself. I was drunk, or something.'

'On the contrary, Faye. You were more yourself than you have ever been. You have started to reclaim your fae nature.' He smiled lazily, watching her.

'What does that mean?' she spat, furious.

'The fae are lustful by nature. It is part of who we are. Part of who you are. My faerie creatures enjoy watching their king and his consort make love. It feeds them.'

Faye was appalled by the idea of being watched at all, never mind the chilling idea that her and Finn's sexual activities in some way fed their onlookers. Fed how?

'And, may I say, it suits you. You were entrancing. Every fae wanted you for their own consort,' he added.

She pushed past him, back into the bedroom.

'How dare you treat me like some kind of... sex slave! I'm not your whore, Finn. I'm not... not anyone's whore—'

He followed her; Faye felt his bare chest press lightly against her back and shoulders.

'Never my whore, Faye Morgan. Only ever my willing lover,' he murmured in her ear.

She was horribly confused. Finn's touch aroused her; it was unfailing, electric. Yet, the fleeting memories of the last few days' revelries fuelled her anger. She had believed this was a place of magic, of beauty. She had come here willingly. But she felt sick, exhausted, and now that the permissive haze of faerie had started to slip, she could see cracks in its beautiful veneer.

Finn touched her shoulder lightly, then walked around the bed to the table where a breakfast had been left. He poured a green liquid into the two goblets and offered her one. Too late, Faye remembered that humans were never supposed to eat and drink in the faerie realms: to do so risked sacrificing their health in the human world.

'I didn't think humans should eat or drink in the faerie world. Perhaps I shouldn't have.' Her head echoed; everything was too bright. She wanted to close her eyes. Her anger sat at the bottom of her stomach, not gone, but waiting.

'Ah.' He smiled and sat beside her on the bed, biting into a fruit that was somewhere between an apple and a persimmon. 'But that rule doesn't apply to you, *sidhe-leth*.'

'Why not?' she asked tiredly.

'I thought you knew. You are half fae. *Sidhe-leth*. I have told you this already.' He chewed the fruit, watching her keenly.

'I still don't believe it.' She sat on the bed.

'You are half one of us, half human. Your father was of the faerie realm,' he added.

Faye gaped at him, open mouthed. 'What?'

'Your father was a faerie king,' he said, sitting next to her and taking her hand.

'My... my father? But I never knew him. He left us,' she stammered. 'He was just some guy. Mum said... he didn't want to be tied down. He was violent towards her, I think. He wasn't... a...' She broke off and stared at Finn, who took another bite of the fruit and shrugged. 'Does that mean... am I... are you... my...?' She felt sick at the thought, but stupid not to have realised immediately what he could have meant.

'No, I am not your blood.' Finn made her look at him, serious now. 'That would not be the way of a king. Your mother loved another.'

'Who?' Faye stood up. 'I demand to know who my father is. It's my right.'

'I will not hold that information from you if you seek it. His name is Lyr. He is the King of Falias, the faerie realm of earth. He rules that kingdom with his sister, the Faerie Queen Moronoe.'

'Lyr.' Faye remembered Moddie drawing his name in the sand. 'He threatened to kill my mother.'

'That is as may be. Still, he is your father. This is how you came so easily into the faerie world, Faye. You would have found your way here much sooner were it not for the fear your forebears instilled in you. Your ancestors were burned for consorting with us, for learning our gifts. And, since your grandmother has passed, you and your mother have lapsed in your responsibilities. You have not honoured us in the way that we demand.'

Faye thought of Grainne Morgan, burned at the stake, spirited away by the Good Folk at the last minute, so that she could avoid the torture of her final moments.

'Indeed. Grainne Morgan was knowledgeable in our ways,' Finn said, as if he was reading her thoughts. Perhaps he was; Faye had no idea if that was something he could do. 'That is why she was saved. Even though Grainne faced persecution for her work, she never failed us. Grainne kept the old ways, made us offerings, observed the seasonal rites. Grainne and the Morgans before her – and the others like her – kept the balance. You do not.'

'But why didn't they tell me about being half faerie? Moddie and Grandmother?' Faye felt sick again.

'I suppose they wanted to protect you. But connection to us is how you gain real power. Your great-grandmothers had real power; they lived alongside us. Learned our ways, honoured our lands. They made the appropriate sacrifices: a baby at Midwinter, a woman at Midsummer.'

'I always thought that was symbolic, the sacrifices. You're not saying that was real?' Faye stared at Finn incredulously.

> *'Midsummer, Midsummer, Midsummer delight;*
> *go to the faeries on Midsummer night*
> *Take thee a maiden, take thee a wife –*
> *Take thee a bairn for the rest of its life –*
> *Midsummer, Midsummer, Midsummer delight;*
> *go to the faeries on Midsummer night.'*

Finn sang the old song, and Faye shivered. She'd never even considered, as a child on the beach with Grandmother, that the song might have some truth in it.

'That's brutal. Who would give a baby away? Or go willingly themselves?' she demanded, appalled.

Finn shrugged again and wiped the juice from his chin. 'Different times take different meanings. The babies, sometimes people would leave us an ailing one in the woods. It would die if it stayed in your world. We could take it and raise it in the faerie kingdom, then use it to strengthen our stock when it was old enough.'

'Stock?' Faye wrapped herself in a silky throw from the end of the bed; an unconscious gesture to somehow protect herself from the truth. Because it *was* the truth; she knew it, instinctively.

'Sometimes, the faerie realm sickens without good stock from the outside to make us strong. And we need to be strong, especially when we are at war.'

'What is this war? You mentioned it before, but I... I was so tired that I fell asleep, and when I woke, we...' She broke off, blushing.

'There are four faerie realms: Murias, of which I am king, Falias, Gorias and Finias. We are the four elemental kingdoms: earth, air, fire and water. In the days when the balance was kept with the human world, we were at peace. The elements were in balance. But we have lost our balance with the human world – in the years since it has decided to rape and pillage and infect the land and the waters with its vile pollution, and in the years when the witches have forgotten their promises to make offerings, keep our sacred spaces and observe the seasonal rites – and the four kingdoms have come to conflict over one question.'

'What is that question?' she asked fearfully.

Finn regarded her solemnly for a moment. 'The question of whether we still try to build bridges with humans, or whether we raze them to the ground, once and for all,' he said finally. 'Falias and Gorias believe that there is no hope left in humanity, and that the balance no longer deserves to be kept. They believe that a new age of faerie is upon us: one where the fae reign supreme, and all humans will become extinct.'

19

'Extinct?' Faye echoed him, in shock.

'Destroyed,' Finn said, expressionless.

'But... you can't do that. There are billions of humans on the planet. Nuclear weapons. Technology. Chemical weapons. You can't just... exterminate everyone,' she protested. The very idea was ridiculous.

'If I wanted to, dear Faye, I could wipe out every single human with a snap of my fingers,' Finn said, placing his finger under her chin and tilting her head up to meet his eyes, which gleamed. 'I command the seas and the oceans. If I will it, tidal waves of such vast proportions you could not even imagine would rise up and flood the land. No one would be spared.' He stared down into her wide eyes for a moment, then let go of her chin. 'And, there would be no foe for humans to perceive or attack. The fae will not come to war on horseback or in tanks. We simply command the elements, and the elements are more deadly than you know.'

'This can't be true. I can't believe...' she began, trying to take in what he was saying, and failing.

'Believe it, my sweet one. Any one of my fellow kings or queens could rain down fire and raise volcanoes, kill with tornadoes or break and decimate human populations with earthquakes. Do not doubt our power. Presently, the only thing preventing the realms of earth and air from enacting the utter destruction of the human race are the kingdoms of Murias and Finias. Water and fire.'

'Why do you… why do you think we should be saved?' Faye asked, terrified at what Finn had just told her. Humanity was unwittingly poised on a precipice of destruction, and it seemed that there was nothing she or anyone could do, if that was what the fae decided.

And she believed him. This wasn't just some delusional, made-up fantasy belonging to some guy she'd met and had a one-night stand with. Faye knew now beyond doubt that she was in the faerie realm of Murias, and that Finn was the king.

If that was true, then she had to believe that what he was telling her was, too.

'Finias and Murias believe that we need to maintain the balance with the human world. That is the old way, and the best way. If we lose humans altogether, we will also die: this is what Falias and Gorias fail to understand. They do not fully appreciate how much the fae realms have always needed humans for stock. Interbreeding. Humans may be a blight on our natural world, but we still need them. Our best bet is to re-educate humans about the balance. And if we cannot do that, enslave humans.'

Finn delivered this in such a matter-of-fact tone that it shocked Faye. 'Enslave us?' she repeated.

'Yes,' he said, standing up and walking to the window that overlooked the vast waterfall. 'But not you, dear Faye. You have a different destiny. You need not worry about becoming a slave. Other than for pleasure.' He gave her that slow, maddening smile.

'Enslaving the human race is still a horrific idea, even if it doesn't apply to me.' She stood up and joined him at the window. 'What would humans do, as slaves? Slavery is inhuman. Evil.'

'You have no argument from me. But we are fae. We are not human. We do not operate with your...' He snapped his fingers, as if he was trying to remember the word. 'Your *morality*.'

He said it with such a sneering tone that she felt mortified she had ever kissed him, ever done the things that the fae creatures had watched and found pleasurable.

'You would take them as lovers, like me?' Her heart sank at the thought that Finn might have brought other women just like her to his bed. It was easy for him to enchant a human woman. They were weak and pliable, unresisting. Like she had been. Like she was.

She refused to meet his eyes. She wanted to cry. She was just the latest in a long line of women plucked from her world to please a bored king. No, not just a woman. Something else; a new identity that she would have to explore. She was half fae – a mongrel. A bitch. A whore. *What am I? Who am I?*

'Sometimes.' He lifted her chin and kissed her softly; he tasted of the fruit he had eaten: sweet and tart. 'Sometimes, humans wet-nurse our children. Sometimes, we breed with humans. Sometimes, we take them for amusement, for work, to use their skills to build things we do not have, to enrich our world. We would have many uses for human slaves.'

She sat up, her heart beating wildly. 'Falias. The realm you are at war with now?' Faye remembered the name now, and Finn nodded.

'Yes.'

'My father is the king of the realm you are at war with?'

'Yes.'

'Then why am I here? Some kind of... strategic point-scor-

ing? Leverage?' She put her hands on her hips, furious. 'I won't
be a part of it! Whatever it is! It's crazy! All of it!'

'Not leverage, no. He knows nothing of you and me.' Finn
stared out at the waterfall. 'There is a prophecy. About you.
Connected to another part of the war between the realms.'

'Another part of the war? You mean there's something else
you all disagree on?' Faye snorted in disgust. 'You think you're
so powerful. So high and mighty. And yet your kingdoms can't
agree about anything, it would seem.'

'Never doubt the power of the elemental kingdoms, *sidhe-leth*.' Finn turned to her and put his hand softly around her
neck. It wasn't a tight grip, but the gleam in his eyes suggested
that it could be. 'Is that understood?'

'I understand,' she said, and he released his hand. Again,
Faye remembered Grandmother's grimoire: *Keep your wits
about you at all times when in the realm of faerie. Tread carefully
there.*

'What is the prophecy?' she asked, narrowing her eyes.

'I cannot tell you.'

'You will tell me, or I won't return here. Ever,' she threatened. 'I have free will. You can't make me stay. I know the rules.
I can leave whenever I want.'

'I can keep you here for as long as I like, Faye.' Finn raised
an eyebrow. 'You are wrong. I am the King of Murias. Within
my kingdom, all obey my will.'

'That's not true.' Faye's resolve wavered, but she tried not to
show it. *Faeries lie*, she reminded herself. *I cannot trust him.*
'What is the prophecy?' she repeated.

He paced the room. 'You will not understand,' he said.

'Try me.' Faye folded her arms over her chest.

'You are insufferable!' he roared suddenly, and Faye
jumped. 'How dare you question me? I am king here!'

'I am Faye Morgan, of the Morgan witches, and you will
answer my question,' she replied firmly. Faye had no idea where

her certainty came from, because her mind had been so foggy since she had been in Murias. But it was as if Grainne and all her ancestors suddenly reached across time and held out a hand to Faye. And in that touch came knowledge.

Faye knew, suddenly – perhaps she had read it in the grimoire, perhaps she had heard Grandmother say it once, or perhaps her ancestors were talking to her – that her heritage as a Morgan gave her power. And she knew that Finn had to answer a direct question if she asked it using his full name, despite the fact that he had forbidden her to call him by his name at all. 'Fintanaeon of Murias, I demand that you tell me: what is the prophecy regarding my interaction with the faerie realms?'

There was a silence. Finn glowered at her. She raised an eyebrow and waited.

'Quite the powerful one, I see. When you are not lusting after my touch,' he said peevishly. 'I told you that I forbid you from using my name. Fine. I will tell you of the prophecy. Not that you will understand it.'

'I still want to hear it,' she said.

'The prophecy says that a half-fae witch of the Morgan line will govern the Crystal Castle of the Moon, taking over from Morgana Le Fae, who has governed it since the beginning of time. I believe that is you. You are destined to rule the Crystal Castle of the Moon, which is the centre of all our power. Hence, with you as my consort, we will place Murias at the centre of all things.'

'What is the Crystal Castle of the Moon?' Faye asked, thinking, *Not if I have anything to do with it.*

'In the middle of the four faerie kingdoms, over the four crystal bridges stands the Crystal Castle of the Moon. That is where She who is the Highest Power resides.'

'I thought there were four faerie realms. The four elemental kingdoms?' Faye said.

'There are four kingdoms. The Crystal Castle is not a kingdom. It is the centre of our realms. Morgana Le Fae herself – Mistress of Magic, the Faerie Queen of the Silver Moon – lives there,' Finn explained mulishly. Faye was enjoying the fact that, by using his full name, she had the faerie king temporarily under her power.

'So, you all think I am... some kind of saviour?' Faye frowned.

'Not a saviour. The future,' Finn said. 'Not all believe in the prophecy, or have interpreted it in the way that I have. But I have seen you there, Faye. I have seen you wear the crystal crown.' He looked away. 'I did not wish to say so much. Not yet.'

'You're right. I don't really understand any of that,' Faye admitted. 'But thank you for telling me, nonetheless.'

'I had no choice.' He frowned.

'Why is Moddie here? Her spirit, I mean. I saw her here.' Faye felt more awake and aware than she had since she had arrived in Murias, and she was determined to find out as much as she could from Finn Beatha.

'I allowed your mother to come here in spirit,' he answered flatly.

'Do you allow many humans to come here after they die?' she pressed him.

He looked away, avoiding her gaze. 'No,' he answered, after a pause.

'Then why Moddie?' Faye sought his eyes. He stared at her, and she could see he didn't want to tell her.

'A bargain was struck. The details are between my sister, Levantiana, and Modron Morgan. I know not what the bargain was.'

Faye paced around the room. Her head was pounding, but now that the veil of illusion had slipped from her a little, she wanted to use her lucidity while she could.

'What was the bargain?' she demanded. 'She's my mother. I have a right to know.'

Finn spread his palms open in a gesture that implied he was being honest; Faye doubted that he was. However, the use of his full name seemed still to be working.

'I do not know. Suffice to say that whatever she offered my sister must have been significant, for her to be allowed to be here in spirit. And...'

'And what?'

'Murias is the realm of water, but we also have a long tradition of magic here. Modron Morgan was a witch in life, though she never fully realised her powers, in the same way as you have not so far. She wanted the power of Murias. She learned it here.' Finn sighed.

'What is the power of Murias?' Faye demanded, feeling her heart lift. *If Moddie learned it, then so can I.*

'It is secret. Not for humans.'

'I am not fully human,' she replied crisply. 'And, you taught Moddie.'

'I did not teach her. The faerie queens are the keepers of the magic.' Finn turned away from her, his voice peevish.

'Levantiana?' Faye continued to push him.

'In Murias, yes. She is the Mistress of the Cup.' Finn was evasive.

'Will she teach me? I am half fae,' Faye repeated. To have the faerie magic would give her the power she lacked in Murias. With it, perhaps Finn wouldn't be able to take advantage of her human weaknesses. And if she met Levantiana, maybe she would be able to find out what the bargain was that Moddie had struck with her – and find her mother.

'No!' Finn shouted, turning to her. There was an uncomfortable silence. 'No, *sidhe-leth*,' he repeated. 'Your mother was a special case. And she had passed from your realm already; she learned the magics once she had died in the human world. We cannot teach the faerie magic to anyone who resides there alive. It is forbidden.'

'Well, then, will I see her again?' Faye's heart sank; she had made her peace with Moddie's death. *When we pass over, we are busy elsewhere,* Grandmother had taught her, though she had never specified where. *We can teach others on the inner planes; we can come into another body for another life; we can heal, we can spend time with our loved ones. All is possible once we have passed, but that person as you knew them, when they are gone from this world, they're gone for good.*

But seeing Moddie again had thrown Faye completely – all those years of grief were unpicked, like wool being wound back from a blanket. Now, she longed for her mother, and it hurt.

'Murias is wide and far-reaching, Faye. Do not expect to see her again.' Finn's voice was soft, but she sensed the firmness of his resolve.

'Why not?'

'She should not have appeared to you. There are rules,' Finn replied grimly.

Faye felt exhaustion take her over, and she crumpled onto the bed.

'I want to go home,' she whispered. 'I'm so tired.' It was a physical tiredness, but the revived grief for Moddie filled her with a heaviness she remembered all too well.

'Try to leave, then, since you think that you can. But you have eaten and drunk here. When you return to your world, you will be weaker. Less immune to the perils of the human world.' He stood over her, toweringly tall.

'You said earlier that wouldn't apply to me, because I am half fae,' she argued. 'Were you lying?'

'No. You will still be affected; less so, because you are part fae. The fae stock protects you, otherwise it would be worse,' he replied.

'I'll take my chances,' she muttered grimly. She was so tired; she longed to sleep again on Finn's soft, palatial bed. But she had to go. She knew that she had already stayed far too long. She hauled herself up.

'Fine. Go. But... you must promise to love only me from now on, *sidhe-leth.* Otherwise, the magic between us will decline. I will treat you as a queen if you honour me as your king. You can gain great power, just by eating our food and drinking our wine and water, sweet one. I need you by my side.' He reached for her wrist and wrapped his hand around it. Faye detected a sense of desperation in him.

'But if my lover loves another, then I will punish him. And you, too.' The threat against Rav was clear.

Faye pulled her arm away from Finn's grasp. 'I can promise no such thing until you treat me as queens should be treated.' She turned to face him. 'Queens rule. They pass judgement. Queens understand the realm they command. How can I be your queen if I've done none of these things?'

His smile vanished and his fine-featured face took on a watchful look. 'I mean that I will treat you as a queen *should be treated*. I will adore you. With my lips, my hands, everything of myself.' He ran his finger up her arm, and she shivered at the electricity that flashed through her body at his touch. 'But I cannot wed you as you do in your world. Such a thing does not exist in Murias, or any of the faerie kingdoms. And you cannot ever be the real queen of this realm. Levantiana is High Queen of Murias, and there is no one else who could be.'

'I don't want to be your *bride,*' Faye snapped. 'I don't know if I ever want to come back at all.'

She also knew that if he touched her again, if his hands held her breasts, if his full, sulky lips found hers again, she might be submerged once more in the erotic lassitude that had kept her here this long. 'I need to leave,' she insisted.

Finn picked up a golden vase and threw it against the wall.

The explosion of reeds and water lilies caught at her skin like a rebuke.

'There is nothing to think about!' he roared; his eyes bulged in sudden fury, and Faye stepped back, her arms over her head as he kicked one of the delicate bedside tables over; it was made of crystal, and shattered on the floor. 'You have no idea! None! How fortunate you are, what I have done to bring you here! Do you think this is how every mortal woman is treated in Murias?' He strode over to her and caught at her hands, but she pulled them away.

'Don't touch me.' Faye was trying to keep her voice controlled, as if calming a wild horse. She felt that if she shouted back, the situation would worsen. She was terrified, but the only way out of this was to pacify the faerie king. *Moddie, Grandmother, give me strength, please help me*, she prayed silently. She tried to visualise the shop, her safe place, her ancestors reaching across time to be with her, like she had felt them before, but she couldn't concentrate.

'Time to think! You don't know what you are *thinking*, Faye Morgan. Few mortals are ever chosen to be the king's consort, to come and go with freedom from his kingdom. You are special, and I offered you more than anyone.' Finn's eyes were flinty. As the anger rose in her belly – *How dare he threaten me, how dare he intimidate me like this* – some of the illusion that had kept her here fell away. SShe saw him for what he was under the cold, powerful, desirous facade: spoilt, insecure, unable to control his emotions.

'I didn't ask for any of this!' she screamed back at him. 'You invaded my dreams. You kept me here as your lover. I want none of it!'

'Then why did you conjure me in your little spell?' he roared at her. 'Yes. I know what you did. You made a poppet of me, and I appeared. Because it is fate that we be together, *sidhe-leth*. I have seen it. And you knew without ever meeting me.

That was why you made an image of me and summoned me to you.'

'I... I didn't ask for a faerie king! I wanted a real lover. A man. To love me. A relationship,' she protested, though she knew that it was true: Finn was exactly like the poppet she had made. How could anyone explain that? Was it fate, as Finn said?

'Fine. Lie to yourself all you like, and deny your destiny. But I will not wait forever for you, and I know that we are meant to be together, as King and Consort, and that you are destined to rule the Crystal Castle with me alongside you. I suggest that you get used to the idea.' Finn shrugged on his clothes and walked out, banging the door behind him.

Faye pulled on her clothes. She had to leave. Now.

He wouldn't change. He couldn't. He was of the oceans, and every ocean held monsters. Finn's realm of water held the deepest, darkest places, where humans could never venture, just as much as it held sunlit bays where warm, transparent seas stretched over white sands. Finn Beatha was the King of Murias; he *was* Murias, and he was unable to be anything else.

The illusion he had thrown over her, like a glamour, like a net over a fish, had shifted, and she knew she couldn't go back to him. She could follow the labyrinth back to the faerie road that ended on Black Sands Beach. She could go home.

However, she was worried for Rav. Even if she never kissed him again, even if nothing ever happened again between them, he was in danger. Finn knew about them, and he was jealous, and she had seen the shadow under his golden magic.

Heart heavy, Faye walked out of Finn's bedroom, out of the castle, through the market and followed the labyrinth home. The way was open – no one stopped her, nothing dallied her. As she made her way back to Abercolme, the grief at losing Moddie for the second time weighed heavy on her, and part of her longed to run back to Murias to search for her mother.

Yet, she sensed that she was on a precipice; nothing could stay the same, now that she had been inside Murias and had become the lover of the faerie king.

She knew in her bones that everything was about to change, forever.

20

Faye woke up in her own bed to the sound of birdsong. She rolled over groggily, patting the quilt for her phone. Locating it by her feet, she pressed the display and looked at the time. Six a.m.

She had left at 1.30 a.m., and she was back a mere few hours later, but she knew that she had been in Murias for days. Time ran differently in the fae realms; she had known that. It was an oft-mentioned part of fae lore.

She swung her feet out of bed and placed them on the wooden floor, then frowned and pulled up her right foot, resting it on her knee. The skin between her toes was sore. She rubbed her foot gently, then took her hand away and felt the sand on her palm.

She stared at the tiny granules of dark sand for a minute or more, feeling unease unfurl in her like a stray ribbon.

Faye stood up and caught her reflection in the mirror. She was naked, and a pile of clothes – jumper, dress, thermals – lay on the floor by the end of the bed as if she had stepped out of them there, but she had no memory of doing so. She knew she had got dressed – when? Last night? A week ago? A month ago?

– and gone to the beach, but then... then, it had felt like a dream.

She went to the bathroom and leaned over to run a bath. As she reached out her hand, she saw the ring on her thumb.

It was a large round opal set in rose gold. Faye gasped and stood up in shock, looking at her hand, which suddenly seemed completely alien. This wasn't any ring of hers; usually she wore a silver pentagram ring that had been Moddie's on her right index finger and a vintage tiger's eye on her left for protection. It wasn't a ring from the shop that she'd slipped on by mistake, either, as she definitely hadn't seen it before.

She held it up to the light. The opal sparkled with unusual gold, pink and orange accents that swirled lazily, as if magic dwelled within it. She stared at it as the bath filled up slowly.

'What on earth?' she opened a jar of her own handmade Full Moon bath salts and shook them into the water. The smell of lavender filled the bathroom. She tried to remove the ring from her thumb, but she couldn't: it wasn't uncomfortable, but it fit tightly and wouldn't come off.

She got in the bath, breathing in the fragranced steam, and let it cover her. She closed her eyes and held the ring to her forehead. It was an instinctive gesture, but as soon as she did so, she saw Finn Beatha in her mind's eye, as if he was with her, in the bathroom. She opened her eyes with a start, but she was alone.

Cautiously, she held the ring to her third eye chakra in the middle of her forehead again and closed her eyes. And then she remembered.

They had just made love – fierce and hot and out of any normal frame of reference – that was something she knew, deep within herself, although she didn't understand it. And, sometime in the night, she had half awoken, twined in his silk bedsheets. He had kissed her awake and, when she roused, sat up in his huge bed, he had placed this ring on her thumb.

'A gift,' he had whispered. 'Wear it and think of me.'

Wear it and think of me. She stared at the ring. How was it possible? Any of it? And *Moddie.* She had seen Moddie there, in Murias. What did that mean?

Finn Beatha wanted her. Wanted her to be his consort, his lover. Finn believed in the prophecy that said Faye Morgan was the heir to the Crystal Castle of the Moon, that sat at the centre of the four faerie kingdoms. He believed that they would both rule it.

It seemed that what Faye wanted was hardly a consideration.

At the thought of him, she felt a rush of desire. Even though he had treated her badly, even though he had been peevish and threatening, Faye still wanted him. The nights and days they had spent together had consumed her. That was the only way to describe it. When she was with Finn, she had felt more alive than at any other time in her life.

He had said that she was coming into her faerie power by being in Murias, by eating the food and drinking the wine, and by being with him. That faerie power was lustful and erotic, and that it was her true nature to be that way.

Instinctively, Faye stroked her own body, thinking of him: his tall, rangy, well-muscled body; his arms, covered in the tribal tattoos; and his lips. His pouty, ever-so-slightly scornful mouth that begged to be kissed, and even bitten. She closed her eyes and turned the hot tap back on with her toe. The warm water covered her fully, and the pleasant heat of the water felt like a kiss on her skin.

Faye wondered about Finn. Now she was back in ordinary reality, she pondered what he had said about his realm being heartbroken about the lack of – how had he put it? – a *balance* with humans. What he had said about the choice between enslaving humans and killing them all hardly made her think well of him.

The arousal that she held felt, thinking about Finn, dissipated. It wasn't exactly sexy, thinking about the annihilation of the human race. She got out of the bath and padded down to the kitchen behind the shop and made breakfast. She was suddenly powerfully hungry. *Probably a good idea to ground*, she thought; the easiest way to ground yourself, to come back to earth after doing magic of any kind – never mind visiting an alternative dimension, or whatever the realm of faerie was – was to eat and drink. She gulped down a mug of strong tea and made some toast under the grill.

Now that she was out of the bath, she suddenly felt shivery and fluey, as if she had a cold coming on. But she knew it was the withdrawal from faerie that was making her feel bad.

When she had finished eating, Faye lit two charcoal discs and placed them inside a large abalone shell, then dropped resinous lumps of dammar gum and frankincense on top of them and rested the incense in its shell on the edge of the shop counter.

The fragranced smoke made the shop smell and feel like a temple, and Faye was grateful for its familiar sweet and sharp tang, which gave her a sense of power as surely as the flagstones under her feet.

Remembering how the vision of the shop and her ancestors had grounded her, even just for a little while when she was in Murias with Finn, Faye opened a sealed display cabinet, reached in and carefully took out a magic wand.

The wand – unlike the rose crystal one she had used in the love spell – was made of wood, with a black glass handle. It was a fine, long and thin wand, the size of a thick knitting needle, and it had words inscribed on it. On one side it read *A rèir an tròcair mhòir, Glòir agus cumhachd do Rìgh agus do Bhanrigh Mhurias, mar a bha e aig an toiseach, agus a-nis, agus gu bràth.*

Faye had always liked the wand. The black glass handle was smooth to touch, and when she held it, the wand always seemed to thrum with magical energy in her hand. She had used it now and again in ritual, to focus energy, to draw the circle. Most of all, she had found that if she held it, she would feel great power coursing through her, like electricity.

Faye spent a few moments holding some of her other favourite curiosities, possessions belonging to other Morgans, from Grandmother and back into the past. There was an ancient, dried lemon stuck all over with pins, which was a protective talisman; Faye thought Moddie had probably made it, but it was as hard as a rock now, a dark brown, and looked vaguely threatening because of the pins which had dried into it. Yet, the idea was a simple one: lemons were known to absorb bad smells, and so it followed that a lemon might also absorb bad energy in a house, with the silver pins stuck in as a way to prick the skin, let air enter the fruit, and provide a spiky outside to the fruit that gave it a threatening, protective vibe.

There was an embroidered garter, which she had never really known the purpose of, and there was also an inscribed copper disc that Moddie had said kept away demons.

However, probably Faye's favourite item was the Morgan family's crystal ball. Not like the acrylic ones she sold in the shop – this was an ancient sphere made of pure quartz. It had one very fine fissure through its middle, like a dim lightning bolt, but otherwise the crystal was without any flaw, which made it incredibly rare and valuable.

The ball was used for scrying – seeing into the future, or seeing visions. It could also be used in healing, as it had a strong, zingy positive energy when you touched it. Children visiting the shop were always drawn to it, inside its glass cabinet; many times, Faye had found a child staring up at the ball, eyes wide.

It had been a long time since Faye had scried with the crystal ball. Today, she wanted the weight of it in her hands, to be reassured she really was back in the ordinary world. Yet, as she turned it over carefully, she thought of all the Morgans who had used it. *Isn't that my power as much as anything? My heritage, the blood of all the other witches that flows in my veins?*

Bringing the ball over to the shop counter, Faye sat down and stared into it, setting it on a circular holder under a piece of black velvet. The velvet meant that no extraneous reflections from the counter would appear when she looked into the crystal; the circular cushion held it in place.

Faye emptied her mind, concentrated on her breathing and entered a meditative state. She unfocused her eyes and stared deep into the crystal, allowing her brain to make patterns and pictures without trying to analyse them.

What she saw surprised her, nonetheless: Grainne Morgan's face appeared in the crystal, and her voice began speaking in Faye's mind.

Remember the rules of faerie, Faye Morgan, Grainne said. *You are unpractised in the ways of the Good Folk. Your grandmother should have made sure that you were properly trained.*

'What must I do?' Faye asked her ancestor. Grainne's face wavered, then became clear again.

Seek the grimoire. Learn from it. Take great care in the realms of faerie. Use the protections against the fae, and do not be deceived. It is our job to work alongside them. Not to be seduced.

Then, Grainne's face disappeared from the crystal.

Faye sat for a moment, stunned, then replaced the crystal ball in its case and locked it. What was that? Grainne had never appeared to her before, but ever since Faye had made contact with Finn Beatha, it seemed that Grainne was showing up for Faye. *Maybe she wants to protect me,* Faye thought. The idea of being protected by her ancestors was a welcome warm thought when she was struggling with the side effects of her time in Murias.

At ten, she opened the shop door and looked out onto the street. She saw Annie a few doors away, coming in to start her shift. Faye waved, and the opal ring on her thumb caught the morning sun.

'Hey! Morning, ma sweet darlin'.' Annie grinned as she walked in past Faye, and instinctively, Faye put her left hand down by her side in the fold of the dress she'd pulled on today. 'Dunno what you've been doing last night, but ye look beautiful,' Annie called out, hanging up her coat in the back room. She returned, sipping a glass of water. 'Ye saw Rav, eh? Out of the bad books, is he?'

Faye twisted the opal on her thumb; she wanted to tell Annie everything that had happened to her. The words lined up on her tongue, but instead of being able to say them, a tightness seized her throat and she coughed.

'Ye all right, pet?' Annie banged her on the back. Faye nodded, and tried again, but the same dry, airless sensation assailed her, and Finn's voice spoke in her mind.

The gift is for you, Faye Morgan. But I am your secret. Tell no one what has passed here tonight, or you may not be permitted back into my realm.

She knew she wasn't supposed to talk about being with Finn, but she hadn't expected his prohibition to be so literal. Annie offered her the glass of water, and Faye took a gulp.

'All right?' Annie looked concerned.

'I'm okay.' Faye nodded, a shiver of unease rippling through her body. She didn't like lying to Annie, but it seemed Finn's enchantment lingered here, in her world. How was it possible that he could completely take her over? *No one controls me*, she thought angrily. *I am a Morgan. How dare he?* 'Phew.' Annie smiled, then looked at her phone and frowned. 'Ah. Slight change o' plan, lassie. All right if I hop off early later? Got an audition. Nice ring, by the way.'

'Sure. Fine. Thanks, it's... new.' The less Faye had to be around Annie today, the better. She didn't want to lie to her any more than she had to. 'Take the day off, if you want? It's going to be quiet, I'm sure.' She dropped her hand by her side to avoid any further comment on the ring.

'Thanks, sweetheart.' Annie grinned. 'I'll stay and have a gossip for a bit, though, aye? I tell ye what, Aisha's been acting odd recently. Have ye noticed?'

Annie was running on about something – about Aisha not turning up for work, about seeing her walking on the beach alone, but Faye wasn't listening. She was twisting the ring on her thumb. She tried several times to take it off but found that she could not. The realisation that the ring was a link from her to Finn, and that he had somehow magicked it to stay on her hand and not be removed, caused a coil of dread to unfurl slowly in her stomach.

She had refused to stay in Murias and become Finn Beatha's whore. And yet he still sought to remind her of him. Why?

21

When the bells by the door jangled the next day, Faye looked up to see Rav's bullish frame instead.

'Hey. I've been messaging you, but I didn't get a reply.' He smiled and Faye looked guiltily at her phone. She realised that she'd spent the last hour staring off into space, pondering her time in Murias; Aisha, who was working that day, had given up talking to her and had turned on the radio.

The fact that Faye was functioning at all after everything that had happened was remarkable, she realised. She still felt unwell, but she was soldiering on, refusing to let faerie get the better of her. Finn had told her, and the rules had warned her that if she spent too long in the faerie realms – if she ate the food and drank the wine – the exposure to fae would weaken her immunity to humanity, once she was back. Less so, as half faerie, but it was still noticeable.

Faye didn't want to believe it, and yet it seemed true. She also didn't want to believe what Finn had told her about the war and the prophecy: it all seemed ridiculous, now that she was back home. Yet, the thought that it might all be true niggled at her. What then?

'Oh. Sorry.' She blushed, unable to explain. Rav looked around at the shop, which was empty apart from Aisha, unpacking a box in the corner, back again at Faye, and at her phone, next to her on the counter.

'It's okay. I was just a bit worried about you.' He looked unsure of her, which Faye could understand. She'd been completely inconsistent with him since they had had their night on the beach.

'You don't need to worry.' She coughed into a tissue. 'Sorry. Just a bit under the weather.'

Dal Riada, there, Scotland's hottest new band, burbled the local radio as the track finished. *Set to be headlining Abercolme Rocks this year; the first Midsummer celebration for many a year up this way. It's gonna be a banger, get your tickets soon cos they're selling out!*

'Are they? Selling out?' Faye gave Rav a big smile, picking up her pack of dog-eared tarot cards she kept at the counter and shuffling them to have something to do with her hands; it made her feel less awkward. She pulled out three cards without any particular questions and laid them on the counter, facing up. The King of Cups on one side, the King of Pentacles on the other, and The Empress in the middle. *Two men that desire you.* Two men – well that was easy enough. The King of Cups was Finn, and the King of Pentacles was Rav. The Empress was herself – sexy, desired, fertile; the ultimate woman. Faye remembered that sometimes the Empress card could mean a Mistress, too; she raised an eyebrow. *Whose mistress?* she wondered.

'Doing all right, yeah.' Rav nodded. 'Word's getting out there. People love that band. Not my thing, but whatever. Sorry you're ill. Can I do anything? Bring you anything?'

'That's sweet of you. No, I'm fine. You know, Aisha really loves Dal Riada. Aish, come and say hi.' Faye beckoned her over.

She pulled out two more cards, more consciously now. On the King of Cups, she placed The Lovers; on the King of Pentacles, she placed the Seven of Swords. The Lovers was obvious. The Swords card meant deviousness, guile – betrayal, sometimes. She frowned and picked up the cards, slotting them back into the deck. *Betrayal*, she thought, avoiding Rav's eyes. *But who betrays who?*

'Hey, Rav.' Aisha finished arranging some new salt crystal lamps on one of the shelves and came over, wiping her hands on her jeans; it was fairly obvious she'd been giving Faye and Rav some space until now. She stuck her hand out and he shook it, hardly taking his eyes from Faye. 'I heard you're organising the festival. Faye's right. I'm a huge fan of Dal Riada.'

'Oh. Cool! Nice to meet you.'

Rav shifted his smile to Aisha. For a moment, Faye saw Aisha through Rav's eyes: young, bright, enthusiastic; Aisha loved music as much as Rav. She had been wearing her hair down more and wore make-up most days now, which made her dark brown, long-lashed eyes look like those of a cartoon doe. Faye had always thought that Aisha was a hidden beauty and had encouraged her to feel more confident about the way she looked, but for the first time, she suddenly felt envious and hated herself immediately for the feeling. *What is wrong with me?* Aisha and Rav were allowed to talk to each other. She didn't own either of them. Faye could feel something encircling her, constricting her throat and casting a kind of haze in front of her eyes. It was a similar feeling to when she had seen Annie yesterday, and had been unable to tell her what had happened with Finn. She shook her head to try and clear the feeling, but it persisted. Was it just the flu? No, it was something else.

'So have you organised a lot of festivals?' Aisha asked Rav.

'A few. Usually, I promote tours, but my company have started moving into festivals now,' he said, his gaze flickering to Faye as he talked to Aisha. 'I've always been fascinated by the historic festivals, you know? Woodstock, that kind of thing. Altamont, Live Aid.'

'Altamont. Didn't people die at that festival?' Aisha asked.

'Yeah. Textbook example of how not to run a festival. Rule number one: don't let the Hells Angels do security.'

'That seems like good advice. What happened, exactly?' Faye asked, trying to shake off the uneasy feeling that refused to go away.

'It was a free concert, 1969. Four months after Woodstock, the Summer of Love.' Rav made the peace sign with both hands. 'Three hundred thousand people, mostly on drugs, descended on this place that wasn't at all prepared. Bike gangs were on security. One woman was stabbed to death, someone drowned in a canal because they were so out of it, two people died in a car accident.'

'Oh god,' Aisha breathed.

'Yeah. It was violent. Chaotic. It was so bad that the Grateful Dead didn't even go on. It's not going to be like that at Abercolme Rocks, however.' He chuckled. 'It's a nice, gentle Midsummer music festival. No Hells Angels.'

Midsummer, Midsummer, Midsummer delight; go to the faeries on Midsummer night; Take thee a maiden, take thee a wife... The song played on Faye's mind again at the mention of the June solstice. Was there a significance about Finn playing Abercolme Rocks that she hadn't dared consider? Was it about more than satisfying his vanity, about more than feeding off the adulation of the audience?

Finn had told her what he thought of humans: that they were, at best, good only for breeding and being slaves to the faerie world. What if his plans for the festival were more heinous than anyone knew?

The image of a rioting crowd, of the out-of-control chaos of the free festival at Altamont filled her mind, and she felt a shiver run through her that she didn't fully understand.

Aisha and Rav were chatting amiably about music, and Faye made herself go and rearrange something on a shelf that didn't need it. *Let them talk*, she told herself, resisting the jealousy that had risen in her.

'If you need any help with the festival, I've got some free time. I'm at university, but I've got a few weeks free at the moment and I love music. I'm really into a lot of the bands on the line-up. I used to run a music blog, so... I mean... it'd be a pleasure to help,' Aisha was saying.

'Oh. Really? That'd be great. I can't pay you, I don't think, though.' Rav sounded apologetic. Faye's heart started beating harder, and she was alarmed at herself.

'Ah well. Festival tickets'd be enough?' Aisha smiled innocently.

'Oh, sure! That I can do.' He nodded enthusiastically. 'You're serious? You can help out? I need admin help, like emails, social media, local advertising, that kind of thing.'

'No worries.' Aisha scribbled her number on a scrap of paper and gave it to him. 'Give me a call. I'm free Mondays and weekends... or evenings, if you need a hand then.'

'Okay, cool. Thanks, Aisha. That'd be a huge help.'

Rav isn't yours, Faye told herself. *You just slept together once. You don't own him.*

Yet, when she looked up from the spell bags she had organised into neat lines, Rav was staring at her. She felt his gaze flicker to her breasts. She looked back at him, not doing anything except accepting his gaze without embarrassment. As she did so, she let the delicious power of faerie suffuse her limbs and her blood. It was suddenly as though all her insecurity had been washed away, replaced by a new seductive power.

Interesting, Faye thought. *It's like Rav's under a spell when he looks at me. My spell.*

She smiled over at Rav, touching her top lip with her fingertip, tracing it along, watching him watch her as she did it. She felt so different, so *good*, suddenly, and she was enjoying it.

Rav followed her across the shop, leaving Aisha to return to her tasks.

'You seem... different.' He blinked. 'Did you... I don't know. Do your hair differently?' he asked Faye, frowning.

Faye ran her hand through her hair, not breaking eye contact with him.

'No. Just the same as always.'

'Oh.' Rav stared at her again, hungrily, his desire open on his face, then looked away, obviously trying to control himself. 'You look... I don't know. Amazing.' He lowered his voice and reached for her, putting his arm around her waist and drawing her to him. 'I mean, you're always sexy, but... fuck. What have you done to me? I don't know what to do with myself around you.'

'I don't know...' Faye said, but she was wondering what had come over her. The glamour of faerie, maybe? That was a thing, wasn't it? She thought she had seen it mentioned somewhere before. A glamour: a magical illusion that made its owner intoxicating in the eyes of others.

'Actually, I wanted to ask you about the' – he lowered his voice – '*faerie problem*. It doesn't seem to have worked, leaving out the offerings.'

'Oh, hasn't it?' she asked, deliberately coolly, though she was loving the way that he looked at her. *What is this power I have over him?* she wondered. 'I'm sorry to hear that. I'll come and take a look for you.'

'Cool... Could you come tonight? It's just that... the noise. I can't sleep. Knocking noises. And it still sounds like they're running through the house. Obviously, whenever I go to investigate, I can't see anything.' Rav rubbed his eyes; Faye could see he looked exhausted.

'Of course I'll come,' she said, feeling sorry for him; the

desirous, wanton Faye receded for a moment. 'I close up around five. I'll come over after. Okay?'

'Thanks so much. It's just, with the festival coming up, I've got so much to do. I could do with some sleep.' He grinned sheepishly and yawned. 'I thought the faeries liked music? Surely, they should be blessing me or something?'

'Who can say what the faeries want?' Faye responded honestly. The past days had been full of extremes, of dramatic emotions and oddness. She felt both wrung out and soaring out of control, hallucinatory, ill, out of sync with her own self.

What is this new, strange power I have over Rav? Was it connected to her visit to Murias? Perhaps enchanting Rav made her more like Finn. And she had no idea whether that was a good thing or not, only that it confused her even more.

She smiled reassuringly and gave Rav a chaste kiss on the cheek.

'I'll see you later,' she said: a friendly tone, nothing more. He looked confused again, and she didn't blame him at all. There was a brief second when she knew he considered kissing her again – she saw it in his eyes – but she stepped back.

Rav met her gaze for a moment, and looked like he was going to say something, but he just nodded. 'Okay. Later.' He let himself out the door, giving a friendly wave to Aisha. Fresh air cut through the shop from the street outside, but right at the edge of her perception, Faye could smell roses.

22

———

'Can't you feel it? It's got colder. And there's this loud knocking, like, pretty much going on all day and all night now.' Rav hugged his arms around his chest and shivered. 'If this goes on, I'm going to have to move. I can't live here with it like this.'

Faye walked slowly around the circumference of the living room, which was still sparsely furnished. In her mind's eye she had a sudden vision of what it could be like – golden shafts of sun slanting through the floor-to-ceiling windows, through diaphanous gauzy curtains that floated on the breeze coming in from the sea outside; soft chairs in neutral pink and silver velvet; elegant, simple furniture, with tall, rose gold lamps in the corners, ready to be lit in the evening when the windows would be thrown open to watch the moon rise over the waves. Above the modern fireplace, in which artificial logs were burning behind a glass screen, she imagined a seven-pointed star, made of opals.

She ran her hand over the leather sofa and caught sight of the opal ring on her thumb. The rose gold lamps were like the precious gold that sang on her skin. Her vision for this room was a kind of homage to faerie, she realised, or, perhaps, a move to bring the house in sympathy with the energy it rested upon and within.

Faye could not feel the cold of which Rav spoke; in fact, as she closed her eyes and saw the room as it should be, she was filled with a warm joy.

'It feels fine to me.' She made her way to the fireplace and stood in front of it, gauging the temperature. 'In fact, I'm actually a bit hot over here.' She took her jacket off and unwrapped her scarf.

Rav looked at her with an odd expression. 'Faye. It's freezing in here. Put your coat back on.'

'No! Really. I'll be too warm.' She shook her hair over her shoulders. 'But this house is built on a faerie road. We may have to do more to mollify the Good Folk.' She wasn't surprised that the phenomenon continued to happen, especially after what Finn had told her about the breakdown of the relationship between humans and faeries. Rav was probably lucky that his house sat on land belonging to Murias; if it belonged to one of the two kingdoms that wanted to wipe out humanity, he might not still be alive.

'There! That sound! You couldn't hear that?' He pointed to the long glass hallway and stared at her expectantly.

Beautiful singing was drifting through the house now; Faye's whole body responded to it with joy. It flowed through the room, a song made of delicate crystal and faint, tinkling bells. Faye followed the lone female voice out to the hallway with a pull of longing in her heart. She walked as if she was in a dream, her arms held in front of her, eyes half-closed. She knew that she was being called by this beautiful song, back across the sea, to the castle of Murias and Finn Beatha's arms, and she felt the enchantment gather its strength again. She had to fight it, because she could feel Finn, under her skin, drawing her back to him. She could feel herself forgetting all the bad things he'd done, replaced with a longing to be back in his bed.

'Ugh. Like someone dropping a pile of saucepans or something.' Rav followed her out to the hall; immediately, the music stopped and Faye felt her connection to faerie severed, savage and sudden. 'Didn't you hear it?'

'Oh, it's gone. It was so beautiful.'

'Beautiful? It's a fucking racket!' Rav shouted. 'I don't get it. What's changed? You got it before, but now you're acting like there's no problem, Faye. I thought you wanted to help me?'

'I do want to help you. It just sounded like nice singing to me. I'm sorry... I... It's complicated. But I do understand.' She shook her head, as if she could loosen Finn's grip on her. The ring tightened on her hand, as if Finn knew that she was trying to resist him and was reaching for her, wanting to possess her.

Rav went to the faerie altar and pointed at it. 'I did everything you said. Milk in the bowl every other day. Flowers, feathers, shells. I've even said a fucking prayer to the faeries every day to leave the house alone, but, if anything, it's got worse. And then you come back here, floating around like some kind of princess, and act like everything's okay! It's not fucking okay, Faye! I feel like I'm going mad!'

'I'm sorry, Rav.' Guilt and frustration gnawed at her, at the way the enchantment Finn had her under was messing with her real life and her relationships.

'I thought you... I thought we had a connection, something... I thought you liked me.' He wiped his eyes in frustration. 'But you're being really weird with me, and I don't know why.'

'I'm sorry,' she repeated.

'I don't know how you didn't hear that banging sound. And the knocking is absolutely doing my fucking head in. I'm... I'm so tired, Faye. I'm not sleeping. And I'm trying to get this festival sorted and all the bands are being completely pathetic, and...' He trailed off and took a deep breath. 'Sorry. You don't want to know about all that. But I am sorry for shouting.'

She approached him cautiously. 'That's okay.' She stepped forward and he opened his arms, accepting a hug. He sighed and laid his head on her shoulder, then pulled back slightly and gazed at her.

'I missed you, too. Can't say that hasn't been part of what's keeping me up.'

Faye felt the energy between them change. She felt Rav's desire for her, as she had before, and she still wanted him.

But the pull of faerie was strong in this house, and she was reminded of Finn's threat to Rav's life. Faye still wasn't a hundred per cent sure that Finn had witnessed her and Rav making love on the beach, but she thought the implication was there that he had. Finn Beatha was jealous, and dangerous. He was also a faerie lover who was so entrancing she could barely remember to eat.

'Why did you run off that night? After we... you know? Were together? You've been so distant. If I did anything wrong, please tell me. I don't want to have hurt you.' Rav stroked her cheek, and Faye looked into his eyes properly for the first time since they had kissed on the beach.

The heady pull of faerie was at odds with Faye as a practical, powerful earth witch. And this Faye, the one whose magic wove the power of crystal and smoke and rain-soaked earth wanted Rav – this Faye wanted a good man she could trust to love her, to honour her as she should be honoured. This Faye was fighting the power of faerie that wanted to overpower her altogether and suck her in its undertow.

'I just... it's hard to explain.' She brushed his lips with hers. 'But I'm here now.'

'Is this happening? Is this for real, now? Because I don't think I can cope if I have you and lose you again. I like you, Faye. Please don't... I don't know. I just want to know where I am with you,' Rav appealed to her. Faye realised with alarm that he was holding back, protecting himself from her.

Is this really who you are now? Faye wondered, stepping outside of herself for a moment. *How have you, Faye Morgan, become someone that inspires such uncertainty? And such desire?* She didn't recognise Rav's vision of her, and it was troubling to have that double sense of herself.

'I like you, too,' she murmured, touching his cheek and meeting his gaze as honestly as she could. She would give him all of herself that she could; he deserved more, but Finn was a secret she was unable to disclose, even if she wanted to.

He returned her kiss like she knew he would.

Faye couldn't deny that there was a chemistry between them. Being with Finn was being inside the addictive, effortless lull of faerie. She was helpless there. A sex slave. Willingly, she submitted to all of Finn's dominant depravities, and she loved every second.

But being with Rav made her feel powerful, sexy and invincible. The difference was, with Rav, she was *awake*. She was sober, and she was in control. Finn led her through a dark dream of excess, but with Rav, she could enjoy his healthy masculinity and feel appreciated as a woman. A woman, his equal, and not a slave.

She didn't know Rav at all, really, but she wanted to; and, when she was thinking straight, she knew she wanted some stability in her life. Usually, the only person in her life who gave her any support was Annie; it would be nice, she admitted to herself, if there could be someone else in her corner.

This wasn't an ordinary dating situation. Faye examined her motives for being here. If it was hard for Rav to compete with a faerie king, it was also true that having been in faerie had given her the confidence to pursue Rav – to respond to him – in a way she wouldn't before.

Rav kissed her hungrily, as if he had been waiting for this. His large, strong hands gripped her waist, and she felt his primal need to have her, to feel her feminine energy meld with his masculine, animalistic need for her. His mouth covered hers easily, and he groaned as he kissed her and hardened against her.

For long, velvety moments, Faye revelled in the kiss; she felt made of honey under Rav's touch. There was something about the way he was, the way he touched her, talked to her – that made her feel queenly, womanly, full of sweetness.

But suddenly, she was pulled away – taken through the air at great speed by rough hands that pinched where they held her.

Faye knew without being told that the faeries had her, though she didn't know how or why. The sound of cruel laughter cut the air, snatching away the air she needed to breathe... *Stay away from the human man, sidhe-leth.* Finn's voice sounded like he stood next to her, but as she whirled around, looking for him, there was no one there. *This is a warning.*

Before she had time to take a breath, she found herself standing over a chasm that fell away to nothing under her, and she reeled from sudden vertigo, slipping from her tenuous footing. She flailed, reaching for mossed rock on both sides of her, not knowing where she had been taken to, and marshalled her instincts as quickly as she could. *What was it that grounded me before?* She reached for the vision of the shop, her place of power. Closing her eyes, she remembered the security of its stone-flagged floor under her feet; of Grandmother, sitting by the fire with a blanket over her knees. *I am a Morgan, you cannot take me. Return me immediately! In the name of my Morgan ancestors, in the name of Grainne Morgan, I command you, Fintanaeon of Murias, return me! I am human, I am of earth, I am a witch, you cannot take me like this.*

Faye's eyes snapped open as she heaved in a ragged breath, doubled over by the – what? A kind of slippage into faerie, an out-of-body experience? – that had just happened. She was back in Rav's house.

'Rav. *Rav!*' She shook him; he looked enchanted, vague. His eyes were misted over.

'Sorry, I... I don't know what happened there. I was kind of... transported. I don't know... I...' he stammered, confusion muddying his expression. 'Were we...? I thought I was kissing you, and then you... disappeared.'

'I don't know what happened. It felt like I was transported somewhere, too. A precipice. It was so real...' She shuddered. Rav stepped back, away from her.

'I don't know what's going on, Faye,' he murmured, rubbing his eyes. 'This is getting weird.'

'I should go.' She frowned. Finn had warned her that he didn't want her to see Rav any more; clearly, he meant it. But Rav looked so disappointed that she felt terrible.

'Please don't go.' He took her hands in his. 'Please, keep me company at least for tonight? I don't want to be here on my own again... Please? Stay?'

'Okay. But this is faerie territory. They were here first... There is supposed to be a balance between them and us. It's a lot to explain, but I guess we have to work harder to appease them, for them to let you live here uninterrupted.' Privately, though, Faye wondered whether the denizens of Murias would ever leave Rav alone, now that their king had decreed that Faye was his. Even if she and Rav never had any contact again, Finn was just that petty and cruel – and Rav's house still sat on the faerie road.

His face brightened.

'Thank you.' He kissed her again, and she felt herself respond. He took her hand shyly.

'Rav... I don't know,' she whispered, taking in a jagged breath as Rav kissed her neck softly, and as his lips found her collarbone. So close to the faerie road, she knew that it was forbidden. She could feel Finn's eyes on her, that same sense of dissociation she had felt at the shop. Unbidden, she heard the faerie king's voice in her mind. *You are mine, Faye Morgan. Remember my warning.*

Forbidden too by the faerie king himself: Faye knew what Finn Beatha could do to both of them if he was displeased.

Faye could feel the electric energy of faerie running through the house. She took a breath and grounded herself, imagined roots growing from her feet deep into the earth, closed her eyes and saw herself as part of the planet, like the hills and mountains and rocks and soil. *You will not command me; you will not control me,* she thought, pushing back against Finn's voice. She could sense him, here, in the room with them. *I come from a long line of witches; you do not control me.*

Suddenly, she thought of the Morgan wand, and what was inscribed on it. Grainne Morgan had told her in her vision to *use the protections against the Fae.* But what were the protections? Was that one of them? She had never thought specifically of the wand as protection against the faerie realm, but perhaps it could be. Faye wished she had the wand with her, that it wasn't sitting in the cabinet back at the shop. She should have brought it.

'I don't expect anything from you. I don't expect to be your boyfriend or anything, if you don't want that. We can take it slow. I just want to be with you. Here and now,' Rav breathed. 'I've tried to be in control of my feelings before, with women. But I can't control how I am with you.'

But there was something about the danger, the prohibition of being with Rav that excited Faye. And her rebellious heart refused to be cowed by Finn Beatha. She had not committed herself to him. *How dare he tell me what to do and who to want. I decide that. No one decides it for me.*

'I can't stop thinking about you; it's like you've possessed my mind,' Rav murmured. 'I've never known anyone like you before. You're like... I dunno... some kind of enchantress.'

He knelt in front of her.

'Perhaps I am,' she replied seriously. She looked around at the room; Finn still lingered here, she could feel it.

Since you like to be watched, perhaps you like to watch, too, she thought wickedly. *Watch, then, if you must. But I banish you, Fintanaeon of Murias. Go, leave us.*

There was a noticeable shift of energy in the room. Finn had gone. Faye felt suddenly euphoric. She had felt so powerless with Finn, but she didn't have to be.

I am more powerful than you think, Finn Beatha. I am a Morgan. The blood of every Morgan witch runs through my veins. Do not toy with me.

Now, Faye felt the energy of the faerie road under her feet and all around her, but rather than it being a threat, she felt as if she was standing in a live stream of power, plugged into it, merged in it like a river. *You gain power from this,* Grainne's voice said, in her ear. *I am with you, and all the Morgan women are with you. And this is one of the secrets that we knew, and that you now know: the faerie road, the faerie magic, the faerie kingdoms, contain power that you can use. You are half fae. Take the power and let it grow inside you.*

'Faye?' Rav touched the hem of her dress. 'Are you okay? You seem a little distracted.'

'I'm fine.' She turned her attention back to Rav, feeling the glittering, swirling faerie power fill her up, as if she had been empty, as if she had only been half living, all this time.

She touched his cheek with her fingertips, and watched his pupils widen, his eyes darkening with desire. 'Am I your queen?' she asked him, savouring the sight of him on his knees. The rush of faerie power flooded her; she would take what she wanted and she would answer to no one.

'My queen, my enchantress. The most beautiful, captivating woman I have ever known,' he breathed, looking up at her in awe.

'Have you ever knelt before a woman before?' she asked, stroking his cheek.

'Never.' His voice was thick with longing.

'Yet, you kneel for me.'

'Yes.'

'Why?'

'Because...' He blinked, and swallowed hard. 'Because I feel compelled to do so.'

She nodded, and slowly unbuttoned her dress, letting it fall to the ground. She took off her underwear and stood in front of him completely naked.

'Take off your clothes,' she ordered him, relishing her new power. And she could see, when he was naked, that he wanted her. His thick, long cock was hard for her. She touched it gently, and he made a stifled noise of want and desire.

'What do you want to do to me?' she asked, running her hands over his broad, muscled chest. 'What will you do to please me?'

'Anything, my queen,' he breathed, his pupils large.

'Are you under my spell?' she asked him, and he nodded.

'Completely.'

'Will you do anything that I desire?'

'Yes, my queen.'

She lay on his bed, her legs open.

'Kiss me,' she said.

He knelt in front of her once more and kissed the inside of her thighs. She spread her legs wider.

'Pleasure me, until I tell you to stop,' she ordered him, and, wordlessly, he bent his head to her, moving his tongue gently in circles around her clit. She caressed his hair, plunged her hands into his thick black waves. Pleasure filled her abdomen immediately; she started to moan, pulling his head to where it needed to go to give her the most pleasure. 'Harder. Faster,' she ordered, and he began lapping her with increased pressure. She let out a long, guttural sigh. 'Damn, that's good,' she sighed.

The familiar tightness and the sweet pleasure began to grow, and she began to breathe faster. 'Don't stop,' she ordered, as her pleasure started to peak. She watched him as she started to climax; wanted to see him kneeling between her legs, worshipping her like a queen, this huge bull of a man, completely in service to her. As she thought that: that he was serving her, like a loyal subject, like a knight pleasuring his queen, she started to come. She held on to his head, ramming it into her, smothering him with her wet pussy, as she cried out, again and again. The orgasm continued, and Rav kept licking her as she rode out every peak, again, again, until it was over, and she pushed his head aside.

She reached for him and lay back on the bed, drawing him to her.

'That was amazing,' he breathed. She kissed him, tasting herself on his lips. 'Thank you for letting me pleasure you.'

'You do it very well,' she replied. 'Now, I want you to fuck me.'

He was still rock hard, and she knew that he ached with desire to be inside her. She wanted that desperately, too. She remembered how good he had felt, before, and she wanted that again.

He grinned. 'As my queen commands,' he said. He kissed her neck, his hands on her breasts, on her waist and then gripping her bottom.

Slowly, he entered her at just the right angle.

'More,' she whispered, her lips full and eyes heavy-lidded with pleasure. He held her, gently but firmly, and drew in and out of her slowly, taking his time, but making sure that he pushed all the way inside her, and then all the way out, repeating the motion until she urged him to go faster.

The sensation of his thickness filling her, stretching her, was almost overpowering. She took in a breath as he pushed inside her, deeply.

She started to moan and writhe as she felt the orgasm coming.

'I want to hear you. I love hearing you come,' he said, gazing at her full lips and then kissing them. 'You're so beautiful. Like a goddess.'

She didn't answer, but pressed his head to her breast. She breathed in deeply as she felt the sweetness build inside her, rising up her body, radiating from her core like the sun, like fireworks, a pure force of pleasure.

'Oh. Oh, Rav, yes, yes, please, yes, yes...' She buried her face in his neck as she came, long and loud, with nonsense words, a guttural cry as something inside her *gushed*. She felt a long spurt of wetness escape her. She cried aloud in surprise, and his cries followed hers; Faye felt him tense as his own climax shook him. '*Fuck. Fuck. Fuck*,' he exclaimed, as his orgasm grew, as he emptied himself inside her. She felt the heat of his thick cum spurt inside her.

'Oh my god,' he muttered, shellshocked. His hair was matted and his eyes were wide. 'I don't think I've ever had an orgasm like that before. You're amazing, Faye,' he breathed.

Gently, he tilted her head up to meet his lips, and kissed her, slowly and passionately.

'That was... amazing. Wow,' he breathed, staring at Faye as if she was covered in jewels; as if she really was a queen who had deigned to take her pleasure with him.

'Yes. That was... pretty great,' she chuckled, reaching up and tracing the line of his cheek with her fingertip. 'I don't think I've ever... you know. *Let go* like that before.' She peered down at Rav's bedsheets, which were soaked.

'Ha. I'm delighted to have made that happen for you, then,

my queen.' He took her hand in his and kissed the tips of her fingers. 'I hope it's the first of many times.'

'Mmm,' Faye giggled, purring like a cat. 'Yes please.' She snuggled into Rav's chest, and he wrapped his vast arm around her. 'I'd like that.'

It had felt good to feel so powerful and in control with Rav. And the fact that he had clearly enjoyed it was amazing: he was grounded in his masculinity, enough of a man to enjoy giving pleasure, to enjoy worshipping Faye like a queen, without needing to subdue and subjugate her. She had never experienced sex like that before. It was... remarkable.

Yet, as she lay with him, breathing in the scent of his sweat and revelling in the feel of her head on his strong chest, him gently stroking her hair, Faye felt a chilling energy ripple over them both like a cold breeze. Rav shivered, and drew the covers over them. But Faye knew that the sudden change in atmosphere wasn't a breeze. She felt Finn's eyes on her, and knew that he was furious.

You betrayed me, his voice intoned in her mind.

I did no such thing, she thought, in reply. *I never agreed to your demands. Leave me alone.*

I will never leave you alone, sidhe-leth, he said. *Never.*

23

Faye woke in the night and rolled over, moonlight illuminating the unfamiliar room. It was Rav's bedroom, she remembered now. But the space next to her was empty.

Despite the late hour, she felt more clear-headed than she had for a while. She sipped some water from a glass by the bed and took in a few deep breaths, feeling them ground her.

There was music coming from downstairs. Faye picked up one of Rav's T-shirts from the end of the bed and pulled it over her head; it was too big for her and reached just to cover her bottom, but the house was cold and she needed something.

Rav sat on the yellow sofa with his laptop, frowning at the screen. Faye recognised the David Bowie album that was playing; the vinyl sleeve for *Diamond Dogs* was propped up on the floor against a cabinet. Rav had put his jeans back on again and wore a sweatshirt and a blanket around his shoulders.

'Hi,' she said shyly.

He looked up and smiled. 'Sorry. Did I wake you up?'

'Don't think so. Maybe it was the moon.' She ran her fingers through her hair to make it less wild.

'Ah, the moon, of course.' He grinned, put the laptop to one side and came to her, wrapping her in his arms. 'Aren't you cold?'

'No. Well. A little. I borrowed your T-shirt, I hope that's okay.' She wrapped her arms around herself.

'Of course it's okay. You look so cute in it,' he murmured, and kissed her on the forehead.

'You couldn't sleep?' She wriggled a little out of his embrace and kissed him softly.

'Mmm. That's nice. No. I'm kind of prone to insomnia, anyway. I'm always on edge in this house. If it's not the weird noises, it's the cold, and this general feeling of unease. Like I'm not welcome here.' He held her to him again. 'I dunno. I really felt that, earlier, before we... you know...'

Faye didn't want to comment. How could she tell Rav that Finn Beatha had forbidden her to be with him – and that she suspected he had watched them make love? That she had openly defied him by being with Rav?

'I really... I really *want* you, Faye, okay? Like I've never experienced with anyone else. I have this completely obsessive, unwholesome passion for you. I mean, it's embarrassing, saying that. But that's how I feel. And I hate it, because I'm not in control of myself around you. That's the one thing I can depend on. I control things, because that's how I feel safe.' He gave her a sideways glance.

He walked to the window to look out over the beach. 'But you seemed to be in control, just then. I've never done that before, and... I guess I'm kind of surprised how much I liked it. Being directed by you. Commanded.'

'Okay,' she said levelly. 'I understand. I... I like you. I've enjoyed it when we've been together. I... I haven't done that before, either. But I loved it. You were amazing.'

Faye followed him and, shyly, wrapped her arms around his waist. 'I want to be here. With you,' she murmured. 'That was a great gift, that you just gave me. It was beautiful.'

'It really was,' he said, staring into her eyes. 'I just...You're doing these things to me that I can't get my head around. You're kind of blowing my mind.'

'In a good way?'

'In a very good way.' He smiled, and kissed her gently.

They stood as they were, with Faye hugging Rav, for a long moment.

'Oh. You dropped something.' Rav bent down to pick something up from the floor; it was the opal ring Finn had given her, and as soon as Faye saw it, she felt a rush of revulsion and desire. *No, no*, she wanted to say, to refuse it. Somehow, she had managed to lose it, even though she had been unable to remove it before.

No. No. No.

Yet, somehow, her body betrayed her, and she found herself offering her hand to him. She didn't want the ring. She had never wanted it. She and Rav had created a moment between them, a realness; they had connected, heart to heart. She didn't want to be shackled to Finn Beatha again.

'It must have fallen off,' she heard Rav say innocently, but Faye was unable to say what she wanted to, and watched in dismay as Rav slipped the ring on her thumb.

There was a sudden rush, and Faye felt as if she had been picked up suddenly and conveyed by powerful hands at an uncomfortable speed – where, she knew not. She had the sense of being underwater again, and helpless. She screamed, but it made no sound.

24

———

'I watched you fuck him.'

Faye opened her eyes to find herself inside Finn Beatha's bedroom and was immediately on her guard.

Whenever she was transported to Murias, it was bodily. She knew that she would have just disappeared in front of Rav, and she could only imagine how distressing that was.

'You kissed him. Made love with him. On my land. When I expressly forbade it. That is not the behaviour I expect from my *sidhe-leth*.' He stared at her harshly, his voice ringing out even among the walls hung with their ornate tapestries. Today he wore something akin to a suit of armour, though it was still finely detailed with the Celtic spirals and intricate knotwork that was everywhere else in the castle, chased into the edges of the golden breastplate which accurately followed the contours of his muscled chest.

'I... I...' Faye's voice wavered; she felt choked by fear, and discombobulated by being spirited away to the faerie realm. Bile rose in her throat: the sudden transition to faerie was too fast, too extreme. Finn's once intoxicating charm seemed like it belonged to another person; now, he was cold and inaccessible.

'How did I get here?' she panted, swallowing the bitter bile in her throat. She shook her head, desperate to get rid of the nausea that was filling her.

Somehow, she had to maintain her strength.

'I can summon you as and when I wish,' Finn said dismissively, looking her over with a frown. 'Though I appreciate you arriving so flushed with pleasure, and scantily clad.' Finn grimaced at Rav's T-shirt. 'Take it off. I will not have another man's cast-offs on my *sidhe-leth*.'

'I am not yours, so don't talk about me as if I were your property,' she fired back at him. 'I will keep it on.'

'You will not.' He stepped forward, grabbed the T-shirt and ripped it from the neck to the hem, then pulled it off her.

Faye cried out at the sudden attack, and tried to cover herself with her hands.

'Perhaps I shall keep you naked here, at my bidding.' Finn smiled, looking her up and down. 'There is no need to hide yourself from me, sweet one. It is nothing I have not seen before. From every angle imaginable.'

'You can't...' Faye wanted to argue, knew that he was wrong, but she was unable to bring the words to her lips. She knew that Finn could not keep her in Murias if she chose to leave, but the effects of being in the faerie world made it difficult to stay clear-headed.

She recognised the delicious haze of fae descending on her, like too many glasses of wine with Annie after-hours in the shop, under the full moon, or luxuriating in an erotic dream, not wanting to wake up but knowing that the real world tugged at the edges of it, waiting for her to return.

'I can, and, if it pleases me, I will,' Finn snapped. 'How dare you take another lover? Am I not enough for you? Am I not everything you desire?' He turned his back on her and paced the room sulkily, prowling like a cat. 'You are not the only lover

I could have, *sidhe-leth*. Many others would willingly take your place.'

Faye couldn't respond: the same tightness restricted her throat, and she knew for sure that it was Finn's enchantment that bound her words. In her right mind, she would have argued back, told him that whatever was happening between them, it was over. That he had no right to treat her like this and that she never wanted to see him again. But her thoughts were disconnected and vague. She felt tears of frustration springing to her eyes.

Finn turned and met her gaze, a speculative expression in his that were the colour of a tumultuous sea.

'I have not stopped thinking about you since the last time you were here. You know I want you; you are unlike a mortal woman, Faye. You and I are destined to be together.'

It wasn't the first time Finn had mentioned destiny. Faye had never known what he meant exactly. Was he talking about the prophecy, that she would somehow, in the future, rule the Crystal Castle that supposedly sat at the centre of the four elemental kingdoms? Or that she and Finn belonged together, entwined in their dark lust? Or something else?

He paused. 'You liked the jewel I gave you, I trust?' He approached her slowly, still prowling, still guarded.

Befuddled, she nodded, looking at the ring on her thumb. Had it brought her here, somehow? It had come off when she was with Rav, and as soon as he had unwittingly slid it back on her thumb, she had been transported to Murias.

'Indeed. See how generous I am, even to my faithless lover?' His voice was cool and steady, but anger still blazed in his eyes. 'You should be so much more grateful than you are.'

As she looked down at her hand, a long, many-stranded rose gold, pearl and opal necklace appeared around her neck, spreading out to her shoulders and down, framing her breasts, the lowest opal resting just above her navel. She realised that she had seen the necklace before: when she had watched Dal Riada play in the pub with Aisha, and been taken into a dream-vision. Then, in the vision, she had found herself at Black Sands Beach, and she had worn a gauzy white dress, and this necklace.

As she watched herself, bracelets of the same rose gold, made of many interlocking spirals, made elegant cuffs on her wrists and ankles, and a thong made of tiny rose gold chains and silky pearlescent fabric, embroidered with pearls and opals, appeared between her legs.

'Since you dislike being naked in my presence, let me clothe you in something... appropriately demure.' He smiled, narrowing his eyes.

She held out her arm and marvelled at the beauty of the design, and as the jewels nestled against her skin, the familiar lassitude of enchantment slipped over her like a robe. She fought it, though it was like trying to hold back a tide. She made herself remember her discomfiture at being transported here without warning; worse, being vulnerable like this, at the mercy of a man dressed for battle. She wondered if he had come straight from the war, or was intending to go to it when she had arrived.

'You like this.' He touched the necklace with his finger. Proprietorial, as if he owned it and her. It was not a question. *You like this.* Yet, Faye was ashamed to admit to herself that she *did* like it. She loved the beauty of the necklace and the ring he had given her, and she loved the way the necklace felt on her body. It seemed to kiss and caress her skin, shimmying delicately against her as she moved.

'Y... yes,' she stammered.

'These are not ordinary human trinkets. The jewels you wear are enchanted fae treasures. They give you such power, and yet you choose to ignore it. Waste it, when you could have a life of delight with me.' He sighed.

'I never... I never agreed to that,' she stammered. The pull and lure of dissolution was almost complete now. In the back of her mind, Faye was aware that the jewellery acted as a kind of cage: it enabled Finn to control her. And yet, the seductive power of faerie was so great that she felt powerless to resist it.

'I give you all of this. I give you access to my kingdom, to my bed, I give you these priceless gifts of power that any mortal would kill for... And yet, you betray me.' Finn's voice was sharp and pointed; icy where once it had been honey. 'When I gave you everything.'

'I'm sorry, I...' She hardly knew what she was saying. *Am I really sorry?* she wondered at herself for a moment. She had felt right with Rav. But Abercolme already felt a million miles and a lifetime away from this moment. *No! I'm not sorry!* She screamed at herself, but the words were coming out and she couldn't stop them: she was under Finn's spell, and said what he wanted her to say.

'Sorry is not enough!' Finn screamed suddenly, picking up one of the small crystal bedside tables and flinging it across the room. 'Sorry is a human word! There are no apologies in faerie. There is love. There is desire. There is service and loyalty to your king. We do not have a single word that makes things right with no effort at all! Sorry is a lie. I do not want your sorrow. I want your love.'

Faye recoiled from his anger. She knew that what he was saying was, in itself, a lie: faeries were by nature deceptive and, by human standards, amoral, but she said nothing. She waited for his anger to pass, her gaze flitting from his face to his clenched fists until they relaxed.

'Promise that you will never see him again.' He stood facing her, and traced his fingertip on her cheek. His voice was calm again, and he kissed her cheek softly, as if she had imagined his outburst. Like it had never happened.

Faye looked up into his ocean-tossed eyes. She knew what had happened, and a part of her felt alarm; there was a warning here, and she knew she should take it. Finn was dangerous; his temper was explosive. But the power of Murias was too strong, and Finn, so close to her, was bright as the sun. Her enchantment was complete; she fell under the waves.

'I promise,' she whispered.

'So be it. I will allow one mistake, Faye. But only one.' He was gentle now, and Faye wondered if she had imagined his anger. He had been hurt. He was emotional. He loved her. That was the truth. Wasn't it?

'The lovers of faerie kings are richly rewarded for their adoration.' Finn Beatha smiled widely and turned her around so that she could look at herself in the mirror.

'They're beautiful,' she murmured, touching the opals. Finn's hand closed over hers, and he traced her own hand over her breasts, her waist and her bottom. She leaned back into him, and felt his arousal against her.

'You are beautiful,' he breathed into her ear, and Faye sucked in a deep breath, feeling her desire for him wash over her like a tidal wave.

'Come.' He held out his hand to her and, at his touch, she felt the seductive, sleepy wave of faerie break over her again, wrapping her in its seawater bliss. 'The faerie ball awaits.'

'So you weren't... aren't...?' She indicated his armour. 'You look like you're ready for battle.'

'The battle is over, for now,' he replied curtly. 'No talk of war now, *sidhe-leth*. Listen to the music. Don't you care to dance?'

'Like this?' Faye hugged her arms around herself, vulnerable. It was one thing to be dressed like this, here with Finn, but quite another for the whole of Murias to see her dressed only in the intricate rose gold chains. 'I... can't I get dressed? For a ball?'

He smiled and kissed her. 'You are the king's lover. In the faerie kingdom of Murias, *sidhe-leth*, I am all-powerful. And you...' He kissed her neck, watching her in the mirror, 'You are the object of my desire. And I desire them to see you as I do. More beautiful than the stars on the night sea. You may wear whatever you please. What do you want?' He caressed her naked breasts softly.

'Something magical,' she replied, and a sudden delight in her own body bloomed like a dark blood-red rose. She remembered the sensation of being watched as she had made love with Rav on the beach, the intoxication of eyes being on her as she claimed her pleasure. 'I want them to see me. Want me as you do.'

He clicked his fingers softly, and Faye felt the softest kiss of silk caress her skin.

'Then you shall have it,' he murmured.

25

As they began to descend the golden spiral staircase, the music stopped and the faerie court stared silently at its king and his lover.

Faye looked down at herself. Any wisp of self-consciousness she might have had was gone, and she felt a wild joy at being in Murias, with Finn. She felt as though she belonged; as if a long-suppressed, shadowy part of herself had finally been allowed to be seen.

A coral-pink gown made of a slightly iridescent, translucent silky material was open to the waist to show off her elaborate necklace and naked breasts. Jewelled straps looped loosely over her shoulders, glittering with opals, pearls and diamonds, and a plain rose gold circlet sat on her forehead, covering her third eye. Her auburn hair had been magically braided around the circlet, and the rest of her hair was a mass of wild curls that spilled over her shoulders.

The skirt of the dress swept the ground at the back but was open to the waist at the front, showing her thighs and the triangle of jewelled thong that sat comfortably against her flesh. A light breeze blew the gauzy material against Faye's skin, and she was aroused by the sensation of the silk – and Finn's hand on her back. She wore flat slippers that seemed to be woven from a soft gold material that was nonetheless spongy and strong when she walked, and protected her feet from the cold marble floors of the castle.

Finn took her hand and bowed before the upturned faces of the court.

'May I present the king's consort, Faye Morgan,' Finn announced to the hall, his voice loud and commanding, then he turned to Faye and, kneeling before her, took her hand and kissed it. 'This ball is in her honour,' he said, smiling up at her, and Faye's heart thrummed with ecstatic joy.

The crowd cheered, and Faye bowed to them. As they continued down the stairs, the music started again and Faye felt her toes twitch. It was enchanted music; it made her want to dance and scream and laugh wildly, to pinch and bite and kiss. And, yes. To fuck wildly, like an animal, as she had done the last time she'd been in Murias.

Finn grasped her around the waist and swung her into the throng. He had changed out of his amour and into a formal outfit; the light from a thousand or more candles glowed gold on his epaulettes and buttons. His eyes were wild, like hers must be, too, she thought; joining the dancers was like going under a magical wave, and not needing air.

Large golden bowls of water alight with floating candles sat on top of numerous gilded pillars around the edge of the wide hall; as they danced, Faye felt the fragranced air on her skin like kisses. Hanging from the ceiling above were strange decorations; some she recognised, like seashells and starfish, and brightly coloured coral that seemed to grow out of the ceiling.

The creatures at the ball were varied, as they had been on the faerie road. Faye sighted human-like faeries like Finn, some with huge, colourful wings and some with scaly skin, like mermaids but with legs; she wondered, for the first time, why

Finn had such a human appearance, when the vast majority of denizens in his kingdom were very far from human. There were blue-skinned, naked female creatures with webbed feet and long, sharp teeth; faeries with long, green hair that wrapped around their drowned-white bodies like shrouds; and frightening, monstrously large sinuous eels that slithered around the ballroom.

'What are the names of all these creatures?' she whispered to Finn.

'The faerie court of water is legion,' he replied, spinning her around until she was dizzy. 'There are dream-weavers, sprites, nixies, river maidens, topsy-turveys. There are frog queens and kings, undines. Many more that have not been given names by humans.'

Yet, as Finn danced Faye around the dancefloor, she started to notice other, more disquieting details.

Among the coral and the roots that hung from the ceiling were charms made from knotted hair and bones. They twirled lazily in the air, animated by the movement of the dancers. As Finn danced her past one of the creations – she guessed it was a charm, though she didn't know for sure – Faye reached out for it, curious and yet with trepidation: it had a dark energy, and yet she wanted to touch it.

Finn grasped her hand and held it.

'Do not touch, *sidhe-leth*,' he warned as they twirled away. 'That is not for you.'

'What are they?' she asked as they danced. Faye was feeling more and more giddy, and yet she didn't want to stop. The dance was intoxicating.

'Magic.' Finn smiled mysteriously.

'What kind of magic?' She closed her eyes for a moment, trying to centre herself, trying to focus.

'Faerie magic,' he replied, laughing. 'It is not your concern.'

'But I am half fae, so you tell me. Aren't I allowed to know?

Did my mother know?' Moddie had been taught the faerie magic, so Finn had told her. 'Is my mother here, now?' The thought suddenly struck Faye, and she opened her eyes, gazing around her at the blur of faces and bodies for Moddie.

'No,' he answered crisply.

'No, she isn't here, or no, I am not allowed to know about faerie magic?' she needled him, trying to find clarity in her thoughts. Some deep part of her knew that she was under enchantment, and that while she was in Murias, she could get Finn to answer her questions... if only she remembered how.

'Both,' he answered, and kissed her cheek. 'Enjoy the dance, my sweet one. You do not need to ask any more questions.'

Again, the lull of faerie descended on her, as if it was a drink and she was getting more and more intoxicated. Faye felt a rush of pleasure fill her as Finn kissed her, and she melted into his arms once again.

As they danced, the panoply of faerie creatures continued to amaze Faye. A frog creature, a naked, otherworldly beauty dressed only in an elaborate crown of pearls, with webbed feet and glistening green and brown spotted legs, danced delicately yet unrelentingly fast with a slim young man who wore a baroque face mask that was as jewelled as her necklace, and a jewelled band around his neck that suggested a collar.

He was human, Faye was almost sure; other than the mask and collar, his chest was bare, and he wore loose trousers in a dark green material. His chest puffed in and out rapidly with the effort of keeping up with the faerie.

Faye watched the frog mistress for some moments as she toyed with her human pet. At the edge of her awareness, Faye felt a sense of unease, but she was so far submerged in the lull of Murias that she was unable to examine her feelings any further.

Finn smiled and bowed to the frog queen and her partner as they passed. Just before the frog queen grasped him by the shoulders and leaped into the centre of the crowd, laughing, the young man's outstretched hand glanced onto Faye's palm, and his eyes, through the slits in the mask, met hers.

As soon as they touched, Faye felt a jolt of pain all the way through her body, like being cut in two. She pulled her hand away. Panic filled her; the eyes that had held hers, she could swear, were full of pain. Was there an entreaty there, a cry for help? But before she could say anything, or hold on to him, the frog queen had dragged him deeper into the crowd.

'Who... who was that? With the frog queen?'

Finn smiled, stroked her face and took her hand. His touch calmed her immediately. 'Her consort, just as you are mine,' he replied simply. 'Do not worry. They come here willingly, like you.'

Then, Faye recognised Finn's sister, the faerie queen of Murias, Levantiana, approaching. Levantiana danced with a young human man – barely more than twenty, Faye guessed – who seemed frail, but who still gazed at the faerie queen as if she was the gleaming spark at the centre of all things, and he couldn't believe his luck that he was the one holding on to her brightness. He wore a mask, as did many of the faeries.

'Good evening, *sidhe-leth*.' Levantiana nodded at her brother, but she addressed Faye. 'How delightful that you are joining us at the faerie ball.'

'I am... I am honoured to be here,' Faye replied, unsure of what she should say. She gazed at Levantiana's dance partner, wanting to reach out to him, wondering if he was here of his own free will, wondering who he was and how he, too, had made contact with the fae realm and its queen. But the young man avoided her eyes. Under and among her intoxication at being in Murias she sensed a black thread of doubt weaving itself silently; she felt the tug of its shadowy teeth, and felt uneasy.

'Indeed, you are.' Levantiana raised an eyebrow. 'Brother, I can see the appeal of this one. She makes a comely whore.'

Rather than defend Faye's honour at his sister's insult, Finn merely nodded. Faye felt as if she had been slapped in the face.

'How dare you!' Faye exclaimed, but Levantiana merely chuckled.

'I dare, sweet one,' she replied condescendingly. 'This is my realm. I may do and speak exactly as I wish.'

'You know so little of us. Stay. Absorb our ways, our culture. Until you know us, you cannot understand,' Finn cautioned Faye. 'My sister expresses herself in a particular manner. Remember that you are my consort, not hers.' He kissed her, and though Faye spluttered with anger, she felt herself growing wet again, and felt the shameless urge to submit to Finn in whatever way he pleased.

'You *are* my comely little whore,' he murmured as he kissed her, and Faye was deeply ashamed at the arousal that his use of the phrase sparked in her. She was aware that Levantiana and her young male dance partner were watching them kiss. Desire washed over her, and she parted her legs readily as Finn slipped his hand between them and stroked the jewelled triangle that only barely covered her. 'See? Dressed like a whore and ready to please,' he chuckled, his voice thick with desire. 'I might have to have you here, now, while everyone watches. You'd like that, wouldn't you?' he asked, as he slid his finger into her. She gasped and arched her back against his hand which pressed firmly against her lower back.

'Yes,' she breathed, shameless and burning with desire.

As she opened her eyes, her gaze alighted on one of the cages that dotted the vast ballroom. They were big enough to hold a person, standing up, and, inside, naked dancers gyrated to the music.

At first, Faye had thought little of it: she knew of nightclubs in the human realm where similar things were a feature and people vied to dance in them.

Yet, as she revelled in the pleasure of Finn's touch, she

realised that, unlike the dancers, none of the creatures in the cages were fae.

They were all human. And though some of them danced, many of them looked exhausted, gaunt and starved. The cage closest to her held an inert, decaying human body.

Faye shivered in horror.

'Finn! Stop!' she cried out, pushing him away. But though he stopped pleasuring her, he continued dancing Faye around the ballroom, while she fought and struggled in his arms.

Finally, she broke free of his grasp, pulled off the opal ring and all of the jewellery that he had draped her in, ripping off the silk dress, too, until she was completely naked, standing in the middle of the vast ballroom. She had no idea why she was able to remove the ring and the rest of it here, when she hadn't been able to back in the human world. But she was grateful to be able to tear it from her hand.

Free of the jewels, Faye's head cleared, and she knew that she had to leave. Without looking back, she ran through the dancers, naked, out of the castle and towards the faerie road. She heard Finn call after her, but she knew that he had no power to keep her in Murias if she decided to leave. And leave she must. Immediately.

26

The walls of Mistress of Magic were no longer enough to protect Faye from Finn Beatha.

Faye wondered if they ever had been; after all, Finn had walked into the shop, the first time she had met him. But she remembered how he had stood at the threshold, how he had asked to be invited in.

Faye could keep Finn away if she tried hard enough; she had to believe that she could. There was no way that she wanted to be spirited back to Murias at the whim of a decadent faerie king who wanted to use her as a sex slave. Finn could spin her stories about how important she was to the faerie realms, how she was some kind of saviour, the subject of a prophecy. But she would never willingly go there again.

What she had seen at the faerie ball had shaken her to the core. The human bodies in cages – left there to starve to death, kept as entertainment for the faerie ball that never stopped. Grandmother had told her about the legendary faerie reels: the never-ending dancing, as if it acted like some kind of gyre or engine, powering the whole realm.

Faye would not be a part of anything that enslaved humans and murdered them in the name of entertainment.

So, to protect herself, she returned to Grandmother's grimoire, just as Grainne had advised her when she sought guidance from the ancient crystal ball. So far, Faye had enchanted mirrors to turn away faerie enchantments, and drawn banishing sigils on their backs. Grateful for the pile of hagstones that she and Annie continually brought back from the beach, she strung them into companion charms for the one that Grandmother had hung by the door and hung them around the house – remembering that, somehow, the charm had not been hanging by the door on the day that Finn had walked in. Was that how he had been able to get to her? she wondered. Had he somehow been able to influence the charm being taken down, to allow him entry?

She had smudged the house with smoking bundles of rosemary and rue for protection, and spritzed the corners and the doors liberally with blessing oils. But was it enough?

It had been a week since Faye had returned from Murias; since she had dragged herself back down the faerie road, feeling the weight of the human world pull her down and down, until, when she found herself on Black Sands Beach – naked and shivering – she had barely been able to move. She had been grateful that it had been the middle of the night when she had reappeared, and had managed to drag herself home, unseen. She had taken a hot shower and wrapped herself in as many blankets as she could find, but couldn't stop the violent shivering. It was hours later when she had finally slipped into a fitful sleep.

Since she had been back, Faye had felt the same flu-like symptoms as before: now, she knew that it was the hangover from being in Murias, and the increasingly toxic effect of the human world on her body. It was worse, this time. She had barely been able to work, telling Annie and Aisha she had flu.

She had heard from Aisha that Rav was away on business. She knew that if she saw Rav, it would endanger him. But she *wanted* to see him, nonetheless. She had texted, aware that she had literally disappeared in front of him when Finn had taken her. But there had been no response.

Faye looked up as some villagers passed by the shop on their way to church. A thick shaft of sunlight sliced through the window and across the dresser where she stacked tarot and oracle cards. Yet, she was still cold.

The protections that she had in place seemed to be keeping Finn from taking her, but he still appeared in her dreams.

Unlike before, where the faerie king had seduced her in her dreams, now, he tortured her.

Every night was the same. Faye would close her eyes when she could not fight sleep any more, and enter a dark room where she lay chained to a black table.

She was naked. Finn Beatha stood over her, smirking, holding a whip with an ornate shell handle and long strips of something like seaweed trailing from it. But when he struck her breasts with it, and her stomach, and her abdomen, before trailing it wetly up her thighs, watching her squirm in fear and discomfort, she realised that it couldn't be seaweed, because it cut her skin, hard.

Did you think you could escape your destiny, Finn said, every night, as she flinched and bit her lip, swallowing the cries that she wanted to scream out loud. *Did you think that I would just let you go, sidhe-leth? You are mine, forever.*

Yet, Faye refused to answer, refused to give him any sign that he was breaking her will, that he was hurting her, though she woke up with the lines of pain still smarting on her skin.

She needed something more. She couldn't go much longer being tortured every night by Finn Beatha, and while she might be safe from him inside the shop, she hadn't yet tried going outside. What if Finn could magic her away to Murias if she left her safely protected home – even without the ring that he had given her? She had found the strength to cast it away from herself on the ballroom floor, but there was no guarantee that Finn wasn't able to transport her to the faerie realm, anyway.

Finn had told her – unwillingly – that Levantiana had taught Moddie the faerie magic of Murias, because Moddie had made a bargain with her. But it was only possible for Moddie to learn the magics after she died and not before. It was forbidden to teach the magics to a living human, even if she was a witch.

If Faye could somehow learn the faerie magic, then surely she would be able to use it to protect herself from Finn Beatha? Coughing, Faye picked up Grandmother's grimoire again and flicked to a section she remembered about the faerie queens. *For the knowledge of and conversation with High Queens of Faerie,* Grandmother had written, *and to learn their magicks.*

Yes. This is it, Faye thought, her heart starting to thrum. *If I can summon Levantiana and persuade her to teach me her magic, that might make me powerful enough to resist Finn.*

She started to read.

First, remember that making a bargain with the fae is perilous, Grandmother wrote. *Be sure that your aims cannot be achieved in any other way. Once you strike a bargain with a faerie – especially a faerie king or queen – they will have a hold on you forever.*

It was dangerous, but Faye was desperate. There had to be some way that she could move on with her life and regain control. She was hardly sleeping; scared to leave the house. She couldn't go on like this.

First, create the environment for the queen of your chosen element, the grimoire began. *To summon Her from her home element, you must create a ritual space of high vibration. Ideally, conduct the summoning as close to the right element as possible.*

There was a note in parentheses which Faye had to bring close to her eyes to read:

High Queen of Murias = tideline
High Queen of Falias = sacred forest
High Queen of Gorias = mountain or storm
High Queen of Finias = ritual fire

Cast a circle. Summon in only the right element for the faerie queen in question. Dance or pace out the circle clockwise and then pace into the centre of the circle as if in a spiral. When at the centre of the circle, call out their full name three times. In Murias, She is called Levantiana, Mistress of the Cup. In Falias, it is Moronoe, Mistress of the Stone. In Gorias, it is Tyronoe, Mistress of the Knife. And in Finias, it is Thetis, Mistress of the Staff. Your calling of the queen should be urgent and passionate, from the heart. Repeat this process, walking the spiral in and out and calling the names, three times.
When you have called their name three times, entreat them to be with you as follows:

Beloved of the Fae, Queen of your Element, Mistress of
Magic,

I seek communion with you; I seek knowledge of you
and your realm,

Bestow your magic upon me, I am fain to know your
secrets,

I am open; fill me with your blessings.

(Name) I call on you.

(Name) I beseech you, enter the space I have prepared
for you.

*(Name) I would love you with my mind, my heart and
my body.*

(Name) I summon you from your kingdom.

*I offer something of mine that I can give freely;
this is the bargain.*

*This is the promise between faerie and human that I
make willingly.*

So mote it be.

The promise between faerie and human that I make willingly, Faye mused, looking up from the book. Faye's own magic might be enough for now to keep Finn away, but she couldn't be sure that it would protect her forever. Here was a way for Faye to at least talk to Levantiana; she could appeal to her better instincts, beg her to teach Faye the faerie magic, if necessary.

At Black Sands Beach, the moon was on its final waning quarter, and the night was dark. If Faye hadn't known the beach so well, she might well have fallen on a rock or a stray branch; as it was, she was careful, and took off her shoes and socks when she was on the sand, placing them on a nearby ledge.

She hadn't brought the grimoire with her, but had copied out the invocation on a piece of paper and had it in her pocket. It was still cold on the beach at night, though it was early summer, so she wore flowered leggings under her red-and-white polka-dot dress, with a green cardigan over the top; a mash-up of styles chosen mostly for warmth. Faye wore a heavy shapeless grey and black coat over the top, like a cloak.

She took a deep breath, nervous about what she was about

to do. Grandmother had hidden this summoning magic for a reason; Faye knew that if Levantiana was anything like Finn, she would be powerful but unpredictable, and vengeful if she perceived she was being wronged. But she needed to be able to protect herself. She knew Finn had meant it when he threatened her, and when he threatened Rav.

Faye began the ritual.

First, she traced a circle at the line of the tide, wide enough to contain her with her arms spread out and with ample room on either side. With her finger, she dug the shallow trench of the circle half in and half out of the sea; the water filled the gap on the sea side of the circle and smoothed it over with the tide as soon as she had done it. She didn't mind; a circle of half sea, half land was right for summoning a fae creature of the water to the land. Faye was meeting her halfway, in a space that belonged to neither of them, an in-between place, a place where magic could be made.

Clouds spread across the black sky, covering the stars until everything above Faye stretched into a blank unity of night. She swallowed nervously, then called out to the sea.

'Powers of the sea, of the ocean, of water, be with me! Fill my circle with your power!' She opened her arms as if to accept the power of water, and felt its energy crashing into her prepared space as forcefully as if she had been standing next to a waterfall.

She started to pace the circle clockwise, as Grandmother had instructed; then, making a spiral, she circled in a smaller and smaller circumference, feeling the energy in the circle compress as she reached the centre.

'Levantiana, Mistress of the Cup!' Faye shouted at the top of her voice, imbue her voice with as much feeling as she could. She imagined Levantiana as she had seen her at the faerie ball, with roses in her golden hair, and her dress of silver and lilac.

Faye paced an unwinding spiral to the edge of the circle,

and felt the energy loosen. She paced to the centre again and felt it contract, like a wave breaking and building. She called out to Levantiana again, feeling the energy rising in her and in the circle. The tide crashed on her feet and ankles as she stood in its shallows; slowly, it advanced into the circle. This was a much greater magic than she had done before, and Faye could feel its toll on her, especially as her energy was still so low. The spiralling energy threatened to engulf her, growing in depth with every contraction; she fought with herself to stay in control.

Faye flicked on a mini torch and read the invocation from Grandmother's grimoire aloud.

> *Beloved of the Fae, Queen of your Element, Mistress of Magic,*
> *I seek communion with you; I seek knowledge of you and your realm,*
> *Bestow your magic upon me, I am fain to know your secrets,*
> *I am open; fill me with your blessings.*
> *Levantiana, Mistress of the Cup, I call on you!*

The tide was coming in, but faster than it usually would; rather than half of the circle being submerged, now three-quarters of it had been erased by the water. Faye steadied herself, breathing deeply and refusing the rising panic that wanted her to give up, to lose her focus. She pushed up the bottoms of her leggings and continued the call:

> *Levantiana, Mistress of the Cup, I beseech you, enter the space I have prepared for you.*

> *Levantiana, Mistress of the Cup, I would love you with my mind, my heart and my body.*

*Levantiana, Mistress of the Cup, I summon you from
your kingdom.*

*I offer something of mine that I can give freely;
this is the bargain.*

*This is the promise between faerie and human that I
make willingly.*

So mote it be!

The tide was much higher now; a cold wave broke and soaked Faye to her thighs, flowing over the last of the circle she had traced in the sand. She still felt the energy of it there, but there was a shift; the power was no longer balanced between earth and water. The tide threw her off balance and she fell forward in the freezing salt water.

Gasping, she pushed herself up onto her hands and knees, the taste of salt in her mouth like blood. *Grandmother, you should have told me,* she thought. *You should have taught me. If you had, I would be stronger now.*

Levantiana stood before her in the water, a tall silver crown on her head, dressed in black robes that merged seamlessly with the waves.

'I am here as you request, Faye Morgan. Be assured that I do not take this summoning lightly,' she intoned, and her voice was like fracturing icebergs.

27

———

Faye felt Levantiana's voice rather than heard it; despite its harsh quality, it was hypnotic like Finn's and drew her into a trance almost immediately.

'Why do you summon me?' Levantiana faced her across the waves which surged around them both. Faye stood up; she was up to her waist now in the water, and she struggled to stay upright, digging her toes ferociously into the wet sand under her.

'I... I... wish to make a bargain.' Faye's teeth were chattering; she was wet through.

'I see. And what do you offer as your end of this bargain, *sidhe-leth*?' Levantiana cast a cynical eye over Faye's soaked coat. 'You hold no appeal to me as a sex slave. My brother is the one you should have summoned. He pines for you, although I have no idea why.' She raised an imperious eyebrow. 'In fact, I should bring him here, and the two of you can continue your tryst.' She raised her hand, as if to snap her fingers.

'Please. No,' Faye cried out. 'Don't. I can't go back to him.'

'You will find that you have little choice in the matter,' Levantiana replied, but she lowered her hand. 'Still. One of your kind has not summoned me for many years, and I find I enjoy being back on your land for a brief moment.'

'Was it my grandmother, E-E-Evelyn Morgan? Who last summoned you?' Faye tried to stop shivering, but it was impossible.

'Yes,' Levantiana answered crisply. Faye noticed that her silver crown featured a crescent moon which curled upwards on her brow like horns. The rest of the points were made of crystal rather than silver, which reflected milky moonlight as the clouds parted and the waning crescent of the moon appeared in the sky above.

'Why did my grandmother summon you?' Faye asked, trying to control the cold that was freezing her from the feet upwards.

'She wished the same as you. To learn our magics,' Levantiana replied crisply. 'She was denied. She had nothing to offer that I wanted.'

'How did you know that was what I wanted?' Faye blurted.

Levantiana laughed. 'It is all you humans ever want. Unfortunately for you, it is not permitted for me to teach our magics to a living human. Congratulations on your power in summoning me here. But that is where this ends.' The faerie queen turned her back and began walking away, her dress merging with the water.

'Wait!' Faye shouted. 'Levantiana of Murias, Mistress of the Cup, I command you to wait!'

Levantiana stopped and turned slowly. 'You have no business commanding me to do anything, *sidhe-leth*. Just because my dear brother is enamoured with you does not mean I am, or that I will do anything for you,' she spat.

'I have something you want. I am willing to make the bargain,' Faye shouted over the waves, holding out her arms to steady herself, teeth knocking together so hard now that her head ached. A shadowy temptation to lie down in the water and never get up crept into her bones.

'You have nothing I want,' the queen sneered. 'I have my choice of human lovers, Faye. You are not one of them.'

'I am Lyr's daughter!' Faye shouted with the last scraps of her strength.

Levantiana stared at her for a long moment, then laughed. 'I know that. Is that your great secret? We all know it. I know Lyr of Falias's ways. That is not a bargaining tool, my dear.' She laughed loudly, and turned away from Faye. 'If I see you again, *sidhe-leth*, it will be when you are naked and jewelled like a whore, on my brother's leash. That is where your kind belong,' she called out. 'If your parentage is all you have for an exchange, then you have nothing of interest to me.' Levantiana's voice was receding, and the waves were dropping. Faye felt herself slump, and pulled herself up as straight as she could. *No.* She had to fight.

'You are at war with Falias. If you teach me your magic, I can be a weapon against Lyr; I have no love for him. I have never known him!' she cried out, remembering Moddie's throwaway phrase, all those years ago: *Almost killed me.* Her father had clearly tried to hurt Moddie, perhaps in anger at being expected to stay and look after her and Faye. She had never known for sure but, ever since that night, the idea of her father as a violent man – a selfish and impatient one, like Finn – had stayed with her.

Faye called on all the strength she had; she reached for the anger she had always kept inside her, a private anger at being left by her father. And she reset her numb feet in the shifting, freezing sand, and pulled up all the energy she could from the earth below her and from the stars above. It was enough to steady her, but only a little. Levantiana was so strong, so powerful. She was the tide: relentless, cold, violent.

'I know that you made a bargain with Moddie, my mother.

She gave you something – information, perhaps, that helped you in your war – in return for staying in Murias after death and learning your magic. I know that you taught her. She was Lyr's lover. Surely, as Lyr's child, you can make a bargain with me?' she added.

'Be a weapon how?' Levantiana's expression shifted; she was still imperious, but curiosity flickered in her eyes.

Faye coughed as a wave hit her chest and splashed hard into her face, filling her nose and mouth with salt water again. *Beware the faeries*, Grandmother's voice echoed in her mind. *They are beautiful, but consorting with them is dangerous.*

'Finn told me about the prophecy. That I would rule the Crystal Castle of the Moon,' Faye said, gasping for breath. 'I would need to know your magic to do that. And if I do rule the castle, I would have the power to kill Lyr. Or overpower Falias. Or do anything that you want me to do.'

'Hmph. Why would I care? Why wouldn't I take on the rule of the Crystal Castle myself and do the things you suggest?' Levantiana sneered, but Faye could sense something behind her words.

Levantiana was lying. And Faye realised that she knew why.

None of the kings or queens of the elemental kingdoms were able to rule the Crystal Castle of the Moon. It was written in the grimoire.

But was Grandmother right? If she was, then whether Faye believed in the prophecy or not, what she was offering Levantiana could be enough of an appealing bargain to get what she wanted: protection for her and Rav.

The last thing Faye saw was Levantiana, tall and black as the waves themselves, advancing through the waves towards her. She closed her eyes as strong arms pulled her up out of the water, and let the dark take her. *Too late, Grandmother*, she thought before she passed out from the cold. *Much too late.*

28

───────

Levantiana, Faerie Queen of Murias, stood with her back to Faye and before a vast sphere of what looked like ice, suspended above a golden altar table. The room was lit by flickering torches that bathed it in warmth.

'Where am I?'

Faye's voice echoed against the stone walls. She swayed on her feet; she was exhausted, cold and still felt awful.

'Take a moment to recover, *sidhe-leth*. You will find that being in Murias has a swift restorative power.' Unlike her voice as she stood in the sea, which had been harsh and sharp, Levantiana spoke now in a voice that sang and flowed like a sweet river.

'You offered an acceptable exchange. I am fulfilling my part of the bargain.'

Faye nodded and sat heavily on a nearby chest, which was draped in luxurious fabrics. She felt the tiredness leave her bones, and strength return to her as if she had drunk some kind of magical draught. Unlike being in Murias with Finn, being with Levantiana felt... restorative.

'Thank you,' she answered wearily. This was what she

wanted, but this was a realm of high magic: there was no going back. 'I just... want to learn what you can teach me. So that I can protect myself from...' She looked away. Finn's name hung between them, unsaid, a phantom.

Levantiana was fine-featured and golden like her brother, and tall and well-muscled; yet there was something more changeable about her, as if she could not be fully perceived. Faye had the sense that the edges of her were fluid like water; that she was everywhere and nowhere at once.

'I know what you wish,' the faerie queen replied, giving no indication of what she felt. Her loyalty would be to Finn, surely. He had told Faye again and again how he and Levantiana were the same, brother and sister, king and queen, the two halves of the kingdom. They *were* Murias.

Faye warmed herself by a great fire in a silver brazier to her left. Around the walls were lamps and silver censers, the censers billowing out smoke fragranced with lavender, rose and jasmine.

'Welcome to my quarters.' Levantiana smiled and bowed slightly at the waist. She stood, looking closely at Faye's eyes. 'I can see Lyr's features in yours. Lyr has taken many human lovers, as humans are most aware of his element over them all, even though you drink our waters and breathe the air and warm yourself in the fire of the sun. Without any of these things you would all die. But the mountains and the trees are the things you feel are the most real. Perhaps it is because you can cut them down and use their stones and logs to make your palaces of money.'

'I'm one person. You can hardly blame me for generations of industrialisation,' Faye argued back.

Levantiana remained impassive. 'I didn't bring you here to discuss such things.' She regarded Faye critically. 'This is what you wanted, wasn't it? To come to my private chambers to learn our magic?'

'Yes.' The blinding pain in her head and her lungs as the water had taken her over was gone, as was the feeling of heaviness in the water, of the shadowy sense of despair. Faye felt a strong sense of trepidation at being back in Murias – what if Finn found her here? She had not asked Levantiana to keep her presence here a secret, nor had the faerie queen offered such a thing.

Still, Faye was determined not to be afraid. Learning the faerie magic was her only chance at being able to stand up to Finn, so she had to risk being here in the meantime, if that was what it took.

Levantiana circled Faye slowly, her blue eyes almost black in the dimly lit room. 'You offered yourself as a weapon against Lyr. That is very serious, Faye. Before we begin, I must know that you are certain. Otherwise, our little arrangement will end.'

'I am serious.' Faye watched the faerie queen pace around her. 'He is no part of my life. I hate him. He broke my mother's heart.'

'But you don't know what that means. To be a weapon against him.' Levantiana delivered it as a statement, not a question. 'You would willingly make a bargain with me and not know the terms. That is rash, to say the least.'

'When you say a weapon, do you mean that it would hurt me in some way? Physically?' Faye cared nothing at all for a father she had never known, but it would be stupid of her to agree to anything that would bring harm to herself.

'No. You are half fae and half human. That gives you certain qualities we do not have; qualities we can use to build power in Murias. Also, Lyr is famously fond of his children. When he knows of you, he will want you with him. We will use that.'

'I don't want him. I don't want to know him at all,' Faye muttered.

'That is your concern. I wish to subjugate Falias and Gorias.

If we can remove Lyr from his throne, that will go a long way to winning the war,' Levantiana said. 'Falias is corrupt, and the High Queen Moronoe spends all her days fucking her slaves. She will be no competition for the throne once Lyr is gone.'

'You plan to take over Falias?' Faye frowned.

'No.' Levantiana gave her an unreadable look. 'I cannot. I am of Murias, and cannot be of anywhere else. But there can be an heir to the throne. A young heir that can be... mentored... before it comes of age.' She smiled, narrowing her eyes.

'What heir?' Faye frowned.

'That is my concern, not yours.' Levantiana shook her head. 'I had forgotten how wilful the Morgan women are. Your mother was the same.'

Moddie. Faye's heart yearned for her mother. 'Can I see my mother? While I'm in Murias?' Faye asked.

'No,' Levantiana said harshly. 'That is not allowed.'

'Why not?'

'Because it isn't,' the faerie queen retorted. 'Do not test me, Faye Morgan, or I will send you back to the human world and you can fend off my brother with your pathetic charms for the rest of your life. Do not think I will not.'

'Will you teach me what you taught her?' Faye persisted. She thought about how different it was, being in Murias and feeling the lushness of the faerie world, and yet not going under and losing control as she did when she was with Finn. In Levantiana's quarters, she was able to think. She could keep her head.

'Yes. I will teach you the same magic as I taught her, because there is only one magic of Murias,' Levantiana replied tersely. 'But do not think that I will reunite you out of the goodness of my heart. I do not have goodness in my heart in the way that humans imagine. My heart is a faerie heart. We are different to you.'

I am closer to you now, Faye thought, ignoring Levantiana's warnings. *I am coming, Moddie. I will find you again. Somehow, I will find you.*

'You will return to live in Murias. That is your destiny, and I cannot argue with his decision. My brother has chosen you as his own,' Levantiana said, as if Faye's will was secondary, and as if Finn's appetites were unquestionable. To Levantiana, she supposed that they were. *I will not*, Faye thought, but she said nothing. *Learning faerie magic is what will protect me from him.*

'If Finn wills it, he may allow you to see your mother, one day. But I doubt that he will.'

'Why? What would be so terrible about letting us see each other?' Faye pressed the faerie queen. 'Levantiana, Queen of Murias, Mistress of the Cup, I demand that you tell me,' she said, using the faerie queen's full name to compel her to tell the truth, as she had with Finn.

'Because it poses too much of a risk to have two Morgan women who know the secret magic in Murias. The Morgan women have been our friends in the human world for the ages, but they have also been our bane. The balance must be kept. The Morgan women cannot have too much power, which is partly why my brother seeks to keep you as his whore,' Levantiana said simply, and then looked shocked at the words she had spoken. 'I... I did not intend to say so much.'

'I want power. I need power to be able to come here as an equal to your brother. I will not be his concubine,' Faye replied.

'I should do nothing other than send you back where you came from and let him use you as he wants,' Levantiana snapped. 'But your offer is interesting; the war goes badly for us, and we need whatever help we can get. If the prophecy is true... and my brother believes it more than I do, but... if it holds some grain of truth, then I can see the logic that it is better to have you on our side. However, the teaching of magic to living mortals is forbidden, so no one can know of our bargain. I will teach you here in my quarters; call me at the tideline and I will come for you. Is that agreed?'

'I agree,' Faye said, steeling herself. She had come too far now to go back, whatever the cost. 'Will Finn know I am here?' She decided to be honest with the faerie queen. 'If he knows I am here, he will take me, and I will not be able to be your student. That would have implications.'

'What implications?' the faerie queen asked, though Faye thought that she knew very well.

'You know what would happen. He would take me to be his... *slut*... and never allow me any power. Hence, I would never be able to rule the Crystal Castle. You know what I need to learn, to take it.'

Levantiana regarded her for a long moment.

'No,' she replied finally. 'I will not tell him you are here. It would endanger our future as a realm for my brother to know. He is...' She broke off for a moment. 'My brother is too in thrall to his desires to be an effective ruler. He is not a strategist.'

Faye nodded. 'What must I do?' she asked, fear gripping her heart. Entering into a bargain with the fae was perilous. She knew that. *Be sure*, Grandmother's voice sounded in her mind.

'We seal our agreement with a kiss,' Levantiana said. 'Repeat after me: *Tha mi a' gealltainn mo ùmhlachd do rìoghachd Murias agus Levantiana a banrigh.*'

Faye repeated the promise. She knew that the words were Scots Gaelic, but she did not know what they meant.

'It means *I pledge my obedience to the realm of Murias and Levantiana, its queen,*' the faerie queen said, and Faye wondered if she could read her mind.

'Now, you kiss me,' Levantiana instructed.

As Faye's lips touched her right cheek, Levantiana said in a low voice, 'Finn will not know. While you are with me, you must not leave this room unless I show you where to go or I am with you. He will not know you are here; my quarters are protected with my magic. But go anywhere else in the kingdom, and he will know. And, outside these rooms, you will feel the effects of his enchantment upon you. You know how that feels by now.' Levantiana's blue-black gaze was penetrating. 'Do you understand?' she said quietly. 'And, when you come back to be his lover,' she said, raising her eyebrows at Faye when she opened her mouth to disagree. 'When that happens, you must not lose your head and tell him the magic I have taught you.'

Faye nodded. 'I understand.'

'Then we will begin,' said the faerie queen, and the flames in the lamps around the walls glowed bright, filling the chamber with blinding incandescence.

29

'This is where you will learn our magic.' Levantiana gestured to the altar table. 'Whether or not you can wield the power is another thing.'

'I'm a quick learner,' Faye said. 'You'll only have to tell me something once.'

'We will see.'

Levantiana took Faye's hand and led her to the golden table and the ice sphere. As well as the sphere which hung untethered above the table, the table held a large, gilded chalice. The bowl of the cup was easily a foot wide, and engraved with the familiar spirals that were everywhere in the castle. Faye recognised the alchemical symbol for water, the triangle with its point facing downwards. The cup was half-full with water which glinted silver in the odd light, and Faye saw a seven-pointed star engraved on its front. Alongside the large chalice, seaweed and shells were strewn on the table, as well as a crystal ball – bigger than the one in the shop, and completely flawless – and a wand. Faye gasped, recognising it: it looked exactly the same as Grandmother's wand, down to the writing inscribed on its shaft.

'You have a matching wand.' Levantiana nodded at the wand. 'It was given to Grainne Morgan, and has remained in the possession of the Morgan women since then.'

'What does this say? My Gaelic isn't great,' Faye asked. 'May I touch it?'

'You may.' Levantiana watched her as she picked up the wand and turned it over in her hand.

'*A rèir an tròcair mhòir, Glòir agus cumhachd do Rìgh agus do Bhanrigh Mhurias, mar a bha e aig an toiseach, agus a-nis, agus gu bràth,*' Faye read aloud haltingly; she recognised the words from the wand in the shop, but couldn't translate them. 'What does it mean?'

'*According to their great mercy, Glory and Power to the King and Queen of Murias, as it was at the beginning, and is now, and forever,*' Levantiana recited. 'It is a wand of great power, made by me from the finest faerie glass and from the wood of our sacred willow grove. I made this one, and the one belonging to your family as a gift. To symbolise our bond and our interconnectedness. The witches honour the fae and the elemental powers, and the fae keep the balance and peace of natural energies in the human world.'

'I had no idea.' Faye felt the same thrumming energy in this wand as she had in the one at home.

'You should. This has been part of the problem; your recent ancestors were too lax when it came to passing on the knowledge they had.' Levantiana looked grave. 'I doubt you even know the power of the wand. What it can do.'

'No,' Faye confessed. 'What can it do?'

'It is from Murias. It has the power to summon water, to cleanse and consecrate, to channel the elemental power of water and, if the power has already been summoned, to send it back. Reverse it, or divert it. It also has the power to protect the user from fae creatures of this realm,' Levantiana explained.

'How would I do that?' Faye asked.

'Hold the wand in your left hand. Ideally, you will be near some source of water, then you need to bring the water into contact with the wand – even a sprinkle will be enough. Then, trace the appropriate sigil in the air in front of you. Here' – Levantiana held up a sigil engraved onto a copper disc. Faye realised that there was one exactly the same in the cabinet in the shop – 'you have one of these, too.'

'Yes. I didn't know what it was for.'

'It is the sacred symbol of water activation. Which any fae in Murias knows, but apparently you do not. Humans are ignorant, but witches should know better,' she said disapprovingly.

'Once activated, and the words read aloud, the sigil cast' – she repeated the Gaelic phrase again – 'the wand just needs your intention. If your powers of visualisation are clear and focused, you will find many uses for the wand.'

'What does that mean?' Faye frowned.

'Imagine it and it will happen.' Levantiana rolled her eyes. 'I wonder exactly what your mother taught you at all.'

'She taught me a lot of things,' Faye argued, protective of the memory of Moddie.

'Not the right things, it would seem,' Levantiana replied archly. 'Try it.' She nodded at the wand. 'Summon the element. Not difficult to do, in the heart of the elemental kingdom.'

'Fine.' Feeling like an errant child, Faye took the wand in her left hand as instructed and read aloud the words on it.

She felt the wand humming in her hand, a subtle but definite vibration. She dipped the wand into the large chalice that sat on the altar, then, looking at the copper disc, copied its shape in the air in front of her. Then, she closed her eyes.

Summon the element.

Faye didn't know exactly what to do, but she thought of a stream of water. A pretty, countryside stream, trickling its way through a beautiful forest. It was gentle and tranquil. She concentrated as hard as she could on the image. She thought about what the stream would sound like, smell like, even.

She opened her eyes and looked down. She felt as though she had stepped in a puddle. But what she saw under her feet made her exclaim out loud. 'Oh!'

A stream flowed through Levantiana's chamber, gurgling over their feet. The water glittered in the lamplight, and Faye knelt down to touch it with her fingertips to see if it was real, or an illusion.

It was real. Tiny, gleaming fish and fronds of green weeds inhabited its flow.

'Oh my... wow.' Faye looked up at Levantiana, who stood with her arms crossed, her expression unreadable. 'I did it!'

'You did, *sidhe-leth*.' The faerie queen inclined her head delicately. 'It looks as if you are not quite as ignorant or talentless as I assumed.'

30

———

'In the castle of Murias, the cup is its magical symbol and greatest treasure,' Levantiana said, watching Faye's face as she admired its beauty.

Now, she waved a censer of sweet-smelling incense over the top of the chalice. 'Pay attention.'

It was two weeks later and Faye's second magic lesson, and she was keen to learn more. What Levantiana had already taught her was incredible. She'd had no idea that the wand was capable of so much. As soon as she'd returned home, she'd taken the Morgan wand out of the locked cabinet and practised summoning water. It was more difficult, outside Murias, as Faye was literally *out* of the element. But it still worked. Faye had managed to make it rain inside the shop, though she had stopped it almost immediately when she'd realised it was going to ruin all of the shop stock.

As Faye gazed obediently into the chalice, where images formed and bled into each other as the candlelight flickered on the water, Levantiana chanted strange words in Scots Gaelic and something shifted. The perspective in the room changed, yet, as she looked around, the room was at normal proportions;

it was the chalice that had grown and was suddenly impossibly large, and she found herself inside it as if she was in a deep golden pool. It made Faye think of *Alice in Wonderland* for a moment. The water was cold but not freezing; her clothes had disappeared and the water covered her naked shoulders as she stood with her feet on the bottom of the... cup? pool? – she didn't know.

Levantiana stood outside of the chalice and stretched into it, pulling her wand over the surface of the water.

'*Mar sin tha deuchainn an uisge cuideachd na leigheas air; mar sin tha draoidheachd an uisge. So is the test of water also the healing of it; so is the magic of water,*' she intoned, in Gaelic and then English, and drew a seven-pointed star on the top of the water. As she did so, the star lit up in blue and Faye felt the temperature of the water change, warming to something more pleasant than the initial cold.

'See your power on the surface of the water,' Levantiana instructed, as images and sequences, symbols and faces came up as if from the bottom of the chalice, breaking onto the skin of the water like drowning faces fighting for air. Faye stepped back, horrified at the effect, but Levantiana held her shoulders and forced her to stay where she was.

'No,' she said, firm but not unkind. 'You must do this. To have the power of Murias, you must accept your shadow and heal it. Our power is different to that which you have been taught, but you must welcome it in. You must integrate your fae and human selves to have the power you desire. You have already met some of your shadow in Murias. You know of what I speak.' Levantiana gave her a meaningful stare, and Faye felt herself blush. She knew what the faerie queen meant: her behaviour with Finn. Playing the slut. The whore. The concubine.

Faye's relationship with Finn was complicated. He had abducted her to faerie and kept her drugged with the magic of his touch, so that she forgot the outside world and wanted only to submit to him. The sexual things they had done together were outside the frame of her usual experience. But she had enjoyed it. She had derived a dark thrill of joy in letting go and allowing him to pleasure her.

On the surface of the water the faces were becoming familiar. They were women's faces, and, Faye realised, they bore a common resemblance to hers. She watched as the features morphed from one woman to another: sometimes a longer nose, sometimes the hair a different colour or style, but all of them somehow similar. She recoiled from them, feeling haunted, but she took a deep breath and gave herself over to it.

It wasn't until Grandmother's face blended into Moddie's and then hers that she realised she was seeing her ancestors, an unbroken line of Morgan women, stretching through the years like a ribbon unrolled. Her voice caught in her throat.

'Oh... I...' She didn't know what to say, and felt tears welling up in her eyes.

'Don't fight it. This is your magic. Take it.' Levantiana's hands on her shoulders felt more like support rather than restriction now, and Faye was grateful for them.

In the water, the Morgan women clustered around Faye, wanting to be acknowledged. Wanting to give her something of themselves. Each one held out a gift, and she knew that she had to take them all, even the things she didn't want to receive.

Some of the women held out bones and skulls. Some held spheres of light or swirling darkness. Some gave her plants and flowers; some handed her crude figures that appeared to be crafted from mud and old pieces of cloth, or swatches from their dresses. Everything she took was made of water and disappeared as soon as she held it, but she had the sense that she retained all the gifts somehow; each was like a memory, firmly committed into her ancestry.

Each Morgan woman said something to her: their voices were real, not imagined.

'I give you my knowledge of herbs.'

'I give you my psychic ability.'

'I give you my insight.'

'I give you my kindness.'

Many of the gifts were beautiful. Faye felt them enrich her soul.

But there were as many women that gave her awful, terrible gifts that made her heavier, darker, sadder.

'I give you my pain.'

'I give you my hopelessness.'

'I give you my loss.'

She took it all, going around and around in the chalice until she had taken everything the women had to give. And then, she stood at the centre of the cup, facing Grainne Morgan.

'To you I give my bravery. You are no man's whore, and no man's servant. Faerie or otherwise,' Grainne said to her. 'Your desires are not wrong. Your desire in whatever form it takes is your power. But do not give yourself to anyone who would treat you less than a queen, dear daughter.'

Faye nodded. She remembered the moment she had witnessed Grainne curse the people who had lashed her to the stake for being a witch.

Confess, and ye shall go to your death godly. Not as the Devil's whore, the man had said to her as she stood defiantly in front of the crowd. *I am no whore. I am Grainne Morgan, Beloved of the Good Folk!* she had replied, and the faerie had spirited her away.

'Are you here, too?' Faye asked Grainne. 'In Murias? Like Moddie?'

'No, child. I was there for a while, healing, but then the fae took me to my rest. I was a friend of Murias, and it was a friend to me, then. But times have changed. You must be careful now.

The faerie kings are corrupt. He would own you, and a Morgan woman will never be owned,' Grainne replied.

'I will be careful,' Faye said.

Grainne took both of her hands in hers. 'I am with you,' she replied.

Finally, Faye stood face to face with her grandmother and her mother.

Moddie. Grandmother.

Tears started rolling down Faye's cheeks as the two people she had loved most in the world walked out of the mist and materialised in front of her.

'Hello, my darling girl,' Moddie said, and enveloped Faye in a hug. 'I cannot stay long. But I give you my love for always, which you already had. And I give you a gift of protection.' Moddie handed her a small silver charm; it looked like it was from a charm bracelet. It was in the shape of a kelpie: a water horse.

'Like poison heals in small proportions, this protects against that which it represents,' Moddie said, pressing the charm into Faye's hand. 'You know of whom I speak. Wear this around your neck and he will not be able to take you. I love you, always.'

Moddie started to fade away.

'Mum. No!' Faye cried out, but Moddie was gone as soon as she had come. A terrible ache of loss filled Faye's heart. 'Please. Come back,' she said, like a child. 'Please.'

Faye turned to her grandmother.

'Grandmother. I have missed you,' she said.

'I miss you too, but I am with you. In the grimoire,' Grandmother answered. 'I give you knowledge. Knowledge is power, my love.' She kissed Faye on the cheek. 'Do not be sad, child. We are all with you, now. Forever.'

They all stepped forward, then, into her.

It was disorienting, terrifying and beautiful at the same

time; Faye heard Levantiana's voice in the distance telling her to 'accept, just accept this'.

'We were always with you,' they said, the mothers and grandmothers who had helped shape every single part of who Faye was. Whose breath was in her lungs, whose blood ran in her veins, whose weaknesses and strengths were hers. They surrounded her in circles, four or five deep and radiating out, outside of the chalice and into the walls of the castle. Faye had the sense that the mothers went on forever, and that from now on they would always be watching over her, loving her, supporting her so she would never feel lonely again.

She felt their embraces and closed her eyes, secure in the love of her grandmothers. It had always been there, waiting: Levantiana had merely shown her the way. And she was only dimly aware of Levantiana snapping her fingers, making the chalice shrink back to its ordinary size on the altar, returning Faye back to normal, standing beside her in the faerie castle.

31

'In the middle of the four faerie kingdoms, over the four crystal bridges stands the Crystal Castle of the Moon. That is where She who is the Highest Power resides,' Levantiana intoned, a week after the cup ritual.

Faye found herself with a foot firmly in both realms. By day she ran the shop, greeting customers, offering advice, and maintaining what normality she could with Annie and Aisha. She still hadn't seen Rav, though. He'd been out of town again, and still hadn't replied to her messages... Every week, in an evening, Faye would summon Levantiana and take up her lessons, and feel her power and knowledge deepen.

The faerie queen was patient with Faye, but there was a remoteness about her that had no conception of human niceties like small talk. As before, Faye had summoned her at the tide-line, this time at the new moon, and Levantiana had transported her to Murias in a moment of swirling hyper-reality. Faye found the transition to Murias was much less exhausting when she was going willingly – instead of being spirited there by Finn – but the spell to summon Levantiana, with its spiralling, all-encompassing power still drained Faye of her energy.

Every night she had vivid dreams that were sometimes nightmares; more than one night she dreamed of Grainne Morgan at the stake. She had been grateful for the mundanities of the shop in the days in between her lessons in Murias; deliveries, customers, pricing and arranging the window display. It had made her feel almost normal.

Rav had finally replied to her texts, but his tone had been brief.

Glad you're okay. I need some time to get over what happened. I haven't ever witnessed anything like that before, he had written. Faye's stomach had dropped when she'd read that; not that she expected anything else, but it was still hard to read.

Okay, she had replied. *I would still like to see you again. When things are back to normal.*

There had been no reply. She hadn't explained much of what was going on: what could she say that Rav would understand?

'The Crystal Castle is not a kingdom. It is the centre of our realms. Morgana Le Fae herself – Mistress of Magic, the Faerie Queen of the Silver Moon – lives there,' Levantiana continued. Today her golden hair was loose and completely straight. She wore a silver circlet that dipped down in a point onto her forehead, and her gown was diaphanous and black, tethered only at the shoulders with clasps in the shape of crescent moons, jewelled with diamonds.

'She's... like an empress, then?' Faye was confused.

'No. She does not rule. She takes no side in war; our disagreements are nothing to her, and we do not involve her in our disputes. She is a neutral place of power. She is eternal.'

'Aren't you all... eternal?' Faye asked. Finn had told her he was much older than he looked, but she didn't know if that meant he was immortal.

'We do not die in the same way as you, but we can be replaced.'

'Wait... you say she's neutral. But you said that I could assume power in the Crystal Castle and then use it to side with Murias.' Faye frowned.

'Just because things have always been one way does not mean they cannot turn another way,' Levantiana said coldly. 'This is the next magic you will learn. You will speak with Morgana Le Fae and bring back whatever wisdom she bestows on you.'

'What will I do when I find her?' Faye asked. '*How* do I find her?'

Levantiana walked behind the altar table and drew aside one of the long curtains that hung on the walls as in the other castle rooms. Behind the curtain Faye saw a tall door, enamelled with what looked like gleaming white shell. Levantiana unlocked the door and beckoned to Faye, who followed in wonder at what lay beyond.

'As you are half fae, you can walk the crystal bridge.' Levantiana pointed out a glistening, silvery-white crystal bridge that stretched across a deep ravine. Below, Faye could hear the sea but not see it. She shivered; the bridge was narrow and had no sides, and it was barely the width of her body. She realised that the faerie queen had not answered her first question.

The bridge was lit with the glow of a vast crystal castle that sat on its own island in the distance. Faye could see its pink-blue sheen reflected in the water.

'That's the... that's where Morgana Le Fae is?' she breathed, gazing across.

'The birthplace of all magic,' Levantiana answered. 'I can teach you little else if you do not experience what awaits you there.'

Faye felt her resolve waver, but if this was her way to power, then she was going to take it. Her life, Rav's life, depended on it.

She stepped onto the crystal bridge, concentrated on putting one foot in front of the other, and didn't look back.

The crossing was perilous. The bridge was so glassy that it was difficult to maintain a grip; more than once, Faye felt herself slip. She only managed to keep her balance by fixing her gaze on the castle and concentrating on her breath.

As she set foot on the island, she heard singing. Faye closed her eyes, and the strange rhythm of the song took her into a light trance; the tune was haunting, and yet it made Faye's heart soar.

After a moment, she opened her eyes and looked up at the castle in the distance. It had seven tall, twisting spires that glowed and pulsed gold, white, pink and blue under a vast moon that hung in the black sky, bigger than it could ever be in the ordinary world. The walls were high and contained no windows, and jutted out in points to her right and left. She wondered if, from above, the castle was the shape of a seven-pointed star, and guessed that it was.

The mist melted away as she stepped forward and followed the path uphill. To her left, the path fell away into a sharp grey cliff that led down to the crashing blue-black sea. Faye felt no fear of it now, but stayed on the path, nonetheless. There was a smell of sea spray and, underlying that, the sour tang of seaweed. It was a steep climb, but there were steps cut into the rough grass and she took them evenly.

At the top, the path gave way to a carpet of pink rose petals, and the fragrance captured Faye in its soft, sweet kiss. Faye felt the sea breeze on her face and held out her arms in pleasure. The energy vibration was high here; it was like standing inside a rose quartz crystal, her favourite stone to use in meditation, in healing, in magic, everything. She liked to have a big piece of it nearby when she made her incenses in the shop. She thought of it, her safe place, for a moment, but not because she needed to protect herself.

As Faye looked up at the castle, a golden door appeared in

front of her where she couldn't have missed it before. A sudden breeze blew the rose petals up around her feet and cleared a path to the door. This was the way in, then.

She pushed the door and it opened easily. Stepping inside, the sound of singing intensified. The space opened up to her as she walked in: a wide, circular palazzo, open to the elements; she could see the seven corners of the castle lead off the main centre. There did not seem to be any other rooms or floors.

The main courtyard was round, open to the stars and circled with gold pillars. She walked to the centre, wondering what she should do.

As Faye stood in the centre of the palace, at the very middle of the circle, looking up at the moon above her which seemed to fill the whole space, three wide moonbeams bathed her in a silver glow. A figure emerged, coalesced from the moonlight. Faye could see silver blood under her black skin. The shape merged and drifted in the moonlight; first, she was a pre-Raphaelite maiden, then a crone, then a harpy that made Faye gasp a little. The figure returned to a silver-haired, black-skinned queen with eyes like diamonds.

She stood in front of Faye and held out her hands.

'My lady,' Faye murmured. 'Am I in the presence of the Faerie Queen of the Crystal Castle of the Moon?'

The woman was more beautiful than any human could be; made of moonlight, she was pure luminescence.

'I am Morgana Le Fae, Mistress of Magic. Blessings on you.' The queen nodded gracefully.

'Blessings on you,' Faye echoed, filled with the over-whelming sense of peace she usually felt when practising magic back in Abercolme; but if that offered a temporary sense of otherworldliness, this was total immersion.

Mistress of Magic. Had Moddie named the shop after Morgana Le Fae?

'You may ask me a question,' Morgana said, the moonlight glowing through her silver hair.

What to ask? Faye wondered, then spoke. 'How can I step into my power as half faerie? Levantiana is teaching me. But I...' Faye trailed off, holding Morgana's hands and feeling her power sing through to her. 'I want more,' she murmured, as the faerie queen's power encircled her like perfume, like lust.

'The fae is in your heart; it is part of you. Relax and let it out. Feel your faerie heart. Hear its song,' Morgana whispered. For a moment, Faye heard the singing again; it was louder, coming from the palace itself. 'You have power. Coming to my realm will help you see it. Navigate the shores and the hills of this place. We are at the heart of the power of the faerie kingdoms: explore and gain your power, Faye Morgan.'

'Thank you,' Faye whispered, feeling Morgana's power fill her; it began in her feet, travelled up her legs and exploded in her body with the power of a kiss, reminiscent of the eroticism of Finn's mouth on her.

Morgana smiled, and where Levantiana's smile was cold, hers was fire.

'This is all you need. I am all, and you must let me in. Find yourself, Faye, remember your heritage, your ancestors, let them hold you. Let me fill you with my magic, and it will stay with you forever.' She leaned forward and kissed Faye gently on the lips. Their mouths lingered together, and Faye felt the fire of Morgana's kiss consume her. Morgana's touch filled her soul with magic.

Morgana pulled away and traced Faye's lips with her fingertip.

'Get to know this place. This is the place of patterning. What you humans call the astral plane,' she said. 'And remember: I am here, forever. No one may supplant me, for I am immortal. You may visit me to refill your cup at any time.'

No one may supplant me. Did Morgana know what she and Levantiana had discussed?

This is the place of patterning.

Faye had spent her whole life learning magic: she knew that the astral plane was the dimension of energy, of being, next to the fully manifest plane of earth. The astral was where spells, once made in the material plane of earth, emanated their magic. The astral was where dreams lived, where ideas formed, where energy was available to be moulded and formed by thought.

That was where her carefully crafted poppet doll had taken its inspiration from, and this is where her instructions – her desires – had entered the ether as she sewed them into the doll. Inspiration flowed to the ordinary world from here; intention flowed upwards, to make patterns which were then transmuted into reality.

Faye nodded, and kissed Morgana's unnaturally long-fingered hands. She had no fingernails, Faye noticed, and her skin was formed of neatly overlapping black scales. When she met the queen of the moon's diamond-like eyes, she was startled that they were not eyes at all, but places where the moonlight streamed through.

Morgana withdrew her hands and stepped back into the three shafts of moonlight, dissolving into them. Faye felt the loss of her keenly and as suddenly as her desire had appeared; she was dazed, aroused and yet fulfilled at once. Morgana had lit something in her soul, and she felt different, though she couldn't say how.

There was nothing to explore inside the Crystal Castle. Faye walked around the edges of the palazzo and in and out of the corners but found only the walls made of their glowing crystalline material. A piece of it came away in her hand, and Faye held it up in wonder. It glowed like a lamp. Carefully, she put it in her pocket, feeling that if Morgana didn't want her to have it, it would not have come away so easily.

There were no other doors in or out except the one she had come in. Only the floor of the castle held any pattern at all, and that was the seven-pointed star of faerie, tiled in what looked like black glass or crystal against a pink-white stone.

Back outside the castle, she walked around it and approached the edge, and the wet grey cliffs fell away under her again.

She felt her breath catch. The drop was high and deep and she felt suddenly afraid, even though she hadn't before. But she took a breath and steadied herself, and let her gaze wander over the surface of the blue-black sea.

As she watched, something broke the surface of the water. She narrowed her eyes; perhaps it was a rock sitting under the water. Though she loved the sea, and her beach at Abercolme, she had always been terrified of deep water – both its power, of the storms that occasionally lashed Abercolme, and what was in it; of mysterious, leviathan-like beings that roamed in the deep oceans, in the dark. Beaches were in-between places, liminal, where water met earth. The deep water was something else.

As Faye watched, a black head emerged from the waves, followed by a large, black-scaled body.

The kelpie rose out of the sea; Faye stood on the edge of the cliff and watched it, her heart beating wildly. Here was her fear made flesh, a creature of darkness, emerging from the impene-trable black water. Scotland was full of myths of them: a black or white horse creature that drowned anyone who climbed on its back. They were said to reside around lochs and rivers, espe-cially at night or at dusk. Like all Scottish children she had been told to beware of them, but had taken it for a cautionary tale to stop children drowning in dangerous water.

The kelpie pulled itself out of the water and stood on the short beach beneath her. She had always imagined kelpies to be very like horses, but its eyes regarded her like marbles of the same blue-black water it had emerged from. It had the head and torso of a vast horse, but its hindquarters were like a long black sea serpent.

It crawled up the cliff towards her; instinctively, she drew back. Dread and panic overcame her and she began to run back towards the castle, but it followed.

When she reached the castle walls, Faye closed her eyes and tried to catch her breath. There was nowhere to go, and her lungs heaved with the effort of running. She tried to quiet herself, to tell herself that there was nothing to fear here, but she was lying to herself.

She sensed the kelpie approaching, and squeezed her eyes tight like a child would, hoping that the monster might disappear, her back pressed into the wall of the castle, her arms over her face. Even after all her experiences in Murias, even knowing that she was half faerie herself, her longstanding fear of the deep ocean and what lay within it almost overcame her. She cried out 'No, no, no, please,' but the kelpie approached her, closer, closer.

No, I won't be afraid. Faye reached down into herself, remembering the ancestors who had appeared to her in the golden cup of Murias. Remembering their gifts, their wounds, their magics, she appealed to them for help, and something came.

The trinket Moddie had given her. As her mother had given her the kelpie charm in spirit, and in the ritual of the cup, her gift had remained in spirit. There wasn't a physical charm around her neck when she was in the human world, but it appeared on a silver chain as soon as she appeared in Murias. It was Moddie's gift to her: a charm that protected her from Finn, a kelpie because of the tattoo that reared up his chest and neck.

But this creature was also a kelpie. Surely, it would protect her from that, too.

She opened her eyes, heart beating manically, her right hand formed into a fist around the charm, her heart aflame with will. *Leave me!* the words were on her tongue, but the kelpie merely licked her hand, like a dog would.

Faye jumped, pulling her hand away.

The kelpie sat next to her, head bowed slightly; it made no move to get any closer.

She watched it fearfully, expecting it to pounce, to move suddenly, to attack her. Yet, it sat next to her peacefully, panting slightly.

She held the charm, watching it. Nothing happened.

Cautiously, feeling her panic subside slightly, Faye laid her palm on the kelpie's nose, ready to pull her hand away at the smallest hint of danger. Instead, she was overwhelmed by a sense of power. The kelpie's energy was pure water, and Faye felt the joyful rush of a waterfall mixed with the furthest, darkest depths of the ocean; it was at once the brightness of a stream in a sun-dappled woodland and the insurmountable grey wall of a tsunami.

Faye looked into the kelpie's unblinking stare and felt her fear melt away as it returned her gaze with its ageless seawater-and-glass eyes. Without thinking, she climbed up onto its black scaly back, and, as if it knew she would, it stretched up into the sky, and then dived back under the black water.

Faye gulped in one last breath of air and went under willingly with the kelpie, just as Grainne Morgan had with the fae that had come to her aid. And, under the water, she released the last of her fear – fear of taking up space, of being herself, and of coming into her full power– in one long, ragged scream that the seawater swallowed as if it had never existed.

Faye felt the faerie part and the human part of her merge, and was filled with the power of both worlds. She plunged down into the deep darkness on the back of the kelpie, and found that she could breathe here, too, and she was filled with a wild exultation. She screamed again, but this time with unfettered joy, and the kelpie under her roared a jangling, unearthly rumble that made the rock shake and pulled all the other water elementals behind them in its wake.

And when she finally returned to Levantiana, the faerie queen opened the door made of glistening shell. And Faye Morgan, who had gone below the waves and returned alive, slid off the black kelpie and strode back into Murias with a piece of pink crystal in one pocket and three rose petals folded securely inside a single black kelpie's scale in the other.

32

'Where've ye been, Faye? It's been three days and nae word.' Annie waved her spare shop keys in her friend's face. 'Just as well I had these, eh?'

Faye went to the kitchen to make herself a tea. In Levantiana's chamber she had walked in the rose-scented air; she had dived into the blue-and-black sea on the back of a kelpie and felt nothing but comfortable. She knew that she was getting stronger, finding the transition between the worlds easier now that she was embracing her power and learning from Levantiana.

'I rang and texted, but there was no answer, I thought ye'd just left. Packed up and gone on holiday or something.'

'Oh... Yes, I was ill again.' Faye grasped at the easy excuse. 'I'm so sorry, Annie. I was so out of it. Hallucinating.' It wasn't even that much of a lie. She'd been in the faerie kingdom, the most hallucinatory of places. She checked her phone; there was a text from Rav and a missed call. *Please, Faye. I want to talk. I miss you.*

She wanted to reply; her fingers hovered over the screen. But if she wanted to keep Rav safe, she couldn't see him – at least, until she had enough power to stand against Finn if she had to.

She pushed the phone away, picking up her tea instead and gulping it down in one go.

Annie watched her warily. 'Looks like ye haven't eaten for a few days, either, sweetheart.'

Faye opened the cupboard where they kept the biscuits and took out a packet of digestives and two cereal bars. She was ravenous. Faye tried to mask her shock that she had been gone for three days, and was making tea to buy herself some time to invent an explanation. She knew time was elastic in the faerie realm, but it seemed it had passed even faster in the Crystal Castle. Levantiana had asked her nothing when she had returned, merely nodding when Faye had requested some time at home.

'No. Starving,' she replied between bites of the bars: vegan ones that Aisha brought in most weeks.

'Okay, well. Next time drop me a text. Or ring and just groan down the phone, eh? I'll know it's you. I'll come round with a takeaway or something.' Annie's tone softened, and Faye smiled apologetically at her friend.

'Okay. Sorry. Love you,' she repeated, and reached for her friend's hand, covered in silver rings. She squeezed it affectionately. 'What would I do without you, eh?'

''I love ye, too, lassie.' Annie squeezed back.

'What did I miss when I was ill?'

'Oh, not much. Aisha did some work for Rav, bit of light emailing. Made him a contact database, apparently. She said the guy has no IT ability at all. Ye didn't see him, then?'

'No, like I said, I was ill,' Faye said, though the thought of Aisha and Rav made her heart ache a little, but she had made the choice not to see Rav – at least, until she was sure she could protect him from Finn. Perhaps it wouldn't be too long now; she was already gaining power. Merging with her ancestors and letting go of her fear about her magic had been two huge steps; she felt transformed.

'Aye.' Annie gave her a funny look.

'What?' Faye snapped.

Annie looked away. 'Nothing. Got some news of my own, that's all.' She looked uncharacteristically shifty.

'What is it?'

'I got a job. Acting.' Annie was trying to hide a grin.

Faye's anger evaporated. 'You're joking! That's fantastic, Annie! Why didn't you say? I don't mind if you're going to be away a week or so. Aisha can cover.' Faye hugged her friend. 'What is it? The role?'

'Ah. That's the thing, see. It's in London. It's TV. A series.'

'A series? Wow!' Faye beamed. 'How many episodes are you going to be on?'

Annie sighed and pulled away from Faye. 'All o' them,' she said. 'It's a new show. They've put me in for six months and see how I go. Maybe permanent. I've got to move away, Faye. To London.'

Faye felt numb. 'London?'

'Aye. I'm sorry. I'm going to miss ye like crazy.'

'But why didn't you say before? That's where your audition was?'

'Aye, well, I didn't think I'd actually get it, did I? Outside chance, I thought, but I had an old girlfriend I wanted to call in on, an'... well. Here we are.'

Tears of shock welled up in Faye's eyes. 'But what will I do without you, Annie?' she whispered, and Annie enveloped her in a hug again.

'Aw, now. Come on. I know ye'll be okay. An' I'll come home for weekends here and there. It's just that the filming's pretty intense, they said. Not many days off for a while, aye.'

What could Faye say? That she really needed her friend,

even though she hadn't yet told Annie anything about Finn or Murias?

But as she looked into Annie's green eyes, she didn't have the heart to ruin this for her. She wouldn't say anything; she could do it on her own. She didn't need Annie looking out for her all the time any more. And this was the big break Annie had been waiting for.

'What show is it? One I've seen?'

'*Coven of Love.*' Annie shrugged. 'Stupid title, aye. But it's about these three modern witches who are looking for love in London. They said they liked my interest in the subject, and they wanted a Scottish witch as a character, so. Life imitates art, aye.' She winked at Faye. 'Maybe it's the spell workin' for me. Tell me you're happy for me, lassie?' she asked, quietly.

Faye smiled through her tears. 'Of course I'm happy for you,' she said, but her face betrayed her, and she sobbed into her best friend's shoulder. 'I'll just miss you, that's all.'

Annie patted her on the shoulder. 'I'll miss you too, you daftie,' she said, but there was a tremble in her voice, too.

'When do you leave?' Faye mumbled.

'Saturday. I'm going to stay with the ex for a while, until I find a place of my own.'

'That's only three days away,' Faye felt her heart wrench further. 'Do you really have to go so soon?'

'Prep starts next week. That's the way of these things, Faye. They have to see me for wardrobe fittings, rehearsals, the lot.'

'Oh.' Her voice was small; she felt powerless, suddenly, like a child. Everything was changing too fast.

'Faye? Are you okay? Is there something you need to tell me?' Annie peered at Faye's tear-streaked face. 'Is it Rav? You'd tell me, aye? If there was something wrong?' She looked worried. 'I don't like to leave ye this upset.'

Faye shook her head hurriedly and wiped her eyes. 'I'm

fine. Really.' She forced a smile onto her face. 'We can have a little party to send you on your way,' she added.

Annie nodded. 'Aye, why not. Say a proper goodbye. I'll miss Abercolme, the old place, aye. But I'll miss ye the most, Faye Morgan. I need to be blasted for the next two days to get through it.'

Faye laughed.

'I'm serious,' Annie insisted. 'Out of it.'

33

———

'He's a nice guy.' Aisha passed Faye a mug of tea. 'Funny. And he let me borrow some of his vinyl. He's got a wicked collection.'

It was Saturday and Faye had a hangover. Annie had got up early for her flight to London; they'd said a final misty goodbye sometime in the early hours before Faye had passed out in her bed. She'd woken up with a headache like a drill.

She'd had to open up, though. Tourists were finding their way to Abercolme for the summer, and Saturdays were her busiest day of the week. Already the shop was full of customers milling between the scented candles and the tarot card display, leafing through the book where Faye kept sample cards of each deck.

She'd been keen to hear about Rav from Aisha. He had texted again: *How are you? I can't stop thinking about you.* But she hadn't replied. She still wasn't sure if it was a good idea.

She had been dreaming of him, though. The dreams with Finn had stopped; Moddie's charm must have been helping. Instead, her nights had been full of longing for Rav.

The dreams were different to the ones she'd had about Finn.

Her dreams about Rav were just dreams, but that didn't mean they weren't full of feeling. The night before, Faye had dreamed that she and Rav were making love on the beach again. But this time she had been dressed like Morgana Le Fae, in a black gown that was part of the sea behind her. In her dream, Rav was naked and she had commanded him to kneel before her and kiss her feet. He did it, and then looked up longingly at her.

How may I pleasure you further, my queen? he asked. She told him to worship her with his tongue, then, and willingly he pressed his face into her. She held his head firmly in both hands, relishing the sweet sensation of his tongue on her, and woke, hungry for satisfaction.

Faye felt jealous of Rav and Aisha: the idea that they might be getting close, sharing laughs, talking about music, all the pleasant, normal things that she could have enjoyed with Rav if she had never got involved with Finn Beatha. Any number of opportunities could present themselves for Rav and Aisha's hands to touch, for them to share eye contact for one micro-second too long. And then, to kiss. To touch. To become a couple. Aisha was a pretty girl. Rav was clearly a man with needs.

'He really likes you, you know. You could be a wee bit nicer to him.' Aisha broke into Faye's thoughts; Faye noticed a blush rise on Aisha's cheeks.

'Who? Rav?'

'Yeah. He talks about you all the time.' Aisha looked down, and Faye wondered if Aisha was jealous of *her*.

'I like him, too. It's complicated,' she said quietly.

'Is it?' Aisha drank her tea and looked innocently at Faye. 'Why?'

'It just is.' Faye didn't want to explain – couldn't explain – about Finn. What could she say? That she was learning faerie magic so that if the jealous faerie king who was now obsessed with her turned on her or Rav, she could stop him enacting a brutal punishment on both of them? For a moment, Faye reflected that she had never before in her life been involved with two men at once (although one wasn't technically a man). She smiled ruefully to herself. Wasn't this what witches were supposed to do? Enchant men and drive them mad with lust? Wasn't that what many innocent women were put to the stake for supposedly doing? The man had whispered in Grainne Morgan's ear that she was the devil's whore, after all.

'Okay.' Aisha looked at the door as some customers walked in. 'I should probably...'

'Sure.'

Faye washed up her cup and pottered around in the little kitchenette. *No good can come of thinking about Rav,* she chastened herself. *You've made your decision – now, stick to it.* She unpacked a box of different-coloured little silk bags, herbal resins in small pouches and some new crystals. The bags reminded Faye that she hadn't made any new incenses for a while, and the shelf where she usually stacked her pretty glass jars, labelled with her own brand, Mistress of Magic, was looking sparse.

'Might go for a forage later,' she mentioned to Aisha, who nodded. Faye made all her incenses with as many locally sourced herbs and plants as she could; there was no need for some of the strange and unusual ingredients she sometimes saw added to herbal remedies sold to burn or to drink. Plants worked best in magic when you used what was local to you, wherever you were in the world; different cultures had plants that essentially did the same things.

'Foraging's definitely a good idea. We're low on love incense in particular,' Aisha sighed. 'I could do with some of that.'

'Love spell not worked yet, then?' Faye said it lightly, but she watched Aisha closely; she couldn't help herself. To see whether there was a twinkle that meant she might have fallen for Rav, or not.

Aisha avoided her gaze and blushed. 'I dunno,' she muttered and turned away to help a woman who wanted to know which colour candle to buy for a protection spell. Faye waited for her to finish her conversation with the woman. Suspicion bloomed in her like a black rose.

'Aish. Are you *sure* you're not into someone?' Faye asked, her heart was beating hard. Aisha shook her head, but Faye wasn't convinced. It must be Rav; it *must* be. She knew it was for the best, but it tortured her, nonetheless. 'Come on. You can tell me. Wallflowers' club, remember?'

She was being disingenuous, and she had betrayed Aisha in a sense – she was certainly no longer a wallflower – but she had to know. Faye had to stay away from Rav, but it would be so hard if he and Aisha started seeing each other. She knew she shouldn't ask; that the knowledge would be like sticking her finger in a cut. But she couldn't help herself.

Aisha smiled awkwardly and motioned Faye towards her.

'I can't say. It's... it's not the time,' she whispered. 'I think we need to talk. Later.' She gave Faye an odd smile and moved away from her, behind the counter to serve more customers.

Faye turned away, saddened. She knew Aisha and Rav had more in common than she and Rav did. Aisha was beautiful, intelligent, she loved music as much as Rav. But Faye wanted Rav. So, where did that leave her?

34

On her foraging walk, Faye avoided Rav's house by the sea, careful also to skirt the faerie path that ran alongside the house. That wasn't why she was here; she was staying in the ordinary world for now.

In the distance, she could hear the sound of clanging as the festival stage was erected, up on the cliffs: Abercolme Rocks was near now, and the village had been busy with trucks and food vendors all week.

She followed her usual path down to the beach. Some things could be collected here: small shells to include in the ready-made spell bags she sold alongside the Mistress of Magic incense. Small spells could still be remarkably effective. Feathers, too; she picked up a few small grey feathers belonging to sea birds, and one black crow's feather.

She walked along the beach, filling a bag with sea buckthorn berries, intending to dry some for incense and make some into the tart jam she liked. She filled another bag with lovage and one with orache, which was better than spinach to eat. Pine was everywhere: she used it in incenses for purification and divination. Faye could never forage without remembering Grandmother – the way she taught Faye which plants could be eaten; which berries could be dried and burned, like hawthorn and rosehip; which looked tasty but were poisonous, like the red yew berries that covered the trees in the churchyard so prettily every year. For an hour or more, Faye lost herself in her foraging, taking pleasure in the small finds along the familiar ways she had trod since girlhood.

As evening came, she turned and followed the coast path back to Black Sands. The pull of faerie was strong now; more insistent than it had been before. Faye recognised the familiar call in her blood as her gaze settled on the faerie pathway outside Rav's house again, and, clearer than before, she found she could see the fae twisting and running along it in their chaotic way.

In the old faerie stories, humans sometimes had their eyelids anointed with a faerie balm that meant they could see faeries in the ordinary world, but this seldom turned out to be a good thing. Faye remembered one story where a cunning woman had taken the balm and put it on her eyes herself rather than the faeries doing it. She had delighted in being able to see the faeries play their tricks on the unknowing humans, until the fae realised she could see what they were doing and struck her blind.

Faye could see the point of the story now. So far, it had felt like a curse to be half faerie.

'I thought you'd be at the shop.' Rav's voice broke into her thoughts, and she looked up, startled.

'Oh. Hi.'

There was an uncomfortable silence.

'Well, nice to see you're still alive, anyway...' He looked at her expectantly.

'I'm alive,' she said slowly. 'I... I wanted to see you, but...' How was she going to explain?

'But what?' His tone was cold. Faye could feel his hurt, and her heart twisted with sorrow.

'I do want to see you. It's just been...' She sighed, not knowing what to say.

'You don't have to explain.' He refused to meet her eyes. 'I thought we had something, but I understand if you don't feel the same way.'

'We do. We did. There's a connection here, between us, Rav. But...' She bit her lip and looked away, unsure what to say.

There were some black clouds coming in, far off on the horizon. Rav nodded to them. 'Black horses coming. Better head in,' he said.

'That's a strange expression.' She was grateful for the change of subject; she sensed that he wanted to stay, to talk to her, and that was something.

'Oh. Is it? My mum used to say it about a storm. Like white horses in the sea.' He kicked at the sand.

'I haven't heard it.' She laid her hand on his arm. 'Look. Can we talk?'

'Sure.' Rav met her eyes with a direct but kind stare; he didn't make any move to either remove her hand or put his own hand on top of hers.

'Okay. So... I'm sorry. About not answering your texts, about being distant. There is a reason, but it's... it's hard to explain.'

'What are we going to talk about if you can't explain anything?' He shrugged and pulled his arm away from her hand. 'Seems to me that you think you want to talk, but I don't think you do. Do you know how weird it was for me to see you just disappear like that? It was terrifying. No explanation of what happened. It's been torturing me. I can't sleep. I feel like I'm going mad.'

'I'm sorry,' she said, feeling hopeless. 'I'm so sorry, Rav. I would like something with you, I just... I just... can't, right now.'

'Whatever.' He turned and started walking away. 'I'll see

you around, Faye. Let me know when you're ready to talk like an adult.'

The storm clouds were growing nearer; the air was changing. Now, it had an electric smell like burnt ozone. Fear contracted Faye's body; she didn't want to lose Rav. Her heart ached, and suddenly she was sick of all her secrets. She knew she had to open up to Rav. To tell him everything.

She ran the few steps between them and made him turn around to face her.

'Please. I will explain. Everything. Just listen.' She reached up to his face and touched his cheek. His eyes met hers again, and she dropped her hand.

'Faye, I don't know...' he muttered, and a distant thunder rumbled in the distance. 'I don't want to get involved if you're going to mess me around. I like you too much.'

She nodded. 'You're right. I'm sorry. You deserve to know everything.'

'Why does it have to be difficult? I like you and you like me. I think you do, anyway,' he murmured, stepping close to her. He pulled her to him and stroked her cheek.

'You know I do,' she confessed, her tone urgent. 'But I've got something to tell you. It's going to sound really strange. But I have to, I think.'

He pressed his finger softly to her lips. 'Tell me later. All I care about is that you like me.'

'I have to tell you, Rav. It's important. Please?' she insisted, fighting the desire to kiss him, to lose herself in him. It would be terribly dangerous, a kiss; the faeries had watched them make love on the beach before. This close to the faerie road, any number of Finn's spies might be watching, or even Finn himself.

'All right.' His lips brushed hers, and Faye felt the heat between them build.

He kissed her. It was a sweet yet rough kiss; his mouth was warm, and her own deep yearning for him responded.

She closed her eyes and surrendered to it, unable to do anything else, despite the danger. His hands pressed into the small of her back; his touch was at once intimate and gentlemanly, and she breathed in his warm, woody smell, remembering how he touched her, how cherished he had always made her feel, how powerful.

The thunder had moved quickly, and the kiss brought on the rain, or so it seemed. The black sky rumbled ominously, and lightning split it like slivers of moonlight. Rav pulled away from the kiss; they both stared up at the storm for a brief moment, startled at its speed, and Faye felt a wave of unease clutch her heart.

'God. Come on, we'll get drenched,' he shouted over the thunder and guided her down the path towards the beach, but the rain came down hard and there was no escaping it.

Faye's gaze flickered to the faerie road alongside Rav's house. There was something odd happening. As she followed him, ducking her head under her arm in a vain attempt to keep off the rain, some of the black clouds had lowered to the path itself, disconnected from the sky, like a stray, angry storm cloud, separated from the rest.

The seawater rose in tall waves and crashed onto the beach, and when Faye looked into the waves, she saw the shapes of horses surging forward, relentless, their glassy black manes driving through the white sea spray. Her breath caught in her mouth. *No.*

She saw the power in their legs, which was the weight that drove the waves forward and rolled underneath them. She knew what the horses were, and why they had come.

Rav started running ahead. He turned back to wave something at her, but she couldn't make it out. He shouted something, but the wind took it away. He pointed to his house. She took it to mean he was going to open up so she could run straight in. She screamed at him, '*No, run, run,*' but he was too far away to hear her over the wind and the crashing waves.

Unlike her, Rav couldn't see the fae or the faerie road. He was completely ignorant of the strangeness ahead of him. And the cloudy blackness was so close to the house that Faye started running after him, a shout growing in her throat, '*No, no, no!*'

Faye watched, aghast, as the black water horses – kelpies – rode out of the sea towards Rav with a white fire in their eyes.

They galloped towards where Rav was standing with his back to the sea, fumbling for his door keys. Their serpent tails powered them along, swishing side to side in the wet sand.

'Rav!' she shouted. '*Rav!* No!'

He hadn't seen them; perhaps he couldn't.

Faye wanted to scream at him to run, run away as fast as he could from the kelpies, but she knew he would never be able to outrun them.

Rav turned around just as a kelpie reared up towards him; its webbed black hoof struck Rav at the side of the head, and he crumpled to the ground. The water horse gripped Rav's arm with its long teeth and swung him onto its back in one lithe, wet motion. Black tethers of some kind lashed him to the horse's back. Sprinting towards him, Faye watched as he struggled but failed to get free.

Faye screamed at the kelpies to free Rav, but they showed no evidence of having heard her. She felt the betrayal slap her in the face; she had ridden a kelpie, she had taken its leathery scale as a token of her communion with it, under the sea. And yet, that meant nothing now. Her hand went to her neck, to the kelpie charm that Moddie had given her, but it was only there in the astral plane, in dreams and in the faerie realm. It couldn't be touched in the human world.

'Rav!' Faye yelled again, panting with the effort of trying to catch up to the kelpie.

The kelpie galloped away, along the faerie road and over the headland. The rain pelted her mercilessly.

'Stop, please stop!' she shouted, trying to run, but no one was listening to her, and the wet sand underfoot grabbed at her, refusing anything other than a fast walk. From the side of the road, tendrils crept out and wound around her ankles; grinning faces appeared on the buds and flowers of plants she could not identify. She shook them off, tearing at their leaves desperately as she tried to run.

By the time Faye had reached the headland and gone on to the gates to the labyrinth, Rav and the kelpie had disappeared.

35

Gasping for breath, she looked expectantly at the same two bearded gnomes that had let her in the first time.

'I need to enter the labyrinth,' she said, her breath ragged. 'My... my friend... has been taken,' she panted.

'She didn't say the magic word, did she?' the gnome on the left said to the one on the right.

'Nope,' said the gnome on the right. He looked up at her expectantly.

'Password,' he said seriously.

'I don't have a password,' Faye snapped. 'I am *sidhe-leth*, half fae. I don't need one. Let me in. I command it!' she said, feeling the now-familiar lassitude of being in Finn's kingdom, but she fought against it and held on to her panic at Rav's abduction into faerie.

'Ooh. She commands us!' The gnome on the left smirked.

'Password,' the other gnome said again. 'Orders from Up High. Even half humans got to give the password or be locked out.'

'Well, I don't know the password!' Faye shouted. 'Just let me in! There must have been some mistake.'

'No need to shout,' said the gnome on the right, looking affronted.

'But... Please.' She knelt down in front of them and looked beseechingly at them both, but they avoided her gaze. 'Please. I'll... I'll see you're richly rewarded.'

Faye had no idea what she was saying or indeed how she would be able to reward anything in the faerie kingdom, but she was desperate. The gnomes conferred between each other and the one on the left pointed to the silver pentagram ring she wore on her right hand; it had been Moddie's.

'We'll have that. Give us that and you can come in,' he said, stroking his beard. 'But you can't tell anyone we let you in. Say it was an accident. You just woke up in the labyrinth. They believe that sometimes.'

'It was my mother's,' Faye appealed to the gnomes.

The gnome on the left pursed his lips. 'We want it, or you don't come in,' he repeated.

'Fine. Yes. Have it!' She pulled the silver ring off with some difficulty – she hadn't taken it off for years – and threw it on the ground between the gnomes.

The gnomes pushed the gates, and they creaked open slowly. Faye barged through. Yet, this time the labyrinth loomed dark in front of her, reaching away into blackness. Faye stopped in her tracks.

'I can't see anything!' She turned to the gnomes, who were shutting the gates behind her; the last shards of the strange golden light of the entry to faerie narrowed to a crack, threatening to plunge her into oblivion. 'Please! Stop!' She ran back, putting her hands in the crack of the gate as it closed, trying to hold them apart. 'I can't see! I need light! Please, I'll be trapped in here!' she cried, but the doors closed and she had to pull her fingers out to avoid them being crushed. Faye heard the gnomes chuckling as the lock turned, and complete quiet and darkness suffocated her.

'No light for traitors, miss,' one of their voices called. 'King's orders.'

Before, the labyrinth had opened to her like a rose; now, it clutched at her with branches and tendrils and refused to let her go.

Faye groped ahead of her in the dark, following only by instinct. Dead silence accompanied her concentration; the only sounds were her jagged breath and occasional cries of frustration as she met one dead end and then another. The stream of faeries that had swarmed around her before, treading on her toes, singing, dancing, rolling and fighting, was gone. It was as though she was alone in the world.

'Help! Please, someone, help me!' she called out, but there was no reply. 'Finn! Finn, I command you to hear me!' she called in vain, but she knew there would be no answer. He had taken Rav, of that she was certain, and abandoned her here to the labyrinth; locked her in like any mortal woman. As a punishment to stop her coming after Rav.

But she was *sidhe-leth*.

If I could come through before, then the only thing stopping me now is Finn, she thought. *So there's no point calling on him for help. He's angry... because Rav kissed me. Jealous.*

Faye stopped running and stood still in the labyrinth, gathering her thoughts and steadying her breathing. There was no point panicking.

She plunged both hands into her pockets while she thought, and her fingers closed around the crystal in her pocket. She brought it out and held it up to her face; it still held a tiny amount of luminescence from the Crystal Castle, but it made little difference to the dark. Yet, she felt it held a power that she could use to help her, if only she knew how. She racked her brain, trying to remember the crystalline singing that seemed to have come from the walls of the seven-pointed faerie castle.

She could remember the words, though she didn't know

what they meant. She began to sing the words softly, and then
louder as she gained confidence. She tried to replicate how it
had sounded.

Tar a thighearna... Tar a thi... She sang the harmony. And, as
she did so, the crystal began to glow, lighting up the dark
labyrinth. The pinkish light filled the pathway, shining into the
overgrown high corners and the mud underfoot.

Faye looked around her; now, at least, she could see where
she was, though she still had no idea where to go. It wasn't going
to be an easy route through this time.

As she took some tentative steps forward, she heard a voice
in the distance.

She listened hard; it was very, very distant.

The voice grew a little louder; still, it was only the volume
of a whisper, and it seemed to be passed leaf to leaf in the dark,
a shushing noise that carried a word.

Faye, Faye, the leaves whispered, circling her like a net.
Faye.

It was Moddie's voice. Faye turned around, trying to find
the source of the whisper. She was *sure* it was her mother's
voice. *Faye. Follow my voice.*

Holding the crystal in front of her for light, she followed
twist after turn, sometimes feeling as though she was walking
uphill, sometimes down. But try as she might, Faye couldn't get
any closer to Moddie's faint call and, all the time, she kicked
away reaching branches and trailing weeds that seemed bent on
tripping her up and holding her back.

She had to keep singing, or the crystal dimmed. *Tar a thighearna... Tar a thi...* she continued, hoping that the crystal
wouldn't fail her.

At the centre of a hedged-in square she found a large silver
bowl of pink roses standing on a golden cube, which reminded
her of the carpet of rose petals that had surrounded the Crystal

Castle. As she stopped to smell them, she looked down and saw the letter M scratched in the dirt by her feet.

Moddie had been here; she was close by. Somehow, she was helping Faye through the maze.

Faye took three of the roses and picked the petals off, scattering them behind her like the breadcrumbs in Hansel and Gretel; she would need to find her way back through the labyrinth, after all.

She followed another twist and another turn and, at the far end of the next pathway, Moddie stood waiting for her, wearing a gown made entirely of rose petals. She held out her hand to her daughter.

'Come on, darling. We don't have much time,' she said, and Faye ran to her, with tears burning her eyes.

36

———

Faye ran through the labyrinth, holding her mother's hand.

'To the castle! We... must... get within the castle gates. We'll be safe there,' Moddie called over her shoulder, and Faye saw that there were tears in her mother's eyes, too.

'I missed you,' Faye called out as they ran, dodging branches and stones along the way.

'The paths are closing!' Moddie shouted, and pulled Faye along faster. 'I missed you, too, my darling.' She stopped briefly and hugged her daughter. 'There's so much I want to tell you, but there's no time. For now, we have to get out of here.'

Faye held the crystal up higher and saw that Moddie was right; the sides of the pathway were drawing together. Some way in front of them she could see the moonlight glinting on the castle in the distance.

'I don't think we're going to make it,' Faye shouted in reply as the tendrils grasped for her more and more aggressively; she tore them away, but they caught her again and again, twisting up her legs and wrapping themselves around her wrists.

Moddie was the same, but different. She had not aged, because there was no ageing in spirit, and in fact she looked younger than she was when she died. And there were other differences, too. Moddie's hand in hers was light and insubstantial and, as they ran, it seemed that Moddie's feet didn't touch the ground.

'We'll make it,' Moddie said. Faye remembered that determined tone. When Moddie wanted something, she usually got it. 'Remember you're half fae. Feel the faerie power as much as you can. You can use it here. Let it fill you.'

Faye focused on the swirling energy of faerie; she called it in, surrendered to it, with as much of herself as she could while running. She felt the power of faerie engulf her, thrill her body, sharpen her senses.

'That's right! More!' Moddie shouted. Faye took in a deeper breath and felt the power unfurl from inside her at the same time it surrounded her; it grew thicker and flowed faster, faster, until she started to lose feeling in her hands and feet. 'I've got you!' Moddie yelled as Faye's feet hovered off the ground like hers did.

The faerie power lit up the labyrinth; the light flashed on the dark hedges, and holes opened up and closed again at random in the walls of the labyrinth. The crystal glowed bright in Faye's hand.

Moddie pulled her towards one of the holes in the hedge, but it was too small for them to fit through.

'Can you make it bigger?' Moddie breathed, glancing around them as the labyrinth continued to tighten. 'When you focus on your fae magic, you can disrupt the illusion of the labyrinth. Can you control it better?'

Faye tried, but she didn't know how. 'Sorry.' She felt like a failure.

But Moddie shook her head impatiently. 'No time for sorry,' she said. 'You'll learn to use it here in time. But for now, we need something else. I can't get us through this on my own. He's too strong for me.'

'Finn?' A part of Faye somehow still hoped that it wasn't her lover doing this; that there was another presence scheming against her.

'Faerie kings are jealous, Faye,' Moddie chided. 'But it's my fault. I could have taught you about your true self, about your father, about faerie, but I wanted to protect you.' Moddie wrapped Faye in a hug and Faye felt the comfort of her mother's body envelop her. 'I'm sorry, Faye. I'm so sorry,' Moddie had started to cry, and grief welled up in Faye at the sound of the sadness in her mother's voice.

She gulped away tears; she had missed Moddie so much that it hurt to see her again now. It was an ache she had become accustomed to forgetting; seeing Moddie renewed the pain of her loss.

'I've missed you so much,' Faye started to cry. It was all too much; she was so tired from fighting Finn, from feeling ill after being in Murias, from worrying about keeping herself and Rav safe, all of it. She wished that she had never cast the love spell. She wished her mother was still alive. Nothing was as she wanted it to be.

'I know, my darling. I know.' Moddie hugged her tight and kissed her forehead. 'We can talk. But we need to get out of the labyrinth first. Okay?'

'Okay.' Faye wiped her eyes and kicked a vine that was trying to snake its way up her leg. 'Hurry! Can you magic us out of here? I know that Levantiana taught you the faerie magic.'

'I can try. What do you know of the faerie magic?' Moddie asked, out of breath.

'I've been learning magic with Levantiana. So that I can come and go freely in Murias without being so... bound to Finn. So I can protect myself.'

'With Levantiana? How?' Moddie spun to face her daughter, panic in her voice.

'The same as you. I made a bargain. On account of being Lyr's daughter.'

Moddie caught her shoulders. 'What? No, Faye. You can't... Making a bargain with the fae is dangerous. You shouldn't have done that. No. No, no, Faye... Please tell me that's not true,' Moddie cried. 'Please. You don't understand how dangerous that is.'

'You did it,' Faye argued.

'I was dead already. I had less to lose,' Moddie answered. 'And I did it to protect you.'

'I didn't know that. You should have told me.' Faye felt a terrible ache in her chest. Dread. Regret. Pain.

'I couldn't. I wasn't allowed to communicate with you. That was one of Levantiana's conditions for teaching me,' Moddie shouted, pulling Faye through the hole in the hedge, which was finally big enough.

'What was the bargain you made?' Moddie yanked Faye through, but the labyrinth tried to stop them, wrapping vines around their legs. Faye kicked them off again.

'Come on. We have to keep moving. There's no time to talk about it now. I offered myself as a weapon of some kind against him, in this war they're having.'

They edged their way down a narrow pathway. Faye felt a wave of oppression wash over her and she tried to take a deep, calming breath, but the denseness of the hedges reaching in choked her.

'No, Faye! You must not...' But Moddie didn't finish her sentence. Something in the hedge reached out, as if it had arms this time, and dragged Moddie back into it. She screamed and tore at the vegetation, but in seconds it had covered her body. Faye rushed to her mother and started tearing the leaves away, but it was replaced with twice as much.

'Mum!' she cried out, trying to focus her magic again to stop the vines.

'Faye. You don't understand, about your father. I—'

'He tried to kill you. I don't care what happens to him!' Faye cried.

Grief twisted Moddie's features. 'No, Faye. That's not true... I—' Moddie choked and spat out the leaves snaking into her mouth.

'You said it. I was eight, I came down that time, you were drinking with that woman from the coven. You said he almost killed you.'

Moddie shook her head, confused. 'No. Faye... he didn't. That's not what I meant.' She coughed again. 'There's no time to explain, but you're wrong. Levantiana... did you visit the Crystal Castle?'

'Yes.' Faye felt branches pull at her clothes, vines wrap around her leg. She felt them circle her left wrist; she pulled away, but they were too strong. Desperately, she stripped vegetation away from Moddie with her right hand. If Moddie didn't mean that her father, Lyr, had tried to kill her, what did she mean? It was so long ago, and Faye had been just a child. What had Moddie's *exact words* been? Whatever this meant, she couldn't think about it now.

'Did you bring back any of the rose petals? From Morgana's castle?' Moddie retched as the hedge reached the back of her throat. Faye nodded, horrified. 'Cast one on the ground. Hurry!' Moddie coughed as the vine disappeared into her mouth.

A leaf brushed Faye's own mouth; she suppressed a scream and reached into her pocket with her right hand, drawing out the black kelpie's scale which she had folded in half like a purse. Its tough, leathery hide had kept the three petals safe.

The plants had both of her legs now and would twist into her mouth the next time she opened it, she knew. They would reach down inside her gullet, like they had with Moddie, spreading new roots inside her lungs and stomach, assimilating her into the labyrinth. She had a sudden vision of herself with leaves and stems sprouting from the corner of her eyes, pulling her eyelids open in an expression of permanent horror as they wove her flesh back into the verdant green.

Faye took out one of the rose petals and threw it into the ground between them. At the same time, Moddie shouted, '*Tar a thighearna... Tar a thi!*'

A scream cut through the air. Faye's last vision, bathed in the light of the glowing crystal, was her mother's face, contorted with pain.

37

When Faye opened her eyes, she was standing behind a pillar in the great hall and the faerie ball was in full swing. She was alone.

She slumped behind the stone and wept, her tears sudden and bitter. To have her mother back so suddenly, after all this time, and have her taken away again so cruelly was like a nightmare, a stab into a heart that had managed to order its grief so that it no longer consumed her. She sobbed like a child, hugging her knees, wanting Moddie back. She had so many questions for her. She whispered her mother's name between her tears, hoping to summon her, but the cacophony of dancers continued behind her, and Moddie did not come.

Faye peered out from behind the pillar at the whirling dancers. Around and around they went, faster and faster, while the pipers and fiddlers played their jig. Faye was reminded of the fairy tale of the red shoes; of the mysterious dancer who would give her shoes to innocent girls but, once the shoes were on, they could never be taken off and would dance the wearer to death. This dance was underpinned with a similar strange kind of desperation. Faye saw more clearly now that many of the dancers were human, but emaciated, being pulled around unconscious like dolls, danced to the point of exhaustion.

She hadn't noticed before, when she was in the dance. Because she had been with Finn, and Finn's glamour masked the things he didn't want her to see. She closed her eyes as a vision of Moddie's face covered in vines struck her like a sword. Was Moddie alive? Was she stuck there in the labyrinth forever, as part of Finn's punishment for helping her daughter? She was in spirit already, and yet the hedge had held her fast. But nothing was as it seemed in Murias. It was a place of illusion, woven with terror and desire in equal measure.

A knot of dancers reeled dangerously close to the pillar; the faeries among them screeched with the wild joy of the dance. Faye closed her eyes and held her breath. If she was seen, she knew she would either be cast out of Murias, or punished in another way.

The dance was slowing. Faye watched Finn Beatha enter the ballroom with Rav in front of him on a leash: Rav was being made to crawl on all fours. He had been stripped naked. Faye gasped in terror as she saw livid weals across Rav's wide, muscular back. He had been beaten.

Rav cried out with pain; his hands and knees were bloody. Finn merely snarled and shoved him forward.

Horror filled her as she watched Rav being treated like an animal at Finn's hands.

The faerie dance slowed to stare at Rav. Faye could feel the rage reverberating from his vast, bloody muscled back; his corded neck was tensed, as if he was ready to spring up and rip Finn's throat out at any minute.

She wanted to go to him, help him, but she knew she couldn't.

Finn strode into the centre of the dance, pulling Rav behind him on the leash. The music stopped; the dancers halted. There was an expectant hush. Now that the dancers had stopped moving, some emaciated human bodies fell to the floor and no one made any move to pick them up. Faye felt bile rise in her throat. Disgust overcame her.

'Be blessed, faeries of the dance, for you have a new dancer!' Finn cried, and the crowd cheered, though Faye could hear forced jollity in the throng. 'This foolish human sought to take my property from me. Perhaps you will all deign to teach him some manners!'

There was a loud cry of approval from the crowd. Faye shivered.

'Use him to slake your deepest desires, my sweet ones,' Finn went on, a terrible fire in his eyes.

The ballroom was darker and more shadowed than Faye remembered, the walls of the castle more soot-blackened. The gold and silver lamps that had glowed so merrily were dirty, the glass smokily opaque; now they cast only a dim, dull orange light. The hammered gold bowls of candlelit water were dark; no light reflected off their surfaces.

Finn pulled Rav onto his feet and pushed him roughly into the centre of the dance. He motioned to the band to start playing.

'Dance, dance!' he cried out as the crowd started its mad whirling once again. 'For you will never stop; the faerie reel is the power of the Kingdom of Murias! Were it to stop, our lights would go out. Our power would dim. So, dance! Faeries and mortals, dance and be merry. For the love of your king!' Finn clapped and danced through the crowd.

Faye's heart beat fast in her panic. She had to get away, and take Rav with her. But how?

The music grew louder. Faye put her hand in her pocket distractedly, feeling the leathery kelpie's scale. She watched as Finn made his way through the crowd, kissing faeries, picking them up, spinning them around and putting them down again with a smile. Faye watched in disgust as the pretty young fae blushed and giggled at whatever he said, and how they watched him as he danced away from them, to the edge of the circle. Finn's power still drew her to him. But she gripped Moddie's charm around her neck, and it protected her.

Then Faye's mouth gaped open when she realised what Finn had meant, and what the fae denizens were doing to him.

Rav had been picked up by a group of troll-like fae and held aloft, like a prize. He bucked and kicked, roaring in displeasure and anger, but they were too strong and too many for him. Naked, his blood-soaked broad back flexed and his tree-trunk biceps flailed as he fought back.

The trolls took him to one of the golden pillars that stretched from the ballroom to the high, vaulted ceiling and, in a cruel reference to Faye's dream of Grainne Morgan, they lashed him to it, both hands above his head and his ankles tied tight.

Then, they began taunting him. Stroking his skin. Kissing him. Taking his large, thick cock in their mouths and sucking and licking it, laughing when he, despite the terror that he must have felt, started to become aroused. Then they would repeat the process, humiliating him, though he never cowered, never looked ashamed, only fierce and angry. Faye watched in horror as two tall, beautiful, black-haired fae women approached Rav, holding long whips. 'No,' she whispered, knowing what they were going to do, but unable to stop it.

Taking turns, they began to rain blows onto Rav's chest, thighs and abdomen. He bellowed in pain; Faye winced and looked away, but not before she saw another fae approach Rav. She was coldly beautiful, in a white ballgown, with hair like ice, and black, soulless eyes. At her touch, he groaned and became suddenly hard and erect; leaning forward to murmur something to him, the fae wrapped the tentacles that she possessed instead of legs around him – appearing from under her ballgown like the slow reveal of a nightmare – and took him into her, as her black-haired fae sisters whooped and laughed.

She had to get him away from here.

Faye waited for a swell of dancers at the edge of the circle to reach where she was hiding, and stepped into the dance just as Finn stepped out of it. The pace had quickened already; the pipers were playing at full speed, and Faye felt out of breath almost immediately.

The shapes and beings passing her were so fast at times that they were only a blur, but sometimes the crowd slowed, seeming to take a temporary breath before it swung around again. In those moments, skeletal faces leered at her and strange faeries with cavernous bodies and upside-down heads and feet that were laced with bulbous veins, or, worse, covered in blood, pressed against her.

The dance swung her around and around, closer to where Finn stood, surveying the dancers with a critical eye. Faye craned her neck to catch sight of Rav; she could see flashes of his black hair through the faeries who spun like dervishes, and she could hear his voice calling out for help. *Just stay there*, she willed him. *Don't do anything. I'm coming to get you.*

But she was being pushed closer and closer to Finn, and Faye couldn't fight against the tide.

Don't look this way, she silently begged. A few more moments and Finn would see her; he'd know that she had broken through the labyrinth, despite his best efforts to keep her out.

Carefully, she reached into her pocket and took out one of the rose petals.

Faye caught another glimpse of Rav and shouted his name, but the music was too loud. *Please see me*, she willed him, but she feared that Rav was too far lost. She could see that a nixie was laughing, pulling at Rav's hair; on his other side, a bare-breasted faerie with beautiful blue wings and violet hair floated in front of him, laughing when Rav pulled away as she tried to kiss him. He was covered in blood, and his eyes were wild with fear and anger.

She could no longer see Finn at all.

Now, Faye said to herself. She thrust her hand up into the air and launched the petal as hard as she could, expecting it to float down to the floor. And as she let the petal go, she shouted the words Moddie had, just moments before in the labyrinth, hoping for the best. '*Tar a thighearna... Tar a thi!*'

The rose petal floated upwards, growing in size.

The music continued and the dance spun Faye around, but the petal spread wider and wider above them until it covered the whole dance, hanging above their heads like a silk barrage balloon. Some of the faeries stopped and looked up, but most were too lost in the dance, and the ones who had stopped were in danger of being trampled.

'*Tar a thighearna... Tar a thi!*' Faye shouted again, and the petal split into a million pieces, falling onto the dancers like rain.

The dance stopped, and every single faerie was frozen to the spot. Only the humans left among them moved; some cried out, but most of them slumped to the ground in exhaustion, their faerie captors no longer whirling them around. One girl, trapped in the frozen arms of her toad-faerie suitor, screamed to be let go, but the toad's legs grasped at her greedily even under the enchantment.

At the other side of the hall Faye saw Finn, rooted to the spot, his gaze trained on her. She halted in fear for a moment, heart beating wildly. Finn's eyes watched her keenly, but he didn't move. *He can see. He knows I'm here.* She had betrayed and disobeyed him, and his eyes burned with fury.

I have made my choice, she thought, and met his gaze. The fury in his eyes was far from the adoration he had shown her before, and it awoke her like a sharp slap. She didn't love Finn; now that she could see him without being under his control, she knew it was not love. It had never been love, and he did not love her. Finn Beatha did not love anyone; he took who and what he wanted and used them until they had nothing left to give.

Faye pushed through the inert bodies, through the strange, gnarled limbs and the ripped wings, to Rav, who was still lashed to the pillar. Pain was written across his face; the skin on his knees was ripped to shreds from crawling on the jagged floors, and blood dripped from his many wounds.

'Rav. Hang on,' she cried.

His eyes widened in disbelief. 'Faye? You're here? How?' he stammered. The sheen of faerie was in his eyes; his pupils were dilated and sweat was pouring off him. Faye could feel Finn's stare burning her back.

'Never mind. I'm going to get you home,' she said, and began undoing his binds.

With Rav leaning on her, they staggered through the ballroom, edging past rigidly still yellow-skinned goblins, diminutive flower faeries and beast-like creatures for which Faye had no name. She turned her eyes away from the humans that lay here and there, bodies that had slowly had the life trampled from them.

They passed a girl who was still alive; her skin was sunken, barely even covering her bones. Too weak to raise an arm, she made a pleading noise as they stumbled past.

'We can't leave them like this.' Faye stopped and held out a hand for the girl; the change in her stance tripped Rav, who stumbled and steadied himself on a pillar. Faye crouched close to the girl, cradling her head on her lap. Faye couldn't carry her as well as support Rav, and the girl was so frail, so thin, that Faye felt she would break if she tried to move her.

'What can I do?' she asked the girl softly, her heart breaking. She felt a rush of anger at Finn. *How could he do this?* And then she was angry at herself, too. For not seeing. Her feet might have trampled this girl as she danced with Finn, heedless of the horrors that lined the great hall. She had been seduced. She had been stupid and powerless. *No more*, she vowed to herself angrily.

'Kill me,' the girl whispered, her voice a rasp of desperation. 'Please.'

'No! I can't leave you here. I'll find a way. Just stay with me, all right?' The girl's eyes fluttered closed; she was barely conscious. 'Stay with me! Come on,' Faye cried, but the girl whispered something; Faye had to put her ear to the girl's lips to make it out.

'It's too late,' she said. 'This is...' The girl coughed and Faye reached for her hand and held it, feeling powerless, hopeless. 'I stayed longer than I should...'

The girl coughed again, and Faye knew she was already too far away.

'I'll stay with you, then,' Faye said, but she could see some of the faeries beginning to break free of the magic she had cast. There were too many of them to be held off for long.

Faye remembered Grandmother telling her: *The fae have their own ways, and it's not for us to judge.* The rules said *Morality does not exist in the faerie realms. Tread carefully there.*

But it was impossible not to judge Murias as she looked around at the twisted and injured human bodies. *I am part of this. I am half faerie*, she thought, and she felt a terrifying guilt consume her. She hadn't brought any of these men and women here, and she hadn't tortured them. Yet, the faerie blood beat in her veins, and she knew what it felt like to revel in the seductive cloak of magic. That made her an accomplice to their suffering.

Rav coughed and Faye looked up; he was pale, and she knew he needed her.

'Leave me,' the girl repeated. 'There's nothing you can do.'

Faye still had the bag of herbs she had gathered at the coast slung across her body. She opened it and rummaged around, watching warily as the faeries started to move slowly.

'I'm sorry,' she said, getting up and placing the girl back on the floor as carefully as she could. She opened the girl's mouth and placed a few flowers onto her tongue.

'Swallow this. It will... ease your journey,' she said, feeling the tears roll down her cheeks.

'Faye...' Rav cried out in pain, and she turned away from the girl, her heart hollow.

'Where are you going?' The imperious voice filled the long hall, and Faye froze.

38

____

'You seem to have a human man with you, *sidhe-leth*.' The voice laughed lightly, and the echo resonated in the quiet. 'That stunt in the ballroom – it seems you have learned the faerie magic all too well.'

Levantiana stepped forward from a dark doorway and dropped her cowled hood. She was wearing a dark blue robe which covered her almost entirely.

'Your brother kidnapped this man and brought him here as a punishment. If he wishes to punish me for supposedly being unfaithful to him, then I will stand his punishment. But Rav is blameless,' she argued.

Levantiana arched a dark eyebrow. 'What makes you think I will let you go? What makes you dare to ask me to ignore my brother's wishes?' she intoned, and Faye felt the ice in her voice fill the hallway; the temperature dropped and Faye was sure she could see icicles forming at the edge of the windows, the glass frosting with an iridescent blue-white covering. Nevertheless, she refused to drop the faerie queen's gaze.

'You thought that because I have taught you, that I have begun to show you the ways of the faerie realm of water, that I am your friend,' she answered crisply. 'Do not make that mistake. I am not.'

'No, but—'

'My brother brought this one here for his own reasons. He will stay here until my brother sees fit to let him go.'

'Since when do you let your brother rule you?' Faye faced Levantiana, who returned her gaze steadily.

'I do not expect him to find fault in my actions, and so I do not criticise his,' Levantiana replied.

'We made a bargain. I am your weapon against Lyr, when you need it,' Faye countered, panicking now. And she was aware that they only had moments before her spell released all the faeries, and they would be caught.

Rav watched the exchange between them with hollow eyes. Faye could see that his ability to fight Finn's power was weakening. He was as strong as an ox, which was how he had made it this far, but Finn was the king of the realm.

'I do not see Lyr anywhere? And I have taught you magic in return. Our bargain is intact.' Levantiana glared at Faye.

'Please.' Faye could hear movement in the great hall. 'I'll do anything. But I have to get Rav home.'

Levantiana looked away and pursed her lips. 'You love this man?'

'I care for him, and I don't want him to be tortured by Finn for something that isn't his fault.' Faye looked down the hall, at shadows flickering wildly in the dim light.

'If you have a great passion for this mortal man, then I do not hear it in your voice,' the faerie queen sneered. She nodded to Rav, who was struggling to stand up.

'Faye. Let's get out of here,' Rav mumbled. 'Please.'

'So you see, Faye Morgan, you have nothing left to bargain with, and I will not allow you to leave. Unless...' Levantiana looked appraisingly at Faye and held out her hand. 'There might be something. But you will not like it.'

Faye's could hear the distant pounding of feet. Someone was coming.

'If this is the only way, then I'll do what has to be done,' Faye answered grimly. 'Will you help us get home? If I agree to your bargain?'

'Of course.' Levantiana's smile twinkled brightly.

'What is it? What do you want in return?' Faye took Levantiana's hand, and the queen waved her other hand at the approaching soldiers; they slowed as if they were running in syrup.

'Something you can make, but I cannot. A child.'

Faye frowned in disbelief. 'A child?' she repeated. 'What? No! That's... inhuman.'

Levantiana laughed. 'I am not human,' she agreed.

'Why... a child?' Faye stammered.

'I have my reasons.' Levantiana regarded Faye impassively. 'Or, I can wave my hand, and they will take you. And they will put you and your lover in the darkest place in this castle and leave you to rot there. It is your choice.' She smiled icily. 'And believe me, *sidhe-leth*, the dungeons here are filled with horrors you cannot comprehend.'

'That is no choice!' Faye cried. 'Please don't ask this of me.'

'Another plea. You humans are full of wants, and yet when your pleas are answered, you do not like the solutions,' Levantiana snapped. 'You are human. You can have other babies; as many as you wish. You will not miss one. And I assure you that it will be well taken care of. It will live as a prince or princess of Murias.' There was no compassion in Levantiana's eyes; no understanding that a baby was anything other than a possession or a pet. 'Choose. Quickly.'

I managed to get Rav away from Finn, Faye reasoned. *So I can make this right, too. For now, I can agree to the pact. I don't have to do it.*

'All right. I agree to your pact,' she said. 'Now. Get us out of here.'

Levantiana smiled. 'You will have to leave a different way than you came in,' she called over her shoulder as she hurried along, pulling her cloak around her. 'He is watching the labyrinth.' She stopped suddenly and opened a golden door in the wall where none had been before.

'Through. Quickly,' she chided. Faye helped Rav over the step of the golden door, and out onto the narrow crystal walkway to the Crystal Castle. He stumbled but managed to stay upright.

'Are you going to be okay?' Faye asked him in a low voice. He nodded.

'I can do it. Let's just go as fast as we can,' he replied, his mouth set in a grim line of pain.

Levantiana raised her arms over her head and called out something in the language of faerie.

There was a ripple on top of the blue-black water, and the head of the black kelpie Faye had only half believed was real emerged from the water. Though she had ridden it successfully once before, now the creature terrified Faye. It had taken Rav from her; it had been Finn's creature as easily as it had been hers.

'Now. There is no time,' Levantiana reprimanded. 'Do not be afraid. It will do as I command.' Full of misgiving, but knowing she had no other option, Faye climbed on the kelpie's back and pulled Rav on with her.

'Put the kelpie scale over the man's nose and mouth,' Levantiana called up to Faye. 'It will enable him to breathe underwater.'

'What about me?' Faye shouted down from the kelpie's back; it was rising up out of the water, readying to dive down into the blackness again.

'Don't worry, *sidhe-leth*,' Levantiana replied, unsmiling. 'You will breathe without it. You did before.'

39

The last of the midsummer sun caressed the stage, casting its twilight warmth onto the audience. Some in the crowd held up their palms to the shafts of twinkling softness that spread over their heads like a spell, stroking their fingers through its sparkle. They were chanting, waiting for the headlining band to come on stage: *Dal Riada, Dal Riada...*

Finn Beatha strode onto the stage, stripped to the waist; his swirling tattoos and the symbols on his warm honey skin were painted over with blue paint, like woad on Scottish warriors going into battle. The side of his face he wore his radio mic on was painted in the same blue, from forehead to chin; on the other side, the audience close to the stage could see a fierce twist to his mouth. Yet, as he bowed to them, the last rays of the setting sun landed on his dark blonde hair, giving him an almost angelic aura.

The first ten rows closest to the stage erupted in a kind of madness: screaming, crying, reaching out for him. Several women sat atop their friends' shoulders. One tore off her T-shirt immediately and threw it at the stage, exposing her bare breasts. He took the shirt from the stage, straightened up, smiled at her and stroked the shirt over his chest, then threw it back. Two young men, probably in their early twenties, also sat on their friends' shoulders; *WE LOVE YOU FINN* was painted across from one's chest to the other. Finn blew them kisses which they grabbed excitedly from the air.

'Abercolme. Finally, we meet!' Finn drawled as the rest of the band took their places alongside him. The crowd roared. 'We've waited so long to be here. And what finer evening to watch the sun set over the sea than at Midsummer?'

He walked from one side of the stage to the other, cupping his hands in front of his face, blowing something from them into the crowd. You had to be very close to see the glitter on his hands; the front row reached out for it.

'Blessings of faerie be upon you all!' Finn cried out, and the crowd laughed and cheered as the first fast riff began, and the music of Dal Riada reached out for them.

Aisha stood in the wings of the stage, her heart in her eyes. This was what she'd been waiting for, what would make all the spreadsheets and phone calls and social media promotion worthwhile. This close, she could see the gold glitter and the braids in Finn Beatha's hair. She could hear his sweet, rough voice in the second before the mic picked it up, sense the easy strength in his languid pose; this close, he was wild, raw, other-worldly.

As she watched Dal Riada spin, scream and weave their first song for the crowd, Aisha felt the same hypnotic pull she always did when listening to them. It was like finding the lull between sleep and dream. The familiar songs made images in her mind; of long, twisting paths through a forest, of gilded corridors, of a dance that went around and around without ever stopping. She closed her eyes and let the fast melody enchant her body. She was dancing now, spiralling deeper and deeper.

She felt her breasts swell, a strange sensation of them being full and aching for release; as she danced, she opened her eyes and watched Finn, imagining kissing him and touching his warm skin. Her body filled with a deeper sweetness; she remembered every moment of making love to him, taking him inside her. It had been unlike anything else she had ever known. She knew it was different than anything she could expect from a mortal man.

Aisha was impatient with the dreams where he came and spoke to her and filled her with unresolved desire, but also came with messages and requests; things he needed her to do for him in the ordinary world. He had promised and promised: a world beyond this one, where she could merge herself into the fabric of all being. He would show her life at the atomic level. He had spoken to her in the terms she understood, had taken the fascination of her scientific work and woven it into the seductive treasure of his faerie domain. If only she would help him, just a little, here and there...

At first, she had connected to Finn through his music. At the concert, before she had taken Faye outside, she too had been transported to a strange place: a room with a golden four-poster bed, a room hung with blue and green tapestries adorned with strange symbols. Finn Beatha had taken her hand and pulled her onto the bed without any preamble; she was naked, suddenly, and he was kissing her. He stroked her thigh, and she had wanted more, oh, so much more, when Faye had jolted her away from her reverie.

The next night, in a dream, he had told Aisha to take down the hagstone charm that Faye kept hanging by the shop door so that he could enter. He had not told her why. She hadn't asked.

He had made love to Aisha a week later on the sheepskin rug in front of the hearth, inside the shop, in the middle of the day; she had locked the door behind him, but had not even thought of being seen through the long windows of the shop. He filled her with an unruly, wild lust that made her not herself; she wasn't Aisha when his fingertips grazed her nipples and she cried out for more; she wasn't herself when he kissed her neck; when he made her strip naked and stand in front of him. She didn't think twice about obeying him when he commanded her to touch herself as he watched and then, when she was almost at climax, her belly hot and sweet, made her kneel on all fours. It didn't escape her that this was the same rug she had, not long ago, sat on while she, Faye and Annie had conjured their love spell. And when he entered her, kneeling behind her, she had welcomed the deep pressure of him bringing her pleasure closer and closer until she ground against him, crying out, and he held her waist and gripped her breasts as he climaxed.

Soon they would be together for ever. He would make her his queen. He had whispered to her in her increasingly hot and fervid dreams, *Midsummer, Midsummer, Midsummer delight; come to the faeries on Midsummer night.* Something big was going to happen tonight. She had done what he asked her in the dreams. She was his faithful lover. She knew her reward was coming, and she ached for its sweetness.

At that moment, Finn Beatha looked directly at her and smiled.

40

———

'Don't go.' Rav reached out for her as she eased him into her bed. 'Please, Faye. I don't trust Finn.'

'It's okay. I'll be all right.' She pulled her old patchwork quilt over him and handed him a herbal tea – a sedative. Valerian and hops would make him sleep, and sleep was what he needed right now. In the distance, she could hear the thump and roar of the festival like a storm off the horizon.

She sat on the edge of the bed and held his hand, waiting for the tea to take effect. They had been back for a day, but Faye couldn't leave it any longer.

'I have to go. I have to face him alone.'

'I should come with you. You can't go alone. He's too powerful.' Rav flinched as he moved in bed, trying to get comfortable. Faye had cleaned the cuts on his back as best she could, but some of them were deep. Rav's knees were a mess and his hands were covered in cuts and bruises. She also suspected that he had broken some ribs.

'Just sleep,' she whispered, and put her other hand on his brow. Rav frowned. 'This is between me and Finn,' she added.

She had walked him back to her house rather than take him

anywhere close to his; that close to the faerie road felt like a risk: would Finn take him again? Levantiana had helped them escape, but Finn had seen them in the ballroom.

Faye felt a stab of grief for Moddie, but she pushed it to one side in her heart. Moddie had died, and was still dead. Whether she remained in Murias in spirit or whether Finn would leave her imprisoned in the labyrinth, Faye couldn't guess. She resolved to return to free Moddie; she shivered as she remembered the leaves snaking down her mother's throat.

Rav's breathing fell into a deep rhythm, and she gently released her hand from his, waiting a few more minutes to make sure he was really knocked out. She looked out of the window to see the sun setting over the ocean, making the island off the shore a brooding silhouette.

She had saved Rav, but had agreed to an infernal bargain in the process; it was exactly like the old stories. *At Midwinter one of the faerie kingdoms of Murias, Falias, Gorias or Finias takes a child, and at Midsummer, a willing woman. The child must be under a year old, so that it can be raised in the Crystal Castle with no memory of its mortal parents, and the woman must be fair, and willing to join the faerie dance for evermore. In thanks, the faerie king and faerie queen will bless the land and grant boons to the villagers of Abercolme for their generous offerings.*

Thinking about it now, Faye shuddered. She had never thought much about having a child herself, but, if she did, she would be damned before she gave it up to live in Murias. Rav started to snore. Faye got up quietly and pulled her coat on properly, then padded downstairs in her socks. She would find a way out of the bargain with Levantiana when the time came; the important thing was that she had saved Rav from a terrible fate.

Downstairs in the shop, the last of the day's light glanced through the plate-glass windows; it was late, past nine, but this was the longest day of the year, after all. Midsummer.

She had to confront Finn. There was a reason Dal Riada were performing at Abercolme Rocks; Finn wasn't just there for the adulation, she was sure. Midsummer was the time the faeries abducted women, to nurse their faerie babies or to live as human lovers, never to return.

Was this what Finn had in mind? Before, she would have dismissed the idea. But now, it seemed all too real. The men and women who lay unconscious on the floor of the great hall, imprisoned in Murias, had come from somewhere. And Faye had experienced Dal Riada's own special brand of enchantment for herself.

She looked around her at the shelves and then behind the counter, at the neatly labelled glass jars Moddie had arranged and which Faye refilled as faithfully as her mother had. What could help her? What would count as strong enough magic against a faerie king who was able to entrance whole rooms of people with his enchantments? A faerie king who made her forget everything except him and the deep desire that thrummed in every part of her body when he was near?

If she was to stop him, Faye had to resist his power.

Moddie had given her the charm, but she needed something more.

She stared at the jars, feeling the pulse of the music in the ground under her feet, pulling her to the abandoned castle. *Not yet, not yet, I'm not ready*, she thought, trying to push against Finn's call, but her faerie blood was responding to his demand. She could feel that familiar lassitude begin to cover her; instinctively, her hands went to her throat, feeling the seductive ghost of the opals against her skin.

'No, no, NO!' she shouted aloud. Moddie had taught her, when she was older and could understand more about magic, sometimes the best way to banish energy was to just shout at it to *go away* or *be gone*, as loudly and definitely as you could. Whatever spell Finn was casting right now – and she had no doubt that he was – he wasn't going to weave her into it as neatly as he had before. She was a different woman now; she had used the faerie magic, or, at least, some of it. She had connected to her ancestors, been given their gifts and their powers. And, she could summon the power of water at will.

Her gaze alighted on the protective charm that hung over the door: a piece of string onto which were tied nine hagstones – pebbles with naturally occurring holes through them. Both the charm and the bells that hung next to it and jangled every time someone came in kept bad intentions and bad doings away, Grandmother said. And, if you looked through the holes, you could see faeries and see through faerie enchantments. Faye unhooked it and took it down gently, putting it in her pocket. It felt wrong leaving the shop and Rav unguarded and taking the charm with her, but her instinct told her that this was the right thing to do, and Faye found that it was usually best to obey her instincts, especially when it came to magic.

Last, she took the wand. That seemed the most powerful of the tools at hand.

She locked the door behind her and set off down the street. The village was deserted; everyone was at the concert, which meant that everyone in Abercolme was currently under Finn Beatha's spell. She quickened her steps and broke into a run as the thump of the music grew louder and more insistent, as the sun set over the ocean, covering Abercolme in darkness.

41

Faye could hear Finn's voice over the PA system as she panted her way through the gates and showed her ticket. He was singing in that strange, otherworldly way he had, and a chill ran up her spine.

'Bit late, miss.' The older man on the gate nodded her through. 'They're almost finished for the night. You'd better hurry.'

'I will,' she gasped, and ran through the field where a number of food and drink stalls were packing up. Some people were chatting at the makeshift bar, and the occasional person too worse for wear was strewn on the grass. But almost everyone was watching Dal Riada.

She was right at the back of the crowd, but there were large screens either side of the stage showing the action on stage. As she looked over the shoulders of thousands of people in front of her, both screens focused in on Finn's face as he held the last note for a long moment. It was jarring to look at him; at the face she knew so well, at the high cheekbones she'd kissed, at the full lips she had bitten gently, had tasted so often. She felt a wave of fear; it was terrifying, how he had been able to seduce her. At the same moment, he opened his eyes and smiled into the camera that fed the screens, and right at her.

It was just a moment, one second, but she knew she had been seen. There was a flicker of displeasure in his eyes.

'Thank you, Abercolme!' he shouted, and bowed at the waist. The rest of the band came to the front of the stage amidst deafening cheering and clapping. The crowd were beside themselves, in the same kind of hypnotised delirium she'd been in that first time, at the bar in Edinburgh.

She looked at the faces of the people standing around her, lit by the fluorescent plastic bangles and necklaces they wore. Some of their faces were painted with rainbows and flowers, some wore glittery faerie wings that picked up the firelight from six tall iron cages that were packed with burning hay. The strange half-light gave them all a wild look she recognised all too well from the faerie ball. They were enchanted, and Finn Beatha had them right where he wanted them.

The band filed off the stage, but the stage lights stayed down, and the crowd started to cheer for an encore. Faye started to push through the crowd. She had to get to the stage and stop Finn.

'More! More!' the crowd were screaming at the stage.

The gap Faye was following closed in front of her just like the labyrinth had, and she was hemmed in by a group of drunk girls – or, at least, they seemed drunk – who wouldn't let her through.

'Eh, stop pushing!' One pushed her back, and her friend shot her an evil, possessive look. 'Get back. We were here first.'

Faye looked around, but she couldn't see a way through. She was starting to panic when she saw Aisha walk onto the stage. Aisha was here! Yes. Of course, she had been so excited about the concert – Rav must have given her a backstage pass. If she could get her friend's attention, Aisha would help her. But

Aisha was on stage, and Faye was still rows away from being able to make herself heard over the chaos.

Faye made her way to the side of the crowd and gestured to a St John Ambulance man, who frowned at her but came over, anyway.

'What is it? Concert's nearly over. If you want the ladies' room, I can't let you through this way.'

'No, I... It's not that. I need to talk to my friend. On stage. It's urgent,' Faye replied as politely as she could, but her heart was pounding with urgency.

'Sorry, love. No can do.' He smiled at her.

'Please. It's that girl I want to speak to. With the dark hair, up there?' Faye pointed to the stage. 'Please, it's urgent. She knows me.'

'Can't it wait, sweetheart? There's still the encore – ten minutes and they'll be finished, this lot. Not that it's my cup of tea.'

'No, really. I need to speak with her now.' Faye gripped the hagstone charm in her pocket. 'Please. It's a matter of life and death.' It wasn't necessarily a lie, she told herself, although she felt like she was being overly dramatic. Still, her instinct was shouting that something terrible was about to happen, and she had to stop it.

The man sighed. 'Ah, all right. But don't tell your friends or they'll all want to get through.' He unhooked the security rope and let her through. 'I've got to search ye, I'm afraid.'

'Fine.' Faye opened her coat and turned out her pockets; the man took the sage bundle from her and sniffed it, then gave it back. 'Going to make some stuffing later, are ye?' He grinned, then frowned at the hagstone charm. 'What's this?'

'Oh, it's... a necklace,' Faye lied.

The man scratched his beard and held up the stones on their ribbon to his eyes. 'It isn't a necklace, sweetheart. These are hagstones.' He met her eyes and stared into them for a long moment, then handed the charm back to her.

'I can go?' she asked, her eyes darting to the stage. The band were coming back on stage; she could hear the guitarist adjusting the tuning on his guitar before they started playing again.

'Aye. Right you are.' He pointed along a walkway that was delineated by traffic cones along the grass. 'That way should take you to the cabins, and the side of the stage.'

'Oh. Thank you!' Faye tried not to show her surprise, but the man nodded.

'I didn't recognise ye at first. You're Modron Morgan's daughter, aye?'

'That's right.' Faye didn't think she knew the man, but he smiled at her again.

'Fine woman, she was. I know better than to disrespect Moddie's kin. Not least anyone who carries those.' He pointed at the hagstones, which Faye returned to her pocket.

'Thank you.' She smiled this time, and pressed his hand. He blushed.

'Get away with ye. Urgent business, ye said.'

She nodded and ran up the walkway. There wasn't time for pleasantries.

Aisha had come off the stage and was standing in the wings watching the band do their encore when Faye found her.

'Faye! Where have you been? Where's Rav?' Aisha turned her eyes away from Finn reluctantly as Faye grabbed her shoulder; Faye could see that whatever spell Finn had cast on the audience, Aisha was caught in it, too.

'There's no time. Rav's safe.'

'*Safe?* I just thought the pressure got to him or something. When he didn't turn up for the concert—'

'No. He was...' Faye shook her head. 'I'll tell you later, okay? But we have to end the gig. Now. Before Finn can...' She broke off, because Aisha had turned away from her and was staring raptly at the stage. 'Aish! Please. We have to stop it. Put the curtain down. Put the lights up. Whatever we have to do to get the people to leave... I...' Faye exhaled in frustration. 'It's dangerous.'

'What? Why?' Aisha's brow furrowed. 'It's all run fine so far.'

'Aisha. Listen to me. He's dangerous.'

'Faye. Please. It's the last song. Stop being a drama queen,' Aisha hissed.

Finn was playing the flute, and the quick trills of notes, up and down, had grown faster and faster. The drummer was playing so fast that the individual beats were hardly discernible.

'But he's not what he seems. Finn Beatha. He's... Look, I know you won't believe me. But he's enchanting this whole crowd. He's a faerie king, Aisha. I know, I've been to the faerie realm. I've seen it. Please. I think he wants to take... a woman, maybe more than one, back to his kingdom. Maybe all of them, I don't know. To be trapped there forever.' Faye pulled at her friend's arm to make her turn away from the stage and, as she did so, her hand slid down to Aisha's wrist, and she noticed the rose gold and opal ring on Aisha's index finger: the same as the one that Finn had given her.

'Where did you get that?' she asked, but she knew the answer. Aisha pulled her hand away.

'So, what if I have it? So, what if I have him?' Aisha scowled at her. 'God, you've always got to be in control, haven't you? Got to be the top dog. Can't stand it that I have Finn Beatha now. He's mine, Faye.'

On the stage, Finn was opening his arms wide as the rest of the band piped and drummed.

'You... and Finn?' Faye's heart felt like it stopped beating as she stared at her friend. She was dimly aware that the crowd had formed a huge circle and was dancing, running around it in exactly the same way as the dancers at the faerie ball in Murias. She stared out at their contorted faces and a dawning horror made her mute.

'Yes. Me and Finn.' Aisha turned her wide brown eyes to Finn, metres away, and he held his hand out to her. Below him, the crowd were no longer dancing; now, it had turned into something else, something darker and more savage. They reeled and trampled each other; there was screaming, but Aisha couldn't hear it, Faye could tell: her face was beatific as she caught and returned Finn's gaze. 'It was the spell, Faye. It brought him to me,' she sighed and then, without warning, ran on to the stage towards the faerie king's open arms.

'Aisha! No!' Faye grabbed for her friend's hand, but Aisha's fingers slipped through hers. Faye ran after her, but it was too late. Finn Beatha picked Aisha up, and glared victoriously at Faye.

'You didn't want me, *sidhe-leth*. Don't blame me if someone else did.' His voice cut through the music as if there was a direct channel between them.

'You can't take her!' Faye shouted, but Finn cradled Aisha in one arm and thrust his other palm out towards her. Faye felt an invisible barrier rise in the space between them.

'You can't stop me,' he replied, smiling, and swept Aisha into his arms so that she lay in them like a child, bewitched. 'I will have my lovers, human or half human; it is no matter to me. We need human blood to keep us strong. Worry not, Faye. I will keep your friend safe in my bed.' He cast a wry glance over the half-naked, cavorting crowd. 'Perhaps with some of these others, too. A faerie king does not like to be bored. And Murias needs stock and women ripe to nurse them when I am done with their mothers...'

Finn was no longer singing and so the drumming reached

fever pitch; everyone in the crowd was leaping and screaming. Their faces were masks, and the sheen of humanity was slipping from them. They were becoming more and more bestial with every passing second.

Faye felt horrified that she had ever desired Finn so deeply. She took out the hagstone charm from her pocket and tried to push through the energy barrier towards him. 'You will not take her!' Faye screamed, holding it up like a lamp in the darkness, but his power was too great and the barrier, whatever it was made of, choked her as if she was drowning.

In desperation, she threw it at him, but he caught it and jumped into the middle of the crowd, which ran to him like rivulets into a stream. He laughed.

'Your charm cannot stop me,' he called as he jumped. 'It protects *you* from my kind like it always has, *sidhe-leth*. But none of these others are so protected.' Aisha clung to him, her arms around his neck, burying her face into his chest, kissing him. Finn threw the hagstone charm away to the far side of the stage.

'Aisha! Don't go!' Faye screamed, but she could see the enchantment in her friend's eyes; Aisha didn't even hear Faye. She knew what Aisha was feeling, and she felt a stab of shame at her own hypocrisy; no one would have been able to call her back from Finn's arms when she had been the one in his favour.

Aisha was at Finn's mercy now. If she displeased him, she would have no defence against his power. She didn't have the magic that Levantiana had taught Faye and she was not half faerie. Aisha might not survive the savage faerie reel if she was thrust into it by a faerie king who had grown tired of her.

Faye watched as others in the crowd grabbed him and went to him willingly, for they all wanted him; they had all been enchanted in exactly the same way as she had.

'Farewell, *sidhe-leth*.' Finn's stormy eyes met hers and she felt grief pass through her. There was a part of her that still wanted him. She knew it was wrong, but she couldn't help it. She steeled herself against the power in his gaze. 'Until our lips meet again.'

'You will never have me again!' she screamed, making her eyes meet his with as much power in them as she could muster. *Resist him, resist*, she told herself, but his power was strong.

Finn laughed cruelly. 'As you will. Go back to your mortal man. But you will always yearn for me.' He smiled, and there was no kindness in his expression, but instead the calculating look of an eagle weighing up its prey. 'And since you have betrayed me three times now – by loving the mortal, by rescuing him from my realm, and for trying to thwart me tonight – I will bar you from entering Murias by any means from now on.'

'I am half faerie. It's my right to be there if I choose,' Faye retorted, but dread twisted her stomach. Murias was Finn's world, and she didn't know if even Levantiana could admit her if Finn had forbidden it. There was no way to stop him, no way she could help Aisha if he took her there.

Finn called out something in Gaelic to the band, still playing on stage; as if following an order, they finished the song, dropped their instruments and jumped into the crowd, grabbing people at random.

It had to be now.

Faye pulled the wand out from her bag, picked up a bottle of water from where it lay at the edge of the stage and splashed some of it onto the end. Standing, she traced the shape of the water-summoning sigil in the air and chanted the Gaelic words:

'*A rèir an tròcair mhòir, Glòir agus cumhachd do Rìgh agus do Bhanrìgh Mhurias, mar a bha e aig an toiseach, agus a-nis, agus gu bràth!*'

Now, Faye closed her eyes and tried to focus.

She had practised before with rain and streams, but now she knew that she had to summon something big. Something that could overpower Finn and the rest of the band. They were fae; they were powerful.

Yet, it was their element: would water even stop them? She didn't know. But she had to try.

Faye thought of Grainne Morgan, tied to the stake, and the way that the water in the bay at North Berwick that day, hundreds of years ago, had risen up and flooded everything and everyone.

She turned to face the sea, and repeated the charm. She imagined the waves growing bigger, but she didn't want the sea to flood the stage and kill everyone. She needed something else.

Faye imagined the sea growing tentacles; with a shiver, she remembered the fae in the white dress who had wrapped her tentacles around Rav and taken him inside her. Screwing her eyes shut, she imagined the tentacles growing longer, thicker, sinuous with seawater, and reaching to the headland.

One by one, she imagined the tentacles picking up Finn and his bandmates and throwing them back into the sea.

She opened her eyes to screams.

Above her, four vast, snaking tentacles made completely of water searched blindly for Finn and the members of Dal Riada. Finn stared in shock at the one coming for him, and then glared at her up on the stage. She saw realisation in his eyes: the knowledge that his own sister had betrayed him.

'You worthless bitch!' he cried out, as tentacles gripped the singer and the guitar player of the band and flung them into the sea. 'How dare you use the faerie magic!'

'I dare because I am half faerie, and it is my right!' Faye shouted back, furious.

Finn pointed his hand at her, and Faye felt a wave of energy emanate from him and pulsate across the whole crowd.

'You have no power, and no rights. I am taking what I want, and you will not get in my way any longer!' he screamed.

Faye fell to her knees as Finn's power knocked her off her

feet. She dropped the wand, and the water tentacles disappeared. An unnatural golden light flashed in the crowd for a moment, on and off. The sudden darkness interspersed with light caught the jerking and flailing movements of the crowd in strange, monstrous angles and shadows. Faye blinked, shielding her eyes as bodies writhed and thrusted.

'Too late, Faye Morgan,' Finn smiled.

The golden light lit the whole crowd for one brief moment. A many-voiced scream, a chorus of the crowd's violent, insane lust ripped through Abercolme, and then, just as suddenly, a dark and dead hush followed it, which was far, far worse.

42

———

Faye ran down the steps of the stage into the crowd. The villagers who were left looked around them as if they were waking up from a dream.

She tried to push her way through the crowd, but they were confused and disoriented. Many were hurt: people sat on the ground, holding arms that might be broken and with cuts and grazes to their faces, legs, anywhere with exposed skin.

Faye looked around in desperation, torn between her instinct to help the wounded and a sense of duty to rescue those who'd been taken. But then, Grandmother's voice spoke in her ear, as if she was suddenly next to her. *Don't judge them for the things they don't understand, Faye,* she said. Faye felt that if she turned around, she'd see Grandmother there, short and round with her long grey hair twined up in a bun and the ghosts of a life of wisdom and kindness etched into her face. *It is your job to help the people, Faye. Never forget that,* Grandmother's voice said.

'But I am trying to help them. The ones who were taken by Finn,' she protested.

Aye, and ye will. Grandmother's voice seemed to come from

all around her; she was in the wind, in the night, in the moonlight that bathed the chaos around her. *But first things first.*

Grandmother was always right; Faye had known better than to question her when she was alive, and she certainly wasn't going to argue with Grandmother in spirit. For a moment, she closed her eyes and breathed in; in a half-second she felt Grandmother's hand in hers, like Annie's that first day at school.

Faye cast one last desperate gaze at the beach below and turned back to the people who needed her.

43

A few weeks later, Faye and Rav lay in Faye's bed, their legs entwined.

'If you go, I'll make you a cup of tea every day for a week,' Faye offered.

'Make me one today, then.' Rav snuggled next to her. 'I don't want to get up. It's too nice in here.'

'If you make it, I'll bring you cake with your tea every day for a week,' she counter-offered. 'Please, Rav. Go on.' She pulled the duvet off his side of the bed. 'See, you're cold now, anyway. Might as well get up.'

'Oh, fine.' Rav got up and pulled on a hoodie over his boxers. 'Only because you might turn me into some reptile or something.'

'Shut up,' she said, then, after a second, called after him. 'An otter. I could turn you into an otter, that would be a cute replacement.'

Faye's smile faded as she stared out through the window at her late-summer herb garden. She had never told Rav about the love spell that had brought him to her; that had also brought Finn Beatha into her life.

She had wanted to tell him, but something had kept her from doing it.

What good was a relationship where you kept secrets? She had tortured herself with the thought, but she didn't want to tell Rav that she had engineered them meeting with magic. She knew that it would worry him, or make him feel that their love wasn't real. She thought that it *was*, despite everything. It was better left.

She hadn't had the time to tend the garden much. Soon it would be time to harvest everything for the winter: the rose hips dried for incenses, or made into a vitamin-rich syrup for coughs and colds. The lavender had to be dried, the nettles, too, for tea or healing tinctures. The apples would be made into apple jam and apple chutney; for a few weeks in late summer, she would fill boxes of the sweet, red fruit and put them outside the shop for anyone to take. The irony of witches giving away free apples wasn't lost on her, but otherwise they would waste.

Rav was recovering slowly. After the concert they'd shut themselves away in Faye's house. She'd closed the shop – not permanently, but until she felt ready to reopen it. She didn't care that news of what happened at the concert – the mysterious disappearance of eighty people – had turned Abercolme into a media circus. She could have opened the shop and talked to all the journalists that had, initially, waited on her doorstep, like they had all the local businesses, wanting a scoop, an insight, some secret that the people of Abercolme were keeping to themselves. She could have made a fortune, selling to all the curious that streamed into the village, determined to uncover the truth behind the rumours of alien abductions, or kidnappings by secret sects within the village. Or, worst of all, that Abercolme was the centre of a black magic community that had sacrificed all eighty to the Devil. Perhaps now the residents of Abercolme would understand how Grainne Morgan felt, all those years ago.

But Faye kept her mouth shut. Nobody talked to the press; not Muriel in the bakery, not Mrs Kennedy, not the minister or anyone else. They kept to themselves, and, slowly, the press began to leave.

Rav had been left weakened by his abduction into faerie. Faye was shocked at how little energy he had for weeks afterwards, and the deep cuts on his back, legs and arms that were only now starting to subside with her repeated treatment of comfrey salve. He had hardly any appetite for the first week, and had gone in and out of consciousness for days until she brought him round, finally, by making him eat some soup.

Midsummer sacrifices. Finn had spoken of it; Grandmother had warned her, in her way. A familiar stab of guilt wrenched Faye's stomach; ever since the concert, after she had limped home in exhaustion, unable to do anything more than slump into her bed, beside Rav, she had felt it. Had she known what was going to happen, would she have been Finn's willing sacrifice? Should she have stayed, so that he didn't have to look elsewhere, and find Aisha and the rest of them?

Midsummer sacrifices. Finn had spoken of it; Grandmother had warned her, in her way.

She had been back to Black Sands, but the faerie road had vanished. At least, it had for her. She knew that Finn had revoked her access to Murias, and Aisha and the others would eventually die if they stayed there. She doubted she had anything left that she could offer Levantiana in exchange for Aisha's release, and a dungeon awaited Faye if she managed to find her way back.

She heard Rav's footsteps on the stairs and sat up in bed, chasing the dark thoughts away for now. Though they were both recovering in their own separate ways, their time together had been sweet. It was just them, eating the food she had in her larder and the freezer, and the ripe fruit and vegetables from the garden.

But Faye hardly slept, racked with worry for Aisha. Whenever she thought about her friend – even though she had gone willingly with Finn – she felt shadow overtake her. Rav found it hard to get through to her at those times. But, nonetheless, she and Rav were talking, sharing themselves with each other. And that, in itself, was a healing. She resolved to get Aisha back somehow.

Faye had failed Rav. She was the reason he had been taken, endangered. *But you're also the reason I'm alive now*, he'd replied, holding her shaking hands when she told him how she had been seduced by Finn, how she was half faerie, and how that had initially blinded her to the darkness of the faerie realm. But there was also something in the shadow part of her that loved faerie and always would. On the nights after Rav had fallen asleep and she sat up in bed, hugging her knees and watching the moon, she worried about Finn. It wasn't over; he had more or less said so. But she wanted it to be. She wanted a normal life.

You can't be anything other than who you truly are, Rav had sighed. *And, now that I know all of it, I can make the choice to be with you or not. Problem is, I can't help loving you. It's not a choice. It just is.*

He set a tray with two of Grandmother's old china cups painted with faded roses, a teapot and a packet of biscuits on the white-painted bedside table.

'I checked the post.' He handed Faye a sheaf of envelopes and papers. She made a face at a couple of handwritten notes from journalists with their business cards attached and screwed them up.

'No thanks,' she muttered.

Faye got out of bed and went to stand at the window; she stared out at her garden, bathed in the rich gold sun of early August. She opened the window and leaned out to breathe in the air; the smell of the wild roses, the raspberry leaf and lavender scenting the soft air.

'There's a card from Annie, too.' Faye felt her heart lift; she missed her best friend terribly. She let out a short laugh when she looked at the photo, which was a London Beefeater mooning the camera; the caption said: *Having a ball in London!*

'Typical Annie.' She showed Rav, who rolled his eyes affectionately.

Dear Faye, Annie had written in her rounded script.

Hope you're okay. I tried calling a few times, but I couldn't get hold of you. I hope you got my emails and letters. I'd come up and check on you, but the filming schedule down here is mad...

Faye hadn't had it in her to reply much to any of Annie's emails yet, except to say that she was all right, that she and Rav were taking it easy together, and that she'd catch Annie up with everything when she was up to it.

Anyway, it's fun. Coven of Love *is kind of cheesy, but I do get to wear great outfits. Plus, things are going well with Suze. Will fill you in more when I see you – come down and see me when you're feeling up to it, maybe. There's room for you here if you want. Thinking of you and love you always, sweetheart. Annie xxx*

Faye smiled and handed the card to Rav, then stared back out at the garden. Roses would always mean faerie to her now: the crystal castle of magic where they were underfoot, the petals she had taken and used, wrapped in a piece of kelpie's scale. It had been the smell of rose in the air when she had first made love to Rav at the beach, almost upon the faerie road. But the wild white and yellow roses that had grown in this garden all her life were a different smell, and they reminded her of Grandmother and Moddie, and playing at witches with Annie in the summers long before Faye knew anything of love.

If she drew power from the realm of faerie, then she also drew it from this house, this garden, and her ancestors, the Morgans. She had absorbed the powers of all of who had come before, and, over time, she would unwrap every piece of knowledge, and know what they had known; feel what they had felt and seen and heard.

'You'll put this right. I know you will.' Rav stood behind her. His arms circled her waist, and she turned around to kiss him. There was electricity between them like there always had been, and there was kindness and warmth, too. For the first time in her life, Faye felt known. And she knew that, in part, that was because she had begun to know herself for the first time, and accept her fae self as well as the self she had always known.

It wasn't over, with Finn, with the war, with all of it. She had only just begun to come into her true power, and she still had more magic to learn, if Levantiana would teach her. *If the prophecy is true, then I've got a lot more to do,* she thought, as she inhaled the scent of the roses. *But I'm ready. Bring it on.*

To be continued...

A LETTER FROM KENNEDY

Thank you so much for reading *A Dance with the Fae*. I hope you enjoyed it as much as I liked writing it. If you'd like to keep up to date with all of my latest releases, you can sign up at the following link. Your email address will never be shared, and you can unsubscribe at any time.

www.secondskybooks.com/kennedy-kerr

I came up with the idea for this book when I was visiting family in Scotland. My uncle, husband and son had gone to the beach in the village of Aberdour, and my aunt wanted to show me a witchy shop on the high street which she said she knew I'd love. Sure enough, I did, and I started thinking about a story that centred around a homely but magical shop that had always belonged to a family of witches.

At the same time, I was reading a lot about Scottish faerie lore and was fascinated with the real-life accounts of men and women in history who claimed to have spent time 'away with the faeries' – and the Seelie Court, a grand place where the Scottish faeries feasted and danced and liked to ride out on grand horses. I started wondering how intoxicating it must be to spend time in such a place – and what would compel a man or woman to remain there...

This series of books is sexier than my Magpie Cove and Loch Cameron series. I wanted to explore some darker themes and more of a fantasy setting. However, even though there is more of an erotic theme in *A Dance with the Fae*, it is still a story about a woman finding herself, stepping into her own power and being brave enough to heal from some difficult experiences. Faye's journey to understanding the complexity of her sexuality – dominant and submissive – is an exploration of her own desires, and that is a strength. Sex is part of our lives as humans, and pleasure is hugely important for our physical and mental health. Especially as women, it is an act of empowerment to learn what we enjoy – whatever it is – and not be afraid to ask for it.

However, if you're looking for heartwarming, clean romance, I heartily recommend the Magpie Cove and Loch Cameron series, which have less sex but plenty of love, hope and healing.

If you have time, I'd love it if you were able to write a review of *A Dance with the Fae*. Feedback is really useful and also makes a huge difference in helping new readers discover my books for the first time.

Alternatively, if you'd like to contact me personally, you can reach me via social media. I love hearing from readers, and always reply.

Again, thank you so much for deciding to spend some time reading *A Dance with the Fae*. I'm looking forward to sharing my next book with you very soon.

With all best wishes,

Kennedy

PUBLISHING TEAM

Turning a manuscript into a book requires the efforts of many people. The publishing team at Bookouture would like to acknowledge everyone who contributed to this publication.

Commercial

Lauren Morrissette

Hannah Richmond

Imogen Allport

Cover design

Alexandra Allden

Data and analysis

Mark Alder

Mohamed Bussuri

Editorial

Kelsie Marsden

Nadia Michael

Copyeditor

Angela Snowden

Proofreader

Catherine Lender

Marketing
Alex Crow
Melanie Price
Occy Carr
Cíara Rosney
Martyna Młynarska

Operations and distribution
Marina Valles
Stephanie Straub
Joe Morris

Production
Hannah Snetsinger
Mandy Kullar
Ria Clare
Nadia Michael

Publicity
Kim Nash
Noelle Holten
Jess Readett
Sarah Hardy

Rights and contracts
Peta Nightingale
Richard King
Saidah Graham

Dear Reader,

We'd love your attention for one more page to tell you about the crisis in children's reading, and what we can all do.

Studies have shown that reading for fun is the **single biggest predictor of a child's future success** – more than family circumstance, parents' educational background or income. It improves academic results, mental health, wealth, communication skills, and ambition.

The number of children reading for fun is in rapid decline. Young people have a lot of competition for their time, and a worryingly high number do not have a single book at home.

Our business works extensively with schools, libraries and literacy charities, but here are some ways we can all raise more readers:

- Reading to children for just 10 minutes a day makes a difference
- Don't give up if children aren't regular readers – there will be books for them!

- Visit bookshops and libraries to get recommendations
- Encourage them to listen to audiobooks
- Support school libraries
- Give books as gifts

Thank you for reading: there's a lot more information about how to encourage children to read on our website.

www.JoinRaisingReaders.com

www.ingramcontent.com/pod-product-compliance
Lightning Source LLC
Chambersburg PA
CBHW030530190726
48283CB00006B/1849